IRRECONCILABLE

DIFFERENCES

GEOFF COOK

Published by Rotercracker Copyrights, 2022
Copyright © Geoff Cook, 2022
Geoff Cook has asserted his right under the Copyright,
Designs and Patents Act 1988 to be identified
as the author of this work

First published in Great Britain in 2022 by Rotercracker
Copyrights
Pacific Heights South, 16 Golden Gate Way, Eastbourne,
East Sussex, BN23 5PU

Paperback ISBN 9789899730083

A CIP catalogue record for this book is available
from the British Library

For more information on
books and plays from Geoff Cook,
please visit
www.geoff-cook.com
https://www.facebook.com/novelgeoffcook/

For Hilary and Stuart
with love and gratitude
for a lifetime's friendship

ONE

CHARLIE AND NORMA

'Irreconcilable differences.' Charlie shook his head. 'Is that what he said?'

Silence.

He swung the chair around in front of the vanity unit until the bed came into view in the mirror. A selection of her make-up bottles rattled on the surface as his knee banged against the side of the unit. She was sitting up in bed, tortoise-shell framed glasses perched on the tip of her nose, her gaze focussed on a magazine.

'Bugger,' he said, as he massaged his knee. 'That hurt. I thought you'd gone to sleep. Did you hear what I said?' There was still no reaction. 'Do you think you could do me the courtesy of turning your attention away from whichever showbiz celebrity is shagging their way around Hollywood and concentrate on the crisis we're facing?' He hesitated. 'And don't look at me like that, Norma. You seem to treat the whole thing as if it's none of our business.' His voice moved up an octave. 'Just explain to me, what are fu—'

'Charlie!' The tone of her voice matched his.

'Sorry, but you can see how uptight I am? Just tell me, what does our son mean when he says they're getting a divorce on the grounds of "irreconcilable differences"?'

She sighed. 'You had the opportunity to ask him, but you were too busy losing your temper and stomping around like a wounded elephant. Do you realise you've been combing the few strands of hair you've got left across your scalp for the last ten minutes? That's my curling comb. Put it back and come to bed, for heaven's sake.'

'Irreconcilable differences?'

'I suppose it means he and Cary can't see eye-to-eye on anything, keep arguing and feel there is no future for them as a couple.'

'Do me a favour, will you? Can't see eye-to-eye? There's not a couple on God's earth who don't fancy wringing their partner's neck from time to time. And so what? You work it out. No way is it a conclusion you reach after

1

ten years of marriage, the responsibility of six-year-old twins and an eye-watering mortgage? A little late to decide you're incompatible, isn't it?'

'Better than reaching the same conclusion after forty, I suppose.'

His chest heaved as he struggled to his feet. 'Is that a dig at us? If so, it's out of order.' He threw the comb onto the vanity unit. 'We may have had our ups and downs, but we always got through it.'

She gave him a sideways glance. 'As I recall, Charlie, most of the ups and downs were you on top of Doris Fairbanks, and it was *you* who was the only one to get through it. I don't remember being consulted, more the role of the priest expected to handle the "I have sinned" confessional and hand out a few Hail Mary penances.'

'Please, Norma, don't go down that road again. I thought we both agreed years ago it was water under the bridge. Let's not go dredging up the past.' He came to stand at the edge of the bed, his hand outstretched.

She pushed the magazine off the sheet, letting it fall to the floor and avoiding his conciliatory gesture. 'Maybe that's my irreconcilable difference,' she said. 'And I've tried to live with it.'

'Can we stop all this "irreconcilable difference" nonsense and get back to the fact that Dominic is talking about getting a divorce?'

'It's more than talking. The paperwork is all done, it seems. Cary has already moved out with the twins.'

'Did he say that? I didn't catch it. Where to?'

'You'd gone off in a huff, effing and blinding. Do you really care that your forty-year-old son is physically scared of you?' She massaged her jaw back and forth. Damn. She hadn't taken out her denture with the two front teeth before going to bed. The Steradent tablet must have dissolved by now. She manoeuvred across the bed away from him, stood up and made her way to the bathroom, closing the door behind her.

'That's nonsense,' he called after her. 'Of course he's not. I was upset. How do you expect me to act?'

It was five minutes before she reappeared to find him sitting on the edge of the bed, flicking through the pages of her magazine. 'I don't know how you can read all this trash,' he said with feigned annoyance.

She snatched the magazine from his hand and placed it on the bedside table. 'What do you suggest I read, Charlie? The Racing Post you have your

2

head buried in half the day?' She sighed. 'If you really want to know, it's pure escapism. It stops me thinking about a sixty-year-old woman, married for forty years to a retired, self-centred used car salesman, during which she has done nothing but produce two children, both of whom appear to be suffering the consequences of their parentage. What an achievement and what prospects for the future.'

'Come on, love. Don't be like that.' He leaned across to take her hand. 'You've always been ashamed of telling people I was involved in the used motor trade, but it's what's given us a good life and let me retire early. You've never wanted for anything, and thanks to Ludo we've got a nice little nest egg to see us comfortably into old age. It's not all bad.'

She shook her head at the hang-dog expression and squeezed his fingers. 'I know. I'm sorry. This business with Dominic got me thinking about just how inadequate we have been as parents. He needs our support, not criticism, or to lose our tempers the moment he opens his mouth. Raise your eyebrows if you like, but you know what I'm saying is right.' She released his hand and snuggled down under the bed covers. 'I'll speak with Cary tomorrow. I expect she and the twins are staying with Len and Muriel until things get sorted out. She'll tell me what's brought their marriage to the brink. I expect Len will have something to say about it as well.'

Charlie struggled to his feet and made an exaggerated sign of the cross, leaving the middle finger of his right hand pointed upward as he completed the gesture. 'God protect us from a gloating Len. How that arsehole must be in his element now. He has all but told me, not in so many words but by his snide innuendoes, how his precious Caroline was too good for our Dominic with her fancy degree in business management and qualification as a certified accountant whilst our lad only had a tech diploma in computer programming. I can see Len standing there now like a thin streak of bacon, sewing his poison, explaining to the twins how they'll be better off with their mum. Believe me, if it comes to divorce, the gloves are coming off. No more Mr Nice Guy Charlie. I can finally tell the wanker what I think of him.'

Norma pulled the sheet over her head. 'Please, Charlie, I'm not defending Len. He can be as obnoxious as you when you're both together. . ..' She pulled back the sheet to register his expression. 'Now is not the time

3

for confrontation. Diplomacy and compromise may not be your strong suits, but you need a dose of reality when the other guy is holding the cards.'

He shook his head. 'You're not making any sense. What cards?' he snapped.

'Think about it. You may not have done too much listening whilst Dominic was here, but, Lord knows, he didn't come to seek our advice on how to save his marriage. He came to tell us it was a *fait accompli*, a decision taken and final. Cary will have custody of the twins and he'll have visiting rights every second weekend or something like that. They both want to start afresh.'

'Well, they can't. I've just said, they've got commitments. You can't just up sticks and wipe your hands of each other like a pair of bloody teenagers.'

'I'm not thinking of them; I'm thinking of us. You dote on the twins. Creedence even said you were cool. Imagine! Syracuse will sit on your lap and listen to your ridiculous stories for hours. The risk is you'll lose all that.'

'I damn well won't. Who's going to stop me?' His fists clenched, cheeks reddened, nostrils flared. 'They're my granddaughters. What are you saying? Cary's going to stop me from seeing them?'

'Please, Charlie, try to stop losing your temper. It's me you're talking to. If you're going to carry on like this, I *am* going to sleep.'

'No, no, don't. I'm sorry. I need to hear what you have to say.'

Norma took off her glasses and rubbed her eyes. 'Just imagine for a moment. Perhaps, "irreconcilable differences" is really a cover for some other reason, and they've both agreed to be kind to each other and not apportion blame. The law now allows for couples to split without acrimony.'

'You're not saying he's got a bit on the side, are you? You're joking? He always looks to me as if just breathing saps all his energy.'

'Maybe, it's Cary. After all, she's the one who has moved out. Normally, it's the husband who leaves.'

'The adulterous little cow!'

'It's just supposition, for God's sake.' She puffed her cheeks and exhaled loudly. 'Get me a glass of water from the kitchen, will you?' Her mobile vibrated gently under the pillow. It was the second time in the last minute. She waited until she could hear him talking to himself as he opened a

4

cupboard door in the kitchen before checking the message. Smiling, she typed one word and sent the reply. He was still talking to himself as he made his way laboriously up the stairs.

'Carry on where you left off, will you?' He handed her the over-filled glass.

'Is this Evian or Perrier?'

'Tap. Is that a problem?'

She put the glass on the bedside table without responding.

'So, you think she's got somebody else and is just in transit at Len's?' he prompted.

'No, I don't. I said it's just supposition to make a point.'

'Which is?'

'Cary's an attractive, intelligent career woman and a wonderful mother. Plenty of men will be queuing up and she doesn't strike me as the single mother type. If she hasn't already, I doubt it will be long before she hooks up with somebody else, and then there is another set of grandparents on the scene. Within six months, you and I are ancient history, occasional visitors who play no active part in the twins' lives. You would hate that. That's why I'm saying you should play up to Len and Muriel in the short term. Be concerned and sympathise. Invite them out to dinner to talk things over. Try conciliation.'

Charlie said nothing as he undressed, lowering the pyjama bottoms to the floor to enable him to step into them and almost losing his balance as he did so. He exhaled loudly with the effort. The mattress groaned as he settled into bed. 'I'll just say this.' His eyes met Norma's. 'Hell will freeze over before I lose my grandchildren. If it means sucking up to that creep, I'll play ball. But when the time comes . . .'

TWO

DOMINIC AND SYLVIA

The van following his car was so close, Dominic could make out the features of the young man behind the wheel and lip read the looped sequence of profanities directed toward him. The tinny sound of the van's hooter in his ears was constant. 'No way,' he said to himself. 'I'm right on the speed limit and you'll just have to wait. Impatience is no virtue. Learn restraint. Don't act like my sodding father and lose the plot.'

The car behind the van had joined in the hooting, a more altogether manly sound, intermittent and demanding. 'Just missing a mellow country beat and we'll have a trio making music.' He found the comment amusing and laughed to himself.

The image in the rear-view mirror caught his attention. The van was moving into the outside lane, ready to overtake. Dominic eased the Volvo to the right, still straddling the two lanes, but leaving no space for the van to pass. The hooting became more frantic. 'Oh no, you don't, you naughty boy.'

Too late, he realised. The space available on the inside lane plus the width of the hard shoulder was enough to let a car overtake him on the inside. Only, this was no ordinary car. The blue light flashed, and a siren wailed. 'Wrong pitch,' he thought. 'Needs to be softer, more warming.' A stern-looking police officer waved him to stop the Volvo on the hard shoulder.

Dominic brought the car to a halt in the service station car park and checked his watch. An hour had passed since the police had pulled him over. His mobile had rung twice, but he had dared not answer it as he would have usually done just in case they were still tailing him. This time, he took the call.

'You said you'd ring me as soon as you left Mum's. You're not still there, are you?' Her voice was unusually high-pitched, full of foreboding.

'No, Sis. I'm sorry. I had a run in with the law.'

'What for?'

He opened the car door and stepped out into the chill night air. It might be the end of March, but there had been a cold snap. He secured the

7

mobile between shoulder and cheek as he buttoned his coat. A hot coffee was required and a quiet Costa corner where he could relax and talk.

'Sorry, you were saying?' he asked.

'What have you been doing to be involved with the police?'

'Reckless and dangerous driving, according to them; possibly aggravated by without due care and attention.'

'Jesus, Dom, you could lose your licence.' She hesitated. 'Your job depends on driving. You could get the sack.' With every sentence, the pitch of her voice rose.

'Calm down, Sylvia. He let me off.'

'He did? You're not just saying that for my sake?'

'Of course not. You sound more nervous than usual. There's nothing to worry about.'

'What happened?'

'I was lucky. One of them sat in the police car checking the legals on the car whilst the good-looking copper came up to the passenger side and started lecturing me. He was just reading the riot act when he caught sight of the file about the divorce I'd taken into Mum's. It had a series of my scribblings on the front. As he hesitated, I said I'd just received the divorce notification from the wife's solicitors and wasn't thinking straight. I apologised for my actions.'

'And it worked?'

He smiled to himself. 'Like a charm. The guy must have read where I'd written "irreconcilable differences" and asked me if it was mutual and amicable. I said, "So far, but you never know." His entire mood changed. "Too bloody right," he said. "Mine's hostile. The cow started off friendly enough. After all, she was the one in the wrong, but the mood changed. She said it was just this one fellow from the wholesale fishmongers and she had got lonely with all the hours I have to put in with the force. What a load of bollocks that turned out to be. I found out she was opening and closing her legs so often, she was creating a fucking draught." I made some sympathetic noises, as you do, and he finishes with "She even had a crack at him." He points to his colleague talking on the radio in the police car. "As far as sex is concerned, he's like that famous pop star, the last of the great mysteries. God knows what turns him on. He's into model railways. Anyway, the bitch isn't happy just splitting what we have today down the middle. Her fancy lawyer is after half my pension rights. Smarmy bastard walks around with a smile on his face. I expect she's giving him a blow job."

'Then, he looks at me like I'm the poor, innocent supplicant and says, "You'll see. In the end, she'll show you no mercy. Now try to keep your shit together and accept the situation's out of control. Don't drive as though you need to keep everybody else's life in order just because yours isn't. Bugger off before I change my mind."'

'That was it?' There was incredulity in her voice. 'You just drove away?'

'He even waved as I pulled out. At least I can thank the divorce for one thing.'

Sylvia giggled. 'You are lucky. Most of the coppers we get in the lab are as sensitive as a wire brush. The number of convictions notched up is their golden chalice. I can be assisting the pathologist on a post-mortem discectomy, and they look at you as though you're not telling them who committed the murder. I feel like turning around sometimes and saying "All finished. It was the butler who did it." But I don't.'

'How's the job going?' he asked.

'Good, but it's no *CSI Miami*. I've just spent a week in a tunnel alongside a sewer where they found what they believe to be a human femur. Unfortunately, the DNA was so degraded and fragmented, we could reach no positive conclusion. Even PCR analysis couldn't amplify the sample.'

'You're losing me, Sis.'

'Okay. In short, they need further body parts, so I have spent daylight hours under arc lights, filtering slop and grime, two hours on, two hours off for five days. I take a shower, but with the scent in your nose, you never feel clean.'

'Are you still seeing . . .? Sorry, his name escapes me.'

She made a clucking noise in her mouth. 'Trevor from Tony Pondy. Him you mean?'

He laughed. 'I think you'll find it's Tonypandy. He's a Valleys' boyo, is he?'

'Yesterday's news, I'm afraid. Made an excuse and left, much like all the others. You'd think a thirty-something-year-old woman would have learnt how to play the field, but no. It's back to the drawing board and the dating agency for me.'

'You don't sound too upset.'

'We'd reached the stage where all those little things in him that annoy you, which you suppress when you're in the first flush of a relationship, suddenly assume humongous importance and really grate. He'd sing the Welsh National Anthem at the top of his voice in the shower and finish by screaming "Wales, Land of my Fathers". I thought it was endearing to start with. After a month, I'd take to singing "Swing Low, Sweet Chariot" at the top of my voice and turn on the hot tap in the kitchen so he'd get doused in cold water in the shower. Doomed to failure.'

'Never mind, Sis. Mr Right will come along, eventually.'

'Talking about Mr Right'–her voice had adopted a serious tone–'how did you get on with Mum and Dad? Did you tell them?'

'Just a minute.' Dominic walked back to the car, his hand over the microphone aperture built into the mobile. How much could he afford to tell her?

'You still there, Dom?'

'Yes. Sorry. As well as could be expected, I'd say. I laid it out in simple terms, chronological order. Mum was paying attention, but I could see the old man chew his lip which, as you well know, is a prelude to Vesuvius erupting.' He put the key in the ignition, hesitating before starting the engine. 'It was when I started explaining the grounds cited on the petition, he went doolally. His idea of an irreconcilable difference is a dissatisfied punter bringing back a used car after a week and asking him for the money back. As far as he's concerned, there's no such thing in personal relationships once baggage is involved. His words, not mine. That's the last sensible comment I got out of him. He was off, marching around the house, talking about ungrateful and irresponsible children. I'll leave out the profanities.'

'Did you say you'd spoken to me?'

'Mum asked. I said you'd been very supportive throughout the whole time.'

'She'll have a go at me for not saying anything to her, but I'll handle that. Dad will be a different proposition.'

'Just say I insisted you keep it a secret. He can't be anymore off with me than he is now.'

There was a moment's hesitation before she reacted. 'Did you tell them everything?' She stuttered as she went to carry on. 'I mean, about the other thing?'

It was his turn to hold back before replying. 'Coward, aren't I?' he said, finally. 'Mum was upset, tears in her eyes and he was still talking to the wall. There was no way I could broach it there and then. It will have to wait for another day. He'll never speak to me again.'

'Maybe it won't be that bad.'

'Don't patronise me, please. Not even you see the old man's script as a self-centred, short-tempered man with misogynist, racist and homophobic traits experiences epiphanic conversion to rational and responsible behaviour. It won't happen.'

'Perhaps not, but don't leave it until it's presented to him as a done deal.'

'Point taken. I'd better be going, but I need your help. Can you take a few hours off work tomorrow afternoon to show a couple of estate agents around the house? I've been given an urgent assignment at work that will take me all day.' He waited for a reply. 'That's great. First one is at three and the last, at four. I'll text you the details. I need to assess the asking price and agree it with Cary before putting it on the market.'

She seemed loth to let him ring off. 'What's the deal with Cary? Fifty/fifty?'

'After we pay off the mortgage, it won't leave enough to buy a parking space, let alone somewhere to live. I'll have to rent.' He keyed the car into life. 'Gotta go now, Sis, the place is in a tip state. I can't let them see it like that.'

She ignored the intended closure. 'I suppose Cary's not overly concerned. From what you told me, her new man is flush with cash: big house in the suburbs; executive car and perks; fancy dinner parties. She'll fit right in.'

Dominic stilled the engine and sat back in his seat, his spare hand pulling the slack on the seatbelt. 'Alex . . . Alex is his name. Did I detect a certain chagrin in your comment, a wish it was me scenario?'

11

'And why not? What's so wrong with a desire for a comfortable middle-class life? I can't understand why it doesn't piss you off how she found it so easy to slip into a new relationship. For all you know, it was going on long before you had your famous conversation.'

'That had occurred to me, but I thought, under the circumstances . . .'

'How do you think her parents will react?'

'Her plan is to leave saying anything for a few days until Len and Muriel have lost that first warm glow of having their grandchildren around. Once they tire of two screaming kids jumping all over the furniture and toys all over the floor, Cary reckons they will welcome the news. After all, the unspoken elephant in the room was always Len's view that mentally I had one leg shorter than the other and needed his Cary as a prop. Of course, his relationship with Dad convinced him the entire family was inflicted with some strain of mental aberration.'

'Maybe we are.'

He restarted the engine. 'Must go. I need to find a suitable wall for my next rant.'

THREE

LEN AND MURIEL

He held the tweezers between gnarled, weather-worn fingers, strangely offset by manicured and polished nails. He closed the tips around the base of the bobble that topped the knitted woollen sock covering the golf club, gradually easing it up and away from the head of the driver. With a grunt of satisfaction, he laid the cover on the kitchen work surface.

'Is it just that one?' Muriel asked.

Len picked up the 3 wood and repeated the exercise. 'It's over all of them,' he replied. 'They were in the hall cupboard. I don't know how Creedence opened the door. It was quite stiff.'

'They're curious about everything at that age.'

'Stating the obvious again, Muriel.'

'Sorry.'

'I don't know what she had all over her hands. I can't tell whether it's that Manuka-style honey or the Dragon Fruit jam that Tansley-Wake gave me. It's the club secretary's grandmother's Malaysian recipe, apparently. You must remember to tell Caroline not to feed them to the children. They're far too expensive. Whatever it was, the four covers are now sticky to the touch.'

He finished removing the last cover from a 5 wood, arranging all four precisely in line. 'Would you mind handwashing them? They were presented to me for winning the four-ball. Hannah Courtney's mother knitted them just before she died. It was her last act, so they say. I'd hate for them to shrink in the machine. We're not teeing off until two thirty, so you have plenty of time.'

Muriel picked up the covers, saying nothing, and walked from the kitchen. Five minutes later, she returned, confirming that his precious covers were on the drying stand.

'Fancy a coffee and a croissant?' he asked.

'You carry on. I need to tidy up the kitchen. It looks as though a bomb's hit it.'

'Caroline did apologise. She says it's important to give the girls freedom of expression at this age and to correct by explanation and to avoid negativity.' He cleaned the shaft of a four iron with the tea towel he had

13

doused under the tap and returned the club to the golf bag. 'My mother relied on a clip around the head as the most effective deterrent and it never did me any harm, did it?'

'Mmmm . . .' She seemed unwilling to be distracted from mopping up milk and sugar puffs from the breakfast bar. 'If you're golfing, you'll want me to pick them up from school?' she said, finally.

He held up a golf glove, the textured mesh puncture with plastic tees. 'Would you look at this?' he said. 'It's ruined. She can't just let them run wild like this. They must learn to respect other people's property.'

'I think you'll find a couple of golf balls rolled under the hall stand.'

'Jesus,' he said. 'What's next?' He took a bite into a croissant, brushing the flakes from his dressing gown onto the tiled floor.

'I asked whether I'm to pick up the girls after school? Remember, Caroline has my car.'

Another cascade of flakes floated to the floor. 'It slipped my mind. You'll have to drop me off at the club. I'll ring later when I need to be picked up.'

'Supposing Caroline's not back from work when you ring?'

'You'll have to bring the girls. On second thoughts, don't worry about me. I'll get one of the lads to drop me back here.' He stood up and gave his dressing gown a last brush down. 'That was good.' He drained the mug of coffee and handed it to his wife. 'I'll use the en-suite. It won't have been kid infested.' He stopped halfway out of the kitchen and adjusted the belt of his dressing gown. 'There's one thing I don't really understand. I spent my life in the force listening to lowlifes telling lies, and I pride myself on being able to distinguish when I'm being spun a yarn.' He raised his eyebrows as she breathed heavily and steadied herself on the counter. 'Are you all right?'

She nodded. 'You were saying?'

'As much as I love our daughter and the twins, I really don't get why she was the one to leave the house and not him. Do you? Her excuse was the place held too many memories, and she felt if she stayed, her resolve to leave might have weakened. Does that ring true to you?'

'I wish they had both stayed and tried to work it out.'

Len shook his head forcibly. 'I have no problem with her ditching him. We'll get rid of that shitbag of a father of his once and for all. I'm only sorry it's taken so long. I told her on the morning of their wedding that she shouldn't worry about the money or the embarrassment. If she was having second thoughts about him, call it off and I'd sort everything out. If only she'd listened to me, but she's stubborn. Takes after your father; like talking to a brick wall.'

'If there is something else, it's bound to come out in the wash. Why don't you get yourself ready?' She turned her back on him. 'Try not to be too late this evening. You remember we're going round to Gerry's for dinner?'

He stopped in his tracks. 'Oh, that's all I need, an evening with my Peter Pan brother. Welcome to the age of Aquarius.' He made the victory sign. 'Peace brother. Do we have to? You walk through the front door, and you feel you're in an opium den. You're high before you reach the living room. Then there's tactile Gloria, the blonde bombshell with a chest that defies gravity and a tee-shirt with a plea to save some obscure species stamped on the front you can't read because the words disappear beneath her bosom.'

Muriel turned back to face him, her fingers trembling as she picked at the curls of grey hair barely intact from last week's perm. 'I'll cancel again if you like. We can stay here with Caroline and the twins. You can interrogate her.'

He hesitated. 'Second thoughts. We've cancelled so many times. Best to get it over and done with. Don't make it too early. It'll easily take an hour to get to Croydon.'

'Really, Len,' she sounded exasperated. 'They moved a year ago. They're in a mobile home now, somewhere near Hounslow. Don't you remember? A group of thirty clubbed together to buy a reclaimed landfill site and establish a commune. It's on the flight path of the third Heathrow runway and scheduled for redevelopment. They plan to hold out against the eventual compulsory purchase order in an organised protest on environmental grounds.'

'Now you say, I recall. It was information I consigned to my loony tunes recycle bin. You mean we're invited to dinner in a caravan?'

'Apparently not. It's some American style, two-bedroom model with all mod cons. Gerry has suggested we might like to stay the night.'

'I presume you said no.'

'I said I'd ask you. He said that was just a polite way of declining.'

15

'Too right. I'm past camp beds, chemical loos and strange individuals walking around in kaftans in the dead of night talking to the moon. I like the comfort of my own bed.'

'When Caroline rings to check on the girls, I'll tell her to be back by seven at the latest. Who are you playing with today?'

'Randy's had to call off. He's the only one still in active service. Another year to go before he can pull up sticks. He's with the ECD and there's a big fraud investigation going on. They've pulled his days off. Otherwise, it's Terry and Nobby from Bishopsgate station. You remember them from my retirement do? We should get around quicker as a threesome.'

'You could always invite Charlie to make up the four. You will have to speak together sometime.'

'You are joking, surely? I doubt he's ever held a golf club and even if he did, by the time he could see the ball over that stomach of his, he'd be too far away to hit it.'

'An exaggeration, perhaps?'

'Forget it. Charlie is the last person I would want to socialise with. We'll talk on another day, hopefully for the last time. Can you make lunch for midday? I don't want to tee off on a full stomach.' With that, he closed the door and climbed the stairs. He began to sing a Jim Reeves classic, "He'll Have to Go."

Muriel stood over the sink, staring out of the window, his coffee mug clasped in her hand. Amid loud, gasping sobs, tears were streaming down her cheeks.

FOUR

CARY AND GERRY

The Seven Bells Wine and Tapas Bar was gradually filling up from the stream of office workers rushing along Chancery Lane during the lunch-hour break. Looking through one of the small bottle-glass windowpanes, Cary could see he was sitting at a corner table, absent-mindedly spinning a coin on the polished wood surface, obviously to the annoyance of the blue pinstripes on the adjoining tables, who, she calculated, might tut-tut, but were unlikely to say anything to such an unconventional looking individual.

Cary smiled to herself as she recalled the story. Gerry was five years older than half-brother, Len, and the result of their father's fling with a West Indian bus conductor, otherwise known as a clippie, whose womanly attributes had apparently transcended the dour dark blue, ill-fitting uniform of trousers and jacket, the silver ticket machine balanced on her chest and the strap of the worn leather money satchel strung around her neck. According to Gerry, his father would spend all day on her bus, snatching a brief opportunity for a conversation every time he bought a ticket, until the day she finally agreed to go on a date with him. Amongst the crews at the bus depot, he was famously known as Randy Routemaster and the regular recipient of unprintable, gratuitous tips on how to handle his red-hot mama.

Gerry would have you believe he was conceived on the bench seat of a number 13 whilst parked up in the North Finchley bus station, but the reality was likely to be much more conventional. In any event, prejudice and attitudes of the time were too strong for the couple to withstand, and the relationship ended before Gerry's father knew of the pregnancy. He was married to Len's mother when a knock came at the door and a three-year-old was standing there, coffee cream features, a shock of blond curly hair and a patois accent calling him "Daddy". It turned out that the boy's mother was of the Windrush generation, judged to have arrived in the country illegally and deported back to Jamaica. The family felt it was only right that the father should know of his son's existence, and to Len's mother's credit, she was aware of her husband's previous relationship and happy to assume responsibility for the child.

Heads turned as Cary made her way across the bar. She had long since realised she had all the qualities to succeed in a man's world, good looks, intelligence, the experience of a woman in her thirties and an air of total self-assurance without appearing conceited. It was a heady concoction for most family-tied men who fantasised about the possibilities. Some even went further and suggested meeting up for a drink. Until recently, she had resisted all the approaches, not out of faithfulness to Dominic but rejection of the messiness and deceit of an extra-marital affair. There had always been too much going on in her world to waste time on seedy hotel rooms and the "how he was planning to leave his wife" bullshit. But circumstances change.

Gerry rose from his chair as he caught sight of her. The fringes on the arms and front of his western-style, suede leather jacket rippled as he moved. He took off the Stetson to let the tinted golden locks bunched up inside fall to shoulder length. The contrast with his Caribbean features was stunning, even for a man well into his sixties.

'Buffalo Bill!' she heard someone say.

'What's all this, Gerry?' she said with a smile as she reached on tiptoe to kiss his cheek. She stepped back to point at the blue denims tucked into cowboy boots. 'Are you auditioning for a part in a Western?'

'Hi Cary. You good? It's the nearest thing I've got to a suit. Better than turning up in the floral shirt and dressing gown I would normally wear at this ungodly hour of the day. I don't know how you survive amongst all these penguins.'

'I dress like one so as not to attract attention.'

'Looking at the eyes following your entrance, I'd say you were failing miserably, if that's really your intention. Can I get you a drink, something to eat?'

'No, it's my treat. I asked you to come. What are you drinking, Cuba Libre?'

'Just Diet Coke. I only appreciate alcohol when it's in excess and today, right here, is obviously not the time or place. Don't look at me like that with your cynic's face on. I still have some social graces.'

Her smile was warm and intimate. 'I admire your restraint. Personally, I need a bloody great gin and tonic and damn the consequences.'

18

Five minutes later, the server appeared with their drinks and two club sandwiches. 'I took the liberty of ordering something to eat,' she said. 'Alcohol on an empty stomach and I'm likely to say something to a client this afternoon I'll later regret. A lack of inhibitions and accountancy don't go together.'

'Sounds dead boring. So, tell *me* something you'll later regret.'

She pulled her chair closer to the table, pushed strands of short, auburn hair away from her mouth, and took a bite of the sandwich. 'I need your advice,' she said, dabbing the paper napkin on full lips. 'Can you treat what I'm about to tell you as confidential, just between us?'

'Not even Gloria?'

'Especially not Gloria. You know what she's like when she's on the wacky baccy.'

'Tricky. She has the most pleasurable and intimate way of eliciting information from me. I find it's irresistible.' The thought prompted a lazy smile and the need to readjust his seating position.

'Well, curb your animal instincts, tell her the first part of what I've got to say and keep the rest to yourself until I've broached the news with Mum and Dad. It's why I need my uncle's input. You know how to appeal to dad's more understanding nature. I don't.'

'I wouldn't put it quite like that. Len gave up on converting me to convention a long time ago. On the rare occasions I now see him, I'd say he tolerates my company and can't be bothered to argue about my life choices. He also finds it difficult to take his eyes off Gloria's chest, a distraction that can make him lose track of the conversation. She is a vital element in the toolbox when we need the occasional loan from him.'

'Go on. Mum says he's never looked at another woman.'

'Muriel will believe what Muriel wants to believe. She used to see the sun as shining out of your dad's bum hole, but I think Len's selfish approach to life in retirement may have jaundiced her opinion.' He said the last phrase loud enough for the couple at the next table to stop their conversation and look around. Gerry raised his Stetson toward them and winked at the woman. He turned back to face Cary. 'Okay, sister. Shoot!'

'Dominic and I are getting a divorce. It's been boiling up over the last six months and has now come to a head. I've left the house and moved in with mum and dad. The girls are with me.'

'How's Len taken it?'

'Telling him I was leaving Dom was the easy part. Dad never really took to him, and he can't stand Dom's father. He hasn't quite got around to saying, "I told you so", but he's close.'

'What are the circumstances?' The straw coursed around the bottom of his glass as he sucked, making a gurgling noise.

'That's where I'm having the difficulty. We agreed on an amicable divorce, no blame, citing irreconcilable differences, but dad's suspicious because I'm the one who's moved out instead of Dom.'

'Len was a copper. He's heard and seen it all. I don't think you'll pull the wool over his eyes. Go on.'

'Six months ago, Dom joined a gym to lose some flab around his stomach. He had a personal trainer, a guy called Lance. A month passes, and he sits me down to tell me his sexual orientation is changing, and he's been taking time off from work during the day to do whatever gays do with Lance. I'm still not sure how it works. He said he still loved me and had, what he called, physical feelings for me, and wanted us to stay together as a family. I told him he couldn't expect to have a normal heterosexual relationship with me if he was in a relationship with another man. I—'

'Let me guess how it pans out,' Gerry cut in. 'You said you'd try to stick with it if he went and saw a shrink to get himself sorted out. He either didn't or he did, and it didn't work out – there's a tongue twister for you – carried on getting himself Lanced, and in the meantime, you felt liberated from the relationship, met Mr X and ended up, metaphorically speaking, in the next hotel room to your husband. Is that about right?'

Her head turned to the side as she studied him. 'That's uncanny. Have you got a spy camera in our house? He saw a psychiatrist - once. The conversation didn't go the way he hoped, so he didn't go again. As for me, I have a client who runs a successful financial investment business. He's in his early fifties, a widower with an adult son. The chemistry has always been there, just under the surface of a cordial accountant/client relationship. He's got a large house near Ashford in Kent. I plan to move in with the girls next week. They should have softened up mum and dad sufficiently to relish my announcement by then.'

'Meaning?'

'Len and Muriel are in the first flush of having the twins stay with them. Give it three days, the novelty will have worn off and the reality of two six-year-old house wreckers causing havoc will make them more amenable to the news of Alex – that's his name – and my new life choice. Creedence has already attacked dad's golf bag with sticky fingers and Syracuse has coloured in one of his cruise magazines. I got them off to school this morning before he discovered the damage.'

'Are you planning to say anything about Dominic? If you don't, Len will think it's your affair that caused the break-up.'

'I know. More than anything, I feel sorry for Dom. I don't think he really knows what he wants, and this affair seems much more an infatuation than a long-term prospect. I gave my word not to say anything until he found the right moment to tell his parents. He's convinced his dad will disown him. Charlie's attitude to dealing with homosexuality is about on a par with Hitler's final solution.'

Gerry reached for her hand and massaged her fingers.

'Did it make you feel inadequate as a wife?' He leaned closer to her. 'You know, lovemaking is such an important part of a relationship. It speaks to your partner when words will not suffice, establishes a state of harmony you cannot recreate in any other way. How *was* the physical side of things with your husband?'

'Inadequate would be the wrong word to describe the way I felt. Confused and disappointed would be better choices. As for sex . . .' She sensed eyes were upon them and quickly withdrew her hand. Her voice was little more than a whisper. 'Since he came out of the closet, intimacy has been restricted to a hug in front of the girls before he leaves for work. Before that, as you might expect after twelve years of marriage, it was a little like painting by numbers, if you get my drift.'

'And with the new guy?'

'Alex? Absolutely mind-blowing. He knows his way around.'

He twirled the Stetson around on his index finger. 'Sounds like my kind of guy. You should bring him along to meet the crew. We have a communal barbecue most nights in the summer. Dress optional,' he joked.

Cary nodded. 'I will. Listen, what I need to ask you is how I should broach the subject of Alex with dad. It's a minefield.'

The wine bar was emptying. The girl from the adjacent table gave Cary an understanding nod of the head as she passed and a questioning glance at Gerry.

He leaned back in his chair. 'As I see it, you have two red zones to avoid. As far as your husband's concerned, protect him, but that doesn't prevent you from saying you're aware or believe he has a new partner, but you have no details, nor do you want to know. Make it sound apparent you have been drifting apart for some time and his new liaison started before you took up with Alex. Then you can say how lucky you are to have met somebody through your work for whom you have strong feelings and who gets on well with the twins, et cetera, et cetera.'

'You think dad will buy that approach?'

Gerry nodded. 'You're halfway there already. He doesn't rate your husband, so you tell me, and he can't stand your father-in-law.' He gave a loud sigh. 'And therein lies your second problem and a much tougher nut to crack.'

'How come?' There was the hint of alarm in her voice.

'On the rare occasion Len confides in me, he comes over as one of those ultra-protective fathers who thinks no man is good enough for his daughter. Not having any kids of my own that I know of, I suspect his attitude is not uncommon, merely exaggerated.'

'He wants to see me happy, surely?'

'Not as much as the subconscious instinct to want his seed to flourish in the future. As his only child and a daughter, your choice of donor is critical to his well-being and, even now, that may still mean hoping for a grandson. Do you envisage having any more children?'

Cary's mouth had fallen open at the turn in the conversation. 'I've never discussed it. The years pass and I'm no spring chicken.'

'Nonsense,' he said dismissively. 'You're barely mid-thirties. Plenty of time. I read about women approaching fifty who are still shucking peas.'

'What an inglorious metaphor. You make dad sound like some pharaoh who dismisses girl babies as irrelevant and recognises only male heirs. Even for him, that's drastic.'

Gerry leaned forward, extending his hands to frame her face between them. He used his thumb to brush the solitary tear from her cheek. 'Don't take my word for it. If you were to become pregnant with a boy, then you can tell me if I'm wrong.'

'Grief, I've never even given the idea a thought. My career path seems set now, and another child doesn't figure in my calculations. Besides, I don't see Alex as welcoming the prospect.'

'Whether you do or don't is between you both and Len's point of view is irrelevant, but consider your new relationship from his angle.'

She sat back, leaving his hands suspended in mid-air. Her stance was defensive. 'I have no doubts about Alex getting on with mum and dad. They have a great deal in common. He'll charm them.'

'Having something in common is great between contemporaries. It's not so great when you're vetting your daughter's partner. Look, I'm sixty-five. Your dad's five years younger. That makes him sixty.'

'He retired from the force on his sixtieth birthday.'

'Right, You're thirty-four.'

'Thirty-five. You missed my last birthday.'

'Sorry. Must have been the curse of alcohol. Obviously, sent your card to the wrong person.'

She laughed. 'You're a terrible liar.'

'Anyway, your new beau is closer in age to Len than he is to you. How do you think Len's going to react when he finds out you're living with somebody almost old enough to be your father and not far short of his age? He's going to hate it. He'll have sleepless nights worrying about Alex's sperm count or whether he's got an adequate supply of Viagra.'

'I can let him rest assured on that score.'

'I'm joking, but take heed. Len will not like it. His relationship with Alex is bound to be frosty. Did Len ever make any sexual movements to you as a child? You know, bounce you for too long on his knee? That sort of thing?'

Cary recoiled in her chair. 'That's disgusting,' she hissed. 'Of course not. How could you think so? Shame on you for even deigning to say such a thing about your brother, Gerry. You have a warped mind.'

'Half-brother,' he corrected. 'It's true, I do. Gloria praises me for it. She says it makes life interesting.'

'Well, I don't.' She reached for her handbag, as if preparing to leave. 'I must be going. I'm late for work.'

'You look a little like Rita Hayworth when you're angry. You won't know who I'm talking about, but Google her. You'll see what I mean.'

'You're a strange man, Gerry,' she said calmly. 'Why did you ask the question?'

'Because it's quite probable that Len will see your relationship with Alex in that light, his contemporary, a predator taking sexual advantage of his precious daughter.'

'Surely not?' She replaced the handbag. 'That's ludicrous.'

'I know your father better than you think. He has a set of standards and you shacking up with a fifty-something year-old is unlikely to cut the mustard. Even Dominic couldn't meet his suitor criteria, could he?'

She was silent as she stared into his face. 'God, you've got me worried now. I'd never even given any of this a second thought. I'll have to sit down with Alex and try to work out a strategy.'

He nodded. 'Don't tell him it was me who put all these weird thoughts in your head. He won't want to come around for the barbecue, which would be a shame.'

Cary stood up, leaned forward, and kissed him on the forehead. 'Remember, no letting the cat out of the bag until I've dealt with dad. He'd be furious if he thought I'd confided in you.'

He squeezed her shoulder as they routed to the exit. 'It's not Len, but Gloria you must worry about. I'll have to work out my story and at what point in the proceedings I crack under her exquisite torture and spill the beans.'

FIVE

DOMINIC AND LANCE

Somewhere in that transition from sleep to snooze, he could sense the refrain of a tune was playing. If he wasn't mistaken, it was one of Cary's favourites, something about wanting to know where love is. This was an instrumental version. The sound in his head grew louder, as did the realisation. Somebody had their finger pressed on the front doorbell.

Cary had made him buy some fancy video security model that offered the choice of a menu of a hundred melodies or the option to download your own. He had tried to raise an objection, but she had insisted. After all, it was her money, she had said. Thinking about it, right from day one, it had never been their money, always his or hers. She would work out their fixed expenses, divide the total in half and deduct it from their net salaries. The surplus was disposable income, and she always had more left on her side of the page than on his. To be fair, she didn't mind spending it on family interests, but it was uncomfortable for him to feel emasculated when she would be the one to ask for the restaurant bill every two out of three times. 'This is female equality,' she would say. 'The ludicrous dogma that the man should ask for the bill and pay is in the past.'

'Are you going to open this door, Dom?' The accented voice shouting through the letterbox was unmistakeably Australian and provoked in Dominic a sensation that was a mixture of excitement and trepidation. He reached behind the bedroom door for a dressing gown. It was one of Cary's, but it would have to do.

'How did you get my address?' He asked, suddenly conscious of the image he must portray in a silk dressing gown with a floral design on the cuffs.

The man who stood on the doorstep was shorter than Dominic, with short, black, cropped hair, shaved around the ears and a square face with a pronounced cleft in his chin. As if in defiance of the blustery weather, his white shirt was open to the waist, revealing a pronounced six-pack and muscular frame. It was a frame that Dominic had come to know in intimate detail over the last five months.

'What are you doing here, Lance? I told you the time is not right yet. The dust must settle.'

'Don't get at me, Dom. I've had a rotten morning. I'm sorry I woke you, but it is nearly nine and I need your help and understanding.'

'What's wrong?'

'I've had to leave the hostel and I need somewhere to crash out for a day or so until I can get things sorted. I looked up your address in the membership records. Not supposed to, but I have nowhere else to turn. You don't mind, do you?' His hand slipped inside the dressing gown and brushed Dominic's underpants. 'I can sense you don't,' he added.

Dominic pulled back and adjusted the belt of the dressing gown. He studied the neighbouring houses to see if Lance's presence was attracting curious gazes from behind net curtains. Everything was as tranquil as normal. 'You'd better come in. Stand there on the doorstep and you'll attract attention.' He ushered Lance into the lounge and pointed to the settee. 'Sit there whilst I make a coffee and tell me what's happened, but be quick. I've got a busy day in front of me.'

As Dominic reappeared carrying two mugs of coffee, Lance patted the area next to him on the settee. 'Come and sit here.' He took the coffee and clasped the mug between his two hands. 'I need this,' he said, blowing and sipping at the liquid.

'Come on then, spit it out, Lance. Why are you here?'

'I blame your bloody Brexit. There was a raid on the hostel at six this morning by the immigration authorities.'

'*A raid?*'

'Well, all right, a visit. Six of them. They were checking our visas?'

'And you don't have one?'

'Wrong. I did. That's to say, three years ago, when I came over to start a degree course in physical education at Northampton, I had a Tier 4 visa. When you graduate, you can apply for a Tier 2 that allows you to remain for a further five years.'

'Great. So, what's the problem?'

'I jacked the course after a year and went to work at a gym. As I failed to graduate and was working over twenty hours a week, I was ineligible to apply for the long stay visa. In the eyes of the authorities, I'm an illegal immigrant. Before all the Brexit bullshit, no one gave a damn. Now, it's sodding 1984 and Big Brother is after me.' He drained the remains of his coffee and rested the mug on Dominic's thigh.

Dominic took the mug, placing it on the side table. Lance's hand remained on his thigh. 'Well, you can't stay here. There's too much going on right now.' He purposefully placed Lance's hand back on the settee. 'My parents could turn up. As it is, I'm on a special assignment today and need to be available for twelve hours from ten this morning. My sister will be here at three to show various estate agents round the house. Because of the divorce, it's going on the market.'

'Surely I could come back after everybody has gone and stay for just one night? I just need to get things sorted out and I'm off.'

'How did you avoid the immigration officers?'

Lance stood up to look through the window at the front garden. 'I always have my bag packed, just in case. When I heard the commotion going on downstairs, I realised what was happening and beat it down the fire escape. I went to the gym, did my nine o'clock Pilates and found my way here. I left my bag under your bush out there.'

'You're putting me in a difficult position, Lance. We had an agreement to meet on neutral territory until I'd cleared the air waves with everybody. One false move and it could put the grounds for the divorce in jeopardy.'

Lance kneeled on the settee and placed his hands on Dominic's shoulders. 'Don't be so melodramatic. I'm only asking for one little night. We can have some fun, can't we? Something to remember during our enforced abstinence. You're so stressed. You need relaxing.' He lowered his hand to feel under the dressing gown. 'I can already feel a big boy here who wants to come out and play.

'I got my head out of the way just in time,' Lance said, a laugh in his voice. 'You've gizzed all over the upholstery. Man, you needed that. Like Cape Canaveral on launch day.'

'Shut up. You're embarrassing me.' Dominic rubbed the sleeve of the dressing gown at the trickle of semen as it ran down the synthetic velvet material. 'Cary wants this settee when we sell up. I said she could have it. Now look.'

'A lasting memento of your creative talents?'

'Don't be sarcastic. I need to get dressed for work. Make another coffee, if you like, but keep away from the windows. Don't let nosey neighbours see you.'

Lance sat cross-legged on the settee. 'Yes, boss. What do you do for work exactly? I know it's something to do with computers.'

'If you're really interested, I sit in a van waiting for a job sheet to appear on the screen. Sometimes it's a new computer installation, sometimes a repair, sometimes a software problem they can't sort out by cloning the client's machine at head office. Sound stimulating?'

'Sounds like you need to be intelligent.'

Dominic finished trying to clean the stain. 'I'll have to wash this to recover the material.' He shook his head. 'You need a mathematical and engineering bent to get on in my line of work. It's like anything. Once you understand the basics and get practical experience, it's pretty much a matter of course.'

The smell of cooking wafted upstairs as Dominic finished showering and dressing. He hadn't shaved, deciding it was time to develop some designer stubble to give him a younger look. He reached for his work jacket with the Byte Man logo and made his way downstairs. 'What's going on, Lance?' He checked his watch. Nine forty-five. They both needed to be out of the house.

'I've rustled up my speciality, a Spanish omelette.'

'We need to be out of the house.'

'You can't go to work on an empty stomach. How long's it going to take to eat it? Five minutes?'

Lance returned his knife and fork to an empty plate. 'Tell me if that's not the best omelette you have ever eaten?'

'It was good. I didn't know you had culinary talents.'

'They begin and end with this omelette, though I'm game to learn.'

Dominic stood up. 'Look, you must leave with me now, only you take the kitchen door, go to the end of the garden and there's a passageway all the way back to the main road. Understood?'

'What time do you want me to return?'

'I don't, but I'll put up with you for one night. Take the same route back around ten and let yourself in. There's a key under the flowerpot. I'll bring back a takeaway. Agreed?'

'Yes, boss.'

'Let's go, before the neighbours talk.'

SIX

LEN, TERRY, NOBBY . . . and MR PAUL BATEMAN

'What are you playing off today, you *pistoleiro*?' Len asked as he bent to tie the lace of his golf shoe.

Terry made to fire an imaginary six-gun. 'As there's only three of us, why don't we make it interesting? How about a fiver a hole and a pony for the winner?'

'Only if I play off fifteen and you off six,' Len retorted. 'Remember, it's the police force that pays your pension, not the Len and Nobby top-up charity. Are you short this month of a few bob, or what?' He checked his golf bag one last time and zipped up his lime green, Lacoste weatherproof bomber jacket.

'Tell you what,' Terry said, pulling the peaked cap over his mop of grey hair. 'I'll give you seven shots and Nobby a shot a hole. How's that?'

'Did I hear my name mentioned in vain?' came a voice from the entrance of the changing room. A balding man with Asian-Indian features appeared around the corner carrying an oversize golf bag.

'You should have left that outside with your trolley,' Terry said. 'It's only Len here and his love affair with his fancy graphite shafts and titanium heads who can't bear to let them out of his sight. I fancy if Muriel won't let him have it, he's out in the shed self-abusing as he worships his nine iron.'

'At least mine's not all shrivelled up and afraid of daylight.' Len shook Nobby's outstretched hand. 'How the devil are you, Mr Clark? Just ignore our friend. He's trying one of his golfing scams to extract money from us. He's even proposed a discount if we pay up before the round starts.'

'All lies. Don't listen to him.' Terry reached over to greet his colleague. 'As we're a threesome, I just wanted to heighten the experience.'

'I'm afraid we're not,' Nobby said. 'We will be a four.' He parked his slender frame on the bench.

'Randy's making an appearance, after all?' Len asked.

'Regretfully not. He had a call at home from Mr Bateman.' Nobby waited for a reaction, but both friends were silent, waiting for an explanation. 'There's a blast from the past, eh?'

31

'One I'd rather not be reminded of,' Len said solemnly.

'Randy said Bateman specifically asked after you, Len.'

'Did he, indeed?'

'Randy told him he was supposed to be playing with us but couldn't, and Bateman said to let the others know he'd make up the foursome. He asked for the tee-off time and said he'd get his chauffeur to drop him off, but not to wait if he was late and missed the first hole. He'd catch up. I've already signed him in as a guest at reception.'

Terry shook his head. 'I've got an uncomfortable feeling about this. Surely, we're no use to him anymore. We've all retired with no influence now everything's tightened up. Darren knows the score.'

'It's not Darren who's joining us,' Nobby said. 'It's his dad, Paul.'

'Woohoo!' Terry interjected. 'I do not like the sound of this. His dad? We barely knew him, even in the heyday.'

'Come on,' Len said. 'We'll miss our tee-off.' He slung the strap of his bag over his shoulder. 'Think about it. There's nothing to worry about. We've retired, left the force and have absolutely no influence with anybody. Fact: whatever Mr Big wants, we cannot help him. Now, let's play.'

They were walking to the third tee before the sound of a golf buggy on the gravel pathway attracted their attention. A club groundsman was at the wheel, accompanied by a man whose outline in the distance was at once recognisable. The buggy came to a halt a good seventy metres from where they stood; the driver moving round to lift out the trolley and clubs before he went to assist his passenger. As Bateman manoeuvred cautiously to plant his feet on the ground, a folded note was forced into the driver's palm. At least twenty quid, Len thought, as he recognised the sudden feeling of nervous apprehension in his stomach.

'Hold up boys,' Bateman shouted. 'I'll be right with you.'

'Take your time,' Terry said. 'The last group has just teed off. It's a par three, so we need to wait until they clear the green.'

Len watched the short, stocky man start walking toward them. He would be around sixty, broad and muscular, with legs like tree trunks and arms to match. At a glance, you could tell he wasn't of British stock. Len could vaguely recall Darren telling him his dad had emigrated in a hurry from

Cyprus as a young man. There was a price on his head set by a mafia group in Limassol, and England was far enough away and a safe enough bet to begin building a new life. According to Darren, the family name matched the length of that famous Welsh railway station, obliging his dad to change it to something considered sober and responsible. Quite how he had funded a refrigerated haulage business on the grand scale was guesswork and although there was no concrete proof, nobody in the City of London CID force was in any doubt as to the answer.

Len's maxim had always been to ask questions relevant to the ongoing enquiry and never stray into areas likely to set him at odds with people more powerful or dangerous than he. That the evangelical police officer rarely made it trouble-free to retirement was proof his philosophy of playing everything by the book paid off.

'Well, look who we've got here.' Bateman's breathing was laboured and his accent pronounced. The golf trolley tipped to one side and clubs began to slip from the bag.

'Bollocks,' he said. 'Stupid game. Only took it up because Darren said it suited my profile. I played ice hockey as a youth in Turkey. That's a man's game with physical contact, none of this fashion parade nonsense.' He pointed at the outfits the three friends were wearing.

Nobby bent to upright the trolley and straighten the clubs. 'Thank you. As I recall, it's Robin Clark, aka Nobby, former police property-slash-evidence custody sergeant at Wood Street? We've also got former DI Len Sheppard and his erstwhile staff sergeant, Terry Corden. I think I'm right in saying you have all benefitted from my largesse in the past and I, in return, from your extra curriculum services.'

'It's all in the past now, Mr Bateman,' Terry said. 'We're retired and long gone. There's a new breed running the show now.'

'That's right. You're all yesterday's men.' He gave a deep-throated laugh. 'The trouble is, the past has a nasty habit of coming back and biting you. None of us need that, do we?'

Nobby pointed down the fairway. 'They're clearing the green. We can tee off.'

Bateman pulled back Terry before he could place his ball on the tee. 'Tell you what, I need a private word with Len here. We'll drive off. If we land on the green, you mark us down for a par. If we land in the rough, we'll drop a shot. Fair enough? We'll join you on the fourth.'

'I doubt I can help you with anything, Mr Bateman,' Len said, but the man wasn't listening.

'How far is the green?' Bateman asked, placing his ball on the rubber mat.

'One hundred and thirty-six yards,' Nobby said.

'What club are you using?'

'A seven iron,' Nobby replied.

Bateman carefully studied Nobby's skeletal frame from top to toe and sniffed air into flared nostrils as he thought. 'It's either a nine iron or a wedge,' he said, eventually. 'Give me the nine.' Nobby dutifully obeyed.

His stance was unorthodox, one foot planted in front of the other, his shoulders almost square on to the green. With almost nonchalant ease and little backswing, the club sent the ball soaring high into the sky. One bounce on the front of the green and the ball scuttled past the flag to come to a stop in the semi-rough twenty feet beyond the hole. 'Should have used the wedge,' he said. 'Put me down for a three, will you?'

Nobody argued. Len chose a seven iron and watched his ball trickle along the fairway to come to a stop just before the front of the green.

'Two pars you can card us for, Robin,' he said as he led Len away from the group. 'Bring our trolleys, will you, lads?' he called back over his shoulder. They walked into the thicket between the third and fourth fairways, stopping out of earshot of anyone approaching. 'We have a minor problem, Len,' he said.

'We? How come?' Len turned to face him.

'Regretfully, yes, *we* and your two partners in crime over there. As you know, things have changed since the good old days when I just did haulage to and from the Continent. I don't do so much in your old patch anymore. Smithfield is not what it used to be. Like the fish market at Billingsgate and the fruit and veg at Covent Garden, plans are afoot to merge three markets into one in Dagenham. I've established my business now in the Midlands. We have a substantial warehouse and wholesale butcher's operation in Wolverhampton, with distribution as far north as Manchester and

Sheffield. My daughter, Dimitra, looks after the day-to-day and Darren takes care of our other business interests.'

'Do I need to know what they are?' Len leaned back against the trunk of a tree and unfastened his golf glove.

Bateman shook his head. 'You got a circulation problem, rubbing your fingers like that?' He looked genuinely concerned.

'Don't know what it is. I get a tingling sensation from time to time.'

'Check it out, mate. At our age, you can't take chances.'

'You were saying?' Len didn't need advice. He knew he should have seen the doctor when it first started, months ago.

Bateman watched as the foursome playing the fourth walked along the fairway. He lowered his voice. 'In the good old days, we used to transport everything in those ten-wheel, refrigerated box trucks, the old Scania P280, six-by-two. It was the biggest unit you could comfortably manoeuvre around the City of London. We've still got a couple on the distribution runs, but all inwards freight from the Continent we now transport in twenty or forty-foot reefer container units loaded onto flatbed rigs.'

'That's fascinating, I'm sure, Mr Bateman, but what's your point?'

'Background, Len, you need the background. Anyway, this Scania I'm going to tell you about had an important modification which I'll explain. Last week, I sent one of the new drivers with this knackered Scania to the breakers. We always use the same guy in Leicester, a trusted old friend, if you get my drift. I told the driver he would receive a grand in readies which he was to bring back and hand over to my daughter. In the event, this man decided to sharpen his entrepreneurial skills and find another breaker who was willing to pay the going rate for the scrap value of the truck. He got two and a half thousand, pocketed one and half for himself and handed the remaining grand to my girl without saying a word. Now, things begin to unravel.'

The sound of strange voices talking and laughing distracted Len and he looked to see a new foursome waiting on the third tee for Terry and Nobby to finish playing the hole. 'You need to accelerate this tale if you want to play the fourth,' he said.

'Fuck the golf!' Bateman hissed, his annoyance apparent. 'None of us will play sodding golf if we're locked up in a cell. Now listen. You need to do us all a favour.'

Len closed his eyes, for the first time wary of what he was about to hear.

'Pay attention. A day after this incident, we send a copy of the logbook over to our breaker who, naturally, asks after the whereabouts of the vehicle. The following morning, we summon the driver and, with a little coercion, out comes the truth. As far as he was concerned, we got our grand, so what was the problem? He'd used his initiative. That was his take on the rights and wrongs of the transaction.

'We sent two guys over to give this second breaker his money back and retrieve the vehicle. By the time they got to the yard, there's a police guard protecting the truck.'

'What the hell!'

Bateman leaned forward and beckoned for Len to get closer. He lowered his voice. 'The breaker had already started to dismantle the coachwork. He must have come across the false aluminium wall separating the refrigerated section from the secret rear compartment. Do I need to elaborate?'

Len shook his head. 'How come the guy had started to break it up without a copy of the logbook?'

'We'd given the driver a letter from the leasing company stating it had no further interest in the vehicle in case he was stopped en route. He left that with the buyer.'

'Looks like you're going to have a bit of explaining to do to the authorities.'

'I sincerely hope not, Len. Such revelations would be embarrassing for all concerned, if you get my drift.'

'I don't see how you can avoid it. If the logbook doesn't show your company name as the keeper, the leasing agreement will. Coupled with that, the police will interview the driver to get the facts.'

'We've put him on indefinite leave, sent him off to have a long and well-deserved rest. Thankfully, to avoid any comeback, he swore he didn't give the breaker his correct name and pretended the vehicle was used by him as a sole trader. He was afraid if he told the truth, the guy would be on the phone to our office to check it out.'

'Pity he didn't, but you're still screwed. As I remember, your vehicles are sign-written and you've got the problem of the documentation.'

Bateman walked out to the edge of the treeline to look back down the fourth fairway. 'I've waved to your two cohorts to play on. We'll drop a ball when they reach us and play up to the green. It will just give me time to explain to you why I'm not the naïve idiot you seem to think I am.'

The three ex-policemen looked on as Bateman hobbled toward the clubhouse door and take the arm of his chauffeur. The man reacted as Bateman spoke and glowered at them.

'Wouldn't fancy bumping into him on a dark night,' Nobby mused.

'Bateman no doubt needs his undoubted charms to perform other services at his master's behest,' Terry said, turning to Len. 'So, tell us. What was all that about? He didn't turn up just to take our money for winning – how many holes was it? Ten?'

'Eleven,' Nobby corrected. 'He claimed you played an air shot on the seventeenth.'

'He's a wanker,' Terry said. 'I was just practising.'

'He'd have won the lot if he had any patience on the greens,' Len said. 'He walks up to the ball and just hits it. No sizing up the putt or the lie of the land.'

'He got really upset with you.' Nobby turned to Terry. 'You take so long studying the terrain, he said you should have been an agronomist instead of a copper.'

'I heard the snide remark, and I heard you laugh, you twat.' Terry smiled. 'Come on, Len, what did the old bastard want?'

'I'll get another round in,' Nobby said. 'We good for time?'

'Not really. I've got a duty dinner tonight.' Len shook his head. 'Last thing I want to do, truth to tell.'

Nobby returned with the drinks. 'We shouldn't speak ill of the departed,' he said. 'He left twenty quid behind the bar.'

'What's he trying to do, Len? Soften us up?' Terry raised his glass in a toast toward the exit door.

It was past six before Len had recounted his conversation with Bateman to his colleagues. The mood was reflective.

37

'These are exactly the questions I posed,' Len said in answer to Terry. 'He had almost all the angles covered. The three vehicles he used for bringing in illegals were owned and leased by a funny money company registered in the British Virgin Islands. I got the impression he had a financial interest in the leasing operation, but in these tax havens secrecy and nominee corporate officials protect the real owners.'

Len explained how, to satisfy vehicle registration regulations in the UK, the leasing company had a branch in St. Albans, which was symbolic, nothing more than a plaque on the wall of a dodgy accountant's office. The logbooks of the three vehicles recorded the keeper as the leasing company at that address, and any correspondence would simply be sent back to the Virgin Islands. The actual operator of the vehicle would keep a copy of the logbook and a letter to "whom it may concern", showing the nominated driver as the rightful user of the vehicle.

'In those days, you could get away with that sort of gimmick. Bateman had three drivers he considered trusties who would keep their mouths shut and, in return, lived well. Of course, none of the vehicles had any external identification and, to ensure anonymity, the insurance was a part of the leasing package and covered by another Virgin Islands registered company. There was never anything to connect Bateman's UK operation to the vehicles. Even the chilled meat transported was invoiced to the driver at Bateman's Dunkirk warehouse and sold back at a profit once the driver arrived at Smithfield. That was how the man got his cut, legally and clean.'

Bateman had not been specific, but reading between the lines, Len assumed the traffickers transported the illegals through the Schengen area to the Dunkirk premises and loaded them into the secret compartment just before the vehicle departed. Upon arrival at the discharging area at Smithfield, Len and Terry would ensure no curious security guard or police foot patrol took an interest in the vehicle or the procession of white-coated porters shouldering carcasses of meat, filing into the cold store and then, one by one, making their way to a passenger minivan parked in the adjacent street.

'With three vehicles crossing the Channel daily, there were weeks when he would bring in up to one hundred illegals. At ten thousand a pop, you can see how he could afford our ten per cent, cover his overheads and have plenty left over for growing his operation.'

'It was a sweet deal,' Terry agreed. 'What with Nobby organising our time records so that we were never in the vicinity at the critical times, IA never got a sniff. Unfortunately, I let it all trickle through my fingers – wine, women and song, as they say.'

Len nodded. Sometimes Terry had needed a sharp word of warning. Once somebody on the force started spending big, rumours would circulate. They had come to blows on one occasion. Fortunately, Terry had seen sense when the money began to run out. 'For years now, Bateman has been striving to legalise the meat haulage business,' Len continued. 'He scrapped two of the dodgy vehicles some years ago. I asked him why he kept the third so long, to which he said something about keeping it for Darren, but he didn't elaborate. When Brexit loomed, he decided to source all his rigs in France, left-hand drive with local number plates and gloriously sign written with his illustrious name. He can't afford a scandal.'

Nobby drained the last of his lager. 'If the scheme is the way you describe it, the nominated driver of this last Scania is the one who will carry the can, not Bateman. I assume if he goes down, Bateman looks after him and the family.'

Len nodded thoughtfully.

'And if the driver squeals and drops Bateman in it?'

'He repeated in so many words how he'd look after the driver and his family.'

'Empty threat, or not?'

A brief smile crossed Len's lips. 'What is it; leopards never lose their spots or tigers their stripes? I can't remember.' He flexed his hand to stop the tingling sensation. 'When I asked him again about the employee who took the vehicle to the breakers and whether he could be relied on in a face-to-face interrogation with the police, he said if they wanted to interview him, they'd need to take a shovel to the meeting. Draw your own conclusions.'

'How do we fit into this?' Terry asked. 'There's nothing to tie us to the vehicle.'

'Bateman wants us to do something for him. It's worth ten grand for each of us, Randy included, plus whatever expense we incur in achieving the objective.'

'Which is?'

39

'Three years ago, this suspect vehicle was pulled over at a DVSA checkpoint en route to Tilbury for a routine weight and document check. There was a tachograph problem, and the Standards Agency officer was just about to write out the infringement notice when the driver complained of a pain in his abdomen. The officer thought he was trying to pull a fast one and ignored the man's protests. As it happened, the man had peritonitis and died on the way to hospital. In all innocence, the lad working with the driver told the officer the vehicle was operated by Batemans and said he would phone for someone to come out to complete the journey. In due course, a fixed penalty notice was issued to Batemans, citing the vehicle as forming part of the company's fleet. The accountant paid the two thousand pound fine by company cheque as a matter of course. Bateman's now fixated with the idea the vehicle will be tied into him.'

'What's he worried about?' Nobby said, turning to Terry for confirmation. 'It sounds like the humane thing for Batemans to do. For God's sake, the man died. Who used the lorry in the intervening three years?'

'As far as I understand,' Len said, 'the vehicle has been laid up in a yard in Wolverhampton, out of commission except for occasional sorties by Darren on whatever he needed it for. During the last twelve months, Bateman doubts it's been used at all.'

'So, what's his problem? No CCTV records, nothing to tie him to the vehicle beyond a good Samaritan act three years ago. What's he wanting us to do?'

'I'm guessing here, something he said about his legacy, but I think someone's tipped him the nod that he's on the cards for some gong or the other in the Queen's Birthday Honours List. They'll be investigating his background to avoid the sort of scandal that bedogged Harold Wilson and his cronies in the seventies. He must be seen as squeaky clean and he's paranoid about this latest development.' Len stopped to appraise the attitude of his two colleagues. He could tell Terry knew what was coming and would protest.

'Bateman remembers how we sorted out an overweight shipment problem for him with the DVSA years ago and he wants us to do the same with the tachograph infringement. He needs the record wiped from the system.'

Terry rocked his head. 'No way. I'm not saying I couldn't use ten grand, but I haven't seen her in the best part of twenty-five years. She'll be married with a family. Even back then, when we were intimate, she was petrified her dad and brothers would find out and disown her or worse.' He smiled weakly at Nobby. 'It's the way you Indian families are, isn't it?'

Len spoke up before Nobby could react. 'Bateman has done his homework. Mahi, now Mrs Mahi Kumar, is an administrative manager with the Standards Agency, working out of Tower Hamlets. I don't doubt with one stroke of the delete button, she can lose the record.'

Terry continued to shake his head. 'Even if I got to speak with her again, why should she do what I ask? I'm probably the last person she would want to see, the reincarnation of a fling she should never have had and has long since forgotten.'

Len's expression revealed nothing. 'If your charms fail to captivate her, that's where Nobby steps in.'

'Me?' Nobby's pencil thin eyebrows were raised in amazement. 'I don't know the woman.'

'No. But you know how things work in the Indian family hierarchy and how distressing it would be if the family got to know about Mahi's liaison with this infidel.'

Terry stood up abruptly. 'I won't do it. She was naïve and infatuated; would have done anything for me.'

'And she did,' Len interrupted. 'Lost a payload sheet before it could be processed, as I remember?'

'Yeah, but she never once believed I'd engineered the relationship just to force her into helping us. She believed I loved her, and I convinced her it was true.'

'And did you?'

'What? Did I convince her or love her? The answer's "yes" to both. I fell for her hook, line and sinker. If I go back now and ask her to do something else, she'll believe I was never sincere.'

Nobby passed his fingers like a comb through greasy, jet-black hair. 'Why can't we tell Bateman it's no go? The likelihood is nothing will come of it. We can ask Randy to keep his ear to the ground as to how the investigation is progressing. If anything transpires, we can act accordingly.'

41

Len laughed. 'That's real politician speak for let's not do anything. You should be an MP, Nobby.' His expression changed. 'You run the risk of Bateman becoming implicated and an investigation into his dealings over the years. He assured me in no uncertain terms he has enough on us to see prison sentences far longer than any term he would collect. He guaranteed if he's implicated, he'll try to deal using us as bargaining chips.' He walked over and placed his hands on Terry's shoulders. 'The choice is we upset a lady with whom you were once in love, maybe to the point of her hating and despising you, or we carry on with the prospect of losing our pensions and a prison sentence which we will never survive. I don't think we have a choice, do you?'

It was seven thirty, and the house was in darkness. The note propped against the empty wineglass on the kitchen island said simply, "Let down, as usual. Taken the car. Get an Uber. Here's the address. Muriel."

Len's mobile vibrated. In the stillness, the noise seemed to be amplified. The caller's name appeared on the screen. He cursed and let the call go to his message service.

'Just checking you're on your way.' Gerry's voice was tinged with a slight alcoholic drawl. 'Only Muriel's a little stressed out. She's had an unfortunate run-in with the police on the way over.'

SEVEN

SYLVIA AND LANCE

Sylvia wheeled around at the sound of a tap on the back door and checked her watch. Dom had said the first appointment was at three. Twenty minutes early. The estate agent must be keen, but why not arrive at the front door like any normal human being? She watched as the man stamped up and down and slapped his arms around a well-developed chest. Good looking, she thought, although it serves him right. Dressed in a sweatshirt and tracksuit bottoms, it looked as if he were out for a jog. Is this the new breed of estate agent – you pay a lower commission, okay, but I'll turn up as I please?

'You're early,' she said, opening the door and standing aside.

'Thanks,' he said, moving into the kitchen and running on the spot as he blew hot air into a fist. 'I left my holdall in the lounge, and it's suddenly turned bloody freezing outside. You must be Sylvia.' He waved a hand without moving his arm.

'I take it from those comments, the unconventional attire and the antipodean accent, you are not from the residential division of Hargreaves and Stour, Estate Agents?'

He chuckled. 'Had it just been the antipodean accent, I might have fitted the bill. Even us Aussies are used to buying and selling homesteads to each other, but, as it is, you are right. If you haven't already guessed, I'm Lance, potential family breaker, failed homosexual and, since nine this morning, a homeless, illegal immigrant and sometime personal trainer, probably by now, out of a job.'

Sylvia collected the long strands of auburn hair from around her neck and expertly pulled them into a bun on the top of her head. She removed a clip from between her teeth to fix the hair into place. 'For somebody boasting such a disastrous curriculum, you appear remarkably well disposed.' She massaged her high cheekbones, drawing her hands down to meet under a rounded chin with a small cleft and finally, pinching the skin together around her neck until her fingers came together in a praying position. Large, hazel-coloured eyes studied him intently. 'So, you are the litmus paper that has changed the colour of my brother's desires and turned his life upside down? You stand there smiling at me like a Cheshire cat, but you are a force to be reckoned with, Lance . . . Lance what?'

'King. King is my family name and I'm very much afraid you've got this whole business back to front.'

'How come?'

Lance moved to sit down, taking a bar stool and suggesting she do the same. They faced each other across the island unit.

'It was very much Dominic who was the driving force in our twosome. He came on to me in the gym like a steam train. I've never thought about a man-to-man relationship in the past seriously until your brother came onto me. I've always played it straight.'

'Is that so?' There was cynicism in her voice. She wriggled her bottom on the padded seat, producing a noise like breaking wind. 'That wasn't me,' she rushed to say, her cheeks flushing.

He made an identical noise. 'That was me,' he said. 'If it makes you feel any better.'

They both laughed.

'Truth is,' he went on, 'I came around this morning to tell him that the affair was over and to reconsider his position before he and his wife took a path which they might later come to regret.'

'I think you're more than a little late as far as that's concerned. The stable door is well and truly shut, and the horse is barely visible on the horizon. How did he react to your announcement?'

'He said he was too busy today to discuss it and suggested I return around ten tonight to "see reason", as he put it.'

Sylvia checked her watch. It was nearly three. 'And will you?'

'I don't know; haven't made up my mind. I don't want to hurt his feelings any more than necessary. He's a great guy, but I feel I should disappear from his life and get on with mine.'

'Which means?'

He thought for several seconds and shrugged his shoulders. 'Sorting out my status in the UK, finding a girlfriend who's on my wavelength and settling into a steady relationship that might move on to bigger and better things. Who knows?'

'And where do you imagine my brother goes from here?'

'If, as you say, his marriage is over, I may be cast as the Svengali who lured an innocent onto the rocks - sorry about the mixed metaphors - but it's far from the truth. For me, a same-sex relationship was an aberration, an adventure into the unknown, prompted by a strong-willed man—'

'Whoa! Hold up. This is my brother you're talking about? Strong willed?'

'Absolutely. He was . . . is totally committed to the relationship. He frightened the socks off me talking about a civil partnership. I knew then things had gone too far, and I needed to back off. I think he finds the male-to-male relationship much easier to assert himself than, perhaps, in the man-to-woman scenario. From what he told me, I guess he felt emasculated by his wife. Could that be the case?'

Sylvia bit her lip and appeared to study the mosaic tiled work surface. 'Perhaps,' she said, finally. 'Cary earns more than Dom, has a high-powered job and insists on a "his and her" split for their domestic finances. He works almost exclusively in a male-dominated world. I recall him saying that in his technical assistance outfit, there are only two women, and they are both in administration.'

'Sounds like a very boring Christmas staff party. No shenanigans in the stationery cupboard. Unless—'

'Quite,' she said, just as the doorbell rang. 'Let me handle this.'

She found a bottle of Chardonnay in the fridge and unscrewed the cap. 'I take my hat off to you, Mr King. That was quite a masterful performance.' She poured a generous measure into both glasses, and they toasted each other.

'I know you said to take a back seat, but from the moment the first guy appeared and treated us as a couple with his male-chauvinist approach, ignoring you and directing his comments at me, I thought I'm going to screw this guy. Not literally, I rush to assure you.'

'I'm relieved to hear it.' She drained her glass and poured them each another measure. 'You played the two of them off against each other. The second man looked shell-shocked as you laid out your demands.'

Lance took the empty bottle and placed it in the recycling section of the waste bin. 'The first one, "Call me Hank" - I thought you're spelling that wrong - he set the parameters. This house is obviously the next step up for the first-time buyer who has got some equity in his existing property and is able to increase his mortgage without too much trouble. The selling price Hank proposed was at a level he knew he had a buyer for. All too easy, so I jacked the price up forty grand, told him about the fictitious sale in the next road at ten grand more than I was suggesting and he's on board for the ride.'

'Dom will be pleased. They both said they had prospective purchasers ready to view. And not only that, they both asked for a two per cent non-exclusive commission rate, and you batted them down to one. I would have just accepted what they stipulated. I'm glad you hung around.'

'Take the credit, Sylvia. Don't tell Dom I was involved.'

'Why not? He knows I'm not a wheeler-dealer.' She punched him playfully on the shoulder. 'Tell him it was a parting gesture of goodwill.'

'I'd rather not create a topic of mutual interest.'

There was a moment of silent eye-to-eye contact that seemed to Sylvia to speak volumes. He picked up on it. 'Supposing we discuss it over dinner. You can choose the place.' He noticed the crease in her brow and backtracked. 'Strictly conversational,' he said, 'and we go Dutch. How's that sound?'

Sylvia took a while to reply, looking down at her right hand as she twisted around her finger the eternity ring Norma had given her. It had been her grandmother's and could be traced back in the family to the early eighteen-hundreds. 'Have you been honest with me? I mean, about your affair with Dom. About your true inclinations?'

'Cross my heart and hope to die.' He made the gesture. 'I just want to talk things through with an understanding friend. We've got to know each other a little over the past couple of hours, and I've found it both relaxing and stimulating. I hope you feel the same.'

'Okay, you're on. There's a Chinese I know where they do an "eat all you can" buffet for a set price. It won't break the bank.' She hesitated. 'Just remember, Lance, I'm used to wielding a scalpel and cutting up bodies, so don't give me any bullshit, all right?'

Bullshit is my speciality, he thought to himself. I sometimes even get it confused with the truth. Out loud, he said, 'I'm shooting straight from the hip with you, sister. You can trust old Lance to give you the unvarnished truth, warts and all.'

46

'I really hope so,' she said with a weak smile.

EIGHT

CHARLIE AND DAVID (LUDO)

The wind was swirling around the forecourt as Charlie pushed the chain-link gate open and stepped back into a world he had known for the best part of forty years. Nothing had changed so far, he thought, but it wouldn't be long before his ex-partner stamped his own personality on the business and lived up to the sign that said, "Under New Management". There again, what did that statement really mean? The inference was the last management had been inadequate and had now changed for the better. Charlie didn't read it that way. He would have written underneath, "Nothing Like as Good as The Last".

Two arc lights mounted on scaffolding cast beams of light along the front row of quality, almost new cars facing the main road. In the darkness, he couldn't see beyond the light to the row of flags he knew were up there, flaying noisily in the gale, advertising "low mileage", "generous part exchange", "zero deposit", "sixty months finance", "fully inspected and guaranteed", "left-hand drive specialist" and a selection of more tired clichés used by motor traders around the country.

Metal rang against metal as the steel rings holding the advertising tarpaulin in place collided with the superstructure, the plastic sheeting flapping like a whale's tail battering the ocean. The lettering was fading. Half of the letter D had become detached from the logo, "Chas and Dave's Quality Used Car Sales - Trade Welcome", and there was a rent in the material by the seam.

How long had the sign been there? Must be fifteen years. He had it made at the time David Logan had accepted Charlie's offer of a partnership and injected much-needed capital into the business. It was all in used fifty-pound notes, it's true, but cash was king during a very difficult trading period and the last thing concerning Charlie was the question of provenance. In fact, there were a great many blanks in Logan's background, but Charlie was not the inquisitive type and asking his partner questions on the subject would only provoke a long, drawn-out monologue full of non-sequiturs, spun-out stories and blatant lies, all delivered in a lazy Irish brogue with a shuddered intake of breath at the end of every sentence after he had said "D'you see?" or "D'you know?".

In fact, the only thing Logan had volunteered about his past with a ring of truth was why everybody knew him as Ludo and not his given name of David. Apparently, his mother, a lay teacher of English in a convent school outside Donegal, had an unrequited crush on a Scottish TV broadcaster and author whose Christian name was Ludovic. Any programme featuring her passion was recorded on a Betamax videotape machine and she would hang on his every word as she faithfully replayed each tape. When she discovered her firstborn was a boy, she insisted on naming him after her hero, but her equally stubborn husband resisted the onslaught, declaring that Ludovic sounded like a Russian homosexual, enunciating the word slowly in five separate syllables as "ho-mo-sex-u-al". Perhaps, in another environment, it would have been a case of unstoppable force meets immovable object, but in Donegal, on such matters as family, the voice of the male prevailed and so, the child was named David. Unwilling to subjugate herself totally to male dominance, his mother persisted in calling the child by her preferred name, which rapidly became abbreviated by school friends to Ludo and remained so for posterity.

He appeared holding the glass door of the small showroom cum office building open against the wind. 'Are you coming in or are you after buying a car?' He shouted across the forecourt. 'There's a special discount for old farts with cockney accents who smell of poncy expensive after-shave which I've paid for, d'you see?'

Charlie brushed the raindrops from his cashmere overcoat and ran his fingers across his scalp. 'Fuck you,' he said, grasping the other man's outstretched hand. 'Buy a car after you've had your head under the bonnet? I've not gone doolally yet.'

'Would you be casting dispersions on my mechanical skills now? I'll have you know I have several diplomas lauding my technical achievements.' Ludo adopted a forced expression of disappointment on his lined and weather-beaten face.

'Diplomas, my fanny! More like commendations from the Provos for the skill in planting explosives under cars.'

Ludo wagged his finger in Charlie's face. 'That is something you never say, not even in humour. Do not walls have ears, d'you know?' He gave a wicked grin and ushered Charlie to a seat in the compact office. There was the lingering hint of stale tobacco mixed with cheap perfume in the air.

'Mandy all right, is she?' Charlie had a soft spot for the part-time bookkeeper, secretary, confidant and coffee maker who had worked for them for over ten years.

'She's grand. Happy as Larry since you pissed off.' His chuckle turned into a racking cough. 'Doc said to give up the fags, but it's hard. Tried one of those frigging vape monstrosities, but every time you go to use it, it's like starting an experiment in a chemistry lab. Not got the patience. Gave it to that homeless who sits outside the Spar. He asked me if it played a tune. I said it was a pea shooter.'

'I expect he didn't have a clue what you were talking about.'

'In truth, a problem with which I'm often faced. Do you fancy a coffee or tea?' Without waiting for an answer, Ludo eased himself out of the chair and shuffled over to a small sink and kitchenette area. 'Which is it to be?'

'Don't care, as long as you wash the mould out of those mugs first and don't give me the cracked one.'

Charlie watched on as Ludo set about his task.

It would have been the turn of the millennium when this fresh-faced man with a mop of tight-curly ginger hair walked into the lot Charlie had at the time and asked for a job in his broad Irish accent. He claimed to have been a motor mechanic since he started with a local garage in Killea as a fifteen-year-old apprentice and had worked in Donegal for twenty years before upping sticks and crossing to the UK. Ludo was vague about his background and the reasons for his sudden move across the Irish Sea, but Charlie had one of his gut feelings and gave the man a month's trial. He wasn't disappointed. Back then, Charlie concentrated on older cars at the less expensive end of the market, aiming for a quicker turnover and a less discerning punter who would not ask troublesome questions, nor ask for an independent examination.

It was thanks to Ludo's skills that, amazingly, most of the cars sold were very low mileage models and purred like new when the engine was keyed into life. If there was one diploma Ludo should have on the wall, it would say something about turning the "sows' ears" which Charlie regularly purchased at the auctions into "silk purses", at least for as long as the three-month warranty period which was generously offered with each sale.

The business prospered, new premises acquired, and Charlie invested every penny of his spare cash into upgrading the profile of the business, discarding the old banger and crash recovery car image for a more middle-class appeal. As luck would have it, the expansion occurred just as the economy took a serious downturn, with the bottom falling out of the used car market, squeezed by both a contraction of consumer finance and desperate moves by the motor manufacturers to seek new car sales.

It was during a casual conversation with Ludo as Charlie was bemoaning his imminent bankruptcy that the idea of a partnership was first muted. A lifeline of thirty thousand pounds for a fifty-percent stake would have seemed ridiculously cheap in normal times, but Charlie was in no position to negotiate, nor did he seriously imagine Ludo could conceivably raise the sum agreed. Once again, he was about to be surprised.

Ludo asked for a three-day leave of absence. Charlie dropped him off at Gatwick and picked him up two days later, complete with a holdall stuffed with fifty-pound notes. Charlie, Ludo and the business never looked back, principally because of the new partner's insistence they look to specialise in the sale of left-hand drive cars imported from the Continent. To Charlie's surprise, demand was firm and the profit margins double that for standard UK models.

It did not prove so straightforward when the time came for Ludo to buy out Charlie's stake in the business. They were carrying more than half a million pounds' worth of inventory on the forecourt, and taking the building and goodwill into consideration, an independent accountant had valued Charlie's fifty-per cent stake at four hundred thousand. Ludo had one hundred and fifty thousand available, but needed to raise the remaining quarter of a million. By whatever means Ludo had financed his initial stake, the same avenue no longer remained open. He had had to look elsewhere.

'Here you are,' he said, slopping tea on the plastic table covering as he put the mug down. 'Disinfected the figgin thing with Dettol but forgot to wash it out.'

Charlie took a sip. 'Tastes like it,' he said. 'Now, tell me. Why am I here?'

Ludo settled back in the synthetic leather executive chair that had once been Charlie's pride and joy. 'Right now, business is shite. Sold a few bits and pieces, a few out and back trade sales to con some additional finance, but the market is confused. Once upon a time, diesel was great, now it's a pariah. Electric's here, but not quite here. Buy a car but drive a hundred miles to find a charging point. Politicians open their gobs with their green timetables, banning this and that. Nobody knows what to do for the best.'

'Where are you going with this? Presumably, you didn't ask me to come just to hear me express my sympathy for your situation?'

'I've had a few problems meeting the repayment schedule for the loan I took, d'you see?'

Charlie held up his hands, palms outwards. 'Stop there, Ludo. We made a deal you wouldn't come sniffing around my backside if you had money problems. I'm not in the banking business.'

Ludo caught his breath and exhaled noisily 'If you'd friggin' let me finish, I'm not after your cash.'

'What I don't want is one of your "round the houses" stories where we end up where you've started, and the real aim is to weasel cash out of me.'

'Jesus, you're an impossible man. I don't know how I managed to put up with you for so long. Just shut up and listen.'

Charlie took another swig of tea, grimaced and nodded.

'You remember recommending I speak to your daughter-in-law, the accountant lady, about the best way of raising the necessary to see you out the door?'

'Cary. Yes. Caroline to you.'

'Well, as you probably heard on your family grapevine, she recommended I speak to a client of hers, Alex Quentin, a specialist in business and personal finance. He was all charm and "How much would you like, Ludo? Three bags full, Ludo." You know the type?'

'I get the picture.'

'But when it got down to the detail, sure, I could have the money, the interest rate was twenty per cent – I could just about live with that – but he had me in a financial arm lock.'

'What's that mean?'

'Guarantees. A charge over the inventory, land and buildings and my personal guarantee for two hundred per cent of the loan.'

Charlie raised his eyebrows. 'How come?'

'It's in the friggin small print. I was going to be late with two monthly repayments, so I made an appointment to see your man Quentin at his office, d'you see. It's next to his detached house, if you can call it that – more like a small mansion – outside Ashford. He's there with a guy he said was one of his chauffeurs. I tell you Charlie; the man must have been close to seven feet and built like a brick shithouse. Albanian, according to your man, but if he can get that frame behind the wheel of a car and drive, I'm the next damn pope.'

'So, you're in bed with a loan shark who has a heavy to enforce the collections?'

'Two heavies, to be exact. As I arrived, your Caroline was saying goodbye to this Quentin and, I have to say, in a most friendly and intimate fashion. Then, a slightly smaller but wider clone of the Albanian ushered her out, d'you see?'

Charlie stared into his eyes. 'What do you mean by "intimate fashion?"'

'Let's say it seemed to me he was trying to lick her tonsils, one of those kisses before you rip off each other's clothes, if you get my meaning.'

'So, you called me here to tell me my daughter-in-law is having it off with someone other than her husband?'

'Bejesus,' Ludo exploded. 'I don't give a shite about who's putting it about in your family. As a matter of passing interest, I thought you should know on your son's behalf. My problem is far more important.'

'Get to the sodding point, then. I haven't got all night.'

Ludo leaned forward in his chair, so close that Charlie could almost tell what type of cheese he'd been eating. 'If you'd do me the honour of listening and not interrupting or pulling your face into that disinterested expression . . .' Ludo waited, but there was no reaction. 'Good. When Quentin hears I'm going to be running late with the repayments, he tells me it would be very unwise. If I've read the contract, I'll know that in the event of a payment default, the interest rate changes from twenty per cent per annum to

54

twenty per cent per week. This means if I owe a grand and delay for two weeks, I must pay back fourteen hundred.'

'That's ridiculous. Can he do that, legally, I mean?'

'Does it matter when the Albanian is nodding his head as if to say "He's right, you know. Don't be a naughty boy."'

'When's the payment due?'

'I'm a week late already. My monthly is five thousand, so I'm already in for six grand.'

'What are you going to do?'

'I've got a short-term proposal for you and a possible long-term fix I thought I'd run past you.'

Charlie shook his head. 'Here we go, round the bleedin' houses and, guess what, back where we started. How many ways are there for me to say no?'

'Don't be like that, Charlie. We go back a long way. I want you to buy a car from me. Take it away on trade plates. I pay the man off and, as soon as business picks up, I buy back the car and no harm's done.'

'And if you don't?'

'You can always eBay the car. I'll make up any shortfall.'

'Can't you give him a car in settlement?'

Ludo shook his head. 'I made that offer. He says he's not into barter. I get the impression he's waiting for me to fail, so he can take over the business. He owns several, so I understand. Builds them up and flogs them off.'

'Got you by the short and curlies, hasn't he? So, what's this long-term solution?'

'You remember the meetings of the regional motor traders' association? I don't have a lot to do with it now, but it used to be useful for moving stock around on the q.t. to raise additional finance or engineer a VAT repayment.' He stopped and laughed out aloud. 'But I forget, you'd know all about that, Charlie, wouldn't you? You're the undisputed champion in organising VAT credits, d'you know.'

Charlie waved away a bad small from under his nose. 'Long time ago and best forgotten, Ludo.' He purposefully looked at his watch. 'You were saying?'

'There was a meeting in Dartford a few weeks ago. As it's close to home, I thought I'd attend, just out of interest. There must have been no more than two dozen I recognised, all with long faces. Do you remember your man Andy from that outfit in Ashford which specialises in reincarnating insurance write-offs? No? Your memory's going, you know that, Charlie? You sure you haven't got that Alf Hammers?'

'You ignorant plonker. It's *Alzheimer's* and, no, I haven't. I've probably forgotten more than you ever knew.'

'No need to get personal. Anyway, this Andy wanted to buy the business he runs from the owner. Like me, he was turned down by the bank even before he asked the manager if he could sit down. He'd heard you'd bowed out and asked me how I'd financed your departure. I told him I'd got a deal, expensive, but doable, and mentioned the name of Alex Quentin. He pulled me to one side of the room as if I'd just confessed to screwing his wife.

'Apparently, at the turn of the year, the police released a series of cars they were storing in the pound at Maidstone, originally held regarding ongoing investigations, since closed or shelved. Andy has a deal with the custody officer to pick up the best of the bunch, one of which was the car Quentin's wife was driving when she was involved in a fatal accident two years earlier. They had examined the vehicle, parked it up and forgotten all about it.'

Charlie checked his watch again. Norma would start to worry. He needed to make a call.

Charlie drove the Mercedes into the drive and parked in front of the garage. He wouldn't activate the remote to open the door. Norma had said she was going to bed, and he didn't want to make any unnecessary noise. Besides, he needed a few quiet minutes to get his thoughts in order.

The new logbook lay on the passenger seat. He glanced over it before shoving it untidily into the glove compartment. He had paid twelve grand for an eight-year-old Volvo estate. It was a bit over the odds, but Ludo had assured him with that coy Irish smile the mileage was very low for the year, and the last owner had been a retired female civil servant and a very careful driver. How Charlie had kept a straight face, he did not know.

The question concerning him was how much to tell Norma about his conversation with Ludo. His wife was close to Cary. She had more in common with her daughter-in-law than with her own children, and Charlie was certain they exchanged confidences.

His first reaction was to blurt out the entire story, but he had learnt, admittedly late in life, in some circumstances it was best to keep your powder dry and use your weapon selectively to inflict maximum impact. If Cary had really discarded her husband in favour of someone with marginal activities and a dubious background, she deserved all she got, provided it didn't rebound on the twins. The additional plus was the impact the revelation would have on that super-smug bastard, Len. The imagined scenario brought a smile to his face.

According to this Andy, the fatal accident had been caused by a steering wheel failure, a bolt with insufficient torque to maintain control over the direction in which the car was travelling. The manufacturer had already identified the defect and admitted liability. The company was recalling around twenty thousand cars so that the part could be substituted. In the case of Quentin's wife, the steering wheel had literally detached from the column, and the car had veered off the road and accelerated into a tree. The airbag had activated, but the ferocity of the whiplash had caused major trauma. Had she been wearing the seat belt and not had traces of alcohol and amphetamines in her system, the out-of-court settlement agreed by the manufacturer would have been substantially greater, but in the event, Quentin graciously accepted the six-figure sum.

In Andy's opinion, the fact the defect was in the public domain influenced both the police examination and the cursory forensic analysis. Andy was far more meticulous. As he dismantled the front end of the crash vehicle, he found two anomalies which cast doubt on the accuracy of the official report. The bolt that had sheared from the steering column was still intact, but at the point at which the bolt entered the nut to create the tension, someone had expertly filed down the thread so that as the chassis reverberated with the car's movement, the torque would lessen, eventually causing the bolt to break loose from its mooring.

'And the second thing?' Ludo had asked Andy.

'A scrap of masticated chewing gum fixed to a fragment of a window display parking ticket had become wedged in the driver's seat belt buckle holding, making it impossible to engage the belt securely. It held sufficiently to extinguish the warning alarm and remain fixed during normal driving conditions, but in any extreme braking or crash scenario, the buckle would spring loose, and the belt retract.'

'You're saying the accident was no accident?' Ludo had asked.

'It looks like it, but I don't want to get involved. I've kept the defective parts in a safe place at home,' Andy had replied. 'Just in case.'

Ludo's dilemma was whether, when faced with the prospect of a further delayed repayment, he should subtly hint of facts in his possession which might influence the imposition of the penal interest clause. 'If I've got something on him, it'll keep him off my back,' was the rationale.

'You'd also be putting yourself and this Andy character in the direct line of fire of two rather scary Albanians,' Charlie had said. 'You're best advised to sit on this information and make a judgement when and if circumstances dictate. Pay the man his money and try to keep up the repayments. As you said, it's a tough deal, but manageable. The way you've pitched it, his interest is to see you fail and then step in and scoop off the cream before the milk curdles. If you keep up the repayments, it's just a financial transaction. Mind you, I'd read the small print in the contract if I were you, just in case. I'll lend you a dictionary for the long words.'

'Fuck you, you Jackeen. Calling me ignorant, is it? Mind you, what you say, surprisingly, makes sense. I'll sleep on it. Now, let me show you the car I have in mind for you.'

'Is that you, Charlie? You're late.'

'Sorry. I was creeping around trying not to wake you.'

Norma laughed. 'Yes, you and a herd of elephants. How did you get on with Ludo?'

He lost his footing as he went to put on his pyjama bottom, one hand reaching out to support himself against the headrest. 'What I suspected.' He finally strained the elastic around his waist and secured the button. It reminded him of tension and torque and a bolt that had been tampered with. 'Had to buy a car from him on consignment until business picks up. I'll collect it tomorrow.'

'It surely didn't take you all this time just to buy a car? It's nearly one o'clock.'

He gave her a sideways glance. 'You know Ludo, plenty of soften-you-up chatter with no substance. I guess he misses not having a partner. It can be a lonely old life sitting there waiting for someone to walk in.' He settled into bed and reached for the light switch.

'If you've got a spare car, maybe we can let Caroline use it,' Norma said. 'Dominic still has their family car. We could give her a helping hand. What do you think?'

The reply was the gentle rhythm of heavy breathing and a rattle in his throat.

She turned away from him and settled her head into the pillow. If you're pretending, she thought, I'll make you pay.

NINE

LEN AND MURIEL

'Thank the Lord that's over,' he said, gazing out of the windscreen to study the route out of the site to avoid careering into the mud. 'Can you imagine living in a place like this?' He felt the wheels lock onto a gravel surface. 'When it rains, it must be like a swamp.'

'I thought the whole evening was delightful,' Muriel said softly, an air of resignation in her voice. 'They are such a happy, loving couple and their friends seemed genuinely concerned about me.'

'You do talk rubbish sometimes, Muriel.'

'So you tell me.'

'You'd be happy and loving if you spent every day studying your navel and imagining you're dancing with the fairies.'

'They do have an argument when it comes to the environmental impact of the third runway at Heathrow. Gerry says they have a social conscience.'

Len let out a long and noisy breath. 'You're a sucker for his brand of flower-power crap. Ask him if he's got a social conscience when it comes to standing in the benefits queue waiting for his handout. They're all spongers, leeches on the rest of us. You're so gullible.'

Her eyes watered. 'So you always tell me,' she repeated.

'And another thing. You don't really believe they're squatting here to save the lesser-spotted, turd warbler from extinction if the hedgerow is demolished by these evil developers? You wait. Their only objective is to make a nuisance of themselves, exploit delays until they get their hands on a nice slice of compensation if they agree to bugger off and find some new cause to profit from.'

'They might say that was very cynical.'

Len shook his head. 'It's the truth and you should know better than to spout their brand of crooked logic.'

Tears drifted slowly down her cheek. 'I like Gerry.'

The defiance in her voice forced him to turn his head. 'What's the matter? I like Gerry too.' He hesitated. 'Up to a point.' He made an illegal U-turn to join the main road. 'Anyway,' he said as he completed the manoeuvre. 'Got away with that.' He sighed with satisfaction. 'What I was asking is what happened to you? I still don't really understand why the police stopped you, but I didn't want to ask too many questions in front of nosey Gloria.'

'I told you. The police did not stop me. I had drawn the car into the kerb on a bus route. The police car came along soon afterwards to check what the problem was.'

'And why had you stopped?'

Head bowed; eyes fixed on her lap. 'I didn't feel well and couldn't drive any further.'

'Couldn't drive? What was it, a pain in your legs?'

She looked up at him, but no further than his chest. 'A little sympathy wouldn't go amiss, Len. You sound more like an interrogator than a concerned husband.'

'It's because I don't understand a sodding word you're saying. Just tell me, please, in plain English, why you stopped.'

Finally, their eyes met. The tears were flowing freely across the broken veins on her reddened cheeks and disappearing into the corners of her mouth. Her voice broke into a staccato squeal. 'I was having a panic attack. I couldn't drive. I didn't remember how to drive, which foot went where, how to change gear, which way to turn the wheel. I had no idea. My heart was palpitating, a sick, empty feeling in the pit of my stomach. I felt deathly cold, yet my forehead was damp with sweat. Now, do you understand?' She waited for a reaction, but his look was one of incomprehension. 'Please don't stare at me as if I'd just come from Mars. Before you ask, no, I don't know why, but it's not the first time. Thankfully, the other occasions were when I was indoors. This time, I felt like opening the car door and just walking into the stream of traffic.'

'How did you get to Gerry's?'

'The policeman was really sweet. He drove the car into a side road and telephoned Gerry.'

'Why not phone me?'

She gave a knowing half-laugh. 'I imagined you would still be golfing, and you wouldn't understand what had happened.'

'I still don't. What in this world have you got to be worried about to bring on a panic attack? Your life is a party, nothing to do but a bit of housework, talk to Caroline, play with the twins. What more could you want? There's the garden. You love your horticulture with all those crazy fertiliser ideas, potato skins, ground eggshells, coffee grouts and God knows what. What's missing? A holiday? Do you want to go on holiday?'

Muriel shook her head slowly. 'No, I don't need a holiday.'

'So, what happened?'

'The police officer said he needed to give me a breathalyser.'

'Oh, fuck! Well, that's it then. You'll lose your licence and get points on your licence. How are you going to handle picking up the twins if I'm not available to drive?'

'I think he realised I might fail and didn't give me one. He was very sympathetic. I began to cry. Gerry arrived by taxi and drove me to his place. He asked if I wanted to go to hospital, but I said I'd be all right.'

'Did he say he was going to charge you?'

'No. He didn't even ask Gerry if he had a licence, which he hasn't. He was banned for driving under the influence six months ago.'

Len put his hand on her arm. 'You had a lucky escape,' he said. 'About time you pulled yourself together, don't you think?'

'Come to my senses, do you mean?' She waved his hand away. 'Thanks to Gerry and Gloria, I'm going to try to be positive, get my life in perspective.'

'That's my girl.' He turned off the dual carriageway, following the sign for Weybridge. 'Could you believe the gall Gerry's got to suggest it might be in Caroline's interest to leave the twins with them for the Easter holidays while she sorts her life out?'

'I thought it was a lovely gesture and would suit everyone. Gerry's always longed for kids, and I know Gloria had a couple with her first husband, but she hasn't seen them in the flesh since they were whisked off to Turkey by their father. It would be nice for her as well. Caroline could certainly do with some respite to make sure the divorce does not become confrontational.'

Len banged his fist on the steering wheel. 'Give me a break, will you? You're talking out of your backside, as usual. We're here to support Caroline and the twins, not to see the girls wallowing around in a field of mud and become marijuana junkies before the age of seven. There is no way I'll allowing Caroline to let the twins stay with him.'

'I don't see it's any of our business.'

'Don't you worry, I'll make it my business.'

They sat in defiant silence until they came to the gated entrance to their estate. Len activated the remote and the barrier swung away. They followed the road past individually designed, large, detached houses set in extensive, manicured grounds until they reached a cul-de-sac comprising a more modest grouping of six smaller, yet substantial, four-bedroom dwellings.

'I was pleasantly surprised by the meal Gloria rustled up,' Len offered as a conciliatory gesture. 'I always enjoy Saltimbocca and the veal was very tender.' He parked and waited for a reaction. 'Didn't you think so?' he prompted.

She continued to look straight ahead. 'I think you'll find it was tofu. Gloria is a strict vegetarian, and she likes to encourage Gerry to follow her lead. But, like most men, I'll expect he'll do what he wants.'

Leaving him sitting there, she walked to the front door, used her key to open it and disappeared into the darkened interior.

Len checked in a trouser pocket for his mobile and the motive for the vibration he had sensed on the journey home. It was a message from D.I. Randall Compton, otherwise known as Randy, suggesting they spoke when convenient. Len reached under his seat for the burner phone he used when a confidential conversation was necessary.

'What's new?' Len asked as the call was answered.

'Just come off a late one,' a tired voice replied. 'Nobby spoke to me about our problem. You want to be kept in the loop circa this refrigerated truck?'

'As much as you can. I appreciate you can't be seen to be over inquisitive. Any feedback so far?'

'I have a mate on the force in West Bromwich. He supports the wrong team, but we have a friendly rivalry.'

'That helps.' He saw the light switched on in the bedroom. 'Randy, I must be quick. I've got a domestic to sort out.'

'Tell me about it. Listen, latest is the forensic team has finished and their report will be sent to Major Crime at Birmingham tomorrow. Unofficially, this secret compartment had blood spatters on the floor and on the container wall. The blood is from two different people and there are textile fibres mixed in with one.'

'I'm surprised SOCA is involved so early on.'

'Me, too. I'll try to get some more info. I'm on again at two tomorrow.'

'Roger that.' Len ended the call and returned the mobile to the fabric pocket under the seat.

He locked the car, straightened his slender frame, and made his way toward the house. 'Another night on the couch,' he said to himself. Just as well. Sleep would not come easily tonight.

TEN

GERRY AND GLORIA

'Poor cow.'

Gerry sat on the floor of the lounge area, his legs apart. Gloria sat between them, the back of her head resting on his chest, hands massaging his thighs. He blew heavily onto the palms of his hands and rubbed them together. Gently, he applied pressure to her shoulders, squeezing and kneading the flesh with his fingers. 'You're all tense,' he said. 'Not too cold, are they?' She often complained his icy hands resulted from poor circulation.

'No, you're fine.'

He took this as an invitation to slide his hands over her shoulders, down beneath her blouse and to lift her breasts out of the inadequate bra she used. He caressed her, slowly playing with her nipples between his thumbs and index fingers.

'I thought you wanted to talk,' she said. 'I feel so sorry for her. She seems like a frightened animal, trapped in the headlights.'

Gerry nodded. 'A cliché, I know, but very apt in the circumstances. Muriel is in crisis and the only person who can really help is Len, either by being there for her or not being there at all.' He removed his hands and coated them from the bottle of jojoba oil he had placed at his side. 'At the moment, he displays an air of total indifference to her, until it comes to criticising whenever she opens her mouth.' He replaced his hands beneath her blouse and began a ritual he knew she adored and how it would end.

Gloria took a deep breath and sighed. 'He seemed particularly strung out tonight. Something troubling him?'

'Not as far as I know, and not that he's likely to tell me, anyway. Maybe they've put up his handicap, or the car needs a repair. I can't imagine what else he has to worry about.'

'He was very complimentary about the meal. It quite took me by surprise.'

Gerry laughed. 'He didn't know what he was eating. I told you to put Marsala in the sauce to disguise the taste.'

Gloria shook the strands of long blonde hair to one side of her head and half-turned to face him. 'That panic attack she had was serious. She needs to talk to somebody. Can't you convince her to see a psychiatrist? She was hanging on your every word tonight. I felt a little jealous at one stage.'

He laughed. 'Muriel has many attributes, I'm sure, but none to compare to yours.' He kissed the side of her head.

'Are you going to speak to Cary and offer to look after the kids?'

'If you're agreeable.'

'I'd love it. We could do such fun things.'

'Then I'll call her tomorrow at work.'

Gloria caught the exhilarating scent of jojoba as she turned her head to face him. She released his hands from her blouse and turned a half circle to face him on her knees. She unbuttoned her blouse and moved toward him. 'My understanding partner deserves a really special treat for being so understanding.'

'I couldn't agree more,' He gulped.

ELEVEN

NORMA AND CARY

Cary had the tall latte glass gripped between both hands as she watched a group of Japanese tourists stream into the ground floor café at Selfridges department store.

'I asked Gerry how and when to tackle the subject with dad, and he made the point about the age difference or, should I say, the proximity of his age to Alex's. Gerry thinks dad is likely to rail against the idea of my going to live with Alex. What do you think?'

'Gosh,' Norma replied with a smile. 'It's a little early in the day to be asking for my opinion on anything. I think the last time I had to get up so early was when I was on the morning shift at the hospital. Since I retired, I'm out of practice of rational thought until, at least, my second Americano.'

'Well, drink up then and put your giving advice hat on. I value your opinion.'

Norma reached across to rest her hand against Cary's. 'That's such a sweet thing to say. Nobody says that to me these days. Charlie uses me as a sounding board, ostensibly seeking my point of view but having already made up his mind about whatever it is. Do you not find that men, either intentionally or otherwise, subjugate you – probably, a little too strong a term, but you know what I mean – or subjugate themselves to you? They rarely seem to treat you as an equal.'

'Honestly, I can see what you mean in the working environment, but, at a personal level. I have to say my relationship with Dominic was very much always one of equals.'

'That's good to hear. Maybe, it's more a feature of my generation than yours.'

Cary released the empty glass and licked the remaining milky froth from her lips. 'So, I'll get your second Americano and you think on what I have said.' She wriggled off the stool and disappeared into the crowd of Japanese.

Norma checked her mobile. The message said he had called twice and where was she? She went to type 'With Cary,' but changed her mind. 'Out on a personal matter,' she typed. 'Speak to Len and invite them out to dinner tonight. Choose a restaurant on neutral territory. Back later.'

Cary returned with two refills. 'You need to take out a mortgage to pay for two coffees these days. These places take the mickey.'

Norma reached hurriedly for her bag. 'Sorry, it was my shout.'

'Don't be silly. I didn't say it for that reason. It's my treat. I suggested the meet and it's the least I can do. I said it because it's a fact. Buy the same thing in Spain and it's a quarter of the price.' She hesitated. 'In fact, I am confident enough in our relationship that I can say such things for you to take at face value. If I wanted your money, I'd ask for it.'

Norma shuffled the purse back into her bag. 'You've embarrassed me now. I only made the gesture for form's sake. I didn't really intend paying.' They both laughed.

'Well, what do I do?' Cary asked as they sipped at their fresh drinks.

'About Gerry's comments? How is your uncle, by the way? It's been years since I've seen him. Last time was when the twins were christened.'

'He never changes. Free love and lots of it is his credo.'

'Not a bad philosophy.' She hesitated. 'Before I answer, does Dominic have a new relationship? He didn't get the chance to expand on the divorce announcement. Predictably, Charlie lost his rag and Dominic retreated into his shell.'

Cary tempered her reply, remembering Gerry's advice. 'The unvarnished truth is that when Dom told me he was in a relationship, it was the proverbial straw. I won't say it was the only reason for the split. Things had been on a downward path for a couple of years, but it pushed me over the edge. Again, I'll admit to having some feelings for Alex some months ago, but I doubt I would have done anything about it and opted to stick with the relationship for the twins' sake. At least, until they were old enough to deal with it without resorting to white lies.' She studied the questioning look on Norma's face. 'You know the thing; "Daddy's not with us because he's working away", or "Uncle so-and-so comes around such a lot to keep mummy company whilst daddy is not here". I hate the idea of hoodwinking the children.'

'Do you know who's in this relationship with Dominic?'

70

'He didn't seem inclined to tell me,' she lied. 'He said it's nobody I know, and I wasn't particularly interested in asking questions other than was he committed to this new relationship, to which he said he was. I suggest you speak in more detail to him, perhaps on your own. He might be more forthcoming.'

'You don't have a name?'

Cary felt that to keep her word to Dom she had to brazen it out, which meant holding her own against another questioning expression. 'No. I'm afraid not.'

Norma shrugged her shoulders and reached into her handbag for a wallet. She pulled out a dog-eared photograph. 'Don't think I've ever showed you this.' She held it out for Cary to look at. 'You won't recognise him, so I'll tell you. It's a picture of Dominic arm-in-arm with a friend from technical college.'

Cary peered at it. 'That long, flowing hair, the puffy cheeks; it looks nothing like him.'

'Charlie said in more offensive language that Dominic displayed homosexual tendencies. I often wondered, but when he met you and your relationship blossomed, I discounted the suspicion as misplaced. But you never know with these things.'

Cary put her foot in the water. 'What would have been the reaction had he been gay?'

'From me or from Charlie?'

'Both.'

'My only preoccupation is his and, by association, your and your family's happiness. His sexual orientation never entered into it. As for Charlie, he would see it as a reflection of his manhood and failure as a father. He only knows one way of expressing these emotions.'

Cary smiled. 'Preoccupation with our fathers' reactions seems to be the order of the day.' She was pleased with the deflection. 'How do you think I should deal with mine?'

'I think your tactic of leaving the topic of Alex for a few days and letting the twins do your work for you is a subtle and devious ploy which could well pay off. If you then bring up the age difference issue, you are drawing attention to an aspect which never crossed your mind until Gerry raised the subject.'

'True.'

'Let it ride. Introduce Alex and if there is a negative reaction from Len, look askance, say it never occurred to you and tell him he's being old-fashioned and you're as young as you feel. Ask Len how old he feels?'

Cary nodded. 'Lucky I didn't ask him this morning. He'd have said about ninety. I think he must have had a bust up with mum. He slept on the sofa and was as grumpy as hell when the kids started jumping all over him. I think something is troubling him, but he'll never admit it. Everything's always tickety-boo.'

'What did Muriel say?'

'Mum was still in bed, and I've had to borrow her car to drop the kids off at school and go on to the station. I couldn't hang around to speak with her.'

Norma waved a fist in the air. 'Thanks for reminding me. I nearly forgot. Charlie bought a car last night - it's a long story - so don't ask me why. It's a Volvo, like the one you and Dominic have. I noticed he was driving it when he came round to see us?'

'Yes. He needs it to get to work. The vans they use must be parked up at company premises overnight; something to do with the insurance. I said to keep it until he can afford something smaller and then he'll give it to me.'

'Well, you're in luck,' Norma said. 'We can lend you this latest Volvo for as long as you need. It's a newer model than yours. I'll get Charlie to put you on his group insurance policy and pay the tax. You won't have to do anything, just drive it.'

As they stood up to leave, two Japanese rushed to occupy the vacated stools. Cary gave Norma a hug. 'That's really generous of you. I don't know how to thank you. It won't be for long, I promise. Dom phoned last night. Sylvia showed some agents over the house yesterday. It's going on at forty thousand more than we anticipated and one of the agents reckons he has a buyer at the asking price. On top of that, Sylvia got the commission rate down. We'll be quids in.'

'Sylvia did? I've never seen her as a tough negotiator.'

Cary squeezed her arm. 'People close to us have a habit of surprising us.'

'I won't say I'm not desperately sorry to see your marriage breakdown. Both Charlie and I are gutted, but you can rest assured about one thing.' She swallowed to remove the lump in her throat. 'Whenever you need us, we'll be here for you. Make sure you keep in touch and give us the opportunity to see the twins on a regular basis. We still want them to be a part of our lives.'

'Of course. How could you think otherwise? The girls never stop talking about you both.'

Cary waved as she left. Norma made a 'call me' sign and rotated her hands to imitate holding a steering wheel.

The message alarm pinged as she was ambling around the perfume franchises on the ground floor. 'Done,' it said. 'Leonardo's in Esher at seven thirty. Muriel answered the phone. I asked if she wanted to check first with Len. She said, "No. It's confirmed." Now, where are you?'

TWELVE

SYLVIA AND LANCE

'The only bath towel I could find was this lemony thing with love hearts all over. I think you'll agree it's rather twee, so I thought I'd wear this.' Lance stood at the foot of the bed with the towel wrapped around his waist, a pink shower cap on his head and a hand on his waist as he turned his elbow outwards. 'What do you think?' he said, twirling around.

Sylvia sat, a sheet pulled up to cover her neck. 'Very fetching. Twee is a good word. It aptly describes the boyfriend who bought it for me.' Her expression hardened. 'Listen, I need to say something.'

Before she could continue, he held his hand out to stop her. 'Let me guess. I think it goes something like, "I want you to know I'm not an easy lay. I don't go to bed with somebody on the first date. Last night was the exception, not the rule. If there is to be a relationship, we need to reset the clock for the future." How does that sound?'

She pulled her knees up under her chin. 'More or less. I hadn't got as far as the sentence about a relationship.'

Lance put on a hurt expression. 'You're not telling me this was just a one-night stand; a quick shag and off to work?'

'I don't know what I'm telling you. This is bizarre. Last week you're humping my brother and now it's my turn. It's like you're working your way through the family.'

'I'll stick. I don't fancy twisting.'

She shook her head. 'This isn't a game of cards. It isn't a game at all. There is no way you can tell Dom about last night. He'll think all sorts of things of me.'

As he moved toward her, his foot pinned the towel to the floor, forcing the tuck at his waist to come free. The towel slipped down his legs and came to rest at his feet. He could sense she was appraising his body, head to toes. He fell onto the bed covers alongside her. 'You don't think I haven't been wrestling with the situation? It's been taxing my mind.'

'I got the impression last night that very little taxes your mind.'

75

'Now you're being unfair. I accept moving on will be difficult, but I really don't want to lose what we had last night without seeing where it can go. Dinner was a revelation, the conversation easy and sincere. Coming back here and what followed was no more than the natural progression between two responsible adults who had found something in common. The lovemaking simply enhanced the experience.'

'Impressive speech. Don't know if I feel the same or not.' She saw his expression change. 'I'm speaking bluntly with no intention of drifting into some illusion from which I eventually wake up and realise it was a bad dream.'

'Are you saying you don't want to see where it goes?'

'I don't know what I'm saying. I need to think it through. I've got to be at work in forty-five minutes, so move yourself.'

'Can I come back tonight to talk it through?'

Sylvia hesitated as she pulled on a dressing gown. 'All right, but we will not end up in bed. Get that straight.'

'I understand. I agree. I'll sleep on the sofa.'

'Who said anything about staying over?'

'I thought you understood my circumstances.' There was a hint of panic in his voice.

'Are you going to speak to Dom today?'

'About what?'

Her brow creased. 'You were going to see him last night.'

'I'd prefer to end it face-to-face. I think it's cowardly to do it over the phone.'

'You can't lead him on anymore. He has a life to rebuild now and needs to know exactly where he stands.' She spun around to face him. 'That's unless you're leading *me* on?'

'I don't know how you can say that after what I've just said.'

'Maybe you'll do or say anything for a bed for the night. If sex comes with it, that's an added bonus.'

He walked across the floor to the dishevelled pile of clothes on the floor. 'We seem to be going backwards,' he said disconsolately.

She opened the bathroom door. 'That's probably a function of moving forward too quickly. As you said, we probably need to reset first.' She went in and locked the door behind her.

They had said very little to each other over a hurried breakfast and her parting words were something he didn't understand about she was off to slum in the sewers. Lance had promised to call Dom and arrange a meeting.

With time on his hands, he decided to earn a few brownie points by making the bed, tidying the flat and washing the dishes.

The door buzzer sounded no more than ten minutes after she had left and found him with sleeves rolled up and soap suds up to his elbows. 'What have you forgot . . .?' The question tailed off as he opened the door and saw the sturdy male figure standing in front of him.

The man was seriously out of breath, his body bent doubled. Glancing up and seeing a stranger, his gaze slowly moved to check the number on the door. Reassured, he looked Lance up and down before speaking. 'Who the hell are you?'

'Sorry?' was all Lance could think of to say.

'Where's Sylvia?'

'She's gone to work. You would be who, exactly?'

'I'm asking the questions? You her latest, are you? Got an accent. Where you from? South Africa?'

'My name's Lance. I'm a friend of Sylvia and Dom and the accent is Australian.'

Charlie went to move into the apartment, but Lance blocked his passage. 'I don't mean to offend,' Lance said, 'but I have no idea of who you are.'

Lance could tell the man was contemplating pushing past, but at the last moment had thought better of it.

'If you must know, I'm Charlie, Sylvia's dad. My wife's not been here, has she?'

'No.' Lance stood to one side. 'Not your day, squire, is it?

Charlie gave a half grin and a cursory look around the lounge. 'You in a relationship with Sylvia?' He studied Lance's rolled-up sleeves. 'Or do you just come by to wash the dishes?'

'I'd call it platonic.'

The comment caused a full-bodied laugh in response. 'Platonic? You youngsters use some strange words. All platonic means is that you fantasise about what she looks like naked rather than experience the real thing.' He gave Lance another once over. 'You're not queer, are you?'

It was Lance's turn to retaliate. 'You old folk use some strange words. You mean am I feeling ill?'

Charlie snorted. 'Cocky sod, aren't you? I like somebody who's got a bit of spunk in them. All this fucking political correctness these days. Load of horseshit. In my day, you gave as good as you got, smiled, and shook hands. What's wrong with that? As it happens, I think the historic definition of gay, meaning merry – and I don't mean tipsy with alcohol – should be preserved and not applied to describe a poofter.'

'You don't approve of homosexuality?'

'Never been confronted by it and I go out of my way to avoid it. As far as I'm concerned, a bolt was made to fit into a nut. Neither two bolts nor two nuts go together. Simple.'

'Maybe life's a bit more complex than that.'

'Let's not get into that. I didn't come round here for a *philo-soph-ic-al* discussion. I came to ask Sylvia to do me a favour. Seeing as you're here, I take it you drive?'

'I've got an Australian licence.'

'Good. I've got to pick up a motor. If you've finished the dishes and cleaned around the rim of the khazi, you can come with me. We'll collect the Volvo which I'll drive on trader's plates. You can follow me back to the house in the Mercedes and I'll sort out getting you to wherever you've got to go. All right?'

'How can I refuse? You're the father I'm supposed to impress.'

'So impress me and bring Sylvia around for dinner at my place tomorrow. I can vet you properly and ensure your attentions to my daughter are honourable.'

'I should ask Sylvia if she wants to bring me.'

'Leave her to me. She'll do as she's told. Come on, let's go.'

If you are going to lie, stick as close to the truth as possible. Those words were repeating in his head as he made the call. Lance could not remember the last time he had felt so nervous about speaking to someone on the phone. It was just lucky it wasn't a video call where Dom could see his face. It would surely betray him.

'I'm driving,' Dom said. 'I'll call you back in five minutes.'

A reprieve, he thought. Just time to order another coffee and move to a seat in the corner out of earshot of the other customers.

It had been an interesting few hours. Driving from Sylvia's apartment to the car stand in South London, he had found it easy talking with Charlie, providing a brief résumé of his personal history, suitably doctored, and his aspirations for the future. Charlie was a keen listener and his questions, pertinent and well-intentioned. Not so the Irish guy who had sold Charlie the car.

The man, Charlie called him Ludo, rambled on incessantly and seemed highly agitated about something or the other. They talked in the office with the door closed. Sitting outside, Lance caught the words spoken when voices were raised, which was most of the time. The Irish guy talked about a visit to Alex and dropping a hint about an accident. Charlie asked him why on earth he had done that when the agreement was simply to hand over the money? It was spur of the moment, came the reply. Alex had warned him to mind his own business or suffer the consequences. Apparently, some Albanian had scared the shit out of Ludo. Charlie said it served him right.

There was a quiet period during which Lance heard very little, except the occasion when the Irishman raised his voice and said the wretched VAT repayment would not only be responsible for Stan's death, but for his as well. Charlie told him not to be so dramatic. A VAT inspection was perfectly normal, and he had nothing to hide, had he?

The last heated exchange was about a box of Stan's personal effects the cleaner had found when clearing out the storeroom. 'Business has been so slack, I had to find work for the guy to do to make-up his hours. Cleaners are like gold dust. When you've got one, you don't want to lose him. The storeroom's been in a mess for years.' Charlie asked what was in the box. Alongside a set of Russian nesting dolls, there were some letters and the photograph Mrs Forbes had claimed they must have lost when they emptied

Stan's desk following his death. 'I'm not taking it to her,' the Irishman had said. 'His mother hates my guts.' Charlie came back with, 'Do you think I'm flavour of the month?' Some toing and froing followed before the Irishman said he'd leave it outside her front door and call to let her know. 'I don't want to bump into Stan's brother either. Roddie's not all there. Thunders around like a mad bull. Mur'drous bastard once pinned me up against the wall and waved his fist at me.'

Lance enjoyed driving the Mercedes. It suited him, he reckoned. He was sorry when they arrived at Charlie's house in Surbiton. He could have driven all day. Charlie parked the Volvo in the drive and shuffled toward the front door. He rang the bell, waited and then returned to the Mercedes cursing and waving at Lance to move over into the passenger seat. 'When I find out where she is . . .' He never finished the sentence. Lance was unceremoniously dumped at the local railway station and a twenty-pound note shoved into his hand. 'See you tomorrow night,' Charlie had said. 'Seven thirty. Don't be late.'

His mobile rang. 'Sorry about that,' Dom said. 'Had to take a business call,'

Lance's body tensed. 'No problem. How are things?'

'I'm missing you already. Truth is, when you didn't come back last night, I know you were doing what I asked, but, secretly, I was disappointed. I'll be glad when this enforced separation is over. I need to pluck up the courage to tell my parents and our friends. It's not going to be easy.'

'I can imagine,' Lance said.

'I'm afraid you can't. You don't know my father.'

'That's what you think,' Lance said to himself.

'Are you still there? Where did you end up last night?'

'I had a stroke of luck.' Here we go, he thought. 'Inadvertently, I'd left my holdall at your place and had to return in the afternoon to collect it. That's when I bumped into your sister, just as the first of the estate agents arrived. He assumed we were a couple, so I stayed on to help out and get a good deal for you. Sylvia was so pleased that when I explained my predicament and your intention that we not be seen together, she offered me a couch at her place for a few days until I get things sorted out. I thought you'd approve.'

80

There was silence on the other end of the line, time enough Lance calculated, for Dom to assimilate the information and react. 'It's not a problem for you, is it?' Lance prompted.

'No. it's just taken me by surprise.' There was a certain reticence in Dom's voice. 'It's very good of her to offer, but she's only got a small place. Silly, you know that, of course . . . The only bathroom is en suite to her bedroom and there's only a WC in the hall closet.'

'It is compact, I agree, but we've worked out a system. Sylvia's on the day shift this week. When she leaves, I get up and shower in her bathroom. I will have my meals out and just come back at night to sleep.'

'Why didn't you call last night to tell me about this development?'

'When I realised you hadn't been contacted, I was beside myself. A misunderstanding, I'm afraid. Sylvia thought I had phoned, and I presumed she would call to get your okay. Sorry.'

There was another silence. 'As long as you can assure me nothing has changed?'

'You're the one who's setting the rules. I'm just trying to react to your guidance and not make life difficult for you. That's what you want of me, isn't it?'

'Try to find somewhere else as quickly as you can. Staying with Sylvia is not a sensible solution. One or both of my parents are as likely to call by unannounced. I'll speak with Sylvia.'

'She's off shift at five. I'd ring after that. She can't get any reception in the underground tunnel she's working in. That's what she told me.'

'I'll do that.' Dom's voice was flat. 'Just tell me everything between us is positive?'

'Why don't we meet up and talk it through? You need to . . .'

'Sorry. I've got a call coming through on my work phone. I'll speak later. Stay strong.'

Lance drained the remnants of a cold coffee. Sylvia's number rang out and went immediately to a beep and an electronic voice suggesting he left a message. 'It's me. I've explained about the invitation for me to sleep on the couch for a few days. I'm waiting to know where and when we can meet to have *that* conversation. Expect a call. A big hug.'

He rang back. 'By the way, met your dad. Got on well.'

THIRTEEN

LEN AND RANDY

Len was in a bad mood. There was a sharp pain in his back from sleeping on a lumpy sofa, and daylight had pierced through the net curtains and on to his face at some ungodly hour of the morning. The noise from the birds nesting in the back garden penetrated and irritated the dull ache in his head he knew had to be attributed to the two double whiskies he had gulped down after Muriel had refused to unlock the bedroom door. To crown it all, he had had the twins to deal with.

They had crept into the lounge just as dawn broke, talking to each other in loud whispers, which he desperately tried to ignore as he feigned sleep. Creedence suggested he wasn't asleep, but had, in fact, died. This prompted a gasp from Syracuse, who stepped back, tripped on the edge of the carpet, and sat down heavily on her backside. 'Come with me,' Creedence had said. 'I know the way to find out.'

He had drifted off into a shallow sleep when he sensed drops of liquid on his cheek and what he calculated was a piece of damp toilet paper stuffed untidily into his nostril. 'If it goes blue,' said Creedence authoritatively, 'He's dead.' There was a distinct scent of urine and he realised too late he was the victim of a rolled piece of toilet paper dipped into the water into which he had urinated during the night and not flushed for fear of waking the household. Drops ran into his throat causing him to choke, sit up and gag spittle onto the floor. There was a flurry of activity as the girls screamed and ran headlong toward the door, arriving together. Syracuse thudded into the door frame as her sister elbowed her to one side. Tearful screams followed as they clambered up the stairs.

Len's shouted, 'Get out!' was swiftly followed by Caroline's stern voice from the top of the stairs asking what the hell he had said to make them cry like that. Her tone changed to soothing as she asked Syracuse how she had got the bump on her head. 'Grandad scared me,' the girl gulped, followed by a fresh outburst of tears

'They were trying to use their initiative,' Caroline said later as she sat opposite her father in the kitchen, mugs of tea in their hands. 'I don't want to suppress their desire to experiment.'

'You condone shoving urine-soaked toilet paper up my nose?' He sounded dumbfounded.

'Of course not,' she said with a conciliatory smile. 'Creedence thought it was just water and wanted to impress her sister with the fabrication. It was your urine, and it didn't kill you, did it?'

'Your idea of stimulating initiative and mine of imposing discipline are thirty-odd years apart and worlds away from each other. The idea kids can run wild is an anathema to me.' He shook his head. 'Frankly, Caroline, I can't accept your explanation for leaving your home and letting Dominic stay there. Logic screams at me you should have remained, and he should have moved out. It makes no sense doing it your way.'

'What was all the noise about?' Muriel stood at the door. She slurred her speech as she leaned on the doorframe for support. 'It sounded as if murder was being committed.'

'Dad has had enough of the kids. He wants me to leave.'

'That's just petulance,' Len said. 'I didn't say that.'

'Of course, you're staying,' Muriel said. 'This is my house as well as his, and what I say goes. Isn't that right, Len?'

'Damn it. I didn't say I wanted her to leave. Obviously, she can stay for as long as needs be. I'm just trying to understand why she moved out.'

Muriel stumbled. Caroline moved to support her. 'Are you all right?' she asked.

'I'm fine. I took some tranquilizers. They've made me a little dizzy.'

'You're taking tranquilizers?' Len sounded confused. 'What for?'

'To put up with you, mainly. You're a selfish, heartless sod when it suits. Let the girl be. She has her reasons, and they are nothing to do with us.'

Caroline held up her hand. 'Stop. I don't want you arguing on my account. I promise to be out of your hair as quickly as possible.' She stopped Muriel from interrupting. 'I know what you're going to say, Mum, and I'm very grateful to you both. Let me answer Dad's question.' She turned back to face Len. 'I suppose I left because I wanted to let Dom know that this time I was serious. There is no going back: no more me in the house listening to a sob story, reacting to his pleas, opening the door and letting him back into my life. I wanted to make the point it was really, unequivocally finished. Does that answer satisfy you?'

Len nodded.

'While I'm here, I promise to get the girls to conform more to your rules than mine. Okay? Mum, you can have your car back tomorrow. I'm getting a lift over to Norma's in the morning. She's lending me a car until things get sorted out financially. It's a Volvo, like the one I'm used to driving, only newer.'

Len rose from his stool. 'She's doing what? Why didn't you ask me? I thought we said you weren't having any more to do with that family. It's him, isn't it? Trying to wheedle his way into your life by offering you a car.'

'For God's sake, Dad, what is it with you and Charlie? Nobody's offering me a car. Norma's lending me a car until I'm financially sorted, and then I'll give it back or, possibly, buy it from them.'

'I don't like it. You should have asked me first?'

'And you would have forked out twelve grand for a car for me, would you?'

'Twelve thousand? Is that how much the charlatan is asking for it? I don't know why you can't carry on using your mother's.'

'I do,' Muriel said. 'I need it. And it's not yours to offer.'

Len scoffed a laugh. 'And you're going to drive doped up to the eyeballs? Do me a favour.'

'I need it. Do I have to say it again?' She clicked her fingers as if something had come to mind. 'Tell you what. We can help you out,' she said, addressing Caroline. 'Norma called me a little while ago. She suggested Len and I join them for dinner tonight. I accepted.'

'You did what?' Len punched a fist into the palm of his hand. 'I'm not going.'

'Charlie will phone Len to arrange the details,' Muriel continued, ignoring the protest. 'And when he does, Len will suggest they come to the venue in two cars. I can then drive the Volvo back here for you.'

'That would be wonderful,' Caroline said, 'But it means you won't be able to have more than one glass of wine. I don't want to spoil your evening.'

'It won't spoil mine. I'd be the one driving home anyway. It's your father who will have to control his intake, but as drink loosens his tongue, that might be no bad thing.'

'I'll tell the arsehole – excuse my French – we can't make it.'

'You'll do no such thing,' Muriel said, a fury in her voice that was strange to them both. 'I have accepted, and we *will* go. Is that understood?'

'Who's got you all fired up like this?' Len said. 'I know, it's bloody Gerry and his "you've got to assert yourself to survive" horseshit. Don't you understand, woman? I cannot stand the man. Don't make me sit down to dinner with him.'

'His son's marriage to our daughter is ending.' Muriel glanced at Caroline and smiled. 'Don't you think we should understand how they see things from their side? Norma sounded distressed and I, for one, don't want to end up in some hostile confrontation when our children appear to be handling this difficult situation in a friendly and mature manner. It's time you grew up as far as relationships are concerned, Len, and it's also long overdue I came to my senses.'

The screen on his burner mobile showed the caller as 'Randy.' 'I hope you've got some good news for me. I'm having an awful day so far and it has little chance of improving, as far as I can see.'

'Blimey, what a greeting. Not even a "How are you, Randy? Okay. Thanks Len, how are you?" What's got at you today?'

'Don't get me started,' Len said. 'The wife's having an independence day; the grandchildren appear to have been possessed by the devil; my daughter is in the middle of a divorce, and I'm forced into having dinner tonight with a couple I can't stand. To top it, I won't even be able to have a drink to blunt the sharp edges.'

'Sounds like fun.' There was a burst of laughter in the background.

'Where are you?'

'In a pub having a liquid lunch,' Randy replied. 'Drowning my sorrows.'

'Not you as well? What's your problem?'

'Our problem, I'm afraid.'

'Go on.'

'The NCA has taken over the case, my contact tells me. Apparently, the discovery of this lorry is now part of a wider enquiry under investigation in London. Obviously, I know people in CSU, but nobody sufficiently well to call on without setting off alarm bells. Do you?'

'With National Crime involved, it's serious. I can put names to faces, but nobody I can ask to keep me abreast of developments. You're working on a major fraud and money laundering enquiry. Can't you try to tie it in?'

There was another burst of laughter at the other end of the line, this time louder and closer. 'Wait until I get somewhere quieter,' Randy said.

Len hung on for what seemed an eternity, a series of background noises and muffled talking before total silence. 'You there?' he said.

'Okay, I can talk now.'

'Did you hear what I asked?'

'Yes,' Randy replied. 'It already occurred to me. There's no obvious linkage, but I'll give it some more thought.'

'It's the obvious point of entry if you can conjure up a connection.' Len knew he would have to keep up the pressure. Randy wasn't one for going out on a limb. 'What was the state of play at the point the NCA took over?'

'There were blood spatters from two different people in the container, smaller drops from one source on the floor and much larger spatters together with fabric thread on the wall. There was a cursory examination by forensics in Birmingham before the vehicle moves to Vauxhall in the morning. What we know so far is a premise that the large spatter resulted from a gunshot, but there is no trace of a bullet or casing. Apparently, the DNA extracted from this splatter matches an unidentified female body recovered from the River Lea near the Vineyard some two months ago. Somebody had tried to weigh the body down, but it had come free and drifted to the bank.'

'Any estimate how long it had been there?'

'My man had no info,' Randy said. 'The only guide was a request from Major Crime in Birmingham to the Met for CCTV images on all roads leading down to the river Lea at that point and surrounding area for the period 1st through 7th of February. Forensics in London will go over the crime scene with a fine toothcomb.'

'There will be a great deal of CCTV footage to scan.'

'National Crime doesn't have our staffing problems. They don't get my sympathy.'

'I'm sure they don't,' Len agreed. 'Is there a match for the smaller bloodstain?'

'Not so far.'

'Do you know if Terry and Nobby have made any progress?'

'Terry rang me from a stakeout in Wembley this morning. He's watching the family home of the woman he knew as Mahi Sharma, who is now Mahi Kumar. She and her husband live in the family home of her father-in-law, retired General Badri Kumar. He has spent thirty years as a military attaché at the Indian High Commission in Aldwych and, as far as Nobby can discover, is a traditionalist, a believer in family cohesion and owns a large property in which alongside the General and his wife, there are three sons, their wives and adult children. Mahi's husband is the middle son. Apparently, they have no children.'

'The point of your stakeout being?' Len sounded impatient.

'Nobby believes we need to establish she is still bound by Indian family social rules and would be receptive to suggestions that the revelation of her fling with Terry would have serious consequences for her within the family. You need to speak with him to get chapter and verse.'

'When do you envisage Terry will be ready to make an approach?'

There was a cynical laugh on Randy's end of the line. 'Like never if it was down to Terry. He doesn't fancy the reception he'll get if he starts rattling her cage. It all happened a long time ago.'

'Bateman's serious. You know that, don't you? If he gets dragged into this and loses his gong or whatever he's expecting, we'll be totally vulnerable. The press will be far more interested in exposing bent coppers than some crooked butcher in the West Midlands. He'll deny everything and blame it all on us if he can.'

'I know. I know. Fuck it. Terry knows he's got to do it. He just hates the prospect of putting the frighteners on someone for whom he has - had the hots.'

'Don't you start getting sentimental as well. Has she got a daily routine?'

'I followed her this morning. She walks to Wembley Park tube station, travels to Liverpool Street where she changes onto the Central Line to Mile End. She walks down the Bow Road, collects a takeaway coffee from a local sandwich bar and passes through a small park to her office just off Grove Road. She's risen to the post of assistant manager in the DVSA traffic enforcement section, has her own office and is a team leader.'

'Where's the best place to intercept her?'

'In the park, I guess. There's CCTV focussed on the entrance and exit, but they can be avoided. There's no coverage once you're past the gate.'

'How do we avoid the cameras?'

'The wire fence has been pulled up over by the Regent Canal footpath in the area where the kids play football. It requires a little limbo dancing technique, but it's more than doable. You've just got to make sure nobody's looking as you slip under.'

'Good. Now all we need to firm up on is when?' Len persisted.

'Terry said he'll sort it out with Nobby. He'll have to follow up with the frightener if she blanks Terry.'

'Tomorrow would be good. I'm arranging to see Bateman to find out how come the vehicle was on the road when he told me it was parked up and why the compartment was not sanitised. It would be convenient to tell him we are making progress. It's Friday tomorrow and with the weekend intervening, developments might overtake us.'

Randy coughed to clear his throat. 'I'd prefer it if *you'd* speak with Terry. He won't take any notice of what I say, even if I impress on him I'm simply relaying your request. If you remember, he used to specialise in questioning orders as if he knew better. You stand more chance of getting through to him.'

'How much does he know about the NCA investigation?'

'Nothing. He was only interested in talking about this Kumar woman. He's still got the hots for her, if you ask me.'

'Tell him he can pin up a picture of her in his cell.'

'Sorry, missed that.'

'Never mind. Leave Terry to me.'

His bad mood worsened as the hour drew nearer to leave for his dinner date from hell, as he had described it to Nobby.

The call had been brief and to the point. Nobby had to establish that Mahi Kumar was subject to the constraints of traditional Indian family life and social behaviour. Had she had freedom of choice, her marriage partner could well have been a non-Indian and her attitudes more liberal and westernised, in which case threats of revealing a pre-marital affair would have no impact.

The converse was true, Nobby had confirmed. The General had left Delhi as a major in his mid-thirties, a firm believer in the caste system, family cohesion and the place of women in the family hierarchy. His father, a senior member of the state legislature, had warned of the creeping danger of western culture in England impacting on family values and the need for his son to adopt strict measures to combat the threat. The son had more than followed his father's advice. As he progressed through the diplomatic ranks, he insisted the household run as if in India, even to the extent the women of the house practiced purdah and wore a suitable veil when in public.

'As far as I can tell from the grapevine,' Nobby explained. 'Mahi's father is a tradesman and of a lower caste. It would have needed a fair amount of arse licking and a sizeable dowry to arrange a marriage for Mahi with the son. As it was, she got the runt of the litter. Neeraj suffers from an emotional dysregulation disorder resulting in highly volatile mood swings, making him virtually unemployable. Dad got him a job at the High Commission as maintenance manager. According to a friend in the visa section, he does very little and spends most of the day in his office.'

'Sounds like misery for the wife,' Len added.

'Her life is her job. She escapes into the normality of an office environment for eight hours before heading back into the time warp of an Indian family life of fifty years ago.'

'Good work. Can we hit on her tomorrow?'

'The sooner the better. It's Terry you need to convince.'

Contrary to his expectations, once Len had run through the details of the investigation, Terry's initial hesitancy evaporated, and he appeared resigned to his role. He admitted to being nervous to approach her and was genuinely concerned she would lose any respect she once had for him.

Len was in no mood to tolerate Terry's emotional concerns. The details needed to be tied up with Randy and Nobby.

'You sound as though you've lost a fiver and found a ten-bob note. Are you all right, Len?' Terry asked.

'The wife is hassling me to leave for a dinner date I really don't need, and my mood will only improve when I'm back home again. I want this Bateman business sorted and out of the way as soon as possible. I've got a nasty feeling about it.'

'That makes two of us.'

Terry's words were ringing in Len's ears as he waited for Muriel to join him.

FOURTEEN

CHARLIE AND NORMA

'Do you mind if I drive the Mercedes?' Norma asked. 'I'm unfamiliar with the controls in the Volvo and I'd feel more comfortable.' She waited for the answer. 'Darling, did you hear what I said?'

She walked across the landing to his bathroom to discover he was no longer there. 'Where are you?' she shouted.

'In the study,' came the disembodied voice. 'I'm registering Cary as a nominated driver on the insurance policy.' He appeared at the foot of the stairs. 'Did you know she's only thirty-five?'

'Yes, same age as Sylvia – a couple of months between them. Sylvia's the younger. Why?'

'Nothing. I was just thinking about the age gap.'

'Dominic's only forty. It's hardly a big difference. These days, nobody gives it much consideration. I doubt their ages had anything to do with the break-up.'

He chuckled to himself.

'Are you ready to go?' She repeated the question about who would drive which car. 'We should be first to arrive as we're the hosts and it's our choice of restaurant. Why did you opt for Leonardo's? We haven't been there in months.'

'He wanted somewhere halfway between us. Esher seemed like a good choice and Leonardo's is the only place I know.'

She wagged her finger at him. 'Promise me one thing. You won't embarrass me by putting on that phony Italian accent and greeting the owner, Livio, as if you are long-lost brothers. All that *Tutto Grazie* and *Come va il family* nonsense. You see him, maybe, twice a year and the only lasting impression you leave is that you sound like Del Boy.'

'Thank you for that vote of confidence.'

'All I'm saying is, don't show off in front of Muriel and Len and start making an order for *Bruschetta* or *Saltimbocca* sound like you're deferring to a mafia boss. I may look like I'm laughing, but inside, I'm cringing.'

93

'It's only a bit of fun,' he protested. 'We've got nothing left to talk about, so it's good to inject a little humour into the proceedings.'

'Humour you call it?' She tut-tutted as she adjusted the knot of his tie and brushed the lapels of his sports jacket. 'Like dancing with that man in the Greek restaurant and shouting Zorba at the top of your voice as you bashed bellies with him. He got so annoyed he sent you sprawling.'

'A miscalculation, I admit.'

'Followed by dropping the twelve plates all at once and sending shards of crockery all over the dance floor.'

'All right, you've made your point, Norma.' He chuckled again. 'We're with company tonight. No doubt, we'll have plenty to talk about.'

'Let's go,' she said.

FIFTEEN

LEN AND MURIEL

Dark thoughts lay heavily on him. A vivid imagination painted scenarios of impending problems he would have discounted with a shrug five years ago. Was it retirement or the approach of old age that accentuated this sense of foreboding? He would never have brooded like this whilst he was on the Force. Perspective. He was losing a sense of perspective, of calculating risk and response to minimise the danger. Now, he just worried. There was no mental progression to seek a solution. All he felt was self-pity, and he despised himself for it.

How long had she been standing there, staring at him? If she had spoken, he wasn't aware of any sound or the movement of her mouth. 'Sorry,' he said, without thinking.

'Whatever is troubling you, put it on hold for the next few hours.' Muriel's voice was starved of any emotion. 'I want to have a civilised meal with two people who are as concerned as we are about the state and future of their children in times of trouble. I want you to curb your impatience and cloak the dislike you have for our dinner companions.'

'I have nothing against her,' Len said. 'Apart from the close relationship she has engineered with Caroline. I find that unpalatable.'

'Has it occurred to you it might be as much of our daughter's choosing as it is of Norma's?'

'Then she should analyse her motives.'

'Doesn't that sound just like the policeman? Must there be a motive? Perhaps she finds something in her relationship with Norma that is missing from the emotional back-up we should have provided. I'll put my hand up and admit I've been far from the supportive mother.'

'You don't know what you're talking about, woman. Caro—'

'Don't you dare address me like that again! I'm not your servant, your woman, around just to do the chores and follow your instructions. I want some life for myself, before it's too late.'

'You have everything you could possibly want.' He sounded indignant.

'Doesn't that statement just say it all? Substitute all these chattels' – she waved her hand around the room – 'for a little loving understanding and togetherness. It's lonely living with you, Len.' She removed her coat from the back of a chair.

'You need to see somebody and talk through all these hang-ups.'

'Maybe I will, but not in the way you mean. Are you ready? I don't want us to be late and I need you to promise you will be on your best behaviour tonight. I'm eager to understand what they feel about the break-up.'

'Hardly as relieved as I am, I guarantee.'

'Do you have any feeling at all for your grandchildren? Their parents are splitting up. Suddenly, Daddy isn't there in the morning anymore, lying alongside Mummy. Maybe there's a man they used to know as Mummy's friend lying there instead. It's a lot for little heads to cope with.'

'Blimey, give her a chance. She's only just breaking up with this excuse for a husband. Let the path of true love take its time. She's not going to exit from one failed relationship to rush headlong into another affair. Caroline is more sensible than that.'

'We'll see. Let's go.'

Len's burner mobile vibrated just as he was about to get into the car. He looked at the name of the screen. 'I've just got to take this.' He moved out of earshot.

'What do you want, Darren?'

'Oh, that's nice, isn't it? Not how's it going, Darren? Long time, no see.'

'Spare me the niceties, Darren. I'm late for a meeting and I can't talk. What do you want, son?'

'Don't call me son. I ain't no relative of yours, thank fuck.'

'The feeling's mutual. Get on with it.'

'Dad wants a meet first thing tomorrow.'

'About what?'

'He's staying down in London and leaving for Wolverhampton tomorrow afternoon. The police have been nosing around the premises. He'll meet you at the normal place in the morning. Eight thirty. Don't be late. He's not in the best of moods.'

96

'As it happens, *I* need to talk to him.' He had no commitments in the morning, but he was through with taking orders. 'Tell him it will have to be nine. I'm tied up earlier.' He rang off before the other man had the chance to answer.

SIXTEEN

CHARLIE AND NORMA – LEN AND MURIEL

Norma could only define the conspiratorial smile she exchanged with Muriel as confirmation the dinner was progressing better than either woman could have predicted. The greetings had been courteous, if not effusive; the conversation banal, but animated, and even agreement between all four that the roasted pear topped with goat's cheese starter would have been more appropriately listed in the dessert section of the menu.

It was midway through their main courses when the subject of family was finally broached. Until that point, the topics of wine, weather, politics and holidays dictated the exchanges with the unspoken aim of attempting to establish common ground before straying onto relationship issues.

It was Muriel who first tested the temperature of the water. 'How's your daughter? Sylvia, isn't it? Is she in a relationship?'

'She's good,' Norma replied. 'It always seems to me work is more important than boyfriends as far as Sylvia is concerned.'

Muriel nodded and smiled. 'She's something to do with a laboratory if I remember correctly?'

'She's a forensic scientist,' Charlie said in his matter-of-fact voice.

'Well, a laboratory assistant,' Norma corrected, deflecting Charlie's reproachful glance with a smile. 'She says it's nothing like the glamorous lifestyle you see on TV; far more mundane and bureaucratic than they make out. Boyfriends seem to come and go.'

'Do you think she'll settle down eventually? She must be in her thirties.'

Norma shrugged her shoulders and adjusted the napkin on her lap. 'Difficult to say. She's the same age as your Caroline, a few months between them. Mid-thirties seem to be the time many people get into serious relationships these days. We keep our fingers crossed.'

Charlie began refilling wine glasses from a bottle of Barolo. Len looked up from a large soup plate full of *ossobuco*, a chunk of braised veal between his teeth, and nodded. Red droplets stained the tablecloth as the wine splashed into his glass. 'Sorry,' Charlie said. 'Got a twitch in my arm.'

Len swallowed the piece of meat, wiped the sauce from his lips, and dried the base of his glass. 'Lots of single girls prefer female company. It's the trend, so I read.'

Charlie turned deliberately to face Muriel. 'I met her new boyfriend this morning. He's a personal trainer from Australia. Got a physique I wish I'd had when I was younger. They're coming around for dinner tomorrow evening. Should be a fun night. It will make a change.'

Muriel held her glass out for a refill. Len shook his head. 'You're driving, remember?'

'I'll be fine.' She waited while Charlie poured the wine, stopping him with the glass barely a quarter full. 'So are you,' she said. 'In a car you're not used to. I think you *are* the one who should watch his intake.'

Len dipped a piece of bread into the remnants of the sauce on his plate. 'No problem. I'm used to driving these old bangers. There's no complicated electronics to worry about. As long as it gets me home before it breaks down.'

'It was very good of Norma and Charlie to sort a car out for Caroline.' Muriel turned to them both with a beaming smile. 'Please tell me there's a chance the two of them will get back together again, if only for the twins' sake.

'We can always hope,' Norma said. 'From what Dominic told us, the divorce proceedings are pretty far advanced.'

'It's the V70 SE LUX model, if you must know.' Charlie leaned across toward Len, cutting the wives out of the conversation. 'There's plenty of electronics, so drive carefully. You don't want to crash it before your girl has the opportunity to get behind the wheel. It had a thirty grand price tag when it was new and it's showing very few signs of age. She'll love it. The last owner was a lady schoolteacher; hardly put on any mileage. Runs as sweet as a nut.'

'Charlie!' Norma reprimanded. 'You're not selling Len a car. Stop the showroom patter.'

'Just saying. It's a later year than the Dominic's Volvo with a bigger luxury spec. The twins will love it.' He put his hands up in a surrender pose. 'Don't look at me like that, doll. I said I was just saying.'

100

'Forgive my husband,' Norma said. 'He's never really retired from the car business.'

Len pulled the starched white napkin from his collar and patted around his mouth, eventually scrunching it into a ball and setting it alongside his plate. 'I said to Muriel the one thing I can't get my head round in this divorce is why Dominic ended up in the house and with their car when it would have been much more sensible for him to move out and leave Caroline and the girls in situ.' He waited until the waitress distributed the dessert menus and retreated out of earshot. Muriel started to say something, but he spoke over her. 'I get the sense he must have a bit on the side and is keen to sell up and move on with someone else. Can't see any other reason. It seems crazy to me.'

Norma reached under the table and dug her fingernails into her husband's thigh. He flinched, but took the hint and said nothing, although his cheeks coloured.

'We haven't gone into details yet with Dominic about his plans,' Norma said. 'We felt it best to give him time to reflect on the enormity of the decision they have taken. Isn't *that* right?'

Charlie mumbled something unintelligible as he flexed his hands into fists.

'I'm sure it will all come out in the wash,' Muriel said. 'We must remember their attitude to each other is respectful and in no way argumentative. I—'

'You're ignoring the impact of his actions on the twins,' Len cut in. 'Those girls are being tossed from pillar to post, but it's happened. I will counsel Caroline to sit the twins down and to explain why their father does not choose to live with them anymore and to establish a . . .' He struggled to find a word. '. . . kind of vacuum in which they can come to terms with the new reality.'

'What does that entail?' Norma asked.

They all fell silent again as the young girl returned to take their order. Both ladies passed. Both men opted for baked apples in red wine. Using the excuse that he needed to make some calls before the night was out, Len proposed they skip coffees and brandies. It appeared that everybody except Charlie accepted the real motive for the suggestion. 'I'll have an Americano and a grappa, *per piacere*,' he said. 'Norma asked you what this proposal of yours involves. Are you going to answer?'

Len sat back in his chair and crossed his arms over his chest. 'They need stability and time to come to terms with a single parent relationship. Their father and his family should keep their distance for as long as it takes; three months, at least.'

Flecks of spittle appeared on Charlie's lips. 'Three months is an eternity in the lives of two six-year-olds.' His voice was soft and measured. Norma squeezed his thigh again, this time harder. She knew this was the calm just before the storm. 'What you want is to see Dominic and us out of their lives forever.' The tone was still measured.

'I think the proposal has merit.' Len said, a tinge of authoritative challenge mixed with smugness in his voice.

The waitress appeared with the two baked apples, which she carefully arranged in front of the two men. 'Anybody else for coffee and liqueurs?' she asked. Norma hurriedly shook her head and signalled for the bill.

Charlie dug the dessert fork forcibly into the apple. 'You know, Len,' he said, his voice rising. 'I've always put you down as a self-righteous prick who fancies himself as one of the elite - what did your dear lady-wife say about your house - where is it? Weybridge, that's it. Fucking Weybridge. Worth well in excess of two million on the market today, is it? Where does policeman plod get enough dough to buy a house like that? Not out of his police salary, that's for sure.' He felt the nails digging into the flesh of his thighs, but not even an amputation would have stopped the maelstrom he felt rising inside of him.

'And what's all this bollocks about a single mum? From what I hear, Cary's already got herself shacked up with a modern-day Shylock. It's no wonder she's in a hurry. He's old enough to be her father and, chances are, when she starts to pound away on top of him, the poor sod is likely to have a stroke – and not the pleasant variety.'

Charlie was standing now, all eyes in the restaurant focussed on him, all conversations reduced to whispers. He held the apple upright by the fork as if it were a microphone. 'That's wiped the smile off your smug face, hasn't it?' He stopped; his brow creased. 'Hang on. You didn't know, did you?' His laugh was genuine. 'Your precious daughter hasn't told you the real reason why she left the house instead of my boy, has she? She probably can't wait to get her claws into her new man and see his will changed before the poor bastard develops dementia. So much for what was how you described it at that tedious wedding speech, "your bond of understanding with your daughter". The poor girl is too afraid to tell you.' His protracted laugh was intended to ridicule.

Len's voice was little more than a whisper. 'I promise you this: if I have my way, you will never set eyes again on the twins. There's a dozen witnesses here tonight who have heard you blaspheming and out of control. I'll get a restraining order to ensure the girls are spared contact once and for all with a monster and his pathetic family.'

'You just try, and I'll see you in hell.' The apple propelled from Charlie's fork splattered into Len's face.

'That went well, didn't it?' Charlie broke the silence they had endured since leaving the restaurant. 'I didn't see. Did you pay the bill?' He turned the car into the road leading to the cul-de-sac.

'I did. I also left fifty pounds to cover any damage, or the embarrassment and inconvenience caused to Livio's clientele.'

'Fifty quid? Are you made of money? We never came to blows.'

'Only because Livio stepped in between you at the critical moment. Len was set to give you a beating.'

'Oh, it's "Len would have given me a beating," is it? I might have given him one.'

'He's thin and wiry, keeps in condition. You're fat and struggle for breath getting out of the bath.'

'I just needed one lucky punch.'

'Forget it,' Norma dismissed the feigned swing at her cheek with a tired yawn. 'You've given me a big problem now. Let's get indoors. I'm tired.'

'He still took the keys to the Volvo, didn't he? Not that proud, was he, the sanctimonious jerk?'

'I apologise if I upset you,' he said, subsiding heavily into the sofa alongside her. He proffered a brandy in an oversize balloon glass, which she accepted.

He leaned forward to pick up his glass from the coffee table. 'Here's to Dominic. Whatever else he's done, he's rid us of his father-in-law from hell.' He took a large swig of brandy. 'I'm starting to feel human again. Anyway, the meal was enjoyable, I thought—'

'Don't say it. If you think I am ever going to set foot in that restaurant again, you can think again. I'd be too embarrassed.'

'Livio wouldn't mind. He's Italian. They've all got short tempers, shouting and gesticulating at each other. It probably reminded him of home.'

'I said "No". Forget it. What I want to know is how you came by the information that Cary was involved with someone else and planned to move in with him?'

'I put two and two together. Ludo was around at the place where this Alex lives to discuss his loan repayment and accidentally saw Cary in an intimate clutch with the guy. Assuming she wouldn't want to be around Len and Muriel for any length of time, I drew the obvious conclusion. According to Ludo, the guy is loaded.'

'Cary's going to think I failed to respect her confidence and told you what was going on.'

'You knew?'

'I met with Cary this morning while you were trying to contact me. She gave me a rundown of her relationship with Alex Quentin. I didn't make an immediate connection with the source of the loan with which Ludo bought you out. Now, I get it. I hope Cary believes me when the fireworks have finished. You dented Len's brittle pride.' She poured the rest of her brandy into Charlie's glass. 'No more booze for me. Do you think he can get us legally banned from seeing the twins?'

'I don't see how. What's his grounds - that I attacked him with a baked apple? Just to be safe, I'll check with Fancy in the morning.'

'I hope you don't call Mr Pantis that to his face. His name is Aziz.'

'Of course I do, same as all his clients. I doubt his mother even calls him by his given name.'

Norma had excused herself and gone to bed. Charlie sat alone in the lounge with the lights dimmed, nursing the brandy glass between his hands. His thoughts ranged over the events of the evening, and he had to admit to himself he was worried. Len was an ex-copper with a lot of friends in the force and, probably, in the judiciary, as well. Now the gloves were well and truly off, he might make things difficult for Charlie, even pry into areas of his life best kept under wraps. Len would calculate somebody who had spent forty-odd years in the motor trade must have a few skeletons and Charlie was no exception, not only in the metaphorical sense. Images of Stanley Forbes flickered into his conscious as if projected by a magic lantern. 'Silly twat!' he said out loud. 'Greedy bastard; you got what was coming to you.'

There had to be something he could dig up on that ex-copper; some pressure he could exert on Len to ensure there was harmony as far as the twins were concerned. It would break his heart to lose contact with the girls. If truth were told, they could generate emotions in him he had not felt for a long time and he enjoyed a sensation akin to that he had experienced when his own kids were young. It was an age of innocence and wonderment, so frail, so easily destroyed.

The one thing about the evening preying on his mind was Len's reaction when Muriel was going on about how much their house was worth. When she said, "well in excess of two million", Len had looked daggers at her as if he was desperate to gag her and change the subject. His expression had deepened into pure hatred when Charlie had questioned how he could afford such a lifestyle. At the time he made the remark, it was simply an attempt to score points by innuendo, but, judging by the reaction, maybe there was some truth hidden underneath the bluster and bullshit that followed as Len angled the conversation away from the subject. Charlie's father had always said that coppers and villains were cut from the same cloth. It was just a matter of luck on which side of the law they ended up.

The question was how and who could he get to investigate Len's affairs? The only person in Charlie's circle who had contact with the police was Sylvia and she was coming to dinner tomorrow - he glanced at the clock on the mantelpiece – correction, today. He would sound her out.

As he climbed the stairs, he could hear Norma's gentle snoring. 'I'll get you once and for all, you arrogant bastard,' he said.

* * *

'I'll make a complaint,' Len said, as he watched Muriel stride toward him after parking their Lexus. 'It constitutes assault.'

'What, GBH with a baked apple? You'll have the local police force in stitches. How did the Volvo drive?'

'Piece of crap, like I knew it would be.'

'Best to ask Charlie to collect it. You don't want your daughter driving a piece of crap, do you?'

'Right now, I don't know what to think of Caroline.' He watched as she filtered the bunch of keys through her fingers to find the one to open the front door. 'Do you think what he said was true, or was he just spinning a line to get me going?'

'Keep your voice down now. Go into the lounge and wait while I take my coat off and make a coffee. What do you want, Ristretto or Latte?'

'Small and black, no sugar. I'll pour a malt. Want one?'

'No more alcohol. I'm turning to a new chapter in my life and the prop of alcohol will definitely not play a part in it.'

'What was that glass in front of you tonight, an apparition?'

'I was just being sociable, playing out my swansong.'

Five minutes later, she returned, clad in a flannelette dressing gown, two coffees on a tray and a blanket over her shoulder. She put the tray down and tossed the blanket onto his lap. 'You'll need that to keep warm. It's colder tonight than last night and the central heating doesn't come back on until six.'

'Not another night. This is down to Gerry, isn't it? He's been putting all these quirky thoughts in your head.'

'Gerry just encouraged me to wake up after decades of living in a trance.'

'Sleeping Beauty?'

'I'll take that as a compliment from you, a rare occurrence.'

'And for how long do you intend to inflict this penance on me?' He drained his coffee and sipped at the glass of malt whisky.

She pulled the belt of her dressing gown tight around her. 'Until the urge has passed to put a pillow over your face whilst you're sleeping.'

'You've got a screw loose, you know that, Muriel? As it happens, I won't object to sleeping down here tonight. I want to ensure I'm up in time to speak to Caroline before she leaves with the kids. I want to get to grips with what that troublemaker was saying. Do you believe him?'

'I asked Norma in the loo if it was true. She said she had no idea. It wasn't anything she had passed on to him. She doubted Charlie would just make it up.'

He slipped off his sneakers and wheeled around to lie on the sofa. 'I'll get the truth out of her in the morning.'

Muriel stood up and once again re-tightened her belt. 'If you're in the mood to take some advice, I'd leave it until she gets around to telling us of her own accord. The way you'll present it will just result in an argument. If you wait, you can then have a conversation to understand why she felt she couldn't tell you earlier. You might learn some home truths.'

He shook his head. 'You're seriously suggesting every question I have here,' he pointed, 'on the tip of my tongue—'

'Swallow them all. If you embarrass her with an accusation, she'll clam up and tell you to mind your own business. And I wouldn't blame her. She's a mature woman who can make her own decisions. Let her handle it and don't try to control her.'

'You're asking me, someone with a copper's background, to suspend the interrogation of a suspect, Caroline in this case, until the information is eventually proffered? It goes against the grain.'

'I'm not asking you to do anything. I know from almost forty years of marriage that you'll do exactly what you want, and, as is the norm, dismiss my advice as unworthy. You should adopt a different approach. That's my suggestion. Give her the space to tell us in her own good time. Don't box her into a corner. If Charlie's right, it won't be long in coming. In the meantime, I'll be in little doubt you'll be doing your background checks into this Alex Quentin, whoever he is.'

He tossed and turned on the sofa, unable to get comfortable, the blanket wrapped around him like an Egyptian mummy. He had relived the events of the last evening over and over, conscious of his rising blood pressure every time he heard in his head the sound of Charlie's mocking taunts. "You didn't know, did you?" He said the words out loud in a high-pitched whine. The indignity of wiping the pieces of wine-soaked apple from his face and shirt;

the urge to launch himself across the table and sink his fist into that fat bastard's flushed face.

Muriel had been stupid, boasting about the value of the house. Charlie had jumped on it with his snidey innuendo. Trouble was, it could prove the one aspect of Len's meticulous financial arrangements to come home to roost. They had paid nine hundred thousand for the house twelve years earlier. Seven hundred had come from the sale of their previous home and forty thousand from their joint savings. The shortfall of one hundred and sixty thousand had been deposited by a Cayman Islands registered company in the offshore account of the UK bank facilitating the mortgage, thereby providing security for the top-up loan needed to complete the funding package. It had been done against Len's better judgement, but they had both fallen in love with the house to the extent he was prepared to take the calculated risk of Internal Affairs becoming alerted to his financial dealings. His aim had been to refinance the top-up loan and release the deposited funds back to the Cayman Islands, but, somehow, he had never got around to doing it and the original structure was still in place. If Charlie went around blabbing to his Masonic friends, it could mean trouble for Len before he had the chance to reorganise his finances.

The only way to stop Charlie in his tracks was to dig up some dirt on him. Nobody could spend a lifetime in the shady world of used cars without falling foul of the law. It was just a question of finding out when and how and he knew just the people to talk to. Comforted by the prospect, he patted down the cushions and turned over. He fell into a deep sleep.

A glance at his watch told him it was past eight. The door to the hall and kitchen had been carefully closed by someone so as not to wake him. From the window he could see that both Charlie's Volvo and Muriel's compact were no longer in the drive. The house was silent, except for the buzz from his mobile on the hall stand where it was charging. There were four missed calls and a message.

The number was Darren's. 'Pissed off trying to ring you. Dad said make it ten thirty in the special place. Be there. Confirm.'

He yawned, stretched and pressed the automatic message reply that said, 'Okay, I'll be there.'

SEVENTEEN

CARY AND ROSE

Cary had expected one or other of Alex's Albanian helpers to open the front door. It was neither Abdyl nor Saban but a rather dramatic looking older woman with short, spiky red hair, blushed cheeks and a gash of maroon lipstick which barely followed the contours of pouting lips. She was small in stature, with a boyish figure clad in a long flowing dressing gown in a vibrant print, which reminded Cary of the curtain material in the hotel room she had regularly shared with Alex in the early days of their liaison. The thick-rimmed, deep turquoise framed sunglasses seemed out of proportion to the rest of her face.

The elderly lady raised pencil-line eyebrows as she studiously appraised the woman standing before her dressed in a business looking dark blue, three-piece suit. Her gaze extended beyond the woman to the car where two identical, small faces stared at her through the windscreen.

'If you're selling children, I'm afraid I've just eaten,' she said with a straight face.

'Sorry,' Cary said, unable to process the context of the words she had just heard. 'I'm looking for Alex,' was her lame response.

'And you are?'

'I'm Caroline,' she replied, slowly gathering her composure. 'Alex is my client.'

The woman frowned and pointed at the car. 'What do the children do, watch?'

'Sorry?' She blushed as the realisation dawned. 'My goodness, no. Nothing like that. I'm an accountant. I hoped to speak with Alex before I dropped the girls off at school.' She sensed she was being played. 'I assume Alex is not at home.'

'You assume correctly.'

'And may I ask who you might be?'

'You may.' She smiled. 'Is there anything else?' She started to close the door.

'Wait!' she demanded. 'Do you know at what time he will be back or if he is contactable today on his mobile?'

'No, and in answer to the second part of your question, I presume if he took it, he intends to make and receive calls.' The door closed.

Cary retreated down the steps just as the anger surged. She walked back up the steps and banged her fist on the door. It opened almost immediately.

'Yes?'

'I'll presume, as the information is not forthcoming, you are a close relative of Alex.' There was no reaction on the elderly lady's face. 'That being the case, let me advise you I am Alex's partner . . . in the relationship sense, and we plan to live together as soon as practicably possible. I came around today to discuss an aspect surrounding the change of our status. That's all I have to say.' She turned as if to leave.

'Wait.' The door opened fully. 'That's better. A statement of facts, not polite waffle. Come in. We'll talk.' For the first time, the woman smiled. 'I'm Rosa, but as it sounds like slang for a policeman, I have become a Rose. It's unfortunate, but there you are. Rosa sounds like somebody with a bit of spunk in her. Rose sounds so acquiescent and subservient.'

Cary gave a reassuring wave to the twins and went to enter the house.

'Are you going to leave them outside?' Rose asked, barring her way.

'I haven't really got much time and disembarking and embarking the girls is such a time-consuming operation. I'm sure they will be fine.'

'Nonsense. They'll fret if they lose sight of you. I'll come and sit in the car.' She extended tattooed legs from within the folds of the dressing gown and fed her feet into a pair of sandals. She tripped down the steps and hurried to the car.

'And who have we got here?' she asked, turning to address the twins.

'I'm Creedence and she is my sister, Syracuse,' a little voice replied. 'She's shy and I'm not. I do the talking.'

'Is that so? Well, I'm pleased to meet you both. My name is Rose, and I need to talk to your mother. Is that all right?' Creedence's hesitant nod said, 'Okay, but don't be too long about it.' Syracuse was busy sucking the cord on her hoodie.

'Alex won't have mentioned me. He rarely invites me because I'm not afraid to criticise his life choices and he's very much like his father, God rest his soul, both unable and unwilling to listen to or accept criticism.'

'You're his mother?' There was total incredulity in her voice. 'Forgive me, but you hardly look old enough to have a son in his fifties.'

'Call it the frivolity of youth, a sexual addict of a tutor at an art college in New Cross and a promiscuous seventeen-year-old, unabashed student who exchanged a lifetime of parental responsibility for a glorious night of total abandonment. The result was Alexander. It was touch and go whether he made it.'

'A difficult pregnancy?'

'Nothing like that. His father offered the option of a backstreet abortion, but, as I sometimes tell my son when he is being obnoxiously pretentious, I should have taken the often selfish and tempting option to flush him down the toilet.'

Cary recoiled at the statement. 'That's a cruel thing to say.'

Her lips parted in a grimace. There were traces of lipstick on her teeth. 'Isn't it just? But heartfeltly meant. Having natured and nurtured him on my own, he turned his back on me, an embarrassment of a mother who could be financially sedated by providing her with the means to live as far away as possible from him.'

Cary saw the woman's eyes fill. Tears were close to the surface, but she was fighting hard to suppress them. 'I have to admit, on the few occasions Alex mentions his parents, he does so in the past tense. I assumed they had already passed away.' Cary turned to smile and assure the girls that everything was just fine. 'I never forced the subject because I sensed a certain reticence to talk about his childhood. I figured it was a conversation for a later day.'

Rose nodded. 'He got quite a shock when I turned up last night. I must see a specialist later today and it seemed a waste of his money to stay in a hotel. By the reception I received, I wish I hadn't bothered. I'll be travelling back to the Lake District before the day is out.'

'Are you ill?'

'Dying, but then, aren't we all?' She held her hand up. 'No platitudes, please. In answer to your next question, I have cachexia stemming from advanced kidney failure. In short, I am gradually wasting away. It's fifty/fifty

111

whether the kidneys pack up first or whether I end up looking like one of those skeletal figures you see in charity pleas.'

'I'm sorry.'

'You're on your own as far as the occupants of this house are concerned.'

'Surely not?'

'It's for you to make up your own mind. Once you're living here, you will have a rounded viewpoint.' She hesitated. 'Tell me, Caroline, do you envisage marriage one day?'

'Good grief, it's never crossed my mind. I'm just moving out of one unfortunate marriage. I'm not planning on another right now.'

'Just as well. There's no stigma attached these days and I can't honestly see him ever having the courage to divorce Rosalind.'

'I'm sorry, you've lost me.' There was panic underlying her voice.

'He hasn't told you, has he?'

'Please don't talk in riddles.' At the change in her tone, Syracuse stopped chewing the cord and looked up. 'It's all right, darling. Mummy's just speaking to the lady.'

'Oh dear, one more reason for him to want to see me banished, I fear. I assumed . . .' her voice tailed off . . . 'he'd told you.'

'Alex told me there was a fatal car accident involving his wife.'

'There was, except it wasn't his wife who died. It was Hannah, their five-year-old daughter. Rosalind was seriously injured. They both went through the windscreen. The doctors held out virtually no hope for Rosalind, but three years after the accident she did awake from the coma with no memory of her past or those close to her. That was twelve years ago. Alex visits the nursing home in Dartmoor once a month. It's a duty appearance. She doesn't recognise him. It's more to impress on the staff what a caring husband he is, but he bears the guilt.'

'In what way?'

'Rosalind was always highly strung. Alex doubtless contributed to her neuroticism. According to Rupert – you've met his son, I guess? No? He's a fine boy; man now; phones me regularly – Alex was supposed to be doing the driving, taking Hannah to infant school, as was the norm. Rosalind would take her medication as soon as she awoke and need an hour to overcome the

112

initial effects of drowsiness and giddiness. On that fatal day, they argued, accusations of his unfaithfulness, and she stormed off in the car with Hannah. The coroner drew the obvious conclusion.'

Creedence stamped her feet on the base of the child seat. 'Too many words', she said.

'All right, darling. We're on our way in a minute.'

Rose had opened the passenger door. 'I've probably said too much and provided another nail for him to put in my coffin. He won't have long to wait.'

Cary smiled and grasped the old woman's hand. 'You can rely on my tact and discretion. I certainly don't intend to say, "Rose told me etcetera". In fact, I don't intend to say I came here, or we met. I'm confident everything you've told me will be revealed without my prompting.'

Rose stood alongside the car, holding the door open. 'I sincerely hope your faith is not misplaced. Bibi girls.' She blew a kiss to the twins. 'Take care of your precious cargo.'

EIGHTEEN

SYLVIA AND LANCE

'You did what?' Sylvia appeared from the bathroom with one towel wrapped around her head and a hand towel held strategically to cover her crotch.

'I thought you'd be pleased. I couldn't say no to him. He's your dad, after all. I told you in the message that we had met.'

'What message? I didn't pick up a message from you. In any event, I've just spoken to him and tried to back out of it, but he says he needs to talk with me, and you had already accepted on my behalf. What the fuck, Lance! How could you?' She traced a line of clothes on the floor until she located the panties and bra he had stripped from her the previous night. 'Who does he think you are?' She started to dress.

Lance smiled as he pulled back the sheet from the bed in which he was lying. 'You're looking really hot in that outfit. You must have a spare fifteen minutes before you leave for work. I'll help you put them back on afterwards.'

'I asked you a question.'

'I said it was just platonic. He could see I was working, tidying up the kitchen. Luckily, I'd already made the bed.'

She continued picking up clothes and putting them on. 'I assume he didn't believe you?'

'I don't think he gets platonic. I went with him to somewhere near Peckham to pick up a car. We got on rather well, if you must know. Now, come on, how about it? It'll be too late in a minute.'

She walked over to the bed, now partially clothed. 'May I remind you, until you meet up with my brother and all the ducks are in a row, you will continue . . . start to sleep on the sofa. It was a lack of willpower last night and your persistence in ensuring I drink enough alcohol to let down my guard for the second time. It will not happen again. Once you've met my parents, we live the lie that we are just friends and I'm doing you a favour until you get a place of your own. Is that understood?'

'I said in the message it was up to Dom to arrange the meet as soon as possible.'

115

'I've already said I didn't get a message.'

He stretched over to the bedside table to retrieve his mobile and activate it. 'Look! Oh shit! I sent the message to Dom by mistake. I must have directed it to the last number on the screen.'

'How could you?' She reached over and grabbed the phone from him. 'Let me read what you said.' She studied the three-line message. 'Would you normally end messaging him with "A big hug" and a kiss?'

'Not really, but he won't take it amiss. I've said nothing to implicate you.'

'All right. I'll be back around six to change. As you've adopted the persona of a home help, there's a fair amount of work needs doing, so act the part. And remember, tonight you come over as a friend, not a boyfriend; a eunuch who helps around the apartment. And none of your smutty sexual innuendoes. Embarrass me and you and your holdall are in the street. Get my drift, cobber?'

'Loud and clear. I'm looking forward to meeting your mum. I'll get her some flowers. Where's the nearest cemetery?'

She picked up one of his shoes and threw it at him.

NINETEEN

TERRY, NOBBY AND MAHI

There was a light drizzle of rain whipped in the wind as they made their way along the towpath, their eyes glued to the wire mesh fence as they searched for the stretch where somebody had forced it free from the retaining post and bent the wire up to provide access.

Nobby stopped to wipe the droplets from his glasses.

'It's over there,' Terry pointed. 'You can barely see it from this side. There's a hump on the grass verge.' He looked beyond the fence to the parkland beyond. 'No sign of anybody. Nobody hangs around in this weather. Let's go.' They clambered through, casting furtive glances around them like errant schoolboys.

'Which way does she enter the park?' Nobby asked.

'From the Bow Road end. If she's aiming for Grove Road, it will be straight down this path. There's a bench underneath the branches of that oak tree. I'll wait for her there.' He hesitated. 'I only hope I recognise her. God, why am I doing this? There's a pain in my guts like a sack of cement. Fuck you, Bateman! Why should I?'

'Just shut up and get it done,' Nobby said sternly. 'If you go like this' - He waved his hand across his stomach like an umpire signalling a four at a cricket match - 'I'll know I must intercept. If you put both hands in the air, as if a six has been scored, I'll keep my distance and just follow her to work in case she tries to make a call on the way there.'

'You Indians are cricket mad. What do you think I'm going to look like dancing around with my arms above my head?'

'Like a crazy man. Nobody will come anywhere near you.'

Terry fidgeted from one side to the other as he waited. Despite the cover of the tree, he was still getting wet and the few passers-by either made a point of looking away or staring at him with questioning expressions.

Here she comes. His heart leapt a beat. She was slimmer, somehow taller than he remembered, and wore a scarf tied over her head and around her neck. As she came nearer, seemingly oblivious to his presence, he felt both the dryness in his throat and the pounding of his heart as old emotions stirred.

117

She was still stunningly beautiful with those large, round, almond-coloured eyes, softened by a misty sheen that made her look as though she was about to cry. Truth is, he had never stopped loving her, and what he was about to do would destroy something so precious and pure.

'Mahi.'

She stopped in her tracks and turned to face him. 'Yes,' she said warily.

'It's me, Ter—' He rose from the bench.

'Terry,' she blurted out. 'I don't believe it.' She moved close to him. 'I never thought I'd see you again.' She tried a nervous smile. 'Not after the way it ended.' Reality sank in. 'What are you doing here?' She looked around to see who else might be within earshot. The look of panic on her face receded.

'I needed to see you. I have a big favour to ask.' He had worked out his strategy earlier. He wasn't going to make small talk. 'I found out where you worked and decided to intercept you for a chat.'

She pulled a retractable umbrella from her bag and gave it to him to extend and hold. 'Let's sit down on the bench. I can be ten minutes late.' She held his arm as they sat. 'You haven't changed much.'

'Liar. I look my fifty-eight years and a good few more besides. I took early retirement. Before I tell you why I need your help, will you allow me to say one thing without wishing to embarrass either of us?'

Her brow creased. 'Of course.'

'Although I cursed you when you walked away from our relationship all those years ago, I came to realise, accept and understand why you had to do what you did. I came to appreciate what pressure you were under to conform to your traditions and the serious repercussions you and, perhaps I, would have faced had you tried to defy your family. You did the right thing.'

'Did I?'

'Let me finish, please. It's a prepared speech and doesn't allow for interruptions to knock me off track.'

She laughed. 'Sorry.'

'A day rarely passes that I don't think about how it was, and I have to say, seeing you now, and how beautiful you are in both body and mind, I doubt a day will pass in the future when you are not in my thoughts.' He smiled. 'There, I've said it. Did it sound like a maudlin old man talking?'

She reached out to put her arm on his shoulder. 'No, although I'd rather have not heard it because I thought I'd managed to break out of the guilt shell in which I've been encased all these years. You have now condemned me to relive my sense of shame and . . . may I say, regret, at my actions.'

'Jesus, I never imagined . . .' He reached out to put his hand on her arm. She recoiled as he brushed the sleeve of her coat. He flung his arms into the air. 'Sorry, I'm so sorry. I didn't mean anything by it. I just felt . . .' The sentence remained unfinished as he realised Nobby would interpret the gesture as indicating no interception was necessary. Good, whatever the outcome of this conversation, he would not have her subjected to pressure on Bateman's account. They could all suffer the consequences of their actions before he would put Mahi's wellbeing at risk.

'It's not that,' she said. 'I had an accident. It's still sore.'

He mumbled another apology.

'You started by saying you wanted a favour from me. Can I ask, is it like the favour you required when we first met?'

'Yes, but . . .' he was about to protest, but she put a finger over his lips.

'Once upon a time, one stranger asked another for a favour. For a while, the lives of those strangers became entwined and emotions exchanged. In a way, you come again as a stranger, but our lives have moved on. Now, we are both the victims of those old emotions. I need time to think before we speak again.'

'When?'

'After work tonight, I have a yoga and meditation class with our *pujari*. I will tell the priest I am feeling unwell and unable to take part. Meet me for a coffee.' She gave him the location. 'We will have an hour to talk things through.'

'But what about your husband?'

She raised her eyebrows. 'He insisted I take the classes to allow him time for his own distractions. You need not worry. I must go now.' She put two fingers to her lips and then on his.

He felt the umbrella prised from his grasp and watched as she made her way towards the exit. The gesture of flinging his arms in the air was more a sense of triumph and relief than a signal to his friend.

'It went well?' Nobby queried as they made their way back to the gap in the wire netting.

'She seems receptive,' Terry said. No way was he going to recount details of their conversation. 'We're meeting tonight for me to give her the details. You can pass that message on for Len to tell Bateman.'

'You seem pleased with yourself. Was she happy to see you?'

'I think so. I feel quite lightheaded. I'm hungry. Fancy a full English? There must be a greasy spoon somewhere nearby.'

TWENTY

LEN AND THE BATEMANS

'What a godforsaken place to meet,' Len complained. 'An open-sided hut in the middle of nowhere, with the rain pouring down. You might have suggested standing under that tree over there in the hope we got struck by lightning.'

'Give it a rest, will you?' the bedraggled man said. 'At least you're dressed for the weather.' Darren stood there in a rain-soaked beige, Cashmere hair suit and a pair of patent black leather shoes that squelched every time he stamped up and down. 'I came straight from the club. His Master's Voice here commanded, and I obeyed.' He fed his fingers through a sweptback mop of greased black hair. 'I'll catch my sodding death of cold.'

I'll pray for that, Len said to himself.

'Stop whining, the pair of you.' Bateman senior sat in the middle of the bench seat, dressed in Burberry galoshes and a treated green raincoat with hood of the same origin. He held a thermos flask between his hands. 'This is known as the weather hut just before the tee for the tenth hole. It marks the furthest point away from the clubhouse, backed by a twelve-foot privet and with views down the ninth and eleventh fairways, providing an unimpeded view of anybody approaching or anybody failing to leave after they have played the tenth.'

'Thanks for that,' Darren said. 'All that's missing are the GPS coordinates. Can we get on with it?'

'Patience,' Bateman snapped. 'I never understand why every spy film shows clandestine meetings in underground car parks. It makes no sense. Normally, there's only one way out, reducing the chance of a quick escape: parked cars and structural pillars making manoeuvres difficult if not impossible, closed-circuit cameras to guard against theft and vandalism, poor light to see anybody approaching, ample opportunity to hide and make a surprise attack. Above all, there you are sitting in a metal box, unable to get out of the way should anybody open fire on you. Think of the possibilities we have here to be forewarned, to disperse and hide amongst the trees. No comparison.'

'Fascinating,' Darren said, his voice heavy with sarcasm and his feet continuing to pound up and down. 'What's all this about?'

Bateman turned to face Len. 'I need to know where we are up to, but before I do, I want to correct some information I gave you. Information I passed on in good faith, I may add. I did not intend to deceive you when I said the lorry the police are investigating has been laid up for three years and not used at all in the last twelve months. It has come to my notice that, unbeknown to me, Darren has been using the vehicle on an average once every three months over the last two years. The last time was two months ago.'

'So what?' Darren protested with a bravado which to Len smelt of fear. 'I needed it for the business.' He looked at his father's expressionless face. 'A business that produces cash for you,' he added.

'I gave specific instructions the vehicle was to be held in reserve for emergency use and exclusively for the butchery business until we had decided on a replacement to take its place. You knew the score, son, but you went ahead anyway and defied me.'

'I didn't think you'd mind,' he said sullenly. 'I had the offer of a group of girls from Azerbaijan with no documents. I couldn't look a gift horse in the proverbial.'

Bateman looked over his glasses at Len. 'Where are the police up to?'

'It's escalated. The case has been taken over by SOCA - Sorry. I keep calling it that. It's the NCA now, as part of a bigger investigation, presumably into human trafficking, I assume.' He went on to detail the blood spattering in the secret compartment and the DNA match with the body recovered from the River Lea. 'I presume she's one of the girls he's talking about.' Darren's expression remained impassive.

Bateman thumped the thermos flask against the bench. 'You fucking idiot! If you weren't blood, I'd peel the skin off your back. If you've cost me a knighthood, I might even yet. You didn't even sanitise the bloody thing, just left it. What was all that about?'

'Bernie lost his rag,' Darren said. 'When he opened the door, one of the tarts went for him with a piece of broken glass, stabbed him in the leg and tried to make a break for it. He said he went to wound her in the arm, but she was too fast for him, darted to the side and copped the bullet in the gut. I went round to see what was going down. As she lay there dying, there was a

122

stampede for the door. One of the girls ran off into the night. He got the rest under control.'

'Isn't that just wonderful?' Bateman retorted. 'We've not only got a high-level investigation on our tail, but a missing girl who could identify both you and this Bernie.'

'I've got people looking for her. She'll have gravitated to her own kind. It's just a question of time.'

Bateman ignored the comment with a put-down wave of the hand. 'Where's it going to go from here?' he asked.

'They will be checking CCTV in the surrounding area to where the body was recovered to identify the vehicle and driver.' Len held Darren's stare. 'As a starting point, they'll have a time window from the pathologist's report of when the girl died.'

'That's a big job,' Bateman said.

Len nodded. 'The NCA can call on as many hands as they want. You'll have to hope this Bernie character kept his face out of view. In any event, he's somebody else you'll have to send on a long holiday and hope there's nobody around who can identify him from whatever image they manage to obtain.'

'It's getting messy,' Bateman said. 'I just cannot afford any links to that vehicle or to this thug of yours, Darren. Make sure he gets good and lost.'

'Any coffee in that flask?' Len asked. 'I could do with a hot drink.'

'Lemon tea any good? Bateman offered up the thermos. 'Doctor said I should drink it to help my gout or my prostate; I can't remember which it is. I work on the assumption that if you don't like it or it tastes like shit, it must be doing you good.'

'I agree the converse is true,' Len said. 'I'll pass on the tea, all the same. Tell me, do you honestly think with all the vetting and checking they do before the Queen awards her gongs, your son's association with gambling clubs, prostitution and drugs is going to pass unnoticed?'

'Give me a little credit, will you? There is no way the Bateman name is in any way connected with the casino operations. We use trusted intermediaries and dummy companies as nominees from the booze and gaming licences down to the season ticket to the car park and the lease on the condom machine in the khazi. No exceptions. The only thing Darren's name is on is the documentation registered with the Charity Commissioners for The Bateman Charitable Trust. He's one of the trustees and disperses funds to worthy causes.'

Len stifled a laugh. 'Who's he donating to, the fund for distressed gentlewomen?'

'Fuck you!' Darren collected the saliva in his mouth and spat on the floor.

'Are you going to be able to keep tabs with what's going on at the NCA?' Bateman looked down at the goblet of spittle and back at his son as if holy ground had just been desecrated.

'The short answer is "No",' Len said. 'Randy and I know a few faces at Vauxhall, but no-one well enough to ask sensitive questions without attracting attention. Terry was seconded there for three months before his minor problem and may be able to help.'

'That's the other thing I wanted to ask you that keeps playing on my mind. How did he get on with the woman about clearing the record of that fine? The further away I can get from any connection with the vehicle, the better.'

'I spoke with Nobby on my way here. It went well. Terry is meeting up with her later today to go through the details. She was receptive, that's the main thing, and it didn't involve any pressure from Nobby to coerce her. The lads are grateful for your generosity. The cash bonus will come in very handy.'

'Get it done and you'll get your money.' His head turned toward Darren. 'As for you, the slapstick way you've handled this has put us all in danger. Make sure you get the wanker driving that lorry out of circulation and find the missing girl. You've made a right cock-up of this and put us all in the firing line.'

'It wasn't me who drove it to the wrong breaker's yard.'

'He's been dealt with.' Bateman held out his hand to Len for help in rising to his feet. 'Give me a pull,' he said. 'I've got stiff sitting here in the damp. See what information you can get without setting off alarm bells.'

'I will,' Len replied. 'Before you go, I need a small favour.'

Bateman flexed his shoulders and exercised his legs by bending his knees. 'Go on,' he said casually.

124

'My daughter is getting a divorce from the waste of space husband I told her not to marry. I've never got on with the guy's father, who's a rude and obnoxious individual, and I want him out of our lives once and for all when the divorce is completed.'

'Won't that happen as a matter of course?' Bateman said.

'Not if this bastard gets his way. The agreement between Caroline and her ex gives her custody of their six-year-old twins, with him looking after them once every second weekend or as mutually agreed. The grandfather, named Charlie Greaves, threatens using legal action to establish a much more intrusive relationship, summer holidays together, weekday stayovers, anything to maintain his hold over the kids. He's a coarse, uneducated tosser and a bad influence on the girls, spoiling them with presents and buying their loyalty. I need a means to dissuade him.'

'How do you propose to go about this?' Darren asked. 'Top him?'

'Of course not. He's spent his life in the motor trade, mainly used cars. You're not going to tell me in those forty years he's not stepped out of line, pulled some fast ones, had a mistress or two; anything I can use to gain a hold over him.'

'What are you asking us to do?' Bateman queried. 'We've never heard of the guy, and it doesn't strike me he's going to have much legal pull as a grandfather.'

'I'm not worried about what he can do personally. It's what he can convince his weak-kneed son to do. That's what concerns me. I need a threat. A threat is something he'll understand and react to.'

'So, we'll ask around,' Darren said. 'Dad's a little out of the London scene now he lives in the Midlands, but I know most of his contacts and I've got sources of my own.' He smiled for the first time. 'You get this lorry business sorted out nice and clean for dad and me and I'll do everything I can. If you can get this type along to our club in Billericay, I'll arrange for one of the girls to do a number on him and we'll take some compromising snaps you can threaten to show his old lady. How about that?'

'Given the choice, I'd prefer financial misdeeds to sexual ones. His wife seems like the long suffering, forgiving type.'

'Leave it with Darren,' Bateman said as he steadied himself to leave. 'You worry about putting this Indian bird into play and trying to find out what's going on with the investigation. Everything else I can control from my end.' He swung around to poke the tip of his umbrella into Darren's stomach. 'And that means you. Before you even think about taking a leak, check with me to see if it's all right to do so. I want no more unpleasant surprises.'

TWENTY-ONE

TERRY AND MAHI

The intense sound of steam released from an espresso coffee machine into cold milk always provoked in him an image of some prehistoric sea creature rising from the depths to surface, recede and reappear as the barista manoeuvred the container to produce the right amount of froth for the next batch of lattes. The rumbling finale preceded a brief silence before an assistant called out 'One skinny, one vanilla latte for Rory.' Terry closed his eyes and imagined a tall, gangly university student type with a stutter and bad breath. Wrong again. The sturdy individual collecting his takeaways was obviously off a building site and boasted tattoos on both exposed forearms.

Mahi stood in front of him, a quizzical smile on her face. 'Why did you have your eyes shut? Were you praying?' She pulled off her headscarf and ran her fingers through shoulder-length, dark auburn hair.

'Yes,' he said, returning the smile, 'Praying that you would show up.'

She moved to sit down opposite him. 'Well, your prayers have been answered. Does that deserve a decaf latte with an extra shot?'

Terry shuffled to his feet. 'Your wish is my command,' he said.

'A *pain aux raisins*, as well, if you're feeling generous.'

As he waited in line to be served, he wondered if any of the strangers sitting around the café would close their eyes and picture him in their mind when the assistant called his name. Would they opt for a non-descript, let's call it late middle-aged man, with receding blond hair, the remnants of freckles on a ruddy face and what a woman PC had once called 'hangdog, sad eyes'? If so, they would be spot on.

'Thank you,' she said. 'It's lovely to be waited on for a change, even if my waiter looks like he's in mourning.'

'Apologies. I was just feeling sorry for myself.' He gave a broad smile. 'A mid-life crisis if you like.'

'How come?'

'The unvarnished truth?'

'Yes, please,' she said avidly, holding out the pastry for him to take a bite.

'I'm here to ask a favour . . .' He stopped to swallow the mouthful but more to try unsuccessfully to censor what he was about to say. '. . .of a married woman I loved desperately twenty-odd years ago. It is an emotion I thought I had long since conquered, yet I find myself in her presence today, still as besotted as I was then. Pitiful. isn't it?'

'You wear your emotions on your sleeve, Terry. It's a novelty in my world to meet a man who admits to being vulnerable. When I close the front door at night, I live in a world where men are the masters, women are subservient and acquiescent to their needs. I survive in a loveless, arranged marriage with a man for whom I have never had any feelings except fear and contempt. In fact, to maintain my sanity in such a state, I have learned to treat the idea of love as a mirage, a vision that simply obscures the truth and, for me, does not exist.' She shook her head and drained the remains of her coffee. 'But let's leave such conversation until later. I assume your favour concerns my work and involves me putting my career at risk?'

Terry sat upright. 'I couldn't possibly ask you to do that.'

'Just tell me.'

He recounted the story of the infringement, the unfortunate lorry driver's demise and how the fine came to be paid.

'How long ago did you say it was?'

'Three years. Thirty-nine months, to be exact.'

She shook her head. 'Your friend really has nothing to be concerned about. After three years, the complete record is reduced to a one-line summary in the diary, showing date, driver or company name, reg number, infringement code and date the fine was paid. As the driver was responsible for the vehicle, it's his name that will appear. It's only when the fine remains outstanding that the entire file is kept. Not applicable in this case.'

'And if he still asks for the record to be erased?'

'Impossible. They run on a consecutive number basis. If one is missing, a default message would signal attention. The only thing possible is to edit the existing entry.'

'Like changing the registration number?'

'Possible.'

'Could you do that for him?'

'I could, but there's still a vulnerability.'

128

'In what way?'

She moved closer to him across the table, her voice lowered. 'Any edit to an entry will appear in the daily journal and stay there, on file, permanently. Let's say I alter the reg number. Both the original and new numbers will appear in the journal. If an enquirer restricts his search request to just the record file, only the new number will appear. If he includes all files in his sweep, the original number will flag up on the journal page, begging an investigation into why it was changed. It's not worth it.'

'Supposing we do nothing, and the number comes up, is there any way the original detail of the case can be restored?'

She wagged her index finger at him. 'That's what I was coming to. The answer is, theoretically, yes. Periodically, one of my staff will perform a permanent delete of the trash bin and reformat the disk segment. I'll have to find out what date sequence we're up to and feed in a batch from the period that includes the one you're concerned about.'

'Won't that appear in the journal?'

'Of course, but it won't ring any alarm bells. Both the system and the hardware are old and awaiting funding to be replaced. Disk space is a constant problem; programmes freeze and give the IT boys a permanent headache. It's the best solution.'

'I'll report to the powers-that-be and get back to you.' He passed her a mobile in its original packaging, together with a Sim card. 'I'll use this to contact you. Don't make any calls on it unless it's to the number I call you on and you urgently need to speak with me.'

'You've been watching too many Hollywood movies, Terry. Is this really necessary?'

'Believe me, it is.'

She sat back in her chair and appeared to be appraising him. 'I made a mistake,' she said. 'Life would have been so different if I'd told my parents to go to hell and brazened it out with you. But I lost my nerve and capitulated in more ways than one.'

'I don't understand.'

'All in good time, Terry. Let me ask you something? Do you have any financial ties to this country?'

He looked at her for some further prompt to understand her line of questioning.

'It's a straightforward question,' she said.

'I've got the apartment I inherited from my mother. I get a police pension, reduced rate because I had to retire early. No real savings.' He thought about the ten thousand Bateman had promised. 'I'm expecting a payday from some work I've been doing. Why are you asking? Do you need money?'

'If I take voluntary redundancy, I'll be entitled to a lump sum and a civil service pension. My husband controls our bank account, but, unbeknown to him, I've squirrelled away around thirty thousand over the last twenty years. It's in a building society savings account.' She hesitated. 'Do close your mouth, Terry. You look like a goldfish.'

'What are you saying?'

She reached for his hand. 'If you really mean what you say, are you prepared to run away with me? I don't mean a hundred miles, a cottage in the country, or a castle in the Highlands. I'm talking about cashing in everything and moving abroad, Spain, Portugal, Greece, anywhere we can relax and enjoy the rest of our days together. Maybe I can even try to love again.'

He looked at her in amazement. 'Are you serious?'

'I spent all day wrestling with my conscience. Life is too short to keep looking back with regret. I need to look to the future with hope and optimism.'

'Let me get this straight. You propose walking out on your family and setting up home with me somewhere outside the UK? You make it sound like a prison break, and I'm the conduit for getting you out.'

'Not an unreasonable analogy, except you are much more than a conduit. I am a prisoner, and the pack of warders will do everything to find us and exact revenge to assuage their damaged pride. You could be putting your life at risk. It's all down to how strong your feelings are for me, especially when I cannot turn around right away and respond as you would like or expect. I was deeply in love with you once. Perhaps I can learn to love you like that again, but I can't give you any guarantees.'

Terry could sense the beads of sweat on his forehead. 'You have no kids?'

'The one essential function of a woman who enters the Kumar hierarchy is that she provides her husband with children, preferably boys and devotes her life to nurturing their bodies and souls until the men of the family can take over and structure their upbringing in traditional moulds.' She took a deep breath and sighed. 'Any chance of another coffee? Make it a decaf this time. After this conversation and caffeine, I'll never sleep.'

He was grateful for the break in a conversation he could never have envisaged taking place in a million years. She had literally taken his breath away, and he needed time to sort out his thoughts and conflicting emotions. He had never imagined a life beyond his flat and the local boozer, a game of golf with Len and the boys, a season ticket to Stamford Bridge. Living abroad and with a partner taxed his imagination, however enticing the prospect.

As hard as she tried to conceal the tears, her eyes were red and swollen when he returned with the two coffees. 'I've gone out on a limb to talk to you the way I did,' she said. 'I know I have no right to ask you to accompany me into an adventure, to take you out of your comfort zone.' She hesitated. 'But, and it's a big but, perhaps you need the jolt to set your life on a different, less predictable course with no predestined conclusion. Is that presumptuous, pretentious? I don't know. You did say the unvarnished truth, didn't you?'

'I did,' he said.

'I have no children. Luckily for me, my husband was blessed with a low sperm count and reluctantly accepts the failure to produce a son might lay with him, although within the family, he vocally puts the blame on me. Also, luckily for me, his attempts to demonstrate virility with a stream of lovers and mistresses – that's where he is at this very moment – have not resulted in a pregnancy. I say luckily not because I did not want children, though I would have felt some trepidation at rearing the product of such a psychotic strain, but had the failure to fall pregnant been attributed to me, I doubt I would be alive and here today,'

'Surely not?'

'You don't know them. They would do anything to protect the honour of the Kumar name. Attributing my death to some infection or disease would be readily signed-off by a doctor friend of the family. My mother, as old and frail as she now is, would understand and accept the decision. The ranks would close.'

'How barbaric.' He sensed her mood had changed. There was no sign of tears, just staring eyes living a scenario inside her head. He said nothing, waiting for her to continue.

The images had passed. Her smile was real, her voice softer. 'As it was, the fault, I knew, was mine. I promise you I had no idea when I broke up with you what I am about to tell you. Two weeks after that fateful day, I found out I was pregnant. My parents had just arranged my marriage to Neeraj at great financial sacrifice after some hard bargaining. I was presented as a mature virgin reaching the end of her sell-by date. I could hardly turn up at the wedding ceremony with a large lump in my stomach.'

'Jesus, Mahi, why didn't you tell me? You were going to have our baby. We could have had a family life together.' There was a tremor in his voice.

'I knew you'd be outraged when I told you, but I want you to understand the pressure I was under. I was a nervous wreck, scared, alone and desperately concerned not to bring disgrace onto my parents. It would have killed them.'

'You had an abortion.' He wasn't asking a question, his voice flat and expressionless.

'A woman who lived in a terraced house in Hendon. I remember walking up the garden path and smelling the flowers. It went wrong. She nearly butchered me. I ended up sterilised. It was God's punishment. The blood I spilled on my wedding night was from the opening of one of my wounds. The pain was intolerable, but I gritted my teeth and accepted my fate.'

Terry slumped back in his chair. 'How could you do this to us? Couldn't you see there was a way forward together?'

'I was scared, desperately alone, fighting a lifetime's indoctrination of the ways of my faith. Castigating myself for having been involved in a relationship with you was the easy way out. I have regretted that decision every single day of my life from the moment I left you standing at the bus stop.' She hesitated. 'I will understand if you say you want nothing more to do with me and it won't influence helping to resolve your problem at work.' She pushed her chair back and got up.

'Please stay just a little longer.' Terry signalled for her to sit down. 'Too much information to process all at one go,' he said. 'I need to digest everything you've sprung on me this evening. It was the last thing I expected to hear, and I feel so many mixed emotions, I don't know where to start. Remember, I'm policeman plod. It takes time for things to percolate through the grey matter. Can I meet you in the park tomorrow morning? Try to come a little earlier than today. Give us time to talk.'

'Of course. The unvarnished truth may not have helped. I'm not asking for your forgiveness, Terry; I'm asking for your understanding.'

He smiled and kissed her softly on the cheek. 'I know. I certainly don't love you less than I did this morning, and I definitely couldn't love you more.'

As he gave a parting wave, he wondered if what he had just said was the unvarnished truth.

TWENTY-TWO

CHARLIE, NORMA, SYLVIA, LANCE AND . . .?

Norma looked up from coating a rolling pin with flour as he came into the kitchen with an empty wineglass in hand. 'I don't suppose you thought to ask Sylvia's boyfriend if there's anything he doesn't eat?' she said.

Charlie opened the door of the refrigerator and retrieved an opened bottle of Macon Blanc, which he held out to her. 'One for you?' he asked.

Norma shook her head. 'Did you hear what I said? The idea of offal puts some people off.'

'Do you honestly think I said to him, "Come to dinner and, by the way, do you have any special dietary requirements?"'

'It would have been both courteously solicitous and totally out of character, so I imagine the answer is "No".'

'Don't worry. These Aussies eat anything that's put in front of them. They love a barbie of grilled kangaroo or roast armadillo. What are you intending to feed him?'

'My steak and kidney pie. It's Sylvia's favourite. I'm just calculating whether to leave out the kidney.'

He laughed. 'At which point, it ceases to be Sylvia's favourite and becomes a steak pie. If he doesn't like kidney, he leaves them on his plate. His fallback position is a Big Mac on the way home.'

'There's no point in talking to you. You're no help at all.'

'Just trying to resolve your quandary, doll.'

She carefully placed the pastry sheet over the dish with the filling. 'Do you think it's serious this time?' She started to trim and crimp the edge. 'It would be so amazing to see her settled.'

'Who knows? Both claim it's just a friendship, and he's a flatmate in transit.' He took a large swig of wine. 'But I got the impression when I talked to her this morning that there's only one bed being made up in the mornings. He's quite a physical specimen, a personal trainer, and I'm guessing he's got a sexual appetite to match. He's not going to look a gift horse in the mouth.'

'You'd know all about that, wouldn't you?'

Safety first. He treated the question as rhetorical and watched in silence as she repeated the process with a fresh sheet of pastry. 'Do we really need two pies?' he asked eventually.

'Just in case,' she said. 'I thought it would be nice to make a family evening of it tonight. I invited Dominic to join us. He's busy finishing a job, but he said he'd be along as soon as he could. I didn't mention Sylvia's boyfriend. I guessed it might sound a little tactless in his present circumstances.'

'Do you always set an extra place for dinner?' Sylvia asked. 'Are you expecting someone from the spirit world to turn up - a dead relative, perhaps?' She giggled, but paused when she saw the frightened look on Lance's face. Still, the penny failed to drop.

'More pie?' Norma held out the dish to Lance. 'You must have a healthy appetite, burning up all those calories in the gym.' She gestured for him to take the wedge she had just separated. 'There's still plenty left for Dominic if he manages to show up. He said he would.' She held a theatrical hand to her ear. 'In fact, I can hear his car pulling up now. Talk amongst yourselves while I open the door. You've met Sylvia's brother before. I remember Charlie saying. At the gym, wasn't it?'

'Yes,' Lance said, but Norma was already out of the room. There came a muffled exchange of conversation from the front door.

Sylvia and Lance exchanged furtive glances. He raised his eyebrows in what she took as a fatalistic gesture.

'Something wrong?' Charlie asked.

Sylvia pushed her chair back. 'Nothing,' she said hastily. 'I need to go to the bathroom.'

'Blimey,' Charlie said to Lance. 'I know the steak pie's potent, but it doesn't normally work through that quick.' He was the only one to laugh at his remark. Lance's eyes were focussed on the door through which Sylvia had just left. He managed a weak smile in Charlie's direction. His body twitched involuntarily as Norma walked into the room. She was alone.

'I told him Sylvia's friend was here,' she said. 'He seemed a bit miffed. I hope I haven't been insensitive at such a difficult time for him. He saw Sylvia go to the cloakroom and said he needed a quick, private word with her before he ate. I'll warm up the veg for him.'

'Bring another bottle of the Rioja, will you? Lance's glass is nearly empty.' Charlie shouted after her as she made her way to the kitchen with a tureen in either hand. He winked at their guest. 'If I said it was for me, she'd conveniently forget. She says I drink too much. I tell her I spill most of it.' He waited for a laugh, but all he got was another weak smile. 'The old ones are the best ones, I guess,' he said. 'Tell me, how you getting on with my girl? She's a lot more sensitive than she appears and I don't want to see her hurt.'

'Like I told you; I know you didn't believe me, but our relationship is as flatmates without complications. We're not in a position where one could hurt the other. Ask your daughter.'

'You can try to feed me that load of old bollocks, Son, but I can guess how it goes down. Sylvia's a good-looking woman, been around the block at her age. You're a randy Aussie. There you both are, sitting in the lounge watching the TV where there's an erotic film playing. You look at her; she looks at you and, bingo, suddenly the TV has got nothing on you two; you're at it like rabbits.'

Lance shook his head. 'We don't tend to be in at the same times and, when we are, we try to give each other space.'

'You make it sound as though you don't fancy her. Are you saying my girl is not attractive?'

'You're speeding down the wrong road, man. Of course, she's got the works, but there's such a thing as mutual respect, you know?'

Charlie laughed. 'Yeah, like saying thank you afterwards and how was it for you?'

'How was it for who?' Dominic said as he hustled through the door.

Lance swung around, his fork falling into his lap. 'Great to see you, Dom. How is everything?' He retrieved the fork and brushed at the gravy stain on his trousers with his napkin.

Dominic nodded without smiling and rounded on his father. 'Mum says you've calmed down today and stopped pacing around in a paddy. Maybe we can talk sensibly in private later?' He turned to Lance. 'My sister tells me you've rented a sofa from her while you find somewhere to live. How long do you expect that to be?'

Charlie gestured for Dominic to sit. 'Have we forgotten all the pleasantries now like, "Good evening. How are you, Dad? Nice to see you, Lance. Thanks for the dinner invite, Mum." You sound like you're about to start a Stasi interrogation. Had a bad day?'

'No, work's great. I just don't like a reception committee meeting me at the front door with my sister waving at me furtively and Mum with, "Your friend Lance is here with Sylvia. Your dad thinks they're getting on well together." She winks at me. "You know what he means." No, I don't know what he means. Do enlighten me; both of you.'

'What in heaven's name has got into you?' Norma returned from the kitchen armed with side plates of steaming carrots and courgettes. 'You seem put out by the fact your sister might have a boyfriend.' She put the vegetables alongside the pie and suggested he should serve himself. 'She's a mature woman. You can't go around trying to act as if you're defending the honour of a younger sister.' She hesitated. 'Or is it her choice of friend you don't approve of?' She smiled at Lance. 'No offence intended.'

'None taken.' Lance beamed a smile back at her.

Sylvia stood framed in the doorway just as Charlie touched a spoon against his wineglass. 'What's all the fuss about?' he said. 'Can't Sylvia have a boyfriend without provoking a bloody inquest?' He reacted to the flash of anger on his son's face. 'I mean to say . . .'

'I feel as though I've been talking into a fog, and nobody is hearing me.' Sylvia returned to her seat. 'Can I repeat that for the last two days, Lance has been staying as a friend at my apartment and has been allocated the sofa, one pillow and a sheet temporarily until he moves to a place of his own? It begins and ends with that. If his presence offends anybody, I shall ask him to find alternative accommodation.' She took a large gulp from a glass of red wine. 'Sorry,' she said, realising the glass was in front of Lance. Her smile was warm, yet apologetic. 'As it is, my friend Holly is coming up from Devon next weekend. She heard about Cary and Dom's split and feels she needs to give Cary some moral support and advice. I've promised to put her up whilst she's in London, so Lance will have to make alternative arrangements.'

'How lovely, dear,' Norma said. 'I haven't seen Holly for years. I didn't even know she was friendly with Cary. Wasn't she your roommate from college?'

'She was. I invited her to their wedding as my partner, so to speak. She got on like a house on fire with Cary and they've stayed in touch ever since.'

'How lovely, dear,' Norma repeated somewhat nervously, obviously unsure how she should interpret the definition of "my partner." 'How is she? A solicitor, as I recall. Married a vet, didn't she? Plenty of work in that neck of the woods, I imagine.' She clapped her hands together, eager to change the subject. 'I've got it. What's wrong with Lance staying with you, Dominic? You'll be in the house until it's sold and there's plenty of room. It makes much more sense than inconveniencing your sister.'

'No!' The force of Dominic's reaction took everyone by surprise. 'I mean, it's part of my agreement with Cary that no third party comes to stay in the house until it's sold. She was quite adamant.'

'Steady on,' Charlie winked at Norma and leered at Dominic. 'You mean she doesn't want some other bird coming around to share the old marital bed? Is that the problem? Is there someone waiting in the wings then?'

'It's nothing like that. We both want to remember the house as it was during better times – just the four of us.'

'If that's the sort of romantic old tosh you're both into, it hardly seems the right emotional reason for a divorce. Perhaps you two should think again.' Charlie waited to assess his wife's reaction, but Norma remained tight-lipped.

'You wouldn't understand,' Dominic countered. 'We have differences in other areas. We've grown apart. We're looking for different things.'

'Here we go again with his irreconcilable differences. You won't explain.' Charlie banged his fist on the table. 'Tell us what they are, and we can try to understand.'

'That's it,' Dominic said. 'Any minute now he'll be patrolling around the house, thumping on walls and talking to himself. How can we ever expect to have a rational conversation?'

Norma patted her son's arm. 'Eat your dinner before it gets cold,' she said. 'I could understand the insensitivity if it were a woman we were talking about, but having a male friend to stay, it's hardly something Cary would object to. Would you like me to speak to her and explain?'

'No, I would not. We made a deal, and we'll stick to it. Don't interfere . . . please.'

'Why not just do it and say nothing to her?' Sylvia suggested.

Dominic shook his head. 'Whenever she next came around, the neighbours would comment. She'd find out and it would breach our trust.'

Charlie guffawed. 'This breach of trust rubbish has got nothing to do with it. It's all about the sodding neighbours finding out and squealing on you, isn't it?' He thought for a second. 'You think if you have a bloke staying there with you,' he said triumphantly, 'people will think you've gone from forward gear into reverse and the happy two plus two family has been substituted by a couple of poofters.'

'Don't use that word,' Sylvia said. 'It's offensive. Being gay is both accepted and integrated into the modern-day social fabric. . . not that I'm saying it's relevant in this instance.'

'Thank God. I was born at a time when being a homo was a crime and people were chemically castrated if they couldn't keep their dicks out of other bloke's arseholes. I was all for it.' He turned to Norma. 'You remember, doll, that film about the homo who helped win the war by solving the code the Krauts used? He got doctored, didn't he? Poor sod. If he'd have been straight and married that bird, well, he'd never have topped himself.'

'That's the point I'm making,' Sylvia insisted. 'He's now recognised as a national hero, posthumously cleared of all convictions and honoured with his image on a banknote. Attitudes have changed. You need to change too.'

'I'm just making an observation. I grew up in another era when it was considered unnatural behaviour and I've always accepted that. I've known plenty of queers in my time, but I'm always uncomfortable around them because I don't understand the motivation and I have this urge to shake them and say, "wake up and act like a real man". I won't change now even if the world has changed around me. Old dogs and new tricks and all that.'

Dominic tossed his cutlery onto a plate still half-full of food. 'It depresses me,' he said. 'You'll never make it into the twenty-first century and understand how people think.'

Heads turned as Lance pushed his chair back and stood up. 'Look. I feel this conversation has evolved purely because of me and I should be the one to resolve it. If it's agreeable to Sylvia, I'll stay on the sofa for the next

140

three days max. During that time, I'll firm up on my new accommodation and be out of your hair for good. How's that?'

'It's no problem for me,' Sylvia said. 'What about you, Dom?'

'Why are you asking him? Charlie interjected. 'Does your brother have to approve who comes and goes at your place? Tell me, does a thirty-something-year-old woman really need her brother as a minder? You invite who you want, girl, and enjoy their company at whatever level you choose. He's not making such a wonderful job of his relationship to ponce . . . poncifi . . . pontificate on your choice of friends.'

With his lips pressed tightly together, Dominic nodded toward his sister whilst his eyes were fixed on Lance. 'All right by me,' he said, slowly.

'If you've finished eating, do you want that chat with me?' Charlie asked.

'Some other time,' Dominic replied. 'It can wait.'

'Is everybody ready for dessert?' Norma asked. 'I'll just put on the custard to warm up.'

Charlie nodded. 'While you're doing that, I'd like a word in the study with Sylvia. Do you mind giving me a couple of minutes, girl?'

Sylvia watched as he closed the door behind her and turned the key in the lock. 'What's all this about?' she said, a puzzled expression on her face. 'You're not going to keep on about Lance, are you? All those silly, smutty innuendoes you come out with. You act like you were a teenager.'

'Just my way of having a bit of innocent fun; no harm intended. But no, forget all that. I need your help with something, if you can, that is?'

'Really? I can't imagine what.'

Charlie summarised his exchanges with Len during their meeting the previous evening. 'That man hates me so much he will do everything in his power to side-line your mother and me from having anything to do with the twins once the split becomes official.'

'I don't see how he can. As Dominic has rights to be with the kids, so he can involve you two as he sees fit.'

'Don't you believe it. Len is evil. He'll brainwash his daughter and it won't take much for her to convince your brother we're . . . I should say I'm . . . a bad influence on them. He's a snob with a fancy house in Weybridge I

141

don't know how he could have afforded, and he treats me as a common piece of whatnot he can just ignore.' His voice rose. 'Well, he's got another think coming. I may be common as muck, but I have a backbone and I'll fight him all the way if he tries to stitch me up.'

'Steady on, Dad. You carry on like that, you'll have a stroke.' She leaned forward in her chair to hold his hand. 'You mustn't let him get to you. You're seeing things out of proportion.'

'Believe me, I'm not.' He pulled his hand away. 'He has it in for me. I want something on him: a blot on his copybook at work, how he got the dough together to buy that house, that sort of thing.'

'All the same, I don't see what I can do to help.'

He chanced a smile. 'What I wanted to ask you was, in your work, you meet plenty of coppers, don't you?'

'Yes,' she replied, hesitantly. 'Mainly from the Met. But I don't know any intimately, so to speak. Our conversations are all confined to forensics.'

'What about the City of London force?'

'The odd case; mainly fingerprinting and DNA requests linked to fraud and money laundering. There tend not to be many homicides in the Square Mile and the latest financial crash didn't send anybody jumping from the roof of an office building.'

'You on friendly terms with anyone from the City?'

'Yes, but not out of work. There was a young DI who invited me for a drink a couple of months back. He's in his late twenties. I put it down as the older woman complex and refused. I suppose I could ring him on some pretence. You'll have to leave it with me.'

'Do your best, Sylvia. I need something on the guy, even if it's just a rumour or something I can develop to make him think I know more than I do. If he thinks I might be a nuisance, I'll get him to change his stance on contact with the twins.'

'It seems a drastic measure to achieve such a well-intentioned desire. Is it really necessary?'

'You don't know him. Len only understands one thing. Influence. He's not into conciliation or compromise. Getting at me is a natural reaction that can only be countered by something to upset his wellbeing. Give me some ammunition and the dickhead will back off.' He went to kiss her on the cheek, but she moved and left his pouting lips suspended in mid-air as she made for the door.

'I'll see what I can do. You should ask Dom to look on the Net. He often discovers some interesting stuff in chatrooms. He won't admit it, but he hacked into Cary's uni website on one occasion. Shall we join the others for dessert?'

Dominic waited until his father had ushered Sylvia out of the dining room and noises from the kitchen showed his mother was busy before he moved around to where Lance was sitting.

'What in God's name do you think you're playing at?' Dominic dug his fingernails through the floral shirt fabric covering Lance's shoulders.

'Hey, leave off, that hurts.'

'It's meant to. I tell you we need to cool things off for a couple of weeks until I can break the news and you turn up two days later, shacked up with my sister and having a pleasant family dinner with my parents.'

'At least, I've seen first-hand what you're up against. Can't you come out first to your mother – she seems like the reasonable sort – and ask her the best way to approach Charlie?'

As Dominic released his grip, he smacked the palm of his hand across Lance's cheek. The reflex response caused Lance to wheel around in his chair, his hands balled into fists. 'What was that for?'

'You've really screwed things up now. How am I expected to break the news and introduce you as my partner when he thinks you're my sister's boyfriend? He takes it you're sleeping with her. You're not, are you? I'll bloody kill you if you are. I didn't sacrifice my marriage to end up with some slut.'

'Why don't you calm down?' Lance was nursing the red mark on his cheek. 'What's got into you? This isn't the place or the time to be having this conversation. Let's meet up and talk this through.'

'You're stalling on me.' Dominic's hands returned to grip Lance's shoulders. 'You are sleeping with her, aren't you? Don't lie. I can tell from the way she looks and acts: the glow in her eyes, the heightened self-assurance, the hand gestures. It all gives the game away.'

For the first time, Lance reacted physically, easily forcing the hands from his shoulders and wheeling the chair around to face Dominic. 'The glow in her eyes? The hand gestures? Dominic! You naughty boy,' he scoffed. 'At sometime in the past, you've screwed your sister, haven't you? Admit it, you dirty old man.'

Dominic recoiled, his gaze a mix of hatred and fear. 'I'll kill you,' he mouthed.

Lance leaned closer as Dominic moved around the table, his fingers closing around one of the serving forks. 'Let me paint the picture,' Lance said, the fervour in his voice apparent. 'You're twenty; Sylvia's fifteen/sixteen and dotes on her older brother, her hero. Her breasts heave as you move toward her. You unbutton her blouse and slip your hands under her bra. She feels you against her. You move her hand down to unzip your fly. She says, "God, you're so *hard!*"'

Dominic raised the fork, preparing to strike.

The kitchen door flew open as Norma shimmied into the room, her hands occupied as she negotiated her entry with a deep dish and large jug. 'Did you just say rhubarb, Lance? That was a good guess. It's Dominic's favourite, rhubarb crumble and oodles of custard. Got to keep his strength up, haven't we? Be a darling, Dominic, leave the fork. I'll clear up later. Call your father and sister before the crumble gets cold.'

Norma studied her face in the mirror as she applied a cotton pad to remove the mascara. She stroked her neck, pulling the skin taut and extending her chin to hide the folds of flesh. 'I'm getting old,' she said, 'and all this business with Dominic and Cary is putting years on me. He was in the strangest of moods tonight, sullen and aggressive. What did you think?'

'Mmmm?' Charlie was lying on top of the bed in his dressing gown, his attention fixed on the centrefold of the *Racing Post*. He lowered the paper just enough for his eyes to appear over the top. 'Sorry, missed that. Say again.'

'I said Dominic seemed at odds with everybody tonight, including himself. He certainly has a thing about Sylvia going out with Lance.'

'Maybe he knows something we don't.' The newspaper rose and fell once more as she spoke.

'What is there to know? Sylvia seems happy enough with her new boyfriend/flatmate, whatever he is. She's old enough to take her own decisions and deal with her own mistakes. That's why I don't understand this ultra-protective and dismissive attitude toward her. Did you see the way he left in a huff? He didn't even touch any of his favourite crumble. He could barely bring himself to say goodbye.'

Accepting defeat, Charlie let the paper slide down to rest across his stomach. 'He's probably regretting letting Cary and the twins out of his life. You know, act in haste, repent at leisure. He could well be jealous of Sylvia's relationship. Personally, I think we should let him get on with it.'

'And what's your opinion of Lance?'

He let the paper fall to the floor and slowly eased himself out of the dressing gown. 'A bit of a chancer, Jack the Lad, but there's something about him that appeals to me. Perhaps I see a little of me in him when I was young and invincible.'

'And six stone lighter?'

'Well, there's that, but I've still got muscles where it counts. Come to bed and I'll demonstrate.'

Norma laughed but made no move to get up from the dressing table. She looked at him through the mirror. 'You know, Cary said it was his affair with someone that caused the break-up. I'm telling you that in confidence. He has said nothing to me, and Cary swore me to secrecy.'

'He's highly unlikely to say anything to me, although I can't see it myself. Maybe the woman's married and decided to stay put.' He hesitated. 'Have you thought, maybe Cary made up his affair to justify her shenanigans with this character Ludo saw her cuddling?'

Norma cast her mind back to an early morning meeting in Selfridges and bit her tongue. 'One way or the other, we need to sit him down and hear the whole sorry story, warts and all.'

Charlie's thoughts were already elsewhere. Get me some dirt to throw, Sylvia, were the words echoing in his head.

'I told you to sleep on the sofa,' Sylvia said. 'After tonight, I'm not in the mood for male company.'

'Just a cuddle. I'm feeling vulnerable.' Lance pulled up the sheet to let himself in beside her back. 'Five minutes. That's all.' He nestled his head into her neck, his hands feeling inside her pyjama top. His teeth and tongue played in and around her ear.

'Jesus, Lance,' she moaned, wheeling around to face him. 'Where's my will power? You're worse than bloody cocaine.'

TWENTY-THREE

CARY AND ALEX

Sleep would not come. The luminous dial on the digital alarm clock meant she had been tossing and turning in bed for the last thirty minutes: thirty minutes that had seemed like two hours, two hours of confusing scenarios, conversations recalled, and unsettling conclusions.

Cary had made a point never to pry into Alex's past life beyond a casual question or a gratuitous recollection prompted by something they were saying or doing. The subject of the tragedy surrounding his previous family life was an extremely sensitive issue, and she had long since reached the conclusion the detail would surface as their relationship evolved. He was a private man, yet naturally sociable, a good listener and participator whenever the conversation was superficial or work related. Yet, whenever the subject encroached into the area of sentiment or relationships, he would stroke the prominent cleft in his chin, close his hazel eyes as if concentrating on an answer and cleverly steer his comments toward more neutral ground. Cary recognised the technique and had spent many a moment at a social gathering, amusing herself by waiting and watching for the gesture.

It didn't seem so funny now. On the occasions their conversation had touched on his wife, he had always referred to her in the past tense, the obvious aim being to steer Cary to the inevitable conclusion that Rosalind had died in the accident. To learn the woman was alive, albeit in a vegetative state, and he visited her regularly was a shock to the system. True, he hadn't lied, just misled her, intentionally, or did he really think of his wife as gone, no longer the woman he once loved? And what was the truth about his mother? Was he genuinely as callous as Rose would have her believe? These were the questions for which she needed answers.

He picked up on the third ring.

'Sorry I'm calling so late, darling,' she said in answer to his abrupt "Hello." 'You must be shattered. I just wanted to know you got back safely.' For a second, she thought he hadn't heard her.

'I don't remember telling you I was going to be travelling today,' he said. His tone, initially cold and defensive, turned rapidly to inclusive. 'I listened to your messages en route, but it was late and knowing of your sleeping arrangements at present, I thought it best to wait until tomorrow morning. Was that wrong?'.

Although tempted to use the opening to launch into the topic uppermost in her mind, curiosity led her to prod a little deeper into the reason for his absence, hoping he might confide in her. 'I couldn't sleep until I knew you were back safely. I called round this morning on the off chance, but your mother told me you were away for the day.'

'Did she?' He failed to add, "What else did she tell you?", but it was apparent from the caution in his voice.

'That's how I knew you were away. Not a problem, is it?'

'Good Lord, no. Nothing like that. I'm afraid my mother is confused and forgetful, a dangerous combination. She lives in a supervised environment but gets out every now and again to attend some medical consultation or the other. She's a terrible hypochondriac, been on death's door for the last thirty years. I expect she'll outlive me.'

'I'd like to get to know her. She shut the door on me quite quickly before we had the opportunity to talk. Will she be there tomorrow?'

'No. She's already left. Next time, perhaps.'

'Was your trip successful?'

'Business as usual. No problems.'

He must have covered the microphone, she thought. All she could hear was him mumbling something unintelligible. Somebody else was in the room with him.

'Sorry,' he said, 'dropped the phone. What is it you wanted to see me about?'

'I know I said we should leave announcing our relationship until my parents had been softened up, so to speak, but I'm afraid events have overtaken us.'

'Sounds intriguing.'

'My mother-in-law left me a message. Apparently, my father-in-law's former business partner saw us being extra-affectionate in your house one day recently and passed on the information. Charlie, that's my father-in-law – I suppose I should say former father-in-law – he ended up in an argument with my father and took dad by surprise by commenting on the aforementioned intimacy. Remarkably, Dad has refrained so far from bringing the matter up with me but, knowing him, keeping quiet must be driving him mad. If you agree, I'll tell him tomorrow and then introduce you as soon as the revelation has sunk in.'

'I've already told you, whenever you feel the time is right, I'll be by your side.'

'Dad can be a little caustic at times. You're not to take offence at anything he says.'

He laughed. 'I've had plenty of experience dealing with tricky customers. I doubt your dad will cause me any distress.'

'I *do* love you,' she said. 'I don't want there to be any secrets between us.'

'Of course not,' he said dismissively. 'Listen, I'm around all day tomorrow. You do what you must and let me know when you want me to appear. Give me a couple of hours' notice. I'll be ready to make a good impression. I must go now. There are a couple of calls to make before I call it a day.'

'Say you love me,' she whispered.

'You know I do,' he said. 'Let's keep the engagement as short as possible, shall we?'

'It's down to the decree absolute. As soon as that's through, I'm a free woman.'

'I love you,' he said. 'Speak in the morning. Goodnight.'

Alex checked the call had disengaged before picking up the second mobile from the table. 'You still there?' he asked.

'That one your latest conquest? Frankly, Dad, I don't know where you get the energy from.'

'*Mens sana in sano corpore*, I think is the appropriate phrase. This lady is to become my next wife. She is an invaluable consort, a first-class tax accountant, and comes with a ready-made family to provide the veneer of respectability which all successful men crave. She also happens to hit my sweet spot, so to speak. You can be my best man, Rupert.'

Rupert barked a gruff laugh. 'Isn't the fact you're still married to Rosalind a minor obstacle in completing this circle?'

149

'A minor inconvenience, easily overcome. I would remind you; I wasn't Alex Quentin when I married Rosalind. Indeed, I don't believe I was even Jeremy Bishop when I was engaged to your mother. She had the good sense to call off the wedding when she realised everything I'd told her about my past didn't quite stack up. Quite put my nose out of joint, but the experience taught me some important lessons. Astute woman, Debbie. How is your mother?'

'Still happily married to the senior partner in a City practice and busy writing freelance for several prestigious publications. Her hubby has tried to recruit me to join the firm, but I can't stand the idea of spending my life conveyancing or specialising in family law. I prefer the rough and tumble of life in the sticks, as you well know.'

'Talking of which, I need your services once again. I have a client who's into me for a six-figure sum and is having trouble with the repayments. He's a used car dealer in South London and has, regrettably, been interfering in my private life. He scraped together the last instalment, but he will not stand the strain for much longer.'

'Send me the file and I'll put the wheels in motion. Same procedure as always?'

'Yes. Be ready to move fast. He's a slippery Irishman with the gift of the gab.'

'We'll go for the statutory demand for five days' final notice, followed by the winding-up petition. I'll put our friendly liquidator on the case as soon as the petition is granted. What do you want out of it?'

Alex felt the adrenalin take effect at the thought of the outcome. 'Selling the vehicle stock at a small discount to market should easily cover my outstanding debt. What I need is a friendly deal on the freehold site from the liquidator. I have an inside source from the local council confirming an outline planning application from the current owner of the adjoining premises for change of use from light industrial to retail. Apparently, Lidl or one of these low-cost supermarket chains is behind the application with an option to purchase linked to planning consent.'

'How would that help you?'

'My contact tells me planning consent would be granted, but with the proviso the owner makes additional car parking space available. For the right price, I would be happy to sell on the used car site. It would be the socially responsible thing to do, after all.' He couldn't help the involuntary giggle as he finished.

'And the upside?'

'Conservatively, at least a million. Maybe double that figure.'

'As your Mr Ten Per Cent, I'll be rooting for you.'

'I'll send you the paperwork tomorrow. Be in touch.'

'Before you go, just one more thing about Debbie.'

'Go on.'

'I know you still have a thing for mum. I'm telling you there's a Do Not Disturb sign on her front door. Please respect it. Any approach from you would only end up in heartache and confusion. Give me your word.'

'Relax. I'll promise you this much. I won't do anything whilst your stepfather is alive. He's a fair bit older than her and, I understand, has a heart problem. He could pass away at any time.'

'What are you saying?'

'Should that unfortunate event come to pass, to cheer her up, I might be tempted to invite her to dinner. Surely, you'd like to see your parents finally reconciled?'

TWENTY-FOUR

JANICE FORBES AND DORIS FAIRBANKS

She had watched through net curtains as the man left the package on her doorstep. It was doubtful she would have chosen to open the door had he attempted to hand it over face to face, but his shameful embarrassment had been averted by taking the cowardly way out. Of course, she had recognised him. He was one of the two men who had sent her blessed Stanley to his death on that lonely road in Torremolinos. Curse his soul for taking one of her boys away before his time and leaving her with the torment that reduced her to tears every time the memory of Stanley came to mind.

Janice Forbes reached for the framed photograph on the mantelpiece and kissed the glass as she sat down clumsily in the armchair, the tears already welling in her eyes. Next month, she would be eighty and her blessed son, pictured here standing arm in arm with his brother, Roddie, would have been dead for nearly twelve years. The photo had been taken on Stanley's thirtieth, all smiles, a glass of cheap fizz in hand and, as a recently qualified bookkeeper, the world at his feet. How cruel fate could be!

It wasn't so much the Irishman she blamed, the one who had just appeared at her doorstep. She couldn't remember his name – something that sounded like a board game – it evaded her. What could she expect at her age? The trivia you could easily forget, but not the important things. The one she could never forgive was Charlie Greaves. He was the person she blamed. She had told the police as much on so many occasions. At first, they had listened, possibly made a few enquiries. After a while, they tried to avoid her, saying there was no more they could do. The Spanish police had confirmed it was a hit-and-run accident in a stolen car driven by a teenage boy. There were no links back to the UK or her son's employer. But she knew better. Stanley always described Charlie Greaves as a lovable scoundrel. They were as thick as thieves. Stanley must have got too close to Charlie, she had long surmised. All he had said was they – whoever they were – had planned a VAT inspection and Charlie had suggested Stanley take a nice long break in the sun, all expenses paid. Charlie had a mate who lived in Marbella with a spare granny annex where Stanley could stay rent free for a month. He was excited. The first holiday he'd had in years, ever since that one time just before his father had walked out on them.

Mind you, this tragedy would never have occurred had Holly not insisted Stanley go for the job interview with this Greaves in the first place. Her daughter had been adamant. It would embarrass her, having taken advantage of her college friendship with Charlie's daughter – what was her name now? Cynthia? No. Sylvia, that was it – to plead her brother's case for an opportunity to meet a prospective employer. Janice had blamed her daughter. All right, maybe it was unfair, but Stanley would never have got mixed up in that evil man's schemes had Holly not been so persuasive. He was in two minds about taking the job and Holly's downbeat talk of unemployment and a tough job market had swayed him. It had caused a rift between mother and daughter that had lasted all these years. They had never seen each other or spoken since. It was only through Roddie's spasmodic contact with his sister that Janice knew she had a granddaughter who would be almost ten now.

The tears began to form rivulets running down her cheeks. She realised she also had herself to blame. At first, Stanley had said he wouldn't go. Who would look after her while he was away? She insisted. Roddie might be a madcap and a milk crate short of a few bottles, as her GP used to say, but he had his heart in the right place and would take care of her, not that the lazy tyke ever did. It was enough to convince Stanley and off he went on the holiday of a lifetime, never to return.

She rose unsteadily from the chair, wiped her face with the sleeve of her cardie and carefully replaced the photograph. 'Let's see what he's left for me,' she said.

The cardboard box wasn't heavy, mainly personal files with bills, bank statements and credit card slips. There was a photograph of her he must have kept on his desk. That brought more tears. She must have been in her fifties at the time it was taken. Although, she said so herself, she had been a good-looking woman in her time. There were a few men who had showed more than passing interest, but their ardour always seemed to dampen after they had met and talked with Roddie. No one had suggested another date.

Amongst a collection of knick-knacks, there were two unopened letters addressed to Stanley which had arrived at the office weeks after his death, Although the stamps bore an image of the Queen's profile, on closer examination she noticed that they included the word "Gibraltar". Both envelopes contained standard letters from Barclays Bank PLC (Gibraltar) advising that there had been an interest rate change on all long-term deposit accounts and the new rate would be applied from the following month. In accordance with the client's wishes, statements would only be supplied on request. She replaced the letters in the envelope. Later, she would ask Roddie what it all meant.

Finally, at the bottom of the box was the set of Russian nesting dolls. How fortuitous, she thought. Her husband had brought them back from St. Petersburg when Stanley was just a boy and how he had treasured the gift. There were six in the set, all hand-painted in blue with white and yellow daisies back and front, replete with smiling faces and blushed cheeks. Janice knew when she opened the set, there would only be five dolls. The smallest had been found in his trouser pocket on the day he died and subsequently returned to her with the rest of his belongings. She retrieved it from the cupboard. It could now be reunited with its five relatives.

Painstakingly, as fast as her arthritic hands would permit, she started to unscrew the largest doll and so on until she came to the fifth in the sequence. Ready to put the sixth back into its place, she noticed the sticky tape covering the base of the fifth doll. As she peeled it away, a piece of folded paper wrapped around something small and solid fell onto the highly polished surface of the dining table. She tutted and, once again, employed the sleeve of her cardigan, this time to buff up the veneer.

Her hands trembled as she recognised Stanley's handwriting, his sweeping, self-confident style, commas and full stops heavily indented as though he had hesitated on the punctuation, pen to paper, as he composed the next phrase. The torn half sheet of A4 paper had been wrapped around a rectangular plastic-coated metal object she recalled him calling a flash drive. He had kept several of them at home and the name had always amused her.

His message, "To whom it may concern" was chilling and suggested to her that he feared for his life. Surely, she thought, nobody says, "If something happens to me", without believing that it might. His request was for the flash drive to be forwarded urgently to a Doris Fairbanks at an address in Canary Walk on the Isle of Dogs in East London. In honour of her dearest departed son, she would not hesitate in complying with his wishes.

On the back of the envelope in which she had sealed the flash drive, she carefully wrote the sender's name as Stanley Forbes (deceased) and his address as Heaven. Unsure of the weight, she had decided on three first-class stamps to avoid any delay caused by insufficient postage. Against her doctor's orders, she would walk the extra distance to the post box near the parade of shops on the main road to guarantee it made the five o'clock collection and would be with this Doris Fairbanks in the morning. Her next task would be to discover the phone number of this lady's office and call in the morning to verify it had reached her.

She had forgotten to take off her apron. How embarrassing. She had walked with it on as fast as she could all the way to the post box. No wonder she could feel the palpitations and the stabbing pain in her chest. She carefully folded Stanley's message and tucked it into the pocket of the apron. The police would have to listen now. No excuses. This would prove Stanley's death was no longer the result of a tragic act by a drugged-up juvenile, but a planned assassination.

Time to sit and rest in her favourite armchair and plan her approach. She couldn't wait to tell Roddie.

At seven-twenty-five that evening, famished after a tiring afternoon in the betting shop, Roddie walked from the front door directly to the kitchen and realised there was no evening meal ready in the oven. He would need to order a pizza delivery. As the last of the money he had borrowed from Mum had gone on a sure thing running in the last race at Wolverhampton, he would have to tap her for another twenty quid. He opened the door to the lounge.

At seven-fifty, the ambulance arrived. At eight-twenty-two, Janice Forbes was pronounced DOA by the acting registrar at Croydon University Hospital. Her apron was packed up with the rest of her clothing to await collection by her relatives.

* * *

What should she tackle first, coffee or cake? That was the choice occupying the mind of Doris Fairbanks as the postboy's trolley slammed into her office door. 'Just three today, Doris,' the teenager said with a wink and a cheeky smile.

'I've told you before, Grant, don't call me Doris. I'm Ms Fairbanks or Madam or Supervisor to you. Have some respect for your elders.'

'I've got a thing for older women,' Grant said as he pretended to assess some weighty issue. 'But, as for geriatrics, maybe I'll give them a miss.'

'You cheeky little sod. Get out!' She took a large bite out of the sugar-coated pretzel and to wash it down, a swig of the Americano with a dash. 'Did you hear me?'

Grant stood, holding the door open. 'There are two old guys in Collections who said you look voluptuous, whatever that means, and you remind them of an older Jayne Mansfield, whoever she is.' He hesitated, registering her expression. 'I won't tell you what else they said.'

She held up a USB stick and checked the text on the envelope. 'Come back here,' she called. Grant ambled back into the room as she scribbled on her memo pad, tearing off a sheet and handing it and the USB stick to him. 'Take this down to Lawrence in IT. I want to make sure if I stick it in my machine, I will not send some deadly virus around the place. Tell him if it's clean, I'd like it back as soon as possible.'

'What's it got on it, porno?'

'No, a photo of you before your arms and legs were broken.'

Grant moved hurriedly to the door. 'All right, I can take a hint. I bet you could throw a punch.'

'You'd better believe it.' She watched him move into the general office, pushing the trolley and exchanging banter with the members of her enforcement team as he made his way.

The envelope she held between thumb and index finger amused her. It was the first time she had ever received a letter from a dead man. Whatever was on the USB stick, it was bound to be intriguing. She needed something or someone to spice up her day. At fifty-eight, with less than two years to go before she took retirement, the workload was already tailing off, the larger

157

investigations going to younger and more career-oriented officers in Her Majesty's Customs and Revenue, London East VAT regional office.

At a personal level, she tended to frighten off most men, and her last meaningful affair had ended nearly five years earlier. She could do with somebody to share a laugh, a bottle of wine, a bloody steak and let's see where the evening takes us. She wanted to be treated like women used to be in the old days before the feminist movement and the 'let's split the bill' bullshit. She had been born thirty years too late. The fifties and sixties should have been her heyday. There had been a few Mr Rights, always married men who had bottled it when it came to the crunch, but she could live in hope. It was still not too late.

She put down the envelope and surveyed the daily work allocation for this week. Boring and tedious. 'Come on, Mr Stanley Forbes, bracket, deceased, bracket, put a little spice into my life,' she said out loud.

TWENTY-FIVE

TERRY AND MAHI AND . . .

Stupidly, he had been waiting in the park since seven thirty, two coffees and a *pain aux raisins* in a compressed paper tray awaiting her arrival. Her Americano would be stone cold by now. Terry had not touched his. The thought of eating or drinking anything enhanced the sensation of nervous anticipation weighing down his stomach, provoking the acid bile to rise into his throat. For the umpteenth time, he checked his watch. Surely, she would appear at any moment now - if she was coming at all. Maybe, she had changed her mind. Perhaps what had seemed like a daring escape from reality yesterday had become a flight of fancy today. Had she sensed the doubt in him? He needed to reassure her of his commitment.

From twenty metres away, she started talking, loud enough for him to hear. 'Don't get up!' she said. 'Pretend you don't know me!' She was ten metres away. He had gone to stand, but her petrified expression was enough for him to stall and sit back on the bench.

Mahi was looking straight ahead, still talking. Another figure appeared on the path in the distance. 'They suspect something's wrong. I'm pretty sure one of his brothers is following me.' She had passed him now, staring straight ahead. 'Ring me on the phone you gave me in thirty minutes, and we'll talk.'

'Buy yourself a coffee at the place we met yesterday before you go into work,' he said. 'Please.'

She was gone, through the gate and out of sight. The Indian man approaching was small in stature, of slender build except for the paunch around his stomach. He had a thin moustache, wire-rimmed glasses and was out of breath as he lengthened his stride.

'Got the time?' Terry asked.

'Sorry, I'm in a hurry,' the man said.

Terry rose from his seat, blocking the man's path. 'I said have you got the time? It's a simple question. You lot speak English, don't you?'

159

The man stopped in his tracks; his gaze fixed on the ground a yard in front of Terry. He pulled back the sleeve of his jacket. 'It's almost eight thirty.'

Terry took a step forward. 'Nice watch that. Rolex, is it? Got that by robbing the poor sods who come into your corner shop, did you? Don't pay your taxes, I guess.'

The man looked anxious. 'I don't have a corner shop and I'm late. Please let me pass.'

'You're not going that way unless you want to end up with a bloody nose and a few cracked ribs.'

The Indian took a step back. 'I don't know you. Why are you threatening me?'

Terry moved toward him. 'You have the gall to suggest I'm threatening you when all I'm trying to do is give you some friendly advice. You lot are all the same. Listen, Curry boy, in half-an-hour, the National Front will be marching to the Town Hall. We're meeting up on the other side of the park. You go that way, and you'll walk straight into the place where everybody's congregating. Believe me, there are guys there who make me look like your fucking fairy godmother, so take my advice, turn around and go back the way you came. It'll all be over by eleven.' He turned to the side and gave a low bow, his arm outstretched. 'If you fancy a bit of rough and tumble, proceed. Be my guest.'

The man gave a weak smile. 'I'll take your advice. Thank you.' He turned on his heels and began to retrace his steps.

Terry sidled up behind her as she stood in the queue. 'Make mine a Mojito on a nice sunny beach,' he said.

There was a look of alarm on her face as she spun around. 'Are you mad?' she hissed. 'He'll see us and tell Neeraj.'

'Relax, he's no longer in the vicinity. That's if we're talking about the thin guy in his late forties with the pencil moustache. I gave a passable impression of a racist thug and he swiftly retreated. I told him if he walked this way, he'd come face-to-face with a National Front demonstration.'

'Are you sure?' There was genuine fear in her voice. 'He's my husband's younger brother, a wicked man who resents my presence in

Neeraj's life. He is a bully and would like harm to come to me. He suspects I'm up to something.'

'How come?'

'He walked into our bedroom without knocking. He knew Neeraj wasn't in and decided I needed another of his lectures on the pillars of Hinduism and the place of the female in the family hierarchy. He normally studies my breasts as he drones on, but this time, his attention was drawn to the packed holdall I had on the bed. I told him it was a collection of old clothing and things I was going to deliver to the shelter for abused women, but I'm sure he didn't believe me. He must have told Neeraj and been instructed to keep a close watch on me. I saw him behind me as I reached the bottom of the escalator in the tube station this morning.' She looked anxiously at Terry.

'I suggest you forget the holdall, walk out of the front door one day carrying nothing remotely unusual, and never look back. I'll be by your side all the way.'

She gasped for breath. 'You mean it? You're going to go with me? I can't believe it. You're not just saying that, are you? You are serious?'

'Totally. I've never been more serious.' He hesitated. 'I have one proviso.'

'Go on,' she said nervously.

'I will need two weeks to organise everything, make arrangements.'

They had reached the front of the queue. He ordered fresh coffees and pointed toward a table at which another Indian man was sitting. 'Let's go over,' he said.

She hovered at his side, unsure of what seemed to her an additional complication. 'I haven't got long,' she said. 'I can't be late for work.'

'This is my friend, Nobby. He's a colleague from my time in the police.'

Nobby rose, offered his hand, which she barely touched before looking questioningly at Terry. 'If we want nothing to go wrong, we need to tread carefully,' Terry said. 'We will have no contact and I suggest you leave the burner phone I gave you at work and use it only in an extreme emergency. To monitor progress over the next fortnight, you can contact me through Nobby.'

'My name's Robin,' Nobby said. 'Robin Clark. As Terry says, we were colleagues and good friends. By good fortune, I am also a consultant on police matters to DOBIS. Have you heard of it?'

She shook her head, plainly still wary of the man.

'The acronym stands for the Development of British Indians in Society. In the time it takes for Terry to get his flat on the market, organise his affairs—'

'I need to get a new passport and International driving licence,' Terry interrupted, turning toward Mahi. 'Do you have over six months left on yours?'

'You bet,' she said with a smile. 'It's locked in my desk at the office.'

'As I was saying, if you two could just control your excitement for a minute, this is important to ensure my communication with Mahi does not raise suspicion within her family. I have told my contact at DOBIS I am working on a podcast to deal with the place of Indian women in the police and public service. As far as everybody is concerned, I have recruited Mahi to prepare and record a section on advancement to seniority in the DVSA, the pitfalls and rewards. Sound authentic?'

'What do you expect me to do?' Mahi asked.

'I suggest you mention it to your boss and promise to provide an advance copy before it's submitted. When I call you or you me, it will be on your regular mobile, and we'll have a spoof conversation about how it's going before we exchange any information. My last call will arrange for us to meet at a time and place. That will be your signal to go to the location and leave with this reprobate. If you want it to work, it must be spontaneous. Do nothing which could raise suspicions within your family.'

'Do I mention the project at home?'

'Treat it as a normal workplace occurrence. If the conversation leads to a point where it would be logical to mention it, then do so. That's how I would play it. The more open and normal it is, the less it will raise any doubts.'

'I'm so excited,' Mahi said. 'I won't be able to do any work today. Two weeks, you say?'

Terry reached for her hand before realising where they were and pulling back. 'Where would you like to go?' he asked.

'Anywhere. Anywhere that's a long, long way from here. You choose.' She leaned over to look at his watch. 'I must go. I can't be late for work. Everything must be as normal. I get that.' She was on her feet and out of the door before the men had time to react.

'Are you sure this is what you want, mate?' Nobby left a moustache of milk on his top lip as he drained his glass. 'It's a big step.'

'There's nothing to keep me here, is there? I can't be sure I'll ever mean as much to her as she means to me, but we'll see. I'm grateful for your help.'

'Believe me, you need it. The Kumar clan has a reputation for being ruthless when it comes to maintaining their status in the Hindu community. When she goes missing, the old man will take it personally, a slur on the family name that must be avenged. He won't stop until you are both brought to their concept of justice.'

'Which is?'

'Use your imagination. You will have both brought shame and ridicule on the Kumar name. There can only be one way of exacting retribution.'

TWENTY-SIX

LEN AND CARY

Len waited until the excited sound of children talking and laughing receded, car doors slammed, and the noise came and went of a throaty diesel engine as the Volvo came to life and eventually receded into the distance. The silence was total.

The sofa bed felt as if it exhaled with relief as he levered himself to the floor and his feet fished around on the bare floorboards until he located his slippers. Pulling on his dressing gown, he made his way downstairs to the kitchen, where the aromas of coffee and porridge hung in the air. Thoughtfully, she had left a half-jug of filter coffee on the machine.

This whole business was getting ridiculous, he thought, as he poured cold milk into an already tepid mug of coffee. Waiting for Caroline to say something was testing his patience to the limit. Ludicrously, it had reached the point where he was now going out of his way to avoid being in her presence should he fail to control the urge to raise the issue of her new relationship. If he did, it was bound to aggravate even further the animosity which Muriel had shown toward him over the last two days. Ever since that bloody evening at Gerry's, she had become openly hostile to him, banning him from the bedroom and answering questions in monosyllables on the infrequent occasions she was in his presence. His temper was at breaking point.

Beyond the wave of self-pity, he became aware of the distinctive engine noise of the Volvo as it came to a stop in the drive. She must have picked up on his anxiety and returned to talk. At last!

She looked harassed. 'Something's wrong with the Volvo,' she said. 'I dropped the girls off at school. I was parked on the kerb and as I started moving off there was a clanking noise from under the bonnet. Best I leave it here and borrow Mum's.'

'Didn't I tell you it would be a load of rubbish? You can't expect anything decent from that man. Probably a big end gone. The engine's had it. Call him up and tell him to send somebody to collect his piece of trash. I'll sort you out with something suitable. The man's a charlatan.' He hesitated.

'Anyway, there's something I need to talk over with you. Have you got a minute?'

Cary raised her eyebrows and deliberately checked her watch. 'I can guess what this is about,' she said. 'I understand you had an argument with Dom's dad, and he said some things which require my explanation.' She finished pouring mineral water into the percolator and switched on the machine.

'Spoken like a true accountant, if I may say so,' Len said. 'He said you are in a new relationship before you're even out of the last one.'

'I've put Colombian instead of Arabica. Are you all right with that?' She didn't react to the disinterested shrug. 'What else did he say?'

'That this latest guy is old enough to be your father.'

She gave an understanding nod. 'Latest? What do you think I have, a string of men? I expect you provoked this outburst from him?'

There was another shrug, this time suggesting an attitude of "so what?" 'I simply said, in current circumstances, I didn't consider it a good idea that he be around the twins. That went for their father, as well. Anyway, what's that got to do with what we're talking about? Bringing the Greaves family into this conversation is not relevant. They're in the past.'

She raised her eyebrows. 'What's got into you today? You're like a bear with a sore head. Maybe here and now isn't the best time to be having this conversation. Don't you want Mum to be involved? It'd save me going through it all twice.'

'For some inexplicable reason, Muriel is upset with something and has hardly said a dozen words to me in the last two days. God knows what's got into her.'

'Perhaps, if you were a little more considerate and attentive to her needs and point of view, instead of treating her as some glorified housemaid, the situation might improve.'

He motioned toward the coffee machine, which was making a noise like a strangled chicken as the last of the water passed into the filter. 'Fill mine up as well, will you?'

Cary ran her tongue around the inside of her teeth and walked slowly around the kitchen aisle to where he was sitting. She said nothing as she refilled his cup. 'Can't you see that?' she said, eventually.

'This profound insight comes from living with us for a few days, does it? In the past couple of years, I could count your visits to see us on one hand. Unless we went out of our way to visit you, we'd have had blessed little contact with the twins.'

'Please, let's not start all this. It was always easier for you as a couple to up sticks and visit us than for us to organise manoeuvres to move the family over here. Surely, that wasn't unreasonable?' She took a deep breath. 'I don't think we're in the right frame of mind to discuss your daughter's happiness, do you?'

'Better now than later. You've left it long enough as it is.'

'All right, have it your own way. First, I'll deal with the history. For three years, I've had a client on my list at work who runs a financial investment business. His name is Alex, a widower. He's a one-man band, operating from his home on the outskirts of Ashford. I must admit, I grew to like the man; quite fancy him, it's fair to say, but it never made me waiver from my commitment to Dom and the twins. As I told you, Dom and I had gradually drifted apart since the twins were born, but we never broached a subject which we both realised would be difficult, possibly impossible, to remedy. We just kept our heads down and carried on.'

'There you go again, sounding like a bloody accountant.'

'I'm sorry my profession offends you so much. Had I been born the boy you always craved, I suspect you would be proud of my career choices. As things are progressing, I expect to be offered a full partnership in the practice within the next year, no mean feat for a woman in a firm where around ninety per cent of the qualified staff are males. Should I apologise for popping out of my mother's womb the wrong sex?'

'Don't be so bloody ridiculous. It's nothing of the sort. I'm as proud as any father could be of your achievements. It's just that you lay out your relationship issues as if you were preparing a spreadsheet, cold and calculated. You talk about career choices. Don't you get angry with yourself for your life choices, that it's taken all these years and two kids to make you realise you chose the wrong man? It was as plain as the nose on your face, right from the start.'

'So you say and have continued saying for God knows how many years. You never lost an opportunity to run down Dominic, criticise his decision making or belittle him. If your aim was to divide and conquer, you achieved the exact opposite. Even when our relationship had started to falter, when the joy as a couple was on the wane, a dose of your nagging him would drive us closer together for a short while. I shouldn't wonder if you should shoulder some of the blame for the sense of inadequacy which drove him into the arms of somebody else.'

'He was having an affair?' His fingertips drummed on the melamine surface.

'That's what I've been trying to tell you. He told me about six months ago. I told him I didn't want to know the details, the who, the when and the where.'

'Why did he tell you? Because he wanted a divorce?'

Cary shook her head. 'On the contrary, he said he would finish with whomever if I thought we had a chance of restoring the relationship and protecting the twins.'

He went to speak but decided to hold back.

'I told him not to bother. The twins would be fine in the long run, provided we did not descend into an acrimonious separation.'

'You made the right decision.'

'I don't need or want your confirmation, Dad. Your position goes without saying. I think Mum sees it differently.'

'She'll come around when she shakes off this malaise.' He looked up at the ceiling. 'So, this tide of events gave you *carte blanche* to get involved with this client. Didn't take you long, did it?'

'There was a strength of pent-up emotion on both sides. It all fell easily into place and I'm thrilled with the way things are progressing.'

'And you plan to move in with him, hence Dominic stays in the house?'

'That's about it. Alex has a large place with a big, enclosed garden for the girls. They know and like Alex. They'll settle in quickly. I'd like you both to meet him.'

Len shook his head. 'How old is he?'

'Early fifties,' she said in a matter-of-fact voice. 'He's a mature, experienced man with a young and positive outlook. We get on well . . . at all levels.'

'You're talking about a difference of almost twenty years. You'll end up nursing an old man. You know that, don't you?'

'I think you should get to know him.'

He shook his head again. 'I don't want to. I won't feel comfortable talking to somebody who's closer to my age than my daughter's in the knowledge they go to bed together. You should wait until the divorce is through, the equity from the sale of your house is in the bank and your head is clear of all past issues before taking any more steps forward.'

'Sorry. We're moving in at the weekend. I'd like you, at least, to keep an open mind until you meet.'

'You're bloody-minded, always do what you want, irrespective of the advice you're given.' He went to get up. 'What does he do exactly?' he said, staring at the tiled wall. 'Charlie called him Shylock. Is he a moneylender?'

'No. He runs an international loan portfolio for second-line clients who, for one reason or another, cannot get finance from clearers or traditional sources. Consequently, his security arrangements with debtors who are unable to fulfil their obligations may involve him standing in their shoes and assuming control of the assets to achieve a successful outcome.'

Len slowly clapped his hands, turning toward her, a twisted smile on his lips. 'Who wrote his CV . . . You? That's real accountancy gobbledygook for "He's a moneylender, full stop." I expect "achieving a successful outcome" involves a few senior management figures who happen to be extremely well-built and know how to put a foot in the door so that "the second-line client" cannot close it.' The smile turned to a forced laugh. 'You see what you want to, Caroline. Don't be fooled by a veneer of respectability.'

'You've got him all wrong, Dad.' There was a strain of desperation in her tone. 'You'll change your mind when you meet him.'

'I'll forego that pleasure for some time. Make sure you don't make a fool of yourself and don't excuse happenings that don't match your allusions. If you've got the beautiful relationship you crave, don't be afraid to ask delicate questions and expect to get back honest answers.'

Cary sat at the wheel of the Volvo. Her hands were shaking, his words ringing in her head. Damn it! There were already questions she needed to ask, questions about his wife, his mother. It had honestly never occurred to her the

169

Albanians might be employed as enforcers. Why had she instigated the conversation with her father today of all days?

He was tapping at the window. 'What do you want now?' she snapped. 'I'm late for work.'

'That's why you've been sitting there for the last five minutes, is it?'

'Just planning my day. Come on, get on with it,' she snapped.

'I need something on Charlie to keep the man in order. It occurred to me you may be able to help.'

'What does keep him "in order" mean, and why do you need to?'

'I know he's going to interfere with the girls' upbringing. You've got the son out of the picture: I want the father to get lost.'

'Dom will still play a big role in the girls' development.'

'That doesn't mean Charlie has to be in the picture.'

'And how do you propose achieving this?'

His face was so close to hers she could detect the aroma of coffee on his breath. 'I've asked my mate, Randy, who's still on the force, together with other people I know, to see if there's some little secret in his past we can use to convince him he is a bad influence on the twins.'

'You mean coercion. You stay clear of the girls, Charlie, or we'll let a and b know about x, y and z.'

'Something like that.'

'And don't I have a say in this?'

'Surely, you as the twin's mother can't accept his wanting to influence the girls' development, spoiling them, using his foul language in front of them?'

'I hold Norma and her opinions in high regard. I don't intend to lose contact with her.'

'That's your choice. I believe in time you will feel obliged to discard unnecessary baggage. Norma will be what's known as collateral damage.'

'This really is your vendetta, isn't it? It's got nothing to do with the girls, has it? You hate the man. Possibly, he hates you and neither will be satisfied until one has crushed the other.'

'You read it as you see it, Caroline. I'm not changing course.'

'Move out of the way, will you?' She leaned her head out of the window as she waved to the figure of her mother, clad in a dressing gown,

170

standing framed in the open front door. 'I've had a conversation with Dad,' she shouted as she continued to wave. 'He'll explain everything to you. I must go to work now, but I'll call you during the day for a chat.'

Muriel acknowledged the comment and beckoned toward her husband. 'Why didn't you come and get me before you had this conversation? Does my viewpoint not count?'

'I assumed you were still asleep. I didn't want to disturb you.'

'You assume too much, as usual. The truth is, you don't attribute any value to what I think about family issues, so I don't need to know. I have to come to my senses or perish.' She turned and slammed the front door shut.

He looked from the closed door back to his daughter as she started the car. 'Bloody women,' he mumbled.

TWENTY-SEVEN

DORIS AND CHARLIE

Unlike her to be so patient. Although the first reaction when the flash drive came back from IT with a clean bill of health was to insert it into the USB slot in the external drive, Doris resisted the temptation. Feeding it into the system linked to the national servers would be an irreversible action, the content automatically copied and filed with a daily journal reference. In truth, the likelihood of anybody else uploading the detail in the future was minimal, but caution as to the implications of what information might surface obliged her to keep the drive locked in her desk drawer for three days until the weekend. Doris had briefly considered taking the flash drive home, but getting it past security would require a senior officer's authorisation, and her inability to provide a logical motive led her swiftly to put aside the idea.

Over the following weekend, the national system would be down for maintenance and the installation of upgrades. Staff on site during this period were permitted to bring personal laptops into the building to send mails or write memos. This would give her the opportunity to copy the content from the drive and consider it at leisure. Something innate was telling her she would not like what she saw.

At eleven, the following Monday, she slipped out of the office to make the call.

'Ludo Quality Cars,' a voice with an Irish brogue announced on the other end of the line. 'How can I help you?'

'Could I speak to Charles Greaves, please?'

'Who's calling?'

'It's a personal matter.'

'Charlie is no longer with the company. It's under entirely new management. We only deal with high quality, nearly new cars now.'

'Do you have a number for him?'

'Who's calling, did you say?'

'I'm an old friend. You're his partner, aren't you? Mr Logan, isn't it?'

'And you are?'

'The name is Fairbanks. I popped in to see him some years back. You won't remember.'

'You're right there. I can't just give out his number, personal data regulations and all that cobblers, but I can tell him you want to speak with him, d'you see?'

'Would you do that? Would you tell him it will be to his advantage to contact me as soon as possible? You have my number?'

'It's here, written on the little screen thing. You make it sound as though he's come into money.'

'You could say his luck has changed. Ask him to call me after seven this evening, will you?'

The wilting page of a magazine with a half-naked, full-page photo of Gerard Butler was precariously propped up in the soap holder as Doris laid in a bath covered with foam. She was close to achieving an orgasm as the mobile on the bath rug burst into life with an instrumental rendition of Tina Turner's 'Simply the Best'.

'*Coitus Interruptus,* your speciality, Charlie,' she said out aloud to herself. She leaned out of the bath and gripped the mobile with wrinkled fingers. 'You certainly choose your time to call, Charlie. I told your mate after seven, not midnight. Had to make sure the wife was asleep, did you?'

'You could say. Am I interrupting something? You *asked* me to ring. I can call back in five minutes!'

'You're a cheeky sod. If I'd have been doing something interesting with someone, a phone call with you would be the last thing on my mind.'

'I'm pleased to hear it. May I ask why you need to speak to me? You *do* know I'm no longer involved with the business?'

'So your Irish friend told me in no uncertain terms.'

'This is a social call, then?'

'Hardly. We need to meet up. Why don't you invite me out to dinner tomorrow?'

'What's this about, Doris? We agreed to finish years ago. Why contact me now?'

174

'Just to avoid you rewriting history, you were the one who finished it after confessing all to your wife. I had no choice. All I did was tell you in anger to eff off.' She waited for a reaction, but he said nothing. 'Does the name Stanley Forbes, bracket, deceased, bracket, mean anything to you?'

'You know it does.' His voice was hesitant. 'What's this got to do with him?'

'I've received a message from the grave; in more ways than one. His mother, it transpires, has also just passed away. I recall poor Stanley was the victim of a hit and run in Spain whilst on holiday, if memory serves.'

'What's all this about?' Hesitancy had changed to impatience.

'Let me know where we're meeting tomorrow night and I'll tell you.'

'Tomorrow may be difficult. It's short notice.'

'I'll hang on until Wednesday. That's my last offer, but the sooner the better.'

'I'll text you.' He had hung up before she had time to reply.

TWENTY-EIGHT

SYLVIA, LANCE AND MORGAN

'Three nights I've slept on that sofa. What more could I have done to show my feelings for you?'

Sylvia shook her head. 'How about finding another place to park your backside, as you told my parents you would, and accepting the sofa so readily only because, as you so romantically put it, "You're on the blob." Does your charm know no bounds?'

'I'm working on a place to stay. Another day or so should do it.'

'Well, you can make yourself scarce tonight. I'm going out with a friend, and we may end up back here. I don't want you around.'

'What sort of friend?' He gave her a sideways glance.

'The friendly sort. What's it to do with you?'

'Nothing,' he said, disgruntledly. 'Other than I see myself as your shining knight in armour, here to protect you from unwanted advances and those bearing false witness.'

'Sounds very much like the conversation of a would-be possessor. Let me tell you, Lance, the idea of somebody attempting to exercise control or question my choices is a total anathema to me and guaranteed to ensure I leave your meagre possessions on the landing before you even have time to mark your territory by peeing on the front door.'

'Graphically put, if I may say.' He held out his arms and gave what he would describe as one of his disarming smiles. 'Can I know if this friend is male or female?'

'If you must know, he is a police colleague from the City of London force who has invited me out for a drink. Satisfied?'

'Do you fancy him?'

She tut-tutted. 'You always reduce everything to the lowest common, just below the belt, denominator. We are going to have a friendly chat, exactly what you should do with my brother and appear to be avoiding.'

'He's the one who's doing the avoiding.' He wagged his finger. 'As it happens, Miss Independent, we've agreed to meet tonight when I intend to tell him I'm in love with his sister.'

Sylvia pulled on her raincoat and swung the strap of her bag onto her shoulder. 'If you expect me to crumble at the knees upon hearing that remark, you have another think coming. The largesse you employ to waft your emotions around the place is boundless and, consequently, meaningless.'

'Is that so?' He wrapped his arms around her and kissed her firmly on the lips. 'It just happens to be true.'

'I'll take that under consideration. Just make sure you're not confusing love with a warm bed and a place to shelter in the rain.' She disentangled herself from him and walked to the door. 'Be gentle with Dom. He's hurting and very vulnerable right now, confused, lacking self-confidence. You don't need to bring me in as the reason for ending your relationship. Treat it as a personal issue and leave as friends if possible.'

He went to say something, but the door had already closed behind her.

It was ten thirty that evening when he heard the key turn in the lock and a male voice project a nervous, high-pitched giggle.

'No,' he heard her say. 'My flatmate is out for the evening. Come in, Morgan. Take a seat. Make yourself comfortable. I'll get a couple of glasses for the wine. Do you need a corkscrew?'

'Not necessary.' The voice was normal now, though slightly strained. 'It's a screw top.'

Lance was sitting on the toilet seat in the en-suite adjoining her bedroom. So far, with the bedroom door slightly ajar and the bathroom door open, he could make out everything that was being said. 'Cheapskate,' he said to himself. 'If you really want to impress the lady, it should be champagne or, at the very least, a decent French wine with a real cork.' He prayed she would come into the bedroom – alone, of course – see him and frustrate whatever plans she or this Morgan creep might have around cosying up for the night.

She had walked back into the lounge from the kitchenette. He could hear the clink of the glasses as she set them on the coffee table. She must have sat next to him on the sofa. Their conversation was reduced to a mumble. From the few words he overheard, she was asking questions about somebody who worked in the City force. There was a sudden burst of laughter before the conversation degenerated once more into a series of mumbles.

Lance was finding the entire business both irritating and soporific. As he changed his sitting position once again, moving from one cheek to another to overcome the numbing sensation, his chin dropped onto his chest, the sensation of release into a semi-conscious state so comforting. It was the sudden change in mood in the lounge that brought him back to full consciousness.

In a more strident tone, she was pointing out that sex didn't follow from a first date, and it was not her time of the month to invite intimacy, even if she did fancy it, which she didn't. He said something to her which Lance didn't catch, but it prompted Sylvia to bark a false laugh. 'When you say, "by making it nice for each other",' she was saying, 'that's malespeak for would I give you a blow job, is it?'

Lance took a deep breath, stood, and rubbed his backside to restore the circulation. Time to make an entry.

The bedroom door crashed open. He rubbed his eyes and yawned. 'Sorry to interrupt, folks. Are you coming to bed soon, darling?' His dressing gown splayed open to reveal a naked torso. 'I've got an early start . . .'

'What the . . .?' Morgan sprang to his feet. 'Who the hell is he?' He stared at Sylvia.

Lance weighed him up: short for a policeman and stocky, broad-shouldered but slightly paunchy around the gut, late twenties, lined, unshaven face, ugly bastard. Lance could take him if need be.

'This is my flatmate,' she said, rather unconvincingly.

Morgan stood, legs apart, in the middle of the room. 'You told me he was out, and you were just mates.'

'Wrong on both counts,' Lance said with a smile. 'Why don't you just leave the lady in peace? What she might have caught sucking your cock doesn't bear thinking about.'

Morgan launched himself toward Lance, his fist clenched, pulled back, ready to strike.

'Please, no violence,' was Sylvia's plea, but it was too late.

Lance moved sideways as the other man neared him, parrying the intended blow to his head with one hand, turning and kicking upward with his right foot to catch his would-be assailant with a deft strike to the crotch. Morgan seemed to stop in mid-step, his expression changing from anger to distress as he yelped and collapsed onto his knees, both hands reaching down to protect himself. Off-balance, he fell sideways with a dull thud onto the coffee table, sending the wine glasses spinning onto the Mexican design rug. Crying in pain, he drew himself into the foetal position, hands between his legs.

'Jesus, Lance,' Sylvia said. 'What the hell do you think you're doing? I can look after myself. You see what you've done?' She pointed to the prostrate figure staring at Lance. 'He's a policeman, for God's sake.'

'I don't care whether he's the head of the FBI, he was still coming on to you even when you were making it plain you weren't interested. What did you expect me to do, stay in my corner and keep quiet?'

'I've told you before, I do not need your protection and you weren't in your corner. You were in my bedroom where you have no right to be without an invitation. Are we clear?'

Morgan was staggering to his feet, his left hand still protecting his crotch. He steadied himself against the sofa. 'Pass me my coat,' he said, looking at Lance, who pointed to the crumpled leather coat on the floor.

'Help yourself,' Lance said. 'Time to go, if it's all the same to you.'

The colour drained back into Morgan's face; his cheeks flushed as the adrenalin rush began. 'You got the drop on me this time, Lance, or whatever your name is. Next time, I'll come prepared, and you'll wake up wishing you hadn't tangled with me.'

'Is that so?' Lance said, as if disinterested in pursuing the conversation.

'And as for you,' – Morgan turned his attention to Sylvia – 'I thought we were really getting somewhere this evening, but it turns out you were only looking for a little diversion from lover boy here. You deserve him. Don't come knocking on my door when you come to your senses. You don't know what you've missed.' He pulled the jacket from the floor and draped it around his shoulders. His path to the door led him right past Lance. 'You can take that smirk off your face,' he said as he gestured for the other man to get out of his way. 'The next time we meet, you'll be smiling through a bloody pulp. Mark my words.'

'I'll bear that in mind,' Lance said, moving two steps back to hold the door open. 'Sorry about the hall light,' he said. 'The bulb has blown. Hope you're not afraid of the dark.' He tried to sound concerned as he let the door swing closed.

'Fuck you, Aussie arsehole!' were the last words Lance heard. He turned back to face Sylvia.

'You're angry with me?'

Sylvia kicked off her shoes and sank back to lie on the sofa. 'I could have achieved the same end without the violence, but you had to stick your oar in and ensure he never speaks to me again.'

'Does that worry you?'

'Our paths might cross. He'll bear a grudge. Tonight's loss of face won't go down well. I should look over your shoulder for a few weeks.'

He sat down on the sofa, lifted her feet on to his lap and began to massage her toes. 'He doesn't worry me.'

'That's nice,' she said. 'Don't stop. He may have some friends with him the next time.' She fished for the wineglass on the carpet and drained the contents. 'I've had too much to drink tonight.'

He kneaded one foot at a time between the palms of two hands. 'What's the score with him? I don't believe you accepted a date from that lowlife without an ulterior motive. He's hardly your type.'

'Nothing special, just a casual arrangement.'

He thrust her feet from his lap. 'I can tell when you're lying. Don't treat me as a fool or the masseuse will go on strike.'

She laughed. 'That's torture.' She wriggled her feet back on to his lap. 'All right, you win. Charlie wanted me to dig up some dirt on Dom's father-in-law, who used to be a detective in the same force as Morgan. They never got to know each other, but tales of good and evil seem to filter down to the rank-and-file. It was the only avenue I could think of.'

'What's your dad hoping to achieve?'

'The two men hate each other, have done ever since Dom and Cary got together. Dad thinks he'll be manipulated by this Len, that's the name of Dom's father-in-law, in to losing contact with his grandchildren.'

'Seems somewhat over-dramatic.'

'You should see them together. They both have a full toolkit, but in each other's company, they only know how to use a hammer.'

He smiled at the comment. 'And did you dig up anything?'

181

She sat up. 'Yes, and no. Nothing concrete, just rumour.'

'Sounds intriguing.'

'Len was viewed as a marginal character in the City of London force, suspected of sailing close to the wind by taking kickbacks from traders in the Square Mile. Nothing was ever proved, but it got to the point where the powers that be recommended to him and a couple of his cronies they should take early retirement to avoid an investigation by the Anti-Corruption Command. Len and his team were suspected of being too close to a butcher named Bateman at Smithfield.'

'How many people were involved?'

'Four, all together. One guy still works for the economic investigation team. They had a nickname because of the link to this butcher. They were known as "meat, gravy and two veg." Apparently, this Bateman moved his operations away from London to the Midlands. His son is still around, runs casino and girlie clubs, mostly around the outskirts of London.' She stopped and swallowed loudly. 'Are you still listening?' One of his hands was now massaging her calf muscle, the other, the thigh on her other leg. 'This technique of yours is becoming intriguing. Why don't we find somewhere more comfortable to lie down?'

'Took the words out of my mouth. Shall we make it nice for each other?' he said with a laugh, as he tried to mimic Morgan's Welsh accent.

'Don't,' she said. 'I've lost the urge already.'

Sylvia squinted through half-opened eyes as she registered the sun streaming into the bedroom through the net curtains. Lance was awake, hands interlocked behind his head, his eyes focussed on the ceiling. 'Morning, did you sleep well?' he asked.

She squeezed her eyes tight before trying to open them. They felt sticky. She hadn't taken her mascara off before going to bed. 'What's wrong? Why are you awake so early?' She wagged a finger at him. 'Guilty conscience for trying to take advantage of such a virginal beauty as I?'

He turned his head to look at her. 'Now we are indulging in the world of fantasy,' he joked. 'Actually, I was thinking about that burke last night and his loud-mouthed threats, then contrasting it with the way Dominic ended our conversation earlier in the evening.'

Sylvia sat bolt upright. 'God, I was so consumed with the Morgan incident, it slipped my mind completely. You were meeting with Dom. How did it go?'

He breathed deeply, expelling the air noisily through partially closed lips. 'If I said all right, I'd be lying. I was in the house for no more than ten minutes. Disconcerting would be too mild to describe the experience. I think he's having some sort of breakdown.'

She gripped the sheets tight around her knees. Her expression told him to continue.

'He blames me fair and square. Imagine the scene. He's sitting at the kitchen table, dirty crockery and fast-food containers covering every surface, broken plates and glasses in the sink. Dom is in his underpants, eating baked beans with a spoon from the tin. By the look of him, he hasn't washed or been to work for the last couple of days. I asked him. He said he'd phoned in sick, something he'd never done before. He's always been on call.'

'Jesus, I need to get over there. He's highly strung, always has been, but this business must have tipped him over the edge. Go on. What did he say?'

'He was perfectly rational, but talking so softly, I could barely hear him. He said he had made a commitment to me, which had brought about the end of his marriage, and I had betrayed him. He accused me of using sex, either heterosexual or homosexual – I was indiscriminate – to gain some advantage, either personal or financial. It meant nothing to me. I had no feelings, no morals, no scruples.'

'How did you react to that?'

'I apologised, not that it did any good. I said that until I met you, there was some truth in what he said, but I felt totally different about our fragile beginnings, and it had never been calculated; it just happened.'

Her eyes were full and looking into the distance. 'I feel like the one who has betrayed him.'

'He doesn't blame you for anything. He sees me as the villain of the piece, manipulating your emotions to suit my ends.' He went to hold her hand, but she held onto the sheet. 'It was the only time he became animated. He scoffed and asked me why I thought it was different with you. I said I'd never

183

felt a thing when any previous relationship had broken up, but if you gave me the heave-ho, I'd be broken-hearted.'

'Is that it? I need to get over there.' She tossed the sheet away from her and began collecting her clothes. 'I'll ring work and tell them I'll be late. Did he say anything else I should know?'

'He said he despised me; I was no better than vermin and, if he had his way, I should be "exterminated" was the word he used. He threw the can of beans at me. I couldn't wait to get out. As I made for the door, I shouted at him to pull himself together and face up to the reality like a man.

'He said he'd see me dead first.'

TWENTY-NINE

LEN AND RANDY

Len dismissed the idea of discussing developments with Randy over the phone, suggesting they meet for a pint at lunchtime in a pub near the Elephant and Castle, where they were unlikely to be spotted by anybody from the City of London police force. In sharp contrast to his friend's upbeat mood, Len projected a sombre and disconsolate image of a man with the problems of the world on his shoulders.

'What's got into you?' Randy asked, two pints of lager in hand as he shimmied through the crowd to an available table next to the slot machine. 'The wife caught you cheating on her?'

Involuntarily, Len nodded. 'Women problems, most certainly, but not the way you're thinking.' He gave a sanitised version of his conversations with his wife and daughter. 'I'm in the doghouse for no good reason,' he concluded, burping loudly as the chilled beer hit his stomach. 'When you lose control of the situation and they start to think for themselves, the outcome becomes totally unpredictable.'

Randy swallowed a laugh as soon as he realised Len was not joking. 'Spoken like a true chauvinist,' he said, attempting to inject a little levity into the conversation.

'I've never seen chauvinism as a curse,' Len said sombrely. 'More as a necessity in preserving domestic sanity.'

There was an uncomfortable silence before Len spoke again, this time his voice more animated. 'Anyway, putting my domestic woes to one side, you sound and look like the cat who's got the cream. What's the score?'

'I've had a good morning.' There was a strong Yorkshire lilt to Randy's accent. 'I was wondering how I could get closer to the NCA investigation when the answer literally fell into my lap or, to be more precise, via way of a video call from a WPC desk operative at Vauxhall. The investigating officers were asking for any file information we had on two refrigerated transport operators working out of Smithfield in the last ten years, namely Bateman and Macario.'

'And that's good?'

'At first, I was alarmed, but when the WPC explained the widow of the original self-employed driver had given these two names as the principal clients for whom her late husband had worked, it seemed a logical request. More importantly, it gave me the 'in' I was looking for. She was very chatty, saw me as a kindred spirit, tied to a screen all day performing routine tasks.'

'Anything on file?' Len asked.

'Nothing much. Bateman's issues are mainly referrals to Health and Safety for complaints on dodgy provenance details and hygiene anomalies. Macario seems to specialise in unregistered workers and threatening behaviour. Everything is years old. For obvious reasons, the investigation is more likely to focus on him than old man Bateman.'

'Good.'

'Apparently, the girl they fished out of the river was identified as having come from Azerbaijan, wherever that is. She had a tattoo inside her thigh which said "little diamond" in their language. According to Interpol, local gangs in league with the Armenian mafia operate illegal trafficking, mainly girls and young women, across Turkey into the EU. These poor souls who think they're going to be reunited with relatives end up in sweatshops or brothels as slaves.'

Len raised his eyebrows. 'Darren mentioned Azerbaijan when he was talking about using the lorry. I'll keep the Interpol connection to myself. Bateman has already flown off the handle with his son. I don't want to make him even more nervous.' He broke off to order fresh beers from the bar. 'You're not in a hurry, are you?'

'Don't spare the thought. Collating dodgy insurance pay-outs can wait another half-hour. You hear about Terry?'

Len shook his head. 'I was just about to ask you.'

'You know he made contact? She's done what he asked? No? Well, he did, and she has. According to Nobby, the deal is, in return for her cooperation, they run away together overseas, far enough away from her husband and in-laws to avoid retribution.'

'You're pulling my plonker? Terry? The local lad who gets homesick if he ventures beyond the M25? I don't believe you.'

'You better had. His flat is on the market; he's cashing in everything he owns and Nobby says he's just waiting for Bateman's pay-out to exit stage left with the love of his life.'

Len smiled to himself. 'I would have never thought he had it in him. Good luck to them both, though I suspect he'll have problems with an Indian bird. There's a big culture gap between a heavily structured lifestyle and farts in bed, smelly socks and takeaway pizza boxes.'

'If it makes him happy, Len, who are we to judge?'

Len shrugged his shoulders. 'I'll get Bateman to cough up. Any other surprises to spring on me?'

Randy nodded and gave a broad smile, revealing a mouth of uneven, broken teeth that gave him a slightly sinister appearance. 'You know you were asking me for anything unsavoury I could dig up on this Charles Greaves character?'

Len leaned forward. 'Now you're talking.'

'I told this WPC from National Crime I was working on a money laundering case and the name of Greaves had come up. Did National have anything on him? To my surprise, just before I left to meet you, she came back to me with a little nugget.' He stopped, relishing the look of anticipation on the other man's face before continuing. 'Around twelve years ago, SOCA, as it was then, processed a complaint from a Janice Forbes regarding the death of her son in an RTA in the Marbella area of Spain. The Spanish authorities were asked to confirm whether the driver of the car involved had any connection with organised crime and if he, his family or associates had any links to a Charles Greaves and/or a David Logan. The reply came back as negative, but the complainant was insistent it could not have been an accident.'

'Why was this Janice Forbes so sure?'

'The summary simply says the woman was convinced her son, a bookkeeper, was being sent abroad whilst a VAT inspection was underway at his employer's premises to avoid disclosures which he might feel obliged to make and which could compromise the employer. No irregularities were discovered during the inspection and SOCA filed the complaint.'

Len massaged the two-day growth of stubble on his chin. 'Fascinating. We don't happen to know who gave the inspection the all clear, do we?'

Randy wrestled a folded piece of paper from the pocket of his jeans. 'It was carried out by London East in Canary Wharf.'

'Do we have a name?'

Randy flattened the creased paper on the table. 'The senior inspector's name was a Doris Fairbanks.'

THIRTY

CARY, GERRY AND MURIEL

It had bugged her all day. A colleague had even commented on how distracted she had appeared at a meeting with a prospective new client the firm was courting. There was a high five-figure sum in audit and tax related fees in play. Cary had apologised and said she hoped her preoccupation with a personal matter had not impacted on her overall performance. She recognised the mealy mouthed support with its sexist innuendo from the audit partner for what it was and acknowledged to herself that if the firm did not get the business, they would lay the blame fair and square at her door. Still, it was her future happiness at stake. Work and career could take second place.

Alex had lied to her about his trip to visit his wife in Devon, failed to mention that she was still alive, if only in a vegetative state, and dismissed his mother's presence as the foible of a deranged old lady. Rose had come over to Cary as both lucid and sane with cogent criticisms of her son's behaviour Cary was not prepared to ignore. She would need to discuss these issues calmly and without distraction with him over the coming weekend, and there would be no question of her moving in until she was confident the man could be trusted.

The number she dialled rang out seven or eight times before the call was answered. 'Can't talk now,' a harassed voice exclaimed. 'My hands are covered in flour, and I have to keep kneading until the pizza dough absorbs the olive oil and the yeast. Tell me your name and I'll call back unless it's a spam call, in which case, forget it.'

'Gerry,' she said lamely. 'It's Cary. I need a favour. Call me back.'

'No problem, darling.' His voice was retreating from the phone. 'Eat your heart out, Domino's. This beauty I'm going to call "the genuine Gerry and Gloria real bollocks of a would-be meat feast only it's for vegans pizza."' She rang off, listening to him singing "Delilah" in the background.

It was gone five when Muriel had called to say the twins had cajoled her into making a detour via the children's playground. So, not to worry if nobody was in when Cary returned to the house. Muriel also said Gerry would be returning Cary's call within the next five minutes.

189

'You've talked to him?' Cary asked, recognising as she did the pointlessness of the question.

'Every day we have a little chat,' her mother said. 'He cheers me up and makes me feel as if my view of things is important.'

'What does Dad think of that?' Cary knew Len had little time for his half-brother.

'No idea. I never tell him. It's got nothing to do with him, anyway. I speak to whom I want. Gerry doesn't take me for granted.' Her tone changed to a soft pleading as she suggested to Creedence it would be nice to let her sister have a go on the swing.

'I'll leave you to it,' Cary said. She had just ended the call when the mobile vibrated in her hand.

'How was the pizza?' she asked.

'Beyond belief,' Gerry replied. 'I grated a little wacky baccy into the cheese before it went into the pizza oven, which Sebastian and his brother, Noah, have built alongside the barbecue. The smell and the taste were just to die for.' He gave an extended sigh. 'Now, what can I do for you, young lady?'

'I need you to meet the girls from school this Friday and look after them for the weekend. Is that possible?'

'Of course. The pleasure and privilege will be ours. There are adventures here just made to occupy the attention of your young maidens.'

'Including making pizzas without mystic substances, I hope?'

'I can assure you no artificial stimuli are required to condition the imagination of a six-year-old.'

'They will be so thrilled. They love the idea of coming to stay with Uncle Gerry.'

'And Aunt Gloria, don't forget. Without her, the world does not turn.'

'What a lovely thing to say. I wish Mum and Dad had your sort of relationship.'

'Are there problems?'

She hesitated. 'On all fronts, I'm afraid. By the time the weekend comes, I'll have been with Len and Muriel for over a week, and I need to give them a break from the kids. I think our presence is causing ructions and hostility between them. The idyllic notion of having their grandchildren around them quickly receded into the reality of noise, domestic chaos, boundless energy, and ceaseless demands for attention. It's very tiring for them.'

'Even so . . .'

'It's not just the kids, if you want the truth. Something's going on I don't understand. Mum seems very anti-Len at the moment and Dad's troubled by something which is centred around his animosity toward Dom's father. Do you have any idea?' For some inexplicable reason, she was suddenly afraid of what Gerry would say.

He had sidestepped the question. 'I assume if you're asking us to look after the girls, your plan must have stalled to move in with your new man once the arrangement with your parents became untenable?'

'Not really.' She brushed the comment aside. 'I need a weekend with Alex to sit down and discuss our future together without the distraction of his work and the demands of the twins. We simply need to put the rosy glow of infatuation, wine and roses behind us and focus on the practicalities of two people with past relationships being totally honest with each other.'

He chuckled. 'You think that's funny?' she said, plainly irritated.

'I suppose I do, to some extent,' he replied whimsically. 'Muriel said your approach to your personal life is very much conditioned to a structured, professional background and I can see what she means.'

'Mum said that? I can't believe it.'

'That's the crux of the reality Muriel is trying to deal with. Over the years, she has ceased to be a person in her own right with no opinions, viewpoints or personality traits that are exclusively hers. Intentionally or otherwise, Len has engineered a relationship, doubtless innocently aided and abetted by you, whereby she has become an adjunct to her husband's take on life, fit only to perform the domestic chores and act as an echo chamber for whatever wisdom he espouses.'

Cary gulped air into her mouth. Her voice shuddered. 'I've never seen her in that light. This change in her attitude is down to you?'

'We just talk. Whatever happens is of her making. Right now, with the need growing for her to be recognised as an individual with a personality of her own, the first reaction is one of resentment, the need to blame someone for reducing her to the status of an appendage. She turns her anger on Len and despises him for what he has made her.'

191

'You must hate your half-brother,' Cary said. 'You've set them against each other.'

'Far from it. I love Len and hate nobody.' Gerry's voice was firm and committed. 'As time passes, I am convinced Muriel will recognise that blaming Len for shaping her destiny is both unrealistic and unfair. As her self-belief and confidence increases, she will come to recognise it is she who allowed herself to be subjugated to Len's dominance. She will cease to apportion blame, draw a line under a past that cannot be changed and live for the future.'

'With or without Len?'

'That will primarily be down to Len. If he can adapt to living with somebody he cannot dominate and enjoy the challenge of sparking off his partner rather than damping the flame, there is hope.'

'So, what about me, Mr Amateur Psychiatrist? Where do I fit into this dysfunctional family?' There was a challenging edge to her voice.

'You're angry with me, I can tell.' He sounded genuinely upset. 'On all that's precious, I'm not trying to pontificate, patronise you or profess to having some special insight. I'm just trying to let you know how I see things so that you can make your own judgements. The Holy Grail is not something I have.'

'I'm sorry, Gerry. I know you care and want to help. To be truthful, I'm just a little uptight about the arrangement I'm walking into. I really am grateful you've agreed to look after the girls.'

'If you knew what pleasure it gives us to have the twins around us, you would realise it's Gloria and I who should say thanks.' Gerry hesitated, as if weighing up his next remark. 'At the risk of really pissing you off, let me say one thing lingering on the tip of my tongue,' he said eventually. 'The periods you describe as "the days of wine and roses" morphing into the practicalities of a serious relationship should not be mutually exclusive. The exhilaration experienced at the start of a love affair can be kept smouldering throughout the day-to-day predictability of living together. It's that shot of adrenalin you both need from time to time to realise just how precious your partnership is.'

'I suppose I know that,' she said. 'Perhaps it's the one thing I'm looking forward to in this relationship which wasn't there in the last. I just don't want there to be any secrets between us.'

'From my experience, a mutual baring of souls is not all it's cracked up to be. Sometimes, keeping secrets which might be misinterpreted or taken out of context is the kindest thing to do.' He giggled at a recollection. 'I've always found Gloria will tell me something new about her past whenever the time is right or circumstances demand. I never pry. I expect she has experiences hidden away about which I shall never know.'

'Aren't you curious?'

'I know enough to understand we love each other passionately. Why should I want to probe any further?'

Muriel had done a good job of tiring out the twins; half-an-hour charging around a playground, followed by a meal at a hamburger restaurant with a children's ball pool and climbing frame. By the time they reached the house, Syracuse was fast asleep and had to be carried to bed. Amidst a series of yawns, Creedence was determined to tell her mother all about the experiences of the last two hours.

'That's wonderful, darling,' Cary said, but the words were already lost on the child whose eyes were now closed, her breathing regular and steady. 'I'll put her to bed. Don't go away. I'll be back in a minute.'

Muriel was sitting at the kitchen island, nursing a glass of white wine when Cary returned.

'Did you put knock-out drops in their ice cream?' she said with a laugh, gently caressing her mother's back as she reached for a spare glass. 'Is Dad not joining us?'

Muriel rested her chin on the palm of her left hand. 'I told your father I hadn't cooked dinner today. I suggested he go to the local Indian or Chinese and get a takeaway for the three of us.'

'I get the feeling everything is not all right between you two. Is it down to having me and the kids around?'

'Good Lord, whatever gave you that idea? I'm thrilled you and the girls are staying with us. Compared to normal, there is so much energy in the house. I find it stimulating. As far as I'm concerned, you can stay forever.'

'Dad told you we'd be moving on soon? About Alex? He didn't seem very receptive.'

Muriel took her daughter's hand and kissed her fingers. 'Don't worry about him. You do what's right for you and don't pay any attention to his "musts" and "must nots". You should live your life.'

'I spoke with Gerry today. He's going to be looking after the twins this weekend. God only knows what they will get up to.'

Muriel's brow creased. 'I thought you were moving in with this Alex? That's what Len told me.'

'Change of plans. There are a few practicalities to sort out at his place. I'll be going over there on Saturday after I've dropped off the twins.'

'Does he know you're not moving in this weekend?'

'I phoned him earlier. He seemed quite surprised, but I told a white lie and said I wanted to decorate the girls' bedrooms with some toys and things from the house before we moved. I want them to feel at home and recognise their possessions, albeit in a fresh setting to the one they are used to.'

'And that was okay?'

'I don't know whether he believed me, but he seemed quite laid back about it and said the timing was up to me.'

'Is there a problem I should know about?'

'No. I know and love the man, but there are subjects mature couples should talk about before they make a commitment and I realised we hadn't got around to doing that yet. There's nothing alarming.'

She interrupted before Muriel could react. 'Gerry's very fond of you. I think he's worried about your state of mind.'

Muriel's face softened as the look of concern was replaced by a relaxed smile. 'I thank God for that man's intervention in my life. We talk every day, and he has taken me from a very dark place to a point where I can understand what has been forcing me down all these years to forego the person I really am and to become the two-dimensional, characterless individual into which my husband has moulded me.' She took another large swig from the glass she had clutched to her chest.

'You blame Dad?'

She held the glass out to Cary for a refill. 'I hold us both responsible: me for my weakness and inability to assert my will, Len, for the callous way he has sought to impose total control over every aspect of our lives together. He proceeds without ever consulting me, riding roughshod over any half-hearted suggestion or objection I may make as if I were a lowly constable under his command. Len always knows better, only now, I don't believe he does.'

Cary realised she had been staring with her mouth open at her mother. 'What do you intend to do?'

'What's the computer jargon your Dom used for drawing a line and starting again?' She smiled to herself. 'A reset! That's it. I'm going for a reset. I intend to put Len in a place where he understands he cannot take me for granted now or in the future. It's down to him how we move on from now and it's thanks to his brother I've slept soundly at night.'

THIRTY-ONE

MORGAN AND DARREN

It was in the car on their way to interview a witness in Southend when the significance of that ill-fated date with Sylvia whatever-her-name-was, suddenly came into focus.

Indiana was driving, but Morgan had stopped listening to his partner's constant commentary on some nugget of trivia he had dug up from the recesses of his mind.

'What did you just say?' Morgan asked out of the blue.

Constable Harris Ford glanced across, his expression one of undisguised surprise. Nobody ever asked him to repeat something he had uttered. They were more likely to tell him to put a sock in it or ask for the radio to be turned on or complain about a headache.

'Which bit?' he asked in his South London accent.

'The bit about the casino,' Morgan replied.

'I said if we take the other road through Billericay, we pass Dreamlands, a casino with a girlie show. Was that it?'

'What else did you say about it?'

'Fancy a gamble, do you? I like a flutter myself, mainly on the horses. Did I tell you when—?'

'Forget that. You were talking about "part of a group" or something.'

Indiana hesitated whilst he concentrated on overtaking a slower vehicle. 'I said there are five or six of these, what you might call adult clubs, spread around the outer suburbs. Billericay's the head office. What you used to get exclusively in Soho has now moved out to semi-rural locations, much like you see in Spain and elsewhere abroad.' He settled back as the Astra rejoined the traffic flow. 'They all have fictional place names, 'Wonderland', 'Lilliput', that sort of thing. The butcher who used to operate in Smithfield, Bateman; it's his son, Darren, who's the head honcho. You've probably heard the name. Old man Bateman used to sail quite close to the wind, but he was friendly with a few lads in the force and kept his nose clean.'

'I've heard all the stories,' Morgan confirmed. 'Meat, gravy and two veg, wasn't it?'

Indiana laughed. 'Len Sheppard and his cronies went for early retirement before the axe fell – saved embarrassment all round.'

Morgan sat back in his seat as Indiana droned on about his gambling experiences. His mind was elsewhere. It was blatantly obvious why Sylvia had engineered the date. What she really wanted was information on Sheppard and his connection to the Bateman family. He had talked a lot, showing off, trying to impress her by exaggerating his importance in CID with his knowledge of the goings-on within the department. She had been clever. Every time he changed the subject, she would channel the conversation back, and he fell for it, hook, line and sinker, spouting facts he had just made up on the spur of the moment.

Cow! She had really played him and just when it was about to get interesting, that muscle-bound Aussie had interfered and taken him by surprise. Revenge would be his, but first, he needed to straighten things out with Bateman. He couldn't risk being exposed for shouting his mouth off about some of the stories he had embellished around the alleged Bateman connection to officers in the City of London force.

The interview with the witness in Southend had been purposely scheduled by Indiana for two thirty to allow sufficient time for a three-course meal on expenses beforehand. Morgan refused the offer of a treacle pudding dessert, leaving his partner to order while he slipped outside to make a phone call.

Darren Bateman was expected at Billericay that afternoon, but according to his secretary, his day didn't start until four in the afternoon. She made a note for a provisional appointment at four thirty. Morgan Priest was an officer with the City of London force who had certain information which he considered Mr Bateman should be aware. Had she understood correctly? Morgan finished the call and returned to the stomach-curdling sight of Indiana starting on a double portion of treacle pudding with two scoops of vanilla ice cream and sugar sprinkles.

There was a change of plans, Morgan announced to his partner. As the regulations required, the witness in the sexual harassment case against the City trader with wandering hands would be interviewed in their presence. By the time it came to the written statement for the witness to sign, Indiana was to handle the transcript whilst Morgan went missing on a personal matter for the hour or so it would take to draft and complete the document.

As it was, Morgan's absence was hardly noticed by his colleague. Indiana's attention span oscillated between the beguiling figure of the witness and the plate of cakes she had laid on the coffee table for them. Homemade, she had said. Living on her own was lonely, and she needed something to occupy her hands.

Darren Bateman was younger than Morgan had envisaged. With swept-back, lacquered, jet-black hair, polished face, manicured nails and dressed in a tailored three-piece suit, the man looked like the archetypal mafia boss. Swop him for Al Pacino, he thought, and the transition would have been seamless.

'I couldn't resist the element of suspense in my secretary's explanation for your visit. How can I help you?' He moved from behind a leather-surfaced partner's desk, his black, patent-leather shoes seemingly polished by the thick-pile carpet as he ushered his guest toward a velour corner sofa unit. The cushions swamped Morgan as he sat, lower to the ground than he had expected. Bateman pulled over a dining chair and sat astride it, the back facing his guest, his arms folded over the top.

'Can we get you anything?' he said, looking down at the policeman.

Morgan shook his head. 'I can't stay long. I'm with my partner on a case in Southend,' he volunteered.

'Fascinating, I'm sure, but not the reason you are here.'

Morgan shook his head again, this time vigorously. There was no reason he should feel this vulnerable, but he did. 'I had a date this week with a woman from our forensic unit. I'm with the City of London force and she started talking about how she was trying to piece together some information about Len Sheppard, who used to be one of our DIs before he retired.'

'What sort of information was she after?'

'Specifically, she said she was interested in the tie-up between this Sheppard and a Mr Bateman who operated around Smithfield. She's got some Australian guy handling the investigation for her. I don't know whether he's a pro or just a friend, but he seemed to have assembled a fair amount of financial information and the Bateman name came up on two or three occasions.'

Darren rocked the chair back and forth. 'And what were you able to add to this information gathering exercise?'

'Nothing. I'm new on the scene. These people are just names to me. Anyway, when I cottoned on she'd come on the date just to pump me for information I didn't have, I blew her out. I told her not to waste my time.' He stopped to register Darren's reaction, but the man's bland expression gave nothing away.

'I wouldn't have thought anymore about it,' Morgan emphasised, 'but as we were literally passing your door today, I thought you might find the information worthwhile.'

'That's very thoughtful of you, Mr Priest. What was the name of your date?'

'Sylvia.'

'Sylvia?' Darren raised his eyebrows in expectation.

'Her last name escapes me. I know her dad used to sell second-hand motors. She told me a few funny stories about his antics.'

'Did she?' He rose from the chair and extended his hand. 'You must come and visit the club one evening. Dinner and the show are on me. Leave your details with Julia, my secretary, and she'll be in touch.'

'That's very thoughtful of you, Mr Bateman.'

'It's Darren. My dad is Mr Bateman. If you hear our family name mentioned in any context at your station, let me know. These rumours can be quite hurtful and sometimes result in serious harm, if you get my drift.'

Morgan let out a serious breath as he walked to his car. If the shit hit the fan now, he was in the clear. He had assured Darren he had said nothing out of turn whilst lining the Aussie up for a rough ride.

Now, what was Indiana up to? He'd wager a fiver there were no more cakes left on the plate when he got back.

Darren came off the phone to his father. The news had got the old man quite worked up. 'It doesn't matter whether anybody knows the truth. Once a rumour circulates, you're guilty by association. Any bad press and I'm screwed. I'll speak to Len. We must put a stop to this nosey cow and her sodding father. Work on something and find out what you can about this Aussie private investigator. Make a plan.'

200

He already had. Darren's idea would leave this Charlie Greaves well and truly compromised. He wouldn't be mentioning the Bateman name now or in the future.

Give it a few months and it might also be desirable to permanently retire that arrogant ex-copper, Sheppard.

THIRTY-TWO

CHARLIE AND DORIS

She was half-an-hour late. Perhaps she wouldn't come. Maybe she had second thoughts. He desperately hoped so. Since he retired, there were few excuses he could offer for an evening away from Norma. His friends were also her friends and there was not one male acquaintance on whom he could count to support the subterfuge. In the end, Charlie had opted to explain to Norma in sombre tone how he needed to provide moral support to his ex-partner during a difficult financial period. He was taking Ludo to dinner, an opportunity to discuss all the options on how to keep the business afloat.

Norma had looked at him askance. Since when had he become the Good Samaritan? His speciality was not only walking on the other side of the road but making sure nobody saw him by hiding in the shadows. He accused her of being unfair, insisting he owed Ludo his support and consideration. Ludo had been primed. Something had come out of the woodwork about Stan Forbes. He would keep Ludo posted. If Norma contacted him, Charlie named a restaurant they both knew and agreed on their fictitious menu selections.

'Is whether I had a salad with the steak not taking it a bit too far?' Ludo had queried.

'Believe me,' Charlie had replied. 'If Norma's suspicious, she'll go into minute detail. Once she gets the scent of dog shit, especially my particular aroma . . .'

The sight of Doris walking toward their table stilled his train of thought and stirred another emotion in him. She had certainly gone out of her way to impress. She was heavily made-up, her hair subtlety highlighted with a blond tint, cascaded in waves down to her shoulders. Charlie mused how the casual look must have taken her hairdresser hours to perfect. Above all, the low neck, contour-hugging blue dress accentuated her voluptuous figure and rekindled in him the impression of a sixties Hollywood glamour puss he had always found irresistible.

With a dozen eyes following her entrance, she bent to kiss Charlie on the cheek, leaving a perfect impression of pouting lips in a deep cherry lipstick on his cheek.

'You're late,' he said. 'I was just about to leave.'

She leaned over to whisper in his ear, her ample breast pressing firmly against his arm. 'You'd stand up a girl who spent a little extra time just trying to look her best for you? Charlie, you haven't forgotten how to treat a lady?'

'Sit down, will you?' he hissed. 'You're making a spectacle of yourself.'

'You've put on some weight, Charlie.' She slid into the chair opposite him. 'Not getting enough exercise of the right sort, I shouldn't imagine.'

'Do you mind telling me why we're here? I thought we had an understanding. For God's sake, it's been how many years? Twelve?'

She tut-tutted with a sarcastic smile on her face. 'Still impetuous as ever, I see. I thought you'd learned how to savour the moment, suppress the urge to explode at the first opportunity. Let's have a drink, choose something to eat and then we can talk about what has brought us together again after all these years. Don't you agree?'

By the time they were finishing their main course, starting on a second bottle of wine and nursing the dessert menus, the mood had changed. From the moment the first slice of fillet steak passed his lips and her bare foot rested on his chair, her toes playing around his crotch, any semblance of propriety evaporated as the meat juices seeped from the corners of his mouth. He felt exactly as he had done all those years ago, scared of where the evening was leading, yet unable to resist the physical desire to possess her. It was like a drug, and he wanted an overdose.

He reached for her hand, the skin still soft, the nails manicured and polished. He reached for her index finger and placed it into his mouth, moving it forward and backward as he played his tongue around, leaving it to her imagination to fill in the blanks.

In a swift movement, she pulled her finger from his mouth, releasing his hand to slump onto the table. She wagged the very same finger at his face. 'You're not getting away with a little erogenous activity, Charlie. I'm here to make a deal with you.'

He looked down. Her bare foot had also retreated and was fishing under the table for the shoe she had discarded.

'What are you talking about?' His adrenalin rush had passed. He felt the dampness. He must have leaked into his boxers. 'What deal?' He took a mouthful of wine. What had seemed mellow and smooth was now tart and acidic. It burned in his throat.

'You remember how we first met?'

'Of course.'

'I was carrying out a VAT inspection of your records. It was hampered by two things. First, your bookkeeper who could have assisted me was absent on holiday in Spain, regrettably a holiday from which he never returned. Second, you seduced me into the start of an affair which ran its course until you developed pangs of conscience and told your wife. During those early days of seduction, I must admit I saw everything around you with rose-coloured glasses and, just maybe, my investigative zeal was not as sharp as it should have been.'

'Where you going with this, Doris?'

'A few days ago, I received an anonymous package at work with a flash drive in it. Until now, nobody else is aware of the contents of the drive, but they are damning and set out in miniscule detail the scheme you used . . .' Her voice was reduced to a whisper. '. . . to defraud the Revenue out of one hundred and twenty-eight thousand pounds. The drive was prepared by your Mr Forbes on the unfortunate premise that he might suffer some fatal accident which, lo-and-behold, came to pass.'

Charlie's teeth were on the point of chattering, but he clamped his top and bottom jaws together.

'You're silent, Charlie,' she went on. 'Would you like me to give you the ins and outs of how you did it: the dummy companies, applying the profit margin basis to a transaction in one company and the full sale value in another? It's all explained in meticulous detail. The complete package is bound to lead the authorities to the conclusion that fraud on a grand scale was perpetrated and the perpetrator also somehow silenced the whistle blower before he could whistle.'

His first thought was to deny vehemently the accusations, but his mind was much more set on settling scores with whoever had opened this can of worms rather than protest his innocence. Besides, she had come to do a deal. Had she wanted to grass him up, she would have done it already. 'You don't know who sent you the drive? No idea at all?'

She shook her head. 'Not a clue. I spoke with Stan's brother, Roddie, is it?'

'Yes. I know him. He's got an anger management problem and a real grudge against me.'

'I got that impression. He said his mother had a visitor on the day she died, a rare occurrence – not her death, that's a one-off event – the fact she had a visitor. If he or she came with a flash drive or if the mother was storing a flash drive prior to this secret visitor's arrival, it wasn't there once he or she left. Whoever it was, they appear to have returned a Russian doll set that once belonged to Stan. Maybe she did a swop.'

'Sounds like the visitor was my ex-partner. The doll set used to be in the office. He wouldn't have consciously passed on a flash drive without checking the contents.' He checked his watch. 'Give me a minute.'

He walked over to the bar area to make a call, returning to find her tapping a fork on the meringue shell of a Baked Alaska. 'I didn't order you anything,' she said with a smile. 'You can have a mouthful of mine.' She waved a spoon at him.

Charlie shook his head. 'Ludo never made it past the front door. In fact, he left a box of odds and sods on the step and beat it before Roddie had the chance to appear. There was definitely no flash drive, nor did he see or talk with the mother.'

'You seem much more interested in its provenance than the impact of the content on your future. For what you did, you could be banged up for five years.'

Charlie allowed himself a private laugh that made his chest heave momentarily. 'You mentioned a deal. I presume your part would be to guarantee these new allegations never surface. My concern is what you want me to offer in return. If it's money, I warn you, Doris, I'm not a wealthy man.'

'How cheapskate of you, Charlie. This isn't a shakedown.'

'What is it then?'

She looked up at the ceiling. 'I never stopped loving you, Charlie. Do you know that?'

Alongside the mildly quizzical look on his face, his entire demeanour had changed to assume a confidence that had not been there before. 'I could have guessed,' he said.

There was an eruption of laughter. 'Bollocks!' she said. 'I never loved you one iota. Just kidding. Like most men, you're an arrogant arsehole, but the one thing you were was a great shag who knew all the moves before, during, and after. You can't put a price on that.'

The quizzical look intensified. 'So? I *asked* where are you going with this?'

She spooned in the last mouthful of meringue and casually licked her lips. 'For the last year or so, life has been a little barren, bereft of a man to satisfy an appetite which, if anything, has intensified. Most men of my age are out of commission. The younger guys sometimes fancy their chances but are too concerned about messing up their hairstyle on the pillow or don't have a clue what they're doing.' There was a moment's reflection. 'Some men see me as too strident and demanding, to the point where they are actually frightened to take the plunge. For God's sake, I don't want to possess their minds, I just want to fuck, savour the experience and go home alone. Is that too much to ask?'

'Always suited me,' he admitted.

'Until you developed a guilty conscience.'

'All good things come to an end.' As the tired cliché left his lips, the realisation dawned.

'That's where you're wrong, Mr Greaves. The deal is: two sessions next week, not consecutive, one session the following week and then, every week for the next three months or such shorter time as I decide. It depends how soon I get fed up with you.'

'You're joking? What you want is for me to service you in exchange for destroying the evidence?'

'Crudely put, but succinct. Corrupting a flash drive so that the content is unrecoverable relies on heat and steam, I am told. When your compliance is no longer required, the drive will be rendered unreadable.'

'How do you know there's not a copy? Whoever sent it to you was bound to have made one.'

She smiled. 'Possible, I agree, but unlikely. Your Stanley Forbes, bracket, deceased, bracket was a smart cookie. There was a note sent with the drive which detailed to whom it should be forwarded in the event it was discovered, namely, to me, and signed off with best wishes and regards from my uncle, Raika.' She made a gesture to the waitress, requesting the bill. 'Don't worry,' she said. 'It's for you to pay. I need to get out of here. Come back to my place for a coffee. It's close by.'

As they strolled along the road, her arm through his, he prompted her to finish the explanation.

'Stanley had encrypted the content on the drive, which was password protected. He'd obviously done his ancestral research on my family and its Hungarian origins. My uncle Raika led his younger brother, who became my father, and a sister to England just as the war was about to intensify. It was Raika who changed the family name from Ference to Fairbanks, probably because he was a movie fan, and the names had some similarities. Understanding that, I knew the password. I doubt anyone else would have readily reached the same conclusion.'

The coffee was from a capsule machine and tasted potent. He drained the last drop as she reappeared from the bedroom and slumped down onto the sofa next to him. He could make out the contours of her breast through the satin housecoat and the white of her thighs when it parted as she sat. 'So, are you on board with my deal?' she asked.

Charlie shook his head. 'It did occur to me, Doris, and correct me if I'm wrong, but it wouldn't sit too well with your superiors if it turned out one of your investigations failed to reveal a major discrepancy and a VAT shortfall running into six figures – allegedly,' he added at the end.

She wheeled around, revealing even more of her thighs and midriff. 'Nice try, Charlie, but no deal, I'm afraid. You see, I never signed off on your inspection. I've left it pending all these years – how did I phrase it? – subject to additional clarification required from the records maintained by an employee, now deceased. As I remember it, I also put something down about seeking the assistance of the Spanish authorities, blah, blah, via Europol or some such nonsense. The paper trail still sits in my filing cabinet. The only thing I would be likely to receive should the information on the flash drive be presented is a commendation for my doggedness in pursuing the investigation to a satisfactory conclusion. Talking about dogging, Charlie, do you remember that weekend in Ilfracombe?'

Her breasts had now slipped free of the housecoat and sat full and firm, the nipples as black as coal and mesmerising him as if they were the eyes of a two-headed hydra. He forced himself to look away, swallowing hard. 'Don't play on the past, please. Things have changed.' He studied the floor.

'Not really, Charlie. You used me back then to try and influence the conduct of the investigation. Don't think I wasn't aware of it. I knew exactly what you were doing. The first time I saw you stripped naked and appraised your tackle, I thought "Shit, I've made a mistake in landing this fish". My concern was happily misplaced. Not only did you know all the right moves, but when it came to the nitty-gritty what you lacked in front you made up for with that pile-driving arse of yours.'

'I don't know whether that's a compliment or I've just been insulted.'

'Don't act the innocent. Somewhere along the line, somebody taught you the real meaning of ambidextrous. I'm not too proud to admit it, but there have been a few occasions when I've been on top of someone and had to close my eyes and imagine it was you in order to finish. Sad, isn't it?'

'If you say so.'

'Now, the boot is on the other foot. I'm the one calling the shots for the next three months. I can tell by the way you've been looking at me all evening you're hot to trot, so say yes and we can enjoy ourselves just the way we used to.'

'You make it sound like being bribed to change electric suppliers with a short-term offer you can't refuse. I may have lacked moral fibre in the past, but your conscience gradually catches up with you.'

Doris moved closer to him and placed a hand on his thigh, running her nails back and forth along his trouser leg. 'I think your biggest worry is about your wife finding out. I don't see morality as a major issue.' She sensed the tension in his crotch.

'Back in the day,' he said, stilling her hand by placing his over hers. 'I had a busy life, meeting people all over the country, travelling abroad, buying and selling cars at all hours of the day. Finding time to be with you was easy. It's all changed now I'm retired. I have very little reason to be apart for very long. Ninety-nine per cent of the time, I do things accompanied by the wife. Finding excuses to spend time with you will be nigh impossible.'

She released his grip and moved her head closer to his cheek. Her fingers adeptly undid his tie and the top two buttons of his shirt. She traced the line in his skin where the ends of the collar had strained to meet. 'Still wearing shirts a size too small,' she said, her hand snaking inside his vest to squeeze his nipple. 'It makes you look like the Michelin Man.'

'Thanks for the compliment,' he said, his voice rasping. 'What do you think you're up to?'

She nibbled his earlobe. 'I can help you,' she whispered, her tongue flicking about the auricle. 'I can be flexible with the day and time. There's always an excuse to be out of the office. Give yourself an excuse for four hours to fulfil your duty call. That's all I'm asking. How did you get away tonight?'

'I said I was meeting my ex-partner for dinner?' He could feel the surge of adrenalin run through his body as she directed him to lie flat on the sofa.

The housecoat slipped off her naked body. 'There you are then,' she said. 'You can say he kept you talking until all hours, and we can have a little tester, a trailer for the next few months.' A hand tugged at his belt, and he felt it move inside his waistband.

'Kiss me,' she said, her mouth open, lips moist as they met his. She felt him straining to kick off his trousers. 'That's my Charlie,' she gasped with anticipation as he moved toward her.

It was close to midnight as Charlie began the drive back across London toward the suburbs.

So as not to embarrass her partner of the moment, she had reminded him, she never used perfume or cologne when seeing a married man. The lipstick on his shirt collar had easily washed off. Even so, the scent of naked animal lust in his nostrils, the demands of violent and conflicting emotions that possessed him - surely Norma would sense he had been with another woman. He had to banish the past few hours from consuming his thoughts, concentrate on how a casual evening with Ludo would have evolved, the topics discussed, a story or two about the industry and the travails of their fellow traders.

His thoughts turned to the appearance of the flash drive in the hands of Doris after all this time. Thinking it through, the likely course of events centred around Stanley's sister, Holly. He must have entrusted the drive to her before he left on holiday for Spain, probably saying it contained financial information about the business and that he'd pick it up on his return. Her brother wouldn't have wanted to alarm her with instructions to deliver it to Doris if something happened to him whilst abroad. He would be content she would read the accompanying note and comply with his wishes in the event of his death.

Either the existence of the drive slipped her mind or, more likely, she preferred not to chance causing any more distress to their mother whilst she remained alive. Whatever was on the drive, and Holly had no way of knowing, the thought that the authorities would start raking over the past would be the death of her mother. She was too frail to withstand any more surprises surrounding Stanley's death, and Holly could guarantee Roddie would lose the plot and start making wild accusations. Subsequently, the sequence of events following the mother's passing probably involved Cary prying on Len's behalf into Stanley's working relationship with Charlie and, lo-and-behold, up pops the flash drive which that snivelling creep, Len, sends on to Doris.

Satisfied he has solved the mystery and laid the blame fairly and squarely at the door of his adversary, Charlie stilled himself for the conversation he was about to have with Norma.

There were butterflies in his stomach as he turned the corner into the cul-de-sac.

The downstairs lights in the house were blazing and two police cars were parked alongside the drive.

THIRTY-THREE

RODDIE, LUDO AND AN ALBANIAN

Roddie Forbes hadn't been seeing things too clearly since his mum passed away. First, there had been that arrogant little prick of a policeman who talked to him as if he was a sodding retard. All right, he might not be the shiniest tool in the box, but don't underestimate him. He would have been man enough to have skewered the copper to the door and disembowelled him onto the kitchen floor. Of course, he didn't. Through the fog of words coming out of the man's mouth, Roddie pictured the scene as the man, still alive, watched the guts slide out of his torso and plop onto the tiles. Mum would have complained about having to clear up the mess, but she wasn't around no more, so he would have had to have done it.

The bloke was talking slowly about the possibility of an autopsy; something about standard procedure in certain circumstances. All Roddie could do was smile at the image in his head and say, 'Okay, mate.'

Then, there were more people. Once the ambulance men had left and the doctor at the hospital had said how sorry he was - although Roddie knew he really didn't give a shit - along came social services like the proverbial bad penny, as his mother would have said. The mousey woman with the thin-rimmed spectacles fussed about, talked of his next appointment with the anger management counsellor, how he needed the stimulus of other people and the possibility of moving into an environment where he would be amongst friends. For a laugh, he asked her what she thought about casual sex with a comparative stranger. She left quickly after that when he said she could stuff her friendly environment. There was no way he was going into some loony bin.

Holly phoned most days. She said she would make all the funeral arrangements, but Roddie had to do something for her. As far as she knew, the Bank hadn't been advised their mum had died, so he should take her bank card and draw out two hundred pounds each day for three days which he must take to the undertaker as a deposit for the funeral costs. Did he understand? Of course he did. What did she take him for? Stupid or something?

At the first attempt, the cash machine swallowed the card and told him to contact his bank. Holly was really pissed. She complained about not having a spare six hundred to pay the man. Roddie told her not to worry. He'd take it from the secret place under the stairs. Mum didn't think he knew about the place where she kept around two grand because she didn't trust the bank. Holly had brightened up and said what was he like. Cool and sexy, he told her.

Holly was coming up from Devon for the funeral, but she had advised Roddie she wouldn't be staying at the house. She didn't fancy walking into all those bad memories, the outcast daughter who could never live up to good old Stanley. Her friend had agreed to put her up for a few days while she finalised the funeral details and dealt with the formality of dealing with their mother's estate, which, as far as Roddie knew, comprised just the house and her personal possessions.

He brushed the seat cushion of mum's armchair, the one she had always sat in. With the wave of a ceremonial hand, he invited himself to take her place. He wriggled his bottom into the cushion and relished the silence. For once there was nobody to disturb his thoughts, no more gibberish to dissect and analyse, no more fancy talkers trying to melt his brain, no shadows hanging over him.

He remembered the last time his mother had spoken with him. It was not so unusual for her to call his mobile. It was unusual for him to take the call. Normally, she could never remember his number, which suited him just fine. Whenever they spoke, it was to reprimand him or to nag or to ask him to do some shopping on his way home. Didn't she realise he had a busy life? Then, some interfering busybody down at the Co-op had suggested she put his number on speed dial. From then on, he had to keep making excuses for not answering. However, on this last occasion, he had answered. His immediate reaction was to tell her he couldn't talk because the big race was about to start, but she started to talk over him. Didn't she understand? A bloke in the pub had given him the name of a horse certain to canter home. The bloody nag had cantered home all right, long after the rest.

She had sounded excited. The Irishman had left a box outside the front door. It was all to do with Stan, and she'd sent the stick thing to the lady just as he'd asked. Half listening and concentrating on the TV screen in the betting shop as they lined up, he had asked her nicely what she was getting so excited about. He hadn't thought anymore about it except to blame her for the horse losing and deciding she would have to reimburse him for the stake money. When it came to horse racing, she was bad luck.

Thinking about it, the only Irishman it could have been was one of the blokes Stan had worked for. His little box of tricks had got her all worked up and must have caused her to have a heart attack. Trust the Irishman and Greaves to be responsible for the death of another Forbes. He would have to go straight over and tell the guy to butt out of his family before there were any more unfortunate fatalities. Do it now, a voice told him. He would, but first he needed to pop into the betting shop on the way over to Peckham. There was an evening meeting at Wolverhampton. He would take the money she owed him from the stash plus a little extra for his trouble. Even if the Irishman had gone home, it wouldn't matter; he would get onto the lot and key a few cars.

* * *

Ludo came off the call from Charlie mildly irritated and wondering what in the name of Dickens was going on. Whatever Charlie might think, this was the first he'd heard of any flash drive. He had sworn on the lives of his unborn children there was nothing like that in the box of odds and sods he'd left outside the Forbes's house.

Judging by the ambient background noise, Charlie had called from a bar or restaurant. Ludo prayed he hadn't been lied to. Charlie had promised he wasn't involving his ex-partner in a subterfuge to cover up an affair. The meeting he wanted to keep secret from Norma related to a business issue he would tell Ludo all about the next time they met.

As a man who manipulated the teachings of Catholicism to suit his convenience and having never been married, Ludo was more than willing to express his disapproval of extra-marital affairs. It was to his credit, he acknowledged, that when Charlie had strayed once before into the arms of that busty bird who had come to check the books, it was he, Ludo, who had stood up for Norma. When the truth came out, he had been the one to offer her his support.

215

Unsurprisingly, he was prepared to admit to himself if his office assistant, Mandy, ever gave him the come-on and was prepared to go behind her bus driver husband's back, he might be willing to acknowledge the codicil of exceptions the Good Lord must have intended when he drafted the ninth Commandment.

Ludo walked out onto the lot. Time to lock the front gate. With the image of a barely clad Mandy uppermost in his mind, he nearly missed the sound of someone scaling the fence from the neighbouring property. As he went to turn, a figure careered toward him out of the darkness, arms outstretched, breathing noisily in loud grunts, exhaling in bursts through his nose. Ludo found himself propelled roughly toward the ground, landing hard on his left shoulder. He yelped as he hit the gravel surface. The sharp pain told him the joint had dislocated on impact.

Ludo was a man of slight build, slender, but wiry with an upper body flexibility derived from a lifetime spent working from above and below the mechanical structure of motor vehicles of all makes, old and new. He would often have to use his agility and deft touch to gain access to a part confined within the engine compartment that would otherwise involve the time-consuming process of dismantling various components.

As the assailant hovered over him, Ludo wriggled on his back toward the showroom until he stopped within the diffused glow of one of the arc lights trained on a row of cars. The assailant followed, his legs moving slowly, crablike astride Ludo's body, but making no attempt to inflict further damage.

Ludo's good arm shot upwards, his hand bunching the neck of a tee-shirt and pulling the assailant's face toward him.

'There's a hundred pounds in the petty cash box,' he said, his voice strained with the effort of holding the man close. 'That's all; no more money on site. Take it and piss off.'

The man's saliva dribbled onto Ludo's face. He pushed him away. 'Haven't I seen you before?' Ludo asked.

'You screwed us over,' the assailant said. 'I'll make you pay for what you did.' He spat on the ground.

Ludo looked up at the quivering lips, the staring eyes full of hate. 'I don't know what you're talking about. Who are . . .?' His voice trailed off. The realisation had just dawned on him. 'Roddie. You're Roddie Forbes,

216

Stanley's brother. I had nothing to do with his death. You've broken my sodding shoulder.' He wriggled further along the ground toward the entrance of the showroom.

Roddie stood still, following the movement with his eyes. 'You're a liar,' he said. 'Mum always said you were hiding the truth and responsible for what happened. Now, she's gone, and it's your fault. You must suffer.' He began edging toward the prostrate figure.

If Ludo had neither the skill nor the will to react physically to his attacker, the one quality which he possessed was the ability to talk, to calm a verbal assault with his soft Irish lilt, conveying reason and serenity in the face of anger and threat. 'Roddie, of course, you deserve a full explanation, and you shall get one. I have never harmed another living soul, I promise. Help me to the office. We'll share a dram of the good stuff and talk this through. I didn't know your mum had passed away. My heartfelt sympathy. I know what it's like to lose a loved one.' Under his breath, he cursed Charlie Greaves.

Roddie helped him roughly to his feet, ignoring the protestations and gasps of pain as Ludo tried to protect his shoulder. With his feet barely touching the ground, Ludo was manhandled across the showroom into the office and deposited into the chair alongside the desk. Roddie bent over double and breathed deeply with the effort. 'For a slim guy, you weigh a bloody ton. Is it your wallet weighing you down?'

Ludo ignored the comment, squeezing his eyes tight as a wave of nausea swept over him. 'I need to get to a hospital,' he said.

'No way,' Roddie said. 'I wanna hear what you got to say for yourself.' He studied Ludo's expression. 'And come off it. I only ran into you. You're like what my mum says about those footballers who get hit by a feather, fall and roll over as if they've been struck by a steamroller. Prima Donna, she calls them.' He took a step forward and poked Ludo in the chest. 'Don't think you can pull one over on me. You ain't leaving here until you tell me what I need to know.' He flexed his shoulders. 'First off, what did you have in that box you left got my mum so worked up, she pegged it?

'Do you know what coincidence means, Roddie?' Ludo pulled out a Jamieson bottle from the desk drawer with his good hand and motioned for the other man to unscrew the cap before taking a long swig. He offered the bottle to Roddie, who waved it away.

'You taking the piss?' Roddie spat out the words.

'Calm down. All I'm saying is I left a box with some of Stanley's personal items on the doorstep. Nothing special, just mementoes. Sometime later, your dear mother, who had a weak heart, passed away. Two occurrences, both unconnected. That's coincidence.'

'Bollocks. You're fucking with me.' He moved closer to Ludo, his fist raised. 'Then why did she sound so excited on the blower? She said the information on it would nail the bastards.'

'I don't know, do I? What is the "it" the information is on?'

'You can't expect me to know. I was paying attention to the race, not listening to her rabbit on about Stan again. There were days she'd never stop going on about him. He didn't stop being her favourite just because he'd died. I'd look at her sometimes and wish I could put a gag in her mouth.' He stopped, realising he'd gone off the point. 'Anyway, there was something in that box of tricks that got her going and you must have known what the effect would be on her.' He grabbed Ludo by the collar of his shirt. 'So, spill the beans before I rearrange your teeth.' He held his fist against Ludo's cheek.

The Irishman shook his head, wincing as the pull on his shirt caused his shoulder to move. 'I swear on the life of my unborn children, I have no idea what could have been in the box to excite your mother. Everything looked totally harmless to me, bits and pieces from his desk, do y'see. I promise, had there been anything unusual, I would have called you first.'

'You're a lying Mick. You don't even have my number.' He pulled the shirt tighter toward him, causing Ludo to scream in pain. 'Tell me what happened to Stan in Spain; how you killed him?' He thrust Ludo back in the chair. 'No lies. I want you to tell me so Mum can rest in peace.' His eyes filled. 'Don't look at me!' he shouted and slapped Ludo firmly across the cheek.

Ludo closed his eyes as he felt the dribble of blood at the corner of his mouth. He knew he had to match force with force and the only way he could do it was verbally. 'Now listen, you. I'll say this one last time and you can choose to believe it or go to Hell.' His voice was rasping. He moved his good hand to wipe the blood from his chin. 'Your brother worked here as a bookkeeper in this office. I was a mechanic working in the yard. We had very little to do with each other beyond sharing the occasional cuppa. He seemed like a friendly guy who was clued into what he was doing. Who worked with him, arranged the flight and holiday, sorted out a place to stay in Spain, paid him his holiday money – that was all down to Charlie Greaves. I had nothing to do with it. If Charlie was somehow involved in Stan's death, which I don't believe he was, only Charlie knows. He has never shared anything with me about the chain of events and I can tell you precisely nothing. So, take your taxi fare . . .' He took the petty cash box from a drawer and slid it across the desk . . . 'and bugger off, so I can call an ambulance and get to the hospital. The pain is killing me.'

Roddie studied the box but made no move toward it. 'Mum said you and this Charlie were as thick as thieves and you must have been in it together.'

'Have you listened to a word I've been saying?' Ludo shouted. 'For Christ's sake, I've got no answers for you. Go see Charlie if you don't believe me.' A jagged pain in his back forced him to lurch violently to one side and howl like a banshee.

Roddie interpreted the sudden movement as the prelude to an attack. He launched himself across the desk with the palm of his hands colliding into Ludo's chest, the force of impact causing the executive chair to fall backwards and toppling the man onto the floor. His head collided with the radiator. Ludo laid still, blood trickling from around his right ear to seep into the fibre of the carpet.

'Jesus, man,' Roddie said. 'Now look what you've sodding done!' He had seen countless films where you put your index finger on the victim's neck to feel for a pulse. 'Jesus, man,' he repeated, nervously removing his hand and wiping the droplets of blood onto his trouser leg. 'The idiot's gone and died on me.'

He reached for the petty cash box and turned the key in the lock. 'You did say take a taxi, after all.' He stuffed all the notes into his pocket and made for the exit, stopping only to turn off the internal lights and close the showroom door. He scaled the fence to the adjoining property and turned into the roadway alongside the retail park. Another hundred yards and he would just be another one of the night-time revellers frequenting the pubs and restaurants along the High Road. He checked his watch. It wasn't even ten o'clock. Time for a beer before he moved on.

As he stood at the bar nursing a pint of lager, he thought about the last hour. He was sorry the Irishman was dead. Mum had said he wasn't the prime culprit, but he must have known what was going on, and that made him guilty. Well, now the Irishman had paid his debt. Mum would be pleased, not only because the man had snuffed it, but nobody knew he, Roddie Forbes, had been anywhere near the place, nor had any reason to have been there. He was in the clear. Even if someone had spotted him, it was an accident, and there wasn't anyone who could say otherwise. Just they dare.

He drained his glass. Time to find out where this Charlie Greaves was hanging out and give him a taste of the same medicine. He was in the mood to slap somebody else around.

The well-built man stood in the shadows, careful to avoid being caught on CCTV. Most of the cameras in the immediate area were directed toward the perimeter of the retail complex and the roads leading to and from the entrance and exit to the parking area. Coverage was sparse along the road leading to the adjoining estate of hybrid retail/semi-industrial units where the used car sales business was situated. By his calculation, if he kept to the left, tight to the fence and in the shadow cast by the hedgerow, he could avoid featuring on the peripheral of one or other of the two cameras at either end of the road.

It wasn't a precaution the other man had taken, Saban mused. He had watched as the man climbed the fence from the neighbouring property and dislodged the wing mirror on a Ford Mondeo as he landed. Muscular, but an incompetent amateur, was Saban's assessment as he followed the assailant's charge into the Irishman that knocked him to the ground.

Saban Sula was not there to interfere. His boss had told him to deliver a default letter to the Irishman, get the copy signed to acknowledge a breach of the loan agreement had occurred and had been rectified. He was used to delivering these letters, waiting for the recipient's reaction, normally one that did not recognise the true significance of the content. It sounded innocuous enough, a statement of fact; the repayment date had been missed but remedied by subsequent settlement. However, if the breach occurred a second time and Saban appeared with another letter, what the punters rarely understood, because they had failed to read the small print, was a raising of the interest rate or, worse still, the lender's right to trigger repayment of the total loan. So far, not a single punter had avoided the inevitable.

With Abdyl and Saban assisting in the enforcement process, once the legal niceties had been completed, their clever boss had taken over some plum businesses, worked some of his organisational magic and sold them on at a healthy profit. With bonuses, Saban had secured the future for his wife and three children in Tirana for the next ten years at least. Make that twenty years if his boss got his hands on this Irishman's business.

As he tried the metal gate and found it pushed open, a smirk crossed his face. Stupid assailant. The fool had scaled a fence when he could have walked right through the front door.

Beyond the beam of an arc light highlighting today's star buy, the ramshackle building was in darkness. Saban squeezed between the two convertibles stored inside, activated the torch function on his mobile and edged around a collection of spare parts and piles of manufacturers' brochures toward what he recognised as the moans of somebody in pain.

As he opened the office door, the beam centred on the figure of a man lying on the floor, his upper body resting on the bars of an old-style radiator.

'Thank the Lord,' Ludo gasped. 'I thought I was going to have to lie here until the morning. Call for an ambulance, will you? I can't get my fingers to work. My shoulder's buggered and my eyesight's all fuzzy.'

Saban took in the scene. One side of the man's face was covered in blood, his left hand clasping what was obviously a badly damaged shoulder.

'Don't stand there looking at me, for God's sake, man. Call nine-nine-nine or whatever you need to do to get me some help.' Ludo hesitated. 'Sorry, I don't mean to offend, but please do as I ask, whoever you are.'

Saban said nothing. The boss always repeated the one thing the Albanian lacked was initiative, and that was why he'd employed him – cue for a derogative laugh. Now, he could show the boss just how imaginative he could be when the situation called for it.

'Who are you anyway, and why are you here?' There was a mix of both fear and curiosity in Ludo's question. He gasped in pain as he tried to change position. 'Please, please, get me some help. Take whatever you want, d' you see.'

221

The beam of light from the mobile played around the room, settling on a cheap white melamine cupboard, the surface covered in several packets and boxes of spare parts. He emptied the contents of a large plastic bag marked 'Fiat 500 – clutch assembly' onto the desk. He turned the bag inside out.

'Who beat you up?' Saban tried to disguise his voice by adopting what he calculated was the accent used by Sacha Baron Cohen when portraying his Borat character.

'I know you, don't I?' Ludo queried. 'You're one of Quentin's heavies, aren't you? How many times do I have to ask for some help?'

'I asked who attacked you?' He dropped the failed impression. 'Who was it?'

'The Forbes boy, Roddie, for God's sake, but that doesn't matter now. We can see to him later. Can you get it into your bone head to call for an ambulance . . . please?'

With a surprising turn of speed for a big man, Saban took a step forward, bent and moved the man toward him, one hand forcing the plastic bag over Ludo's head and squeezing the aperture tight around his neck. From a look of surprise to blind panic, Ludo reacted. Releasing the damaged shoulder, his left hand clawed first at the plastic covering his nose and then at the hand securing the bag around his neck. The plastic was sucked into his mouth and rapidly exhaled, the bag clouding as he consumed the fast-depleting oxygen within. For thirty seconds his movements became ever more erratic until, suddenly, his body relaxed, dead eyes fixed on his killer as if pleading for mercy.

Saban cursed as he removed the plastic bag from the corpse. The wound on the side of the man's head had opened as he had struggled, and blood spatters now decorated the front of Saban's beige bomber jacket. Still cursing, he replaced the clutch assembly back into the bag, found a cloth to wipe clean the exterior of fingerprints and returned it to the cupboard, discreetly placed, hidden under a collection of brake pads.

Normally, he would have worn gloves if a visit was likely to involve violence, but delivering an arrears letter was hardly likely to have turned out the way it did. His fingerprints were bound to be on various surfaces. He was cuter than the boss could imagine. He took the letter from his pocket, unfolded it before placing it in the middle of a small pile of bills and circulars on the desk. Yes, he had been there, but much earlier during the day. The Irishman was fine when he left.

Back in the deserted street, he looked over toward the supermarket car park where he had left the Range Rover. People were milling about. It was too risky. He took off the bomber jacket, folded it inside out, and draped it over his arm. He might look stupid on such a chilly night dressed in a tee-shirt with a jacket for decoration, but it was safer. As a matter of course, he had parked in an area out of range of the CCTV cameras and he was confident that walking around the perimeter fence away from the entrance, he was unlikely to have been picked up on a screen.

The current burner phone he removed from under the seat had not previously been used and would be discarded when he had finished the call.

'Police', he said in answer to the question which emergency service he required. He tried to speak like the boss with an accent someone had described as 'posh'. 'I've just witnessed a break-in and a fight going on at a car sales place.' He gave the name and location. 'The bloke who runs the place keeps calling out for Forbes to leave him alone, but the other bloke keeps hitting him. He's going crazy. I think he saw me. I don't want him coming after me. I'm scared.' He rung off before the operator could ask for his personal details.

Saban sat back in the driver's seat, a satisfied smile on his face. The boss would be pleased with him. The permanent injury or death of a client triggered full repayment of the loan plus accrued interest until the loan's original due date. They would get hold of the site a lot quicker than his boss could have calculated. That was worth another grand on his bonus, at least.

Five minutes later, the sound of a siren grew louder as it entered the adjacent road. Good. He would dump the bomber jacket en route, go home for another coat and pay a visit to a lady friend of his who knew all about the art of bondage. Tomorrow, he'd break the news to the boss.

THIRTY-FOUR

CHARLIE AND DOMINIC

Dominic was sitting cross-legged in the middle of the three-seater sofa when he heard the tapping of a coin on the glass insets on the front door. 'Piss off!' seemed an entirely appropriate comment coming from somebody dressed in nothing more than the only pair of laundered underpants he had found three days earlier. How was he expected to attend to visitors at this hour virtually naked with some pretty aggressive gay porn on the television and a selection of empty pizza boxes and spent extra-strength lager cans spread around the floor?

The tapping had resumed, this time on the panel of the French windows beyond the drawn jade and gold velvet curtains which Cary had spent days agonising over before coming to a buying decision. 'They were expensive,' she had admitted. 'But you can sense a discerned taste when you look at them.'

The bile rose in his throat. 'Piss off, whoever you are,' he shouted. 'I'm not in the mood for socialising. I'm busy.' Defiantly, he thrust a hand inside his briefs.

The tapping was incessant. For a fleeting moment, his heart leapt. What if it was Lance, eager to apologise and admit how wrong he'd been and how he wanted to make amends? He leapt to his feet and flung the curtains apart. 'Jesus! You!' he gasped. 'What are you doing here?' It was still raining. Standing before him was the bedraggled figure of his father, clothes soaked, rivulets running from his head down through the rugged features of his face as it pressed against the double-glazing, his mouth moving in what could only be a series of obscenities.

Dominic closed the curtains and scrambled for the remote to turn off the television and kick-shuffle a selection of the fast-food containers and beer cans into a corner. As he opened the French windows, he caught the tail-end of a vicious string of invective.

Stumbling into the room, trailing a small suitcase on wheels, Charlie collapsed into an armchair. 'What took you so long? I tried ringing the bell, banging on the front door. Have you gone deaf?' He studied Dominic before casting his gaze around the room. 'You all right?' He peeled off a layer of saturated clothing. 'You're nodding your head, son, but you don't look all right to me. When was the last time you shaved or took a shower?'

'What's it to you?' Dominic hitched the pants up above his waistline, as if addressing an attack of modesty. 'Anyway, would you mind telling me what you are doing here at close to midnight? I was just going to bed.'

'I need to stay for the night.' He took a deep breath. 'Ludo's dead and your mother has kicked me out of the house?'

'Ludo's dead?' He took a step back. 'Did you have anything to do with it?'

'Of course, I bloody didn't.' He released the braces holding up his trousers, causing a trickle of water to emerge from his waistline. 'Though I'd be better off if I had done. At least, I'd be tucked up nice and dry in some warm police cell and not standing here leaking all over the sodding carpet.'

'How did he die?' There was a hint of panic in his voice.

'The coppers waiting for me at the house said it was too soon to draw any conclusion. Apparently, he was the unintended victim of a robbery that went tits up.' Charlie took pity at the confused look on his son's face. 'Look, you deserve a full explanation, but I'm totally sha. . . bushwhacked. Can we leave it until the morning? I need to get out of these clothes and dry off. Where can I crash?'

Dominic hitched his pants up once more, glanced down at the sofa and then up at the challenging expression on his father's face. 'You'd best take our bedroom,' he said with obvious reluctance. 'The beds in the girls' room are too small and I've converted the third bedroom into an office.' He turned away and slumped onto the sofa. 'I'll watch a bit of telly and sleep here. The bedroom has an en-suite, so you can take a shower and clean up. The bed's not made up, but . . . with only me here . . .' He shrugged his shoulders.

As Charlie turned to walk away, the wheels on his suitcase squeaking in protest as they bounced onto the solid wood flooring that ran along the hallway, Dominic called out. 'Is mum all right?'

Charlie kept walking. 'She's got the wrong end of the stick she's beating me with,' he said with resignation in his voice.

THIRTY-FIVE

LEN AND AN EARLY MORNING VISITOR

As far as he was concerned, there are only two sets of people in society who bang on your front door rather than ring the bell and only a single exponent who does so before the sun has even got a peek at the dew on the grass.

As the second barrage sounded on the solid oak door, a barely awake Len discounted the prospect of facing a disgruntled neighbour. He yanked the door open. There was something vaguely familiar about the man holding out a warrant card for him to study, but right now his one desire was to turn around and slam the door shut in the man's face. He didn't. Instead, he opted for the reaction of the righteous offended. 'What time of day do you call this to come banging on my front door? Didn't you notice the bellpush?' He looked past the man at the WPC hovering uncertainly three steps behind him. 'God knows what time he must have woken you up or did he just have to nudge you in bed with "time to make a move"?'

The young woman's cheeks coloured as she went to answer, but the man took a step closer to Len, his hand raised, as if to say, leave it to me. The twang of his voice announced his Caribbean heritage. 'Detective Inspector Sheppard, I presume.'

'You presume incorrectly . . .' He motioned the man to raise the warrant card he was still holding. 'DS Washington Moses, is it? I'm now retired and just plain Mr Sheppard. What can I do for you, son?'

Moses ignored the intended offensive putdown. 'I'm with the IOPC, Detective Inspector. Your attendance at Canary Wharf is respectfully requested.' He gave a sarcastic bow of the head.

'What is this, some sort of joke?'

'Afraid not. DCI Brannigan instructed me to tell you it's to clarify some issues which have come to light. Nothing formal . . . at this stage,' he added.

Len shook his head. 'I could have guessed Flaky would be the one behind this dramatic early morning wake-up call. The man's been snapping at my heels for the last ten years, looking for an excuse for Internal Affairs to pin something on me. It's chemistry, you see, DS Moses. We're not compatible. Flaky has an enormous chip on those slender shoulders.' He went to close the door. 'You'll need to tell him I'm busy and will try to fit him in soon.'

'I can't do that.' Moses went to wedge a foot in the doorway.

'Meaning what?'

'I'll make it formal, if you like, Sir. WPC Roberts can confirm I've read you your Miranda rights.'

'Arrest me? You've got a fucking cheek.' His voice had risen an octave.

A female voice called down from the upstairs landing. 'What's going on?'

Len fully opened the door again. 'Nothing to concern you, Muriel,' he called out. 'Got to go out with some colleagues from the City force for a while. They need my help on an old case. I won't be long.'

'You need to change out of that old track suit? You can't go out looking like that.' Muriel's voice echoed around the hall.

'It's all right, love. There's no dress code for retired coppers. Best to get it over and done with.' He pulled the door shut behind him before she had a chance to react. 'Come on,' he said to Moses. 'I'll expect a lift back when Flaky's got whatever it is off his chest.'

'Whose made the allegations?' Len was slouched in a chair set back from the desk occupied by the neatly turned-out figure of DCI Brannigan.

The slender man massaged the stubble on his chin with the palm of his hand and looked from the window of his office on the fourteenth floor of the towering building that sat above Canada Square station. He watched as the last carriage of a Docklands Light Railway train veered out of view on its way toward the Tower of London.

'Are you going to answer me or just ignore the question?' Len persisted.

Brannigan looked over heavy-rimmed glasses as he flared the nostrils of a delicate, aquiline nose. 'You know the form, Len. I can't divulge that information. The allegations are quite specific. The letter we received states you used funds from a named offshore bank account to finance the purchase of your home. We need to know how you came by the account and by what

228

means it was funded. You know also that serving officers are specifically forbidden to operate bank accounts in jurisdictions outside of the UK unless specifically approved.'

Len leaned forward; a clenched fist planted on the edge of the desk. 'Somebody's flying a kite, Brannigan, and whoever it is has sucked you into a private issue I happen to have with someone. There's a second-hand car dealer, an arsehole who's got it in for me because my daughter is divorcing his useless twat of a son. He's jealous I've got a nicer house than his and he has tried to dig up some dirt to smear my reputation. He's using some amateur private dick who must have come across somebody else's information and decided it was good enough to get the IOPC all sexed up.'

'Is that the case?' Brannigan gave a questioning smile.

Len's fist contracted, turning his knuckles white as the flow of blood was restricted. 'It's all bullshit, believe me.' He thumped the desk hard.

'You don't or, should I say, never had an offshore bank account?'

'Of course not. It's bad enough trying to deal with the bloke at Barclays, let alone some wallah sitting on an island in the middle of the ocean with an abacus and a satellite phone.' He sat back in his chair and studied the flakes of dandruff on the other man's jacket lapels. It was the origin of the nickname and a curse with which Brannigan lived. He hated having it drawn to his attention.

Len's hand moved to where his lapels would have been had he been wearing a jacket. 'Need to brush yourself down,' he said, stroking the area. 'My wife mentioned a good shampoo the other day. I'll give her . . .'

'Forget it, Sheppard! Don't try to wind me up.' He flicked his fingertips at the white flakes. 'We're talking about a bank account in the Cayman Islands and monies transferred into your domestic account from an offshore company called Pitchfork Holdings. Ringing any bells?'

Inwardly, he was raging. The image was of Greaves slumped, bound in a chair, begging for forgiveness, pleading for his life, suffering the retribution he deserved. 'Can't say it does,' he replied laconically. 'Say again, when was this?'

'I've already told you. The accusation is that at the time you purchased your house, you needed to top-up the mortgage with a little nest egg you'd put to one side. Correct?'

Len should his head slowly from side-to-side. 'Pissing up against the wrong leg, I'm afraid, Chief Inspector. I don't remember the name of the company making the transfer, but it was a bridging loan from a second line mortgage lender. I'll go through my files and get the paperwork for you to peruse.'

Brannigan straightened a small stack of papers on his desk, tapping the corners into order. 'You do that, Sheppard. Let's say tomorrow, same time, shall we? If you don't appear of your own accord, I'll make this official. Get my drift?'

Len extended his hand, but instead of grasping the other man's, he moved his palm upwards to brush the lapel of the jacket. 'Can't have you looking like it's snowing, can we?' He was at the door before the expletive came.

Len's call to his daughter must have taken her by surprise. A change of heart? No, not that. He recognised reality had to be faced. Yes, there were reservations, more concerns for her happiness than his own prejudices, but he should get around to meeting the man she loved and there was no time like the present. To her amazement, he suggested the three of them get together for dinner at home that evening. Yes, it was short notice, but he had an invitation for a week's golf in the sun and might not have another opportunity before she moved out. Also, it would go a long way to getting back into Muriel's good books.

She had called back within fifteen minutes. Alex would be delighted to accept, but he couldn't make it before eight thirty. Caroline seemed genuinely amazed but delighted with her father's change of heart. 'We'll see you later,' she said. 'And thanks for being so understanding.'

Len checked his watch. Ten thirty. It was now or never. At ease around the dining table, coffee and liqueurs on offer, the consensus must be the evening had been a success. He had to admit a grudging admiration for Caroline's choice of partner. He was everything Dominic was not. There was a controlled self-assurance in the man, yet a willingness to listen instead of talking, picking up on the points of importance and the ability to give a straight answer to a direct question. There was only one stage during the evening when Alex had appeared distracted and missed a couple of observations Muriel had made about caring for the twins.

Just after nine, Charlie had dropped off his daughter's boyfriend to collect the Volvo and Caroline had gone outside to hand over the keys. From the floodlight outside the garage, Alex had watched the two in conversation. She was genuinely amused at something he had said, her hand resting on his shoulder as their heads came closer and he whispered something in her ear, which caused another outburst of laughter.

Had the exchanges gone on much longer, Len guessed Alex would have been out of his seat to break up the *tête à tête*, but a final peck on the cheek and wave of the hand signalled their goodbyes. Just in time, he thought. Nothing like a little dose of jealousy to sharpen the emotions.

'Sylvia's boyfriend is certainly a live wire,' Cary had said as she returned to her seat. 'He's an Aussie, built like one of those tanned surfers you see wandering around Bondi beach in Speedos. Good for her. He's quite a catch.'

'What's he doing over here?' Alex had asked.

'Helping Sylvia with some project she's working on. He didn't go into details. Made a joke about it which had me in stitches. I like dry humour with a little sarcasm in the mix.'

The conversation moved on. It was varied, positive and good-natured, despite Muriel's stubborn insistence on probing into Alex's background, a subject which both Len and Caroline tried to deflect.

'I was sorry to hear about the car accident,' Muriel had said. 'Both your daughter and wife were victims?'

Alex had hesitated. Caroline had stopped eating. Her face tensed. 'Yes,' he said, finally.

'Are they buried together?'

There had been a long pause. The sound of a knife clanged against a plate. Alex looked directly at Muriel. 'I should point out two things, Muriel, so that you understand my position whilst I try to satisfy yours.' He took out a handkerchief to clear his nose. 'I find talking and dealing with the past very difficult to handle. My sense of guilt for not being in the driving seat on that day will never leave me. To her credit, Caroline has never probed into the detail, and I have felt no need or desire to explain. Perhaps now is the right time to come clean with the facts, a once only experience, if we are all agreed?'

He took the embarrassed mumbling as the prompt to continue. 'It's only right you should want to know the history of the man who loves and wants to share his life with your daughter. I've been involved in the world of finance all my working life and until fifteen years ago, you could say I had a conventional lifestyle with a house in the suburbs, a wife and a five-year-old daughter. My wife, Rosalind, and I had a silly argument. She stormed out of the house and drove off with Hannah. That was the last time I saw my wife and daughter as I remember them.' He exhaled deeply into the silence. 'Both of them went through the windscreen. Rosalind survived in a coma for three years before waking in a vegetative state. She has no recollection of any worldly thing. I visit every month as a penance, really. She has no idea who I am or that I am even present. The vibrant, exciting woman I knew is dead, replaced by a physical clone with no apparent sense or feeling. I look upon myself as a widower.'

Had it not been for one of the twins waking and crying out, the room might well have remained in silence for some time. Len watched as Caroline reached for Alex's hand, squeezed it tight and whispered something to him, just before leaving the room to attend to her child. Masterful performance, Len thought. He'd get one of his contacts to look out the accident report and check the facts.

Muriel asked if anybody wanted more coffee. Nobody did. Len sensed the evening was about to draw to a close.

'Do you girls mind if I have a private word with Alex?' Len said. 'I'd like to get a few practical issues straight in my mind.'

Caroline gave him a puzzled look, but at Alex's prompt, followed her mother into the kitchen.

'I've got a feeling I'm about to hear why I was really invited here at such short notice.' Alex gave a broad smile.

Len nodded. 'I'll not beat about the bush. Under normal circumstances, I'd have left it a week or so before getting together with you, but I need your help with a little local difficulty in which I find myself.' He held his hand up. 'Before you say anything, it's got nothing to do with borrowing money.'

'Go on.'

Len gave a sanitised version of the events earlier in the day and his run-in with an old police colleague out for revenge. 'It's personal,' he concluded. 'And I need to nip it in the bud before this guy makes it a big issue.'

Alex rolled the brandy glass between his hands and raised it to his lips. 'One benefit of having a driver is I don't have to worry about this.' He took a sip and savoured the taste in his mouth. 'It's a fine cognac. Thank you.' He could tell just how much his delay in reacting to the other man's sense of urgency was beginning to annoy and frustrate in equal measure. The greater the need, the broader the scope of opportunity. Beneath the veneer of nonchalance, this man was desperate.

He deliberately took another sip and sighed at the effect. 'Cutting through the detail,' Alex said, finally, 'you want me to stand in the shoes of a would-be lender and provide you with evidence of a loan from an offshore company which I control?'

Len's nod was hesitant as he considered the question.

'Otherwise, you will provoke a full-scale investigation into your affairs, expose yourself to criminal charges and lose your pension. Is that about it?'

Len nodded again.

'Timescale?'

'Tomorrow,' Len said. 'He's expecting me in the morning, but I can probably hold him off with some excuse until late afternoon.'

'If you want my help, we will have to do it by the book. I don't want the police turning up phoney data, which prompts further investigation into my activities.'

'We're talking about the confidentiality of an offshore company and bank account.'

'Don't be naïve, Len. Nothing is sacrosanct these days. Look at the Panama papers scandal. Hackers can get in almost anywhere.' He held his glass out for a refill. 'If you want my help, you will need to advise your contact in the Cayman Islands to establish a name I give you as the ultimate beneficial owner of this company and to backdate the authority to a date prior to transferring funds to the UK.'

233

'Can he do that?'

'My experience is these bogus lawyers will do anything for the right fee.'

'Okay, I'll tackle it first thing in the morning.'

'Too late. You need to do it now. It's close to six in the evening now in the Caymans. If you leave it until tomorrow, we can't start the ball rolling until two or three in the afternoon.'

'What else?'

'I'll draft a loan agreement for you to sign. The interest on the hundred and sixty thousand will be rolled over until the due date, when the entire amount becomes due and payable. Let's say, by the end of this year.'

'Will that do it?' Len pulled nervously at the skin under his chin. 'How do we unravel it at the end of the year?'

'You'll have a copy of the loan agreement and a letter from my holding company confirming beneficial ownership of whatever its name is.'

'Pitchfork Holdings.'

Alex smiled. 'Whoever thought that one up?'

'It was on a list of names to choose from.' He realised the question was rhetorical. 'Sorry, I interrupted.'

'By the end of the year, you've been to your bank, pointed out by how much your house has increased in value and asked to increase your mortgage. You pay back the loan; we transfer the funds to the Caymans and onwards to another offshore you've set up in a better location together with any other monies Pitchfork is holding. How much more is there in the Caymans?'

'Getting on for three-hundred thousand.'

'Really? You have been a busy boy with your ex-curriculum activities.'

Len ignored the comment. 'I appreciate your help. Tell me, what are you expecting out of this?'

Alex lifted himself out of the armchair. His hand rested on Len's shoulder. 'I'd better be going now if we're going to set this business in motion and you need to talk sharpish to your man in the Caymans. Create a new email account, let me have it and I'll get my legal assistant to send you a list of the personal details he'll require as at the date you entered into the transaction. He'll draft up the agreement and send it by courier for you to sign in front of a witness who would have been present at the time. We'll keep each other posted.

'As to what I want from you, let's say a positive and productive relationship with the parents of my sweetheart into the future. If we get that, we couldn't have asked for more.'

* * *

The soporific effect of the alcohol and the smooth ride in the Mercedes had caused Alex to fall asleep. The ring tone of his mobile jarred him into wakefulness. Glancing at the signpost, it showed they were approaching Maidstone. He had been asleep for the last half-hour.

'Alex, is that you? It doesn't sound like you.'

'You woke me up, Rupert. Has he been in touch?'

'He's hot to trot, this one. I've already got all the info back from him. He's also confirmed somebody in the Caymans is onside. I said I'd pass the message on. What's the story?'

'I'll bring you up to speed in the morning. Give him the minimum interest rate, but with standard terms and conditions.'

'How much is in play?'

Alex prompted the driver to speed up. 'Close to half a million. I need to work on it. The situation is entwined with my current relationship. Worst way, dumping him may spell the end of the affair, but it needs some thought and a little guile.'

'I'm intrigued.'

'It's too good to pass up. Speak in the morning.'

THIRTY-SIX

RANDY AND DORIS

Randy awoke with a start, unsure of his surroundings. The pillow was not the ergonomic, fit the contours of your head model he had at his place. It was soft and fluffy, full of feathers and with that Estee Lauder scent to provoke his memory into gear through the fog of a massive hangover.

Slowly, as his head turned, he brought into focus the woman snoring in a series of soft grunts, her pillow stained with make-up foundation and crimson lipstick. Had he really described her looks as angelic? As the events of the last twenty-four hours percolated through his brain, her features seemed to contort into the visage of a witch from Macbeth. Had he really? He lifted the sheet. He was totally naked, and Estee Lauder was replaced by the waft of bodily fluids exchanged. Yes, he . . . they definitely had. He reached onto the bedside table for his watch. Seven. His movement had stirred her. God, please don't let her wake up.

For DI Randall Compton, aka Randy to friends and colleagues, yesterday had started full of good intentions. The call from Len changed his mood. Although Len had now squared his problem with the IOPC using some moody documents, he was obviously deeply troubled by the turn of events and Brannigan's continued suspicions, encompassing Randy and the others, Len had emphasised. If somebody was feeding information to Brannigan and his team, God knows how much of their clandestine activities would come to light. There was only one source from where it could have come, and Greaves was obviously getting help from somebody on the inside doing the investigative work. The quicker they could shut up Greaves and his cohorts, the better.

The sense of urgency had prompted Randy to pick up on the only lead he had and take the Docklands Light Railway from Tower Hill to the Isle of Dogs. The post room boy who showed him to the supervisor's office door leered as he made a large bosom gesture with his hands and shunted his hips back and forward in an unmistakable gesture. As he ushered Randy through the door, the wink left no room for misunderstanding.

237

Supervisor Doris Fairbanks was certainly an impressive-looking woman, the right age, but definitely not his type. She gave the impression of the buxom, homely farmer's wife who would suffocate you with affection. How wrong first impressions can be.

Randy preferred the slender, bird-like oriental look, just like Chantana, his Thai wife, who was no more. Weighing at her heaviest just eighty-five pounds, she had been so flat-chested, he could count the ribs poking through the pallid skin. But she was wiry and strong. How she hated and fought against the restraints he insisted upon when taking her. Her face was impassive to the end; that was the trouble with her. If she had reacted like any normal person. He shook his head. Now wasn't the time to go over all that. She was back somewhere in Pattaya City, south of Bangkok, wasn't she? Her brothers were troublemakers. They blamed him.

'Are you all right?' Doris enquired, rising from her seat behind the desk. 'You wanted to talk to me, DI Compton?' Taking the time to study his physique, she gestured for him to sit down.

'Yes, I'm fine. Sorry. I had something else on my mind.'

He had carefully prepared a storyline to explain how he was involved in a money laundering investigation, and the name of Charles Greaves had come up in connection with his enquiries. He knew there had been a suspicious death following a VAT investigation in which she had been involved.

'I've got a vague recollection,' she said. 'The bookkeeper died following a traffic accident abroad, wasn't it?'

'Spain,' he confirmed. 'You don't recall the outcome of the VAT inspection, do you?'

'Now you're asking. I pride myself on my memory, but in that particular case, afraid not. I can look it up and get back to you.'

'When can you let me have something? It's urgent.'

She studied his face. He was a few years older than her, probably close to retirement. He wore a wedding ring on his finger, but she'd never worried about such trivial detail before. 'I've got a suggestion,' she said.

Her workload and deadlines were demanding, she explained. There was no way she could take time off to help him during working hours. It might sound unconventional, but how about she arranged a dinner reservation somewhere and she would bring whatever information there was with her? They could then discuss it at leisure in pleasant surroundings.

She raised her shoulders and gave a make-believe grimace. 'That's if your wife wouldn't mind?' she said, demurely.

'I'm no longer married,' he said. 'There's no problem on that score.'

She exhaled as she smiled. 'Give me your number and I'll tell you where and when.'

They met up that evening in a bistro restaurant off Clapham Common. It was one of her favourites, she told him. The owner, Albertina, and the staff certainly knew her as a regular.

'I had a good look at the file before I left the office,' she said as they studied the chalkboard listing the desserts. 'Think I'll go for the chocolate chiffon pie. How about you?' She leaned across and squeezed his knee. 'You've got to keep up your energy level, honey.' He gave a weak smile and said he'd wait for coffee.

Until now, the conversation had ranged over a host of uncontroversial topics, the getting-to-know-you variety in which she was well-versed, even if attempts to get him to say anything meaningful about his private life had so far proved fruitless. She sensed his interest was waning. He needed to be brought back onside.

'You say your concern with this Greaves character is to do with money laundering?' She registered the nod, and the spark rekindled in his eyes. 'I recall the man and, frankly, the nearest I could see him coming to laundering money is if he left a fiver in the pocket of his trousers en route to the dry cleaners. That's if my judgement is anything to go by.'

Randy laughed. They were on positive ground. 'It's the Spanish connection interests me,' he said.

Over her dessert, coffees and two rounds of a house brandy especially imported, she gave him a summary of the inspection and the bare facts she had on the accident in Spain. There was no mention of the new information on the flash drive she had received. She would need a lot more from him before that confidence was shared. 'The file on the inspection is still open, believe it or not,' she concluded. 'There are unanswered questions which may remain unsolved unless a paper trail can be established. We issued fines for non-compliance and raised a default assessment, but it was pennies rather than pounds. That's about all I can tell you.'

If he thought the evening would reach a conventional finale, a peck on the cheek and hot-air suggestions about meeting up again, he was badly mistaken. Her insistence on a nightcap at her place, a top-floor flat in a converted Victorian terrace house on a side road off the common, was the prelude to an experience he had never encountered before. There was no preamble, no foreplay. She was on him the moment he sat back on the couch. He loved domination, until now, always his, but this woman's brand of control he had never come across. In some primeval way, it really roused him, and she took full advantage. Three hours later and heaven only knows how many times she had climbed onto him, he finally slept.

Her eyes flickered and immediately registered his presence. She looked wary of what he might say. There was no sign of last night's dominance, just a fleeting glance before she pushed the duvet to one side. 'I'll take a shower first,' she said. 'I take longer to dry my hair.' She gave a watery smile. 'Make a coffee if you fancy it. I've got to be at work early this morning.'

Randy's brow creased. 'Are you all right? You seem off with me? I'll go now, if you want.'

'No need,' Doris said. 'It took me a while to nod off. You talk in your sleep, loud, you know that?'

'Really? How would I? I don't share my bed with anyone now.' He stopped. 'She left me,' he added. 'What did I happen to say?' He looked into her eyes.

'God knows. Apart from one word you kept on repeating that sounded like "sultana", the rest was all garbled.'

His smile returned. 'Just as well,' he said

Even Grant noticed the supervisor wasn't her normal self this morning. 'You all right, Doris?'

'I've told you not to call me that.'

'A thousand apologies, *Herr General*. Get out of bed on the wrong side? No bonking last night? Could you be suffering from sexual deprivation?'

240

'Piss off and I mean it.'

Damn it. Whether or not it was her business, she could at least give him the heads-up. She now had his number on speed dial. 'Doesn't sound like you, Charlie,' she said.

'I've got problems,' he said. 'My ex-partner was topped the night before last. It looks like the other Forbes brother was involved. He's on the run, apparently. The wife kicked me out when I had to admit where I'd been. I'm surprised they haven't already been on to you for confirmation.'

'I've got a message to ring a DI Cross. He called yesterday afternoon, but I had to visit the archives to check out something and left straight for a dinner date.'

'You don't waste much time, do you?' Charlie sounded indignant. 'You're sex mad, you know that, don't you?'

'Do I detect a hint of jealousy?' She adopted an American drawl. 'Why, Charles, I have my needs, just like you.' She listened to his snort and reverted to speak normally. 'I'll ring this Cross now. I take it you told Norma you had strayed.'

'She won't forgive me this time. I'm having to reorganise my living arrangements.'

'Whoa there, boy! Even if the thought had fleetingly crossed your mind, forget it. Long gone are the days when I wash a man's shitty underpants or check he's taken his pills. As far as I'm concerned, cohabiting is a swear word and I don't use bad language.'

'I wasn't. Don't worry. I'm praying for the miracle of redemption, not condemning myself to an eternal purgatory.'

'Well, that's not a gracious thing to say to somebody who rang with the best intentions of passing on some information you might find helpful.'

'Go on. I'm up against it at the moment. Len has got it in for me, getting that flash drive into your hands. I'm still looking for something to put him under the cosh.'

She spoke, almost in a whisper, enunciating each word carefully. 'I had a visit from a copper who was trying to dig up dirt on you. Don't worry, I was discreet.'

'Name?'

'DI Randall Compton.'

'Never heard of him. Which force is he with?'

'City of London. He's a desk wallah, majors in fraud and money laundering. He was especially interested in the accident involving your bookkeeper in Spain.'

'He'll be one of Len's cronies. What's he like?'

'Getting on but fit.'

There was a mix of amazement and resignation in his tone. 'Don't tell me he's the guy you ended up in bed with?'

'Since when are you my conscience? As it happens, he was and, as it happens, I wish it hadn't happened. Does that make sense?'

'Come on, Doris. What's the punch line? I haven't got all night.'

'I'm telling you. The guy talks in his sleep. Weird stuff. He kept me awake. Talking about somebody with a name sounded like "sultana". He was going on about "the island". I think he mentioned Sheppey and something about marshlands and keeping it hidden under water. He seemed in distress, moaning and cursing himself.'

'Do you know what it's about?'

'I've got no idea, but the guy's deeply troubled and all this babbling on really gave me the jitters. I'll be busy washing my hair if he calls again.'

Charlie rang off. Maybe something, maybe nothing, but he'd ask Sylvia if she could get some information on this Randall Compton and his connection to Len and the Isle of Sheppey.

THIRTY-SEVEN

MAHI, NOBBY AND THE KUMARS

Back pressed against a concrete wall plastered with graffiti, Mahi nervously looked for movement at both ends of the alleyway bordering the railway line. Her hands trembled as she slowly keyed the message into her mobile and waited for the reply.

Two minutes. He would be there in two long minutes. What if Neeraj or his brother showed up in the meantime? She was certain they were on to her, somehow tracking her movements, suspicious of her communications with Robin Clark, the validity of his podcast claims and the interest of DOBIS in the role in society of working Asian women.

The subject of the podcast had cropped up one evening over dinner, as she was about to rise from the table to clear the main course plates. The General's casual observation that she seemed distant and preoccupied caused her to panic and use the topic as an excuse for her disrespectful behaviour. Nobody pursued it at the time, but the following Sunday, the General summoned her to his office, where Neeraj and younger brother, Vijay, were waiting for her. The grilling was intense. Suspicion fell on her motives, the relationship with this former police officer, Clark, the activities of the organisation for the Development of British Indians in Society and the restricted role of a woman in the Kumar household.

Vijay suggested a sexual liaison was taking place with Clark under the cover of this phoney podcast. Neeraj had struck her and called her a whore. Her protestations went unheeded. He had banned her from any further contact with Clark and put on a strict daily timetable which would take her to and from work with no distractions. They would be watching, the General promised. Step out of line and she would be punished.

'You've come,' she said nervously, as Nobby strolled untroubled toward her. Her gaze flittered incessantly between the two exits. 'Thank you.'

'What's wrong? Why not use the burner I gave you?'

'I just have a feeling it's not safe. My family is suspicious of my involvement with you.' Her hands trembled as he reached for them. In an instant, she pulled away. 'They accused me of having an affair.' She studied the ground in front of her. 'With you.'

Nobby burst out laughing. 'You're joking. With me? How did we fit this in? With you standing against the wall in this alley?'

She rocked her head. 'Don't be crude. It's no joke.' She pulled away the scarf covering the gash on her cheek.

'Jesus,' he said. 'Who did that?'

'This is just a taste of what's to come, believe me. They are capable of anything. You must tell Terry to hurry.'

Nobby put his hands on her shoulders. 'Calm down and stop shaking. I spoke to him this morning. He said next Friday.'

She wriggled his arms away from her. 'It's too late. I could be dead by then. Tell him it's next Wednesday at the latest or I'm backing out.'

'It's not leaving much time.'

'Even then, it may be too late. If we're not gone by Wednesday, I'm taking sick leave and not moving from the house.' Tears welled in her eyes. 'I'll leave for work as normal. Terry meets me en route and we leave forever, or I go to work, return home and never see or speak to him again. It's my ultimatum. I don't want to die, Mr Clark.'

Terry answered the call on the second ring. 'How is she, Nobby?'

'Petrified. Afraid for her life.' He lost the signal briefly as he exited the Northern line station at East Finchley. It was a ten-minute walk to his terrace house in Muswell Hill, a stone's throw from the ice rink at Alexandra Palace.

'You there, Nobby? I asked you what the problem was?'

As he strolled along Fortis Green Road and turned away from the traffic toward the secondary school, Nobby relayed a summary of his conversation with Miha.

'Wednesday?' Terry queried. 'That's tight for me. I can leave a few things pending, but I'll need that ten grand from Bateman as seed money to get us started.'

'I'll speak to Len, ask him to get the old man's authority for Darren to pay you. It might mean a detour to Billericay before you can make tracks.'

'That will be the least of my worries.'

The white Transit van pulled up a few yards in front of Nobby. The man who exited from the passenger door was wearing a scarf across his nose and mouth. Had it not been for the element of surprise coupled with the fact he was still talking on the mobile, Nobby might have put up more resistance. Extending an arm to stay the man's hurried advance was all he could do. His attacker was of a similar stature and build, but younger and fitter. The side door of the van creaked open, and the force of the push sent him sideways into the darkness. Hands grabbed him from inside the vehicle, forcing his arms behind his back. His mobile danced across the ribbed metal flooring. He felt the ties tighten around his wrist and ankles. 'What the . . .!' he exclaimed, looking up into the partially covered face of a second man.

'*Suprabhat, Srimana Clark.*'

'Don't you fucking "good morning" me. *Tum kya chaahate ho?* Who are you dickheads?'

'You'll find out soon enough. In the meantime, have a little sleep.'

Nobby recognised the scent of chloroform a split second before the cloth covered his mouth and nose. The last thing he heard was a concerned voice coming from his mobile asking what was going on and was everything all right?

THIRTY-EIGHT

LEN, ALEX AND A COINCIDENCE

'You look worried about something.' Alex took the offered glass and studied the contents. 'I never understand why pubs sell expensive drinks in understated glasses. I'm sure it influences the taste.' He held the glass out. 'Cheers, anyway. Sorry to mess up your day, but I need some background information.'

Len was still reeling from the price he'd had to pay for a double twenty-five-year-old Glenmorangie. He'd queried the amount with the barman, whose stoic expression had been sufficient confirmation. 'I'll pay by card,' he had said.

'Something on your mind?' Alex persisted.

'Nothing to concern you. It seems one of my friends might be in some trouble. We can't contact him.'

'Anything I can do to help?'

Len shook his head. 'Actually, no. It would help if you told me why we're having this meet in a godforsaken pub in the middle of nowhere. I need to be on my way as soon as poss.'

Alex sipped his malt whiskey. 'I've been invited – is that the right word? – to a police station in Walworth this afternoon for a friendly chat with a DI Cross. Would that be something to do with this loan deal we've set up?'

'I don't think so.' Len centred his glass of lager precisely on the beer mat, carefully flattened the bent-up corner, and looked up to meet the other man's eyes. 'The enquiry into my finances is run by a DCI Brannigan at the IOPC from Canary Wharf. I can't see how an officer out of Walworth could be interested. It must be something else.'

Alex nodded slowly. 'We never really discussed how the police came to investigate you. Presumably, somebody made an allegation?'

'An anonymous letter with details of the transaction with the Cayman Islands naming the offshore and the bank.'

'Who sent it?'

Len drained his glass. 'There's only one suspect, Caroline's father-in-law, a former used car salesman and a rough-and-ready individual. Back in the day, I used to assist a family in the meat trade, the Batemans; the son, Darren, runs brothels posing as casinos/nightclubs around London. He got some information from a bent copper. This man, Charlie Greaves—'

'The name rings a bell,' Alex interrupted. 'Used cars, you say? He has a partner, an Irish guy. Is that the man?'

'No idea. I never discussed his business with him. Not interested.'

'You follow the news? Somebody topped a used car dealer in South London a few days ago. A burglary gone wrong is the official line. They're looking for a suspect. Could there be a connection?'

Len shrugged. 'Feasible. I'll ask around. Anyway, as I was saying, this Greaves character is using his daughter, who has police connections, and some Aussie private investigator, to dig up dirt on me.'

'An Australian?' Alex's casual air had turned serious. 'The guy who came to collect the Volvo at your place. He was Australian. Cary said so. She spent ages talking with him. They seemed to get on very well. Could this be your nemesis?'

Len frowned at the hostility in the man's voice. 'More than likely, I guess,' he said with a nod of acceptance. 'He's thick with Charlie. I hadn't realised Cary had struck up a conversation. I wasn't paying attention to who took away that piece of junk. Whether or not it's him, they've found the information from somewhere.'

Alex shook his head. 'It doesn't fit. There are only two potential sources. Either the Cayman Islands lawyer's records were hacked, which would require highly specialised skills, or somebody got at your documentation. You keep details on your laptop?'

Len ran his finger around the rim of the empty lager glass. 'Don't treat me as naïve, Alex. Until my retirement, I kept a single sheet of paper in my safe at home with the details, username, passwords etcetera. When I left the force, I scanned the page, subscribed to an encrypted cloud service and destroyed the original. The cloud support officer guaranteed me there had been no unauthorised access to the file nor any download until the day before yesterday when I needed sight of the key table to authorise the transfer of the beneficial ownership into your name.'

'Well,' Alex said, 'somebody with computer know-how has gained access or your controls are not as watertight as you claim. Any suggestions?'

Len's mouth was open. 'Jesus, it never occurred to me to make the connection. The man is such a damp rag, it didn't cross my mind.'

'Who are we talking about?'

'My current son-in-law; the man Caroline is divorcing to be with you. He's a computer nerd, works for a company sorting out all technical problems for their clients. It must be. The only thing in life that stimulates him is talking a load of technical jargon about software issues, which nobody understands. Jesus, why didn't I think of him before, the snide?'

'Has Caroline ever had access to this famous sheet of paper?'

'What do you take me for? I have never shown it to a living soul.'

Alex savoured the last mouthful of his whiskey. 'Well, it's out there now and you have to ensure this Charlie Greaves pulls no more rabbits from the hat. Haven't you got anything unsavoury on him you can use to shut him up, something in his past?'

'There's a lead. A friend on the force is doing some digging into a VAT irregularity and the death of his bookkeeper in Spain from a hit-and-run. Maybe something, maybe nothing. He's shagging the VAT inspector.'

'Who? Charlie?'

'No. My mate. He reckons he'll get something concrete next time they meet up.'

'Let's hope it's not an STD. Has Charlie got any history of sexual misadventures, straying from the marital bed?'

Len stroked his chin. 'Caroline mentioned something once. She's in thick with her mother-in-law, Norma. Gets on better with her than she does with her own mother. He had an affair once. Hit his wife hard. She took a long time to get over it and forgive him.'

'Really?' Alex leaned across the table. 'I've got a suggestion to shut him up for good. Listen to this idea.'

Saban drummed his fingers on the steering wheel of the Range Rover. The last two nights he had hardly slept. He had done plenty of bad things to people in his time, but he could not forget the face of the man with the plastic bag over his head struggling for breath. It was ridiculous. The man was dying anyway. He'd just helped him along and somebody else was in the frame for his murder. Saban had nothing to worry about. Then why was he on edge? He cursed loudly in his native tongue. Why was his boss taking so long in this pub? What was going on?

As if on cue, Alex emerged and hurried to the car. 'Set the GPS to Walworth police station,' Alex said.

'Why we go police station?' Saban used the back of his hand to wipe the sweat from his forehead.

'Because I say so. Now, get going.'

Saban pulled into the traffic, forcing the driver of the approaching car to brake suddenly and keep his hand pressed on the horn. Alex did not register. He was already on his mobile.

'Rupert, can you talk?'

Saban slowed the car as he concentrated on the phone conversation.

'Make sure the paperwork is in order the moment the next payment is due. Now he's dead, the demand will have to be addressed to his executors, I assume?'

Through the rear-view mirror, Saban watched him nod as the other man spoke.

'Okay, I'll leave it with you. Just don't miss a trick.'

Another pause.

'I'm due at Walworth police station to speak about Logan's death. Obviously, they've discovered the loan agreement and want clarification, last contacts, that sort of thing.'

After a longer interval, he spoke again. 'It's the sort of thing my guys would do. I don't get involved, and taking along a solicitor at this stage might suggest I'm implicated. If, for any reason, the conversation becomes difficult, I'll break off and call you, but frankly . . .'

Saban swerved to avoid a mother pushing a pram on a crossing.

'For God's sake, man, concentrate on the road. What's got into you today, Saban?'

'Sorry, boss.' The sweat was almost impairing his sight. He shook his head like a dog drying off after a soaking.

'Are you all right?'

'Fever, boss. Probably, the flu.'

'You should have changed with Abdyl. Don't breathe in my direction, spreading your germs.' Alex pointed at the car reversing into the road. 'Park outside the front door. Take the space that car is vacating.'

Saban watched his boss push open the red double doors of the police station and disappear inside. His hands were shaking. He fumbled to loosen his tie and undo his shirt button. His eyes nervously settled on two uniformed police officers as they made their way indoors. He couldn't stand much more of this.

'Grateful you could come at short notice.' DI Cross nestled into a carver chair and pulled down his jacket sleeves before resting his hands on the battered-looking table separating him from Alex. 'You met Sergeant Moses in reception, I believe.' He acknowledged the man sitting alongside him. 'Moses is from a special branch of the service concerned with police conduct.' He hesitated. 'Probably here to check up on me.' He laughed loudly at his aside, strands of saliva visible between bulbous lips, the folds of fat around his bull neck vibrating and almost eclipsing his chin. 'Just my little joke,' he said unnecessarily in a broad Geordie accent as he registered the stoic expressions on the faces of the two men. 'Now, down to business.'

He opened a manila file and shuffled the pages together. 'We're investigating the suspicious death of David Logan, whom I believe you know. Can you tell us about your relationship?'

Alex took a deep breath before launching into a brief, but succinct chronological account, starting with Cary's introduction of the buy-out loan scenario through to the current status of the debt. 'Mr Logan was late with his last monthly repayment, which automatically triggered serving a default notice,' he concluded.

'I'll come to that,' Cross said. 'Why do you think Logan came to you rather than a high street bank?'

'It's all to do with risk and security. Used car dealers aren't on the list of gilt-edged borrowers favoured by the clearers. I deal with second and third tier clients who have been rejected by their bank. When I consider the risk justified, I offer my company's support. Such was the case here.'

'You charge a higher rate of interest and strict default conditions if the loan becomes overdue. Were you putting pressure on Mr Logan? When did you last see him?' The tempo of Cross's questioning had increased, his tongue flicking between his lips to clear the ever-present strands of saliva.

'Interest rates are determined in function of the risk. Bitter experience has taught us clients who default persistently are unlikely to fulfil their obligations during the term of the loan. Better to nip the problem in the bud than a long-drawn-out saga, which often reduces or destroys the value of the security. By pressure, if you mean the default notice, the first is normally a wake-up call. From then on, I'd call it pressure to accept reality.' He stopped for breath. 'Finally, Mr Logan came to my office about a month ago – I'll get the exact date for you – to renegotiate his loan agreement; unsuccessfully, as it happens.'

'You didn't visit his premises two nights ago to serve him this default notice?' He waved a sheet of paper in the air. 'Perhaps there was an altercation and things went too far?'

'I've told you when I last saw him,' Alex replied icily. 'I've driven past the premises, but never been inside. And, finally, I don't handle the serving of default notices. That is left to one or other of my employees.'

'You would know who and when they served this notice?'

'Who, yes. When, not exactly. They will be given three or four at the same time and left to serve them as soon as their timetable permits. I don't supervise the process.' He shook his head in apparent frustration. 'Is all this necessary? According to your press conference, it was a robbery gone wrong and you have a suspect. Why quiz me?'

Cross ignored the outburst. 'This default notice; I assume the debtor signs and dates a copy to acknowledge service?'

'Correct.'

'So, you will be able to tell me who served the notice and the day on which they did so, but not the exact time?' He reacted to the nod. 'Can you ask someone in your office to give us this information?'

'You'll have to wait until I get back. The phone is switched to the answering service. I have a very lean operation.'

'As soon as possible, please. Could we ask you and the employees who do this work to provide fingerprint and DNA samples?'

'What in Hell's name for? I'll need more than your standard blurb of "to eliminate you from our enquiries".

Cross leaned across toward Moses and let out a loud burst of wind. 'Sorry, couldn't hold it in anymore. Bit of a stomach problem.'

Alex grimaced and deliberately pushed back his chair, but Cross remained unphased. 'Have you heard of lubricating oil mist?' he asked.

Alex shook his head. The first unspoken question to enter his head was, "Is that what came out of your backside?", but he suppressed the temptation.

'It's used to conserve machinery parts. We found traces of this oil on the face and neck of the deceased. It was also present in a plastic bag containing a clutch assembly found in the same room. The inside of the bag contains DNA from the saliva of the victim and the cursory attempt to clean the exterior of fingerprints left a perfect set around the aperture where the murderer squeezed the bag around the neck to restrict the flow of air. That's why we need fingerprints and DNA from all persons who were on the premises and, as you so succinctly put it, to eliminate them from our enquiries. Satisfied?'

'So, apprehend your suspect – the news bulletin said he's on the run – and match up your evidence.'

Cross grimaced as he leaned forward across the table. 'It's not as simple as that, I'm afraid. Alongside the victim and his office assistant, we have two sets of fingerprints, one matching the suspect and another, as yet unidentified, namely the set on the plastic bag.'

'You're saying there were two robbers?'

'If it were just a robbery, freeze and flight normally apply. Staying to fight rarely occurs. This looks like a premeditated murder, not the unlucky consequence of a botched robbery. Somebody wanted Mr Logan dead.'

'Why suspect my organisation?'

Cross poked the point of his finger into the dimple on his chin and squeezed together the surrounding flesh. 'I didn't say I did. I was on the loo and had a quiet fifteen minutes reading the terms and conditions of your loan agreement. If the borrower steps out of line, albeit marginally, your sword of Damocles soon comes crashing down on his head. It struck me, with Mr Logan dead, you are the most likely candidate to be resting your feet under his desk, if you get my drift.'

Alex erupted into a burst of false laughter. 'You're not seriously suggesting I'm desperate enough to contemplate murder to get my hands on a failing second-hand car business at the undesirable end of South London? Come on now, Cross, get some perspective.'

'It's the one thing I always strive for, Mr Quentin. Unfortunately, it's also the one thing of which some greedy people lose sight.'

PC Oliver Wright, better known by his nickname of Orville, rose from his chair in the staff canteen and gestured to his partner, WPC Cheri Sobers, better known by her nickname of Tipsy, that they were about to start the second half of their day shift patrol along the Walworth Road to East Street Market.

Tipsy held the door open for him, immediately sensing the change of temperature from the air-conditioned interior. It was one of those cloudy, humid days when the weather was depressingly uncomfortable. 'Some people can't read,' she said, pointing at the emergency vehicle parking space occupied by the Range Rover.

'Or don't accept it applies to them,' Orville added, strolling purposefully toward the vehicle. He registered the startled look of the swarthy man in the driver's seat as he motioned for the window to be lowered. The man was sweating, hardly unexpected in a stationary vehicle with all the windows closed. The man appeared to ignore him. He repeated the gesture, but the driver remained motionless, his eyes darting from one uniformed officer to the other.

'He must be foreign,' Tipsy said as she neared the vehicle. 'Tell him to open the door and step out.'

As Orville took a step forward, his arm outstretched, the door was flung open, crashing into his leg and shattering his knee. He collapsed to the ground as if poleaxed, his high-pitched screams reverberating around the entrance to the police station.

The giant of a man exiting the car leaped over the writhing body and started along Manor Place, pushing pedestrians to one side as he gathered pace. Only Tipsy stood in his way and, legs astride, teeth gritted, she appeared determined to stop him.

Tipsy pressed the transmit button on her chest-mounted two-way radio. 'Officer down; Ambulance, Walworth station; suspect attempting to flee the scene.'

The man was almost upon her. To his credit, she thought, he was attempting to swerve to avoid her. She moved sideways, directly into his path.

A week had elapsed since she passed the OST/ELS training course, and this was the first time she put into practice her new skill. The taser was out of its holster quicker than Billy the Kid could have drawn his Colt. The giant of a man was close enough for her to smell the scent of fear as she released the protective cover, and in a single movement, flicked off the safety and pulled the trigger. Eyes focussed on the five-second digital countdown, she kept her finger pressed tight. The crackling sound was inches from his chest. His forward impetus knocked her breathless to the floor. He was out cold.

Everything was hazy. Officers gathered around to help her to her feet. Some were dragging the unconscious man into the station. Others were tending to Orville as they waited for the ambulance. Passers-by had stopped, looking on in stupefaction at the surreal scene. One old man was clapping loudly. There was a single thought in her head. She could really murder a mug of tea in the canteen.

DS Moses had just asked his last question as the sound from the commotion outside the building filtered into the interview room.

Alex ignored the interruption as he addressed Cross. 'You've had your pound of flesh, Inspector. I didn't expect to be answering questions concerning confidential information about another of my clients.' He glared at Moses. 'For God's sake, man, Len Sheppard is a respected, retired detective inspector. There is nothing improper about our relationship. I provide loan finance. He borrowed money and provided the appropriate security – end of story.'

The noise outside the building continued. Cross excused himself. 'I'll be back in a minute if you can just hold on.' He shuffled out the door.

The two men sat in silence before Moses broke the silence. 'Can I ask you when you first met Mr Sheppard?'

Alex puffed his cheeks and exhaled loudly. 'Offhand, I don't remember. Is it important? Around the time he purchased his house, I suppose.'

'Was it an introduction?' Moses persisted. 'How did you come to meet?'

'Really?' Alex screwed up his face into a look of disbelief. 'His daughter is my accountant. She approached me on his behalf.'

They lapsed again into a strained silence. It was some minutes before Cross reappeared.

Alex went to stand up. 'Good, can I go now?'

Cross gestured for him to sit back down. 'Unfortunately, no. We are waiting for your employee, Saban Sula, if that's his correct name, to regain consciousness. It was necessary to immobilise him. For starters, we will be charging him with assault of a police officer. I suggest you request the attendance of a solicitor. In the meantime, we would like to complete your DNA and fingerprint examination.'

'On what grounds?'

Cross gave him a wry smile. 'Shall we say to eliminate you from our enquiries?'

THIRTY-NINE

CHARLIE, SYLVIA AND DOMINIC

'Dom's sleeping,' Charlie said. 'I've been kipping down in his bed while he stays up all night staring at the TV and watching nothing. His mind is somewhere else. God knows where. He looked so terrible when I got up this morning. I told him to go to bed and when he woke, to shower and shave before coming down for breakfast.'

Sylvia took off her raincoat and draped it over a stool at the breakfast bar. 'I really didn't think he would get into such a state.' She pulled over another stool and sat down. 'I'm on my lunch break. Should I wake him?'

'Leave him. He needs the rest. Maybe he'll start thinking straight, if he'll listen to me and I can put some sense into him.'

'Does mum know?'

'No, and don't you go telling her. When the time is right, we'll arrange a family meeting. Everything will come out in the wash, and I'll try to make amends. I can't carry on like this.'

Sylvia drummed her fingers on the melamine surface. 'What does that mean, exactly?'

'We've all got stuff to talk about, haven't we? I've been intent on trying to strong arm Cary's father into ensuring we don't lose contact with the twins. Out of the blue, he phoned me this morning. Suggested we needed to cease getting at each other, calm down, meet and talk things over like two sensible adults rather than gladiators. I agreed.'

'Wonders will never cease.'

'He's suggested we make a night of it at a casino club near Billericay. He's a member. Dinner, a show, a flutter at the tables. If it gets too late, there's a motel alongside to stay the night.'

'Sounds like progress.' Breaking off, she turned her head toward the door. 'I heard a noise. Is that Dom stirring? If so, great. I can have a word.'

Charlie appeared irritated by the interruption. 'I didn't hear anything. Let me finish. Anyway, I told Len I wouldn't be staying the night. He suggested I invite someone to drive him there. Did I have anybody I could call on? So, I hope you don't mind, I phoned up your man and asked if he'd do the honours.'

'You mean Lance?'

'Who else? He's a star, your Lance; jumped at the invitation.'

'He's not my Lance. I keep telling you.'

The kitchen door banged open against the rubber stop. Dominic was wearing the same grubby tracksuit bottoms and stained T-shirt he had been using for days. 'Hi Sylvia. Good to see you,' he said dismissively, with a cursory nod to his father.

'I told you to have a shave and a shower,' Charlie said. 'You stink.'

Dominic took a carton of milk from the fridge and drank. He wiped his mouth with the back of his hand. 'All in good time. What's new?' he said, turning to his sister.

'SSDD,' she replied. 'I was worried about you. Came around in my lunch hour to see how you were. Dad's been saying he's going to get us all together for a heart-to-heart with mum.'

A laugh rattled in Dominic's throat. 'That'll be enlightening,' he said. 'How does he explain he's been seeing some other woman? A shag for the sake of the family?'

'I told you that in confidence.' Charlie's voice rose a tone. 'To get you to open up about your own troubles. Unsuccessfully, I might add.'

Dominic looked straight at his sister. 'He is an absolute hypocrite, isn't he? Telling me in confidence in one breath and, to you, how he's going to confess all in the next?' He took a deep breath. 'My troubles? I'll tell you. I lost my wife and family to another man for the sake of a relationship with somebody who deceived me and consigned me to the scrap heap. I'm feeling angry with the world and desperately sorry for myself. I'm in a mid-life crisis with sexual hang-ups and I'm searching for an answer. Does that do for starters?'

It was seven thirty as Dominic watched the Volvo pull away from the drive with his father in the passenger seat and an over-zealous, smiling Lance behind the wheel. How he could have seen anything in that shallow personality and superficial attitude was beyond him. Lance was a worthless vacuum of a man.

Dominic had felt decidedly better since the outburst in front of Sylvia and Charlie. So much so, he had followed the advice and cleaned himself up. He had even made a surprise appearance at the company's depot, confirmed he would return to work the following day and signed out a van to complete an assignment that was still pending. Ignoring company procedures, he had parked up the van in the drive. It was all part of the plan.

He was feeling decidedly hungry. There was next to nothing in the fridge. He would drive to that Greek restaurant in Vauxhall for a Moussaka with all the trimmings. There was no point in setting course for his final destination until around ten.

The night was young and, for once in a long time, Dominic knew he had an objective to achieve.

FORTY

LEN, TERRY AND DARREN

Repeating the same story in that stuttering, nervous style was a sure sign Terry had passed the worry stage and was now sick with fear. It had happened once before in the early days of their clandestine association, when Len had asked him to help Randy with a harrowing personal issue. Terry had become a gibbering wreck, and it had needed all of Len's persuasive powers to calm down his colleague and make him come to terms with reality. The same remedy needed to be applied now.

'You know nothing,' Len had said. 'You're just surmising. Focus on what we can do to establish the truth. Speak to the woman; ask her to do some sniffing around. If you're right—'

'I know I'm right,' Terry interrupted. 'They must have suspected something and got hold of him. It's my fault. He's going to need his blood pressure tablets. What have I done? Why in Hell's name did I get Nobby involved?'

'Stop blaming yourself. Nobby got involved because his participation was a strand in the plan. If it's gone wrong, we will sort it out, but we need intelligence: where, when and how. If the woman is intent on running away with you and you say you can't leave until you discover what's happened to your friend, she'll react. Believe me.' Len sounded more convinced than he felt.

'She'll put herself in danger,' Terry said. 'God knows what the family is capable of.'

'I understand your concern, but your first responsibility is to your comrade.' Len deliberately chose a military association. 'Remember where your loyalty lies.'

'I'll call you back.' Terry had rung off as Len was about to speak.

'What an unreal mess,' Len said to himself as his main mobile vibrated in his trouser pocket.

'Is it sorted?' Darren asked, ignoring an introduction or preamble.

'He accepted the invitation willingly. I sounded quite humble and conciliatory. The prick swallowed it hook, line and sinker.'

'Do what?'

Len sighed. 'Charlie's hot to trot. It's up to you now.'

'What about his Aussie mate?'

'I suggested he bring somebody along to do the driving. He agreed. That's about as far as I could go. I couldn't tell him who to appoint as his chauffeur, could I?'

Darren took a few seconds to react. 'There's this copper I've invited from your old force who has got a serious grudge against the Aussie and your man's daughter. With any luck, he'll do the heavy lifting and we can keep our noses clean.'

'We? I'm not intending to be there, am I? I've invited some friends around for dinner. Mind you,' Len said with a laugh. 'The wife's not thrilled about last-minute guests, but I'll get one of those delivery companies to bring some ready cooked stuff.'

'Fascinating, I'm sure.'

'Charlie's going to know it's a set-up when I don't make an appearance.'

Darren laughed. 'Don't worry, old man. By the time he realises you're not coming, his pants will be around his ankles, and he'll have forgotten all about you.'

Late in the afternoon, Terry rang back to find Len in a sombre mood.

'What's the problem?' Terry asked, panic in his voice. 'Have you heard something? Is Nobby all right?'

'Calm down, for God's sake. It's nothing to do with Nobby. I'm in the middle of a domestic. The wife's got the hump with me. That's all. So, talk to me.'

'I did as you said. Went round to her office, bold as brass. Said to the receptionist I was from DOBIS, the organisation Nobby's involved with. Mahi's nervous. I told her I was fine about leaving next Wednesday, but we'd only go once I knew Nobby was safe.'

'Does she know anything?'

'Something's up, she thinks. The men in the house are acting unusually secretly. Neeraj – that's her husband – let slip he would be at Vijay's place – that's her brother-in-law. He imports religious artefacts from

Nepal. Mahi says he has a storage unit on an industrial estate in Wembley, but she doesn't know where.'

'It can't be that difficult to find out. We'll get Randy and go mob-handed just in case there's resistance. Is she sure that's where he'll be?'

'She can't think of anywhere else. She says her mother-in-law seems more nervous than usual – raised voices between her and the General.'

'Everybody has a domestic now and again.' Len cast his mind back to an hour earlier and Muriel's heated outburst, criticising his thoughtless selfishness.

'Not in the Kumar household, apparently,' Terry said. 'The men rule, and Mahi has never heard the General's wife raise her voice to him.'

'Find out what you can and call me back. I'll put Randy on standby.'

Toward the end of a rather sterile dinner party during which most of what Muriel had to say to him had been in monosyllables, Len excused himself to check the message on his mobile. He had fully expected it to be from Darren with an update on Charlie and company, but it was a brief note from Terry advising the address of the storage unit and suggesting a time to meet up in the morning. After a heads-up to Randy and an affirmative reply to Terry, he returned to the dining room. Both his guests were standing, ready to leave. The woman looked daggers at him. She had never been so insulted in her life. The man wagged a finger at him. The membership secretary at the golf club would hear about this. If this was the sort of people they were, Len would be well advised to consider his position.

He watched the couple walk to their Jaguar. 'What on earth did you say to them?' he asked.

But Muriel had already left the room. Len heard the door slam upstairs.

FORTY-ONE

CARY AND RUPERT

The reception waiting area at Walworth police station comprised one padded bench seat set against a grimy white painted, pebble-dash wall and two uncomfortable looking metal chairs. A series of public information sheets fixed to the wall with 'Tack-it' adhesive clay fluttered in the draught created every time the entrance door opened.

Rupert perched on the edge of a bench seat as he watched the rather attractive woman speak to the duty counter officer. She was plainly nervous as she asked for information concerning the irregular apprehension of Alex Quentin. A knowing smile creased Rupert's lips as he watched the officer's blank expression and codfish-like eyes as he ignored the question. In a disinterested monotone, he repeated a request to record her name and relationship to the person in custody. It was a scene he imagined repeated in a thousand police stations across the land. Pointing toward the waiting area, the counter officer said he would advise the OIC.

Cary sat on the bench, leaving a conventionally acceptable gap to Rupert. Her brow was creased as she caught his eye. 'Do you know what OIC means?' she asked. 'The only thing that came to mind was the Organisation for Islamic Cooperation. Clearly, that can't be right.'

Rupert laughed, to which she reacted with a smile. 'I'm out of my depth in these places,' she offered.

He turned toward her. She was radiant, he thought, a real stunner with those glazed come-to-bed eyes and slender, yet curvaceous body barely visible under that unflattering raincoat. Even in her concerned state, with her flaxen hair windswept, her face pallid behind the hurriedly applied blusher on her cheeks, he could certainly understand what had appealed to Alex. Like all his women, she would be hard and defensive on the outside, but soft as marshmallow on the inside. Right now, she seemed so vulnerable and confused. He ached to put his arm around her. Instead of doing so, he said, 'I guess he means the officer in charge. I doubt there's an outpouring of Islamic cooperation in this place.'

They laughed together. He sensed she was starting to relax. 'I heard you asking after Alex. I perform two functions as both his legal representative and his son. You must be the lovely Cary. I have heard a great deal about you and surprised we have never met before. You do his accounts. I cover his legals. You would think our paths would have crossed.'

Her face was alive, her eyes searching and appraising the man. 'You're Rupert?'

'Don't sound so amazed. I'm not that frightening, am I?'

She shook her head. 'I'm sorry. You've taken me by surprise. I imagined Rupert as a young man in his early twenties, recently qualified. No offence intended, but you must be around my age?'

'Thirty-six last month. I think he was a young man sewing his wild oats when he impregnated my mother. She had just finished her A-levels. I was a love child, my mother says.'

Her expression changed from one of enthusiastic interest to concern. 'I was very sorry to learn about her condition. It must be difficult for you.'

'Her condition?' He gave a false grimace. 'You've lost me.'

'The car accident; the death of your sister.'

He smiled involuntarily. The deceiving old bastard. Alex had kept this woman totally in the dark about his past. He felt the anger surge inside him. 'Sorry,' he said. 'You've got the wrong end of the stick. Did he tell you I was Rosalind's son?'

Cary hesitated; conscious she had just put her foot in it. 'I guess I just assumed you were. I was talking to Rose. She mentioned Rosalind and talked about you. I made the association.'

'My gran's a sweety, but she knows too much about his past for her own good, so he tries to keep her out of public view as much as possible.' Rupert knew he was being deliberately provocative, but, irrationally, he really wanted to get this woman onside.

'What do you mean?' There was hesitation in her voice.

'Mr Quentin.' The officer called from behind the counter. 'DI Cross will be with you in a few minutes.'

'Thanks.' Rupert turned to face Cary. 'You know what's going on here?' He didn't wait for her to respond. 'They've got Alex in here for questioning concerning the suspicious death of one of his clients. You watch these police programmes on the telly?'

'Now and again.'

'You're led to believe this is the softening-up period following the initial interrogation. The suspect is left alone to pace around the interview room while a room full of detectives and police psychologists analyse his movements from close-circuit cameras. "Give him another thirty minutes, one says, and we'll hit him double-handed, good cop, bad cop style. He'll soon break and confess." You familiar with the scenario?'

'It rings a bell.'

'It's all nonsense, I'm telling you.' He inched closer to her. 'They terminate the interview because they've run out of questions and need to think up some more or to comply with union guidance and take a rest break or for the DI to take a call from his wife to ask him to bring home a pint of milk or, possibly, from his mistress to remind him it's his lucky day or because his stomach's rumbling from last night's curry and chips or to help the Chief Constable finish the Times crossword. It's got absolutely nothing to do with the mental state of the detainee, who everybody has conveniently forgotten.'

They laughed together. 'Seriously,' she said, composing herself. 'Do you suspect Alex has anything to do with this?'

'Probably, but indirectly and obtusely. They will need me to witness fingerprint and DNA sampling, officially to eliminate him from the enquiry; unofficially, desperately hoping they can link him to the scene.'

'You make it sound like a game.'

'In a way, it is.' He hesitated. 'Your smile is a lot like Rosalind's. Forgive me if I say you look similar in many ways to the woman she was before the accident.' He moved his head from side-to-side as if bemused. 'From photos I've seen of her in her youth, you could also put my mother, Debbie, into the same category. Perhaps, he always goes for women with lookalike features. It's never occurred to me before. I'll have to see if it holds up with the others.' He knew he was being deliberately provocative.

'The others? You make him sound like a serial womaniser.'

'That's a great and totally fitting description. His inability to remain faithful whilst in a stable relationship cost him his future with my mother – they got engaged when he knew she was pregnant, but she broke it off when it turned out he'd been sleeping with two of her best mates – and, if I'm being brutally honest, it was unfaithfulness which brought about the accident that caused the death of his daughter.'

She swallowed hard. 'What a terrible accusation! You really believe that?'

He waited and then nodded slowly. 'Rosalind discovered he had sacked the au pair because she was about to confess to having been seduced by him, fallen pregnant and encouraged by him to agree to an abortion. The girl was on the point of a nervous breakdown. There was a bitter row and Rosalind stormed off with Hannah.'

'You don't appear to like your father very much?'

'I love the old rogue. I just don't approve of his womanising. And I'm not being sanctimonious. I'm thirty-six, unmarried and never been in a serious relationship. That says something about the impact of his behaviour on me, doesn't it?'

'I wouldn't know. Perhaps you're gay.'

He laughed. 'Never been my predilection.' He stood up. 'I'm going to grab a coffee from the machine before I see the old man. Can I interest you in one? Don't bother to choose; they all taste the same.'

She nodded, but he could tell her attention was elsewhere.

When he returned, she was nowhere to be seen. Rupert looked around. 'She left,' the counter officer said. 'Must have been something you said.'

'Must have been,' Rupert agreed, offering the man the spare coffee.

FORTY-TWO

CHARLIE, LANCE AND DARREN

Charlie twisted around in the passenger seat. 'Let's give the Volvo a good, long run just to check there is nothing wrong with the engine. I don't want her sending it back again.'

Lance turned into the traffic on the trunk road toward central London. 'Should be all right going through Town this time of night. Better than circling around the M25.' He listened to the instructions from the navigation system. 'Anyway, what was wrong with the car?'

'Bugger all. Mr "Know-it-all" Len Sheppard told his daughter it was a big end, and the car was crap.'

'I drove it back from his house. There was a clanging noise.'

Charlie exhaled loudly. 'If you'd bothered to open the bonnet, the problem was staring you in the bloody face. The plate securing the battery had worked loose and was banging against the superstructure. Thirty seconds with a spanner. Job done.' He tut-tutted. 'Big end, my fanny!'

It was almost ten thirty as they drove into an almost deserted overflow car park. In the darkness, the only illumination was a flashing neon sign above the entrance to a single storey building.

Charlie cast his eyes around at the half-dozen cars scattered around the parking area. 'Dreamlands seems a very appropriate name for the place,' he said, showing where he wanted Lance to stop the car. 'It looks like everyone is asleep.'

'Why here when we could park outside the entrance? We're miles away.'

'Caution, my boy, caution. There are two CCTV cameras I can see, one covering the front of the building, the other in the main parking area. Until I'm sure this invite is kosher, I'd prefer we keep a low profile. Something's been troubling me. Len and I both live on the other side of London. Why invite me to this place when we could have met up the road from home? There must be a motive.' He got out of the car and pulled the hood on his topcoat over his head. 'The place is like a morgue.'

'These sorts of places don't liven up until midnight.'

'And what "sorts of places" would this be?'

Lance studied Charlie's face. 'You're pulling my leg,' he said with raised eyebrows.

'I wouldn't touch any part of your body with a bargepole. Go on, elucidate me.'

'Members' club: bars with table companions, if required, casino, small restaurant for intimate dining, girlie show, probably motel attached for after-hours activities. You get the picture?'

'A high-class brothel?'

'Optional, I'd suggest. The more respectable aspects fill the licence application; the more carnal guarantee its approval.'

Charlie winced as he went to laugh. 'You mean a backhander and the promise of a BJ for the mayor and half the councillors?'

'You are just an old cynic.'

The man at the door towered over them, his upper body appearing as if set to burst through his suit jacket. Without a word, he ushered them inside toward a reception desk and an equally imposing middle-aged woman in a black cocktail dress barely restraining an overripe bosom.

'Temporary membership, is it, honey?'

Charlie tried to concentrate on the start of a moustache sprouting through the amply applied foundation on her top lip. 'We're here as guests of Len Sheppard.'

She ran an excessively long false nail on the end of a stubby finger down a list of names, stopping halfway down the page. 'Honey,' she said to the doorman, 'take these VIP guests to the Yankees saloon where Mr Bateman is waiting for them.' She winked at Charlie. 'You have an enjoyable night, darling. Make the most of the facilities.' Her laugh was a rich baritone.

The double, frosted glass doors opened into a subtlety lit room, a long, curved bar leading onto a tiny dance floor and a pianist at an upright piano working his set with some innocuous background music. Behind the bar, the walls were decorated with American baseball shirts and equipment.

Nearly all the seating was taken, a spattering of couples, but the majority, men in twos or larger groups. There must have been forty people in total. A young man with slicked-back dark hair introduced himself to the new arrivals as Darren Bateman.

'I expected the place to be empty,' Charlie said.

'I think you must have come in from the Perry Street end and found the overspill carpark. The main parking area is valet controlled between the motel complex and the golf course clubhouse.' Bateman held out two flutes of champagne. 'Compliments of the house.' He turned to speak to Charlie. 'Unfortunately, Len phoned to say he's running late, so I've volunteered to look after you until he turns up. Down the hatch.' He held up a glass of lager but did not drink.

'Interesting décor,' Lance said. 'You a Major League fan?'

'All American sports. We've three bars here, all themed. Alongside baseball, we've an American Football and Ice Hockey selection. You're right though. My preference is baseball. Once you know the rules, it's a fascinating game.'

'I thought it was a take on rounders,' Charlie said.

Bateman laughed. 'Popular misconception. The sport is electric and big money.' He pointed to the gnarled-looking wooden bat in a glass case fixed to the wall. 'That's the bat Babe Ruth used to hit his sixtieth homer in the 1927 season. It's worth well into six figures.'

'Careful somebody doesn't steal it,' Lance joked, but Bateman's face stayed deadly serious. He gestured to the barman, who reached under the counter.

'Professional bats have to be made from a single piece of wood, but this beauty is used to deter anybody with thieving intentions. Feel it.' He held out a metre long bat by the tip, levelling the handle first toward Lance, then to Charlie. 'Feel the weight,' he said. 'It barely weighs ten ounces yet could knock a man senseless with one blow.'

Charlie held the bat in both hands and made a playful swipe in Lance's direction. 'What's the metal?' He rubbed his fingers along the matt silver surface.

'A mix of aluminium and magnesium alloys.' Bateman said, reclaiming the bat and placing it on the bar. 'We call it the widow maker. There are various dotted around the club.'

Charlie nodded and checked his watch. 'Can't we give Len a ring and establish at what time he's going to get here?'

271

'I'll do just that,' Bateman said, nodding toward the barman. 'Tell Jocelyn to contact him, will you?' He turned back to face his guests. 'In case Len shows up, we'll leave Lance here. In the meantime, let me show Charlie the rest of the facilities.' He refilled both glasses of champagne. 'The next bar we call The Patriots. It's named after an NFL team from Wisconsin.' He strode toward a set of double doors at the far end of the bar, with Charlie attempting to keep pace.

Lance pushed the second glass of champagne back across the bar. He had never enjoyed sparkling wines. They gave him an acid reflex in his stomach that repeated and seared his throat.

'I've got Fosters if you're feeling homesick,' the barman said.

'You psychic?' Lance asked.

'Come again?'

'I make one comment with my back to the bar and you standing ten yards away, yet you can not only hear me, but recognise the accent. You must have ears like antennae.'

'I picked up on the Australian twang.' The barman gave him a 'so what' shrug. 'Half or a pint?'

Lance shook his head. 'I'm driving. Where's this Jocelyn hang out?'

'You passed her on the way in; onetime Joseph, now Jocelyn.' He finished cleaning a glass. 'We cater for all tastes here. *Sure* I can't get you anything?' He winked at Lance.

'No. I need to check if this guy is on his way or not.' Immediately, with his first step, he experienced the light-headed sensation he recognised after drinking a skinful, except he hadn't. He wheeled around to face the barman. 'What was it, GHB, Ketamine? I felt there was a slight salty tang to the champagne. Why don't you come this side of the bar and we have a little chat about it?' The man blinked rapidly and retreated to serve a group of customers some distance away.

By the time he made it to the reception area, Lance's head was spinning. He steadied himself with both hands on the counter as Jocelyn looked on, a twisted smile on her face. 'Not feeling so good, honey?' she said.

He raised his head to look into her uncaring eyes. 'As if you didn't know. Where's the nearest John?'

'Use the employees' changing room just down the corridor.'

The place was deserted. He fumbled on the wall to find a light switch and staggered toward a double-sided bench separated by a row of clothes hooks which he clung onto. He had to keep standing. If he sat down, he'd pass out.

He needed to drink water, flush the crap out of his system, find Charlie, and get out of this place. He staggered in the direction of the washroom and stood in front of the mirror. Cupping his hands, he forced water down his throat until he sensed the need to vomit. The sink was blocked. He ran more cold water, splashing handfuls onto his face. His shirtfront was saturated. He remembered arriving in a bomber jacket. Where was it now? He must have hung it up.

The door to the changing room opened and closed behind him. He needed to find his jacket with the car keys in the pocket. He was feeling slightly better. Drink more water. He raised his head. Someone was behind him, staring into the mirror. He tried to focus. Whoever it was, wore a mask.

'Who—?' He had barely finished the word when he felt the searing pain in the small of his back. His chin grazed the edge of the sink as he slid to the floor. 'This is a set-up,' he said, just as the blackness descended.

Charlie was coming to the same conclusion as his guided tour of the club reached the third floor of the motel. Bateman had marched him through bars, a restaurant, a walk around the perimeter of the casino, and finally, toward a locked double door with a keypad entry control. He had barely stopped throughout the brief tour and Charlie found himself a little lightheaded and, most definitely, out of breath.

Bateman had stopped in front of the doors and pointed at the various young women in tight-fitting, provocative dresses lounging expectantly on seats or already engaged in conversation with someone.

'This is the casino entry into the motel,' Bateman had said. 'It allows clients who have met a friend to gain private access to their rooms without passing through the main reception.'

'How does that work?' Charlie asked. He was losing his sense of balance, as if attempting to walk on a tightrope. Whatever they had put in his drink, thank God he'd had the sense to get rid of most of his. Whilst Bateman was talking to Lance, he had surreptitiously poured the contents of the flute into the base of a decorative, artificial yucca plant. Even so, the few sips were taking effect.

'Members have access to an app which works throughout all the clubs. Drinking, dining or gaming, you can book a room in an instant for the time you want and the app charges your credit card, provides the room number and a QR code to let you in.'

'What happens if you don't have the app?'

'The girls have it on their mobiles. They just feed in your credit card detail and you're in business.' He flashed his mobile at the VR screen and the double doors opened into a small, enclosed lobby with two elevators. He used his mobile again to open the elevator doors. 'You can't move around the motel without using the QR. If you stay beyond the time you booked, your credit card will be automatically charged for the excess.' As they exited on the third floor, he laughed. 'Strangely enough, the punters never argue.'

Charlie's nostrils flared as he recognised the scent of cheap perfume. 'What if a member doesn't want the charge to appear on his statement and prefers to pay cash?'

They stopped at a door displaying the number thirty and the name *Juliet*. 'The narrative simply shows up as roaming costs. If cash is preferred, visit reception on leaving and the charge will be reversed.' The mobile he used to open the door to the room vibrated. 'Excuse me. I must take this.' He listened briefly. 'I'll be right down. Wait until I get there.'

Charlie gave a polite smile, a knowing smile, as he would have described it. Bateman was apologetic. He would have to leave Charlie for a few minutes to deal with a problem in one of the bars. 'You in there?' he called.

Seemingly from behind the door, a young woman appeared. She was petite, with shoulder-length raven hair, mascara-accentuated hazel eyes, and full lips. Her curvaceous body just about fitted into lycra-tight, black sequined dress. 'This is Indemira,' Bateman said. 'I'll leave her to look after you while I attend to the matter.' Before Charlie could react, he had turned back toward the elevator.

'Come in,' she said, pulling at Charlie's coat sleeve. 'Let me make you comfortable.' There was an edge to the way she spoke. Even through the thickness of her accent, Charlie sensed she was apprehensive, reciting a script she had to follow, unsure of how to proceed.

She tried to push him to sit down on the bed, but he resisted. Her eyes blinked feverishly, her breathing quick and stuttered. 'I want to make things nice for you,' she stammered.

Charlie wrapped his arms around her shoulders and pulled her towards him, bending his head to align with hers. 'If you don't want to make things worse for yourself,' he whispered. 'Listen to me and stop shaking. Say nothing until I tell you to. Do you understand English beyond the sex chat?' She went to speak, but he squeezed harder. 'Nod or shake your head.'

She nodded.

'I know this is a set-up,' he whispered. 'How many cameras? One. Two?'

She froze. 'Please don't hurt me,' she mumbled.

'I asked how many cameras? Squeeze me back when I say the right number. One? Two? . . .'

She squeezed.

'Both in this room, focussed on the bed?'

She squeezed again.

'None anywhere else? Squeeze for no.' He felt the pressure around his midriff as she responded.

He released her. 'Do you know what?' he said out loud. 'Before we get down to business together, let's take a shower. You can soap me down just the way I like it.' He retrieved his mobile from an inside pocket as he tossed his jacket onto a chair. 'Lead on,' he said, bundling the frightened woman in front of him toward the bathroom.

Sitting her on the toilet seat, he cast his eyes around the bathroom, examining any fixture which could conceal a camera or microphone. Satisfied, he turned on the recorder function on his mobile and set the shower to the maximum cold pressure. The noise was comfortingly loud. However minimal the dose, the drug was having both a mild numbing and aphrodisiac effect on his senses. He stared down at her. 'What did you say your name was?'

'Indemira,' she said. 'Indemira Taskin.'

She was beautiful, he thought, with that pert little turned-up nose, delicate chin and kissable lips. Perhaps . . . An image of Norma filled his head. Get a grip, he said to himself. He allowed himself to slide his back down the wall, coming to rest seated on the tiled floor opposite and looking up at her. He placed the mobile on the floor between them.

'Indemira,' he said, 'I didn't come here for sex with a prostitute, nor do I intend to hurt you. Someone I know imagines this clumsy set-up will provide evidence to blackmail me. Do you understand? Don't nod. Talk, so that my wife will understand what is happening.'

'I understand,' she whispered.

'They tried to drug me before they left me with you. I'm still feeling the effects, even though I drank next to nothing. Who told you what to do?'

'We are guarded by two minders, and the freak you must have met at reception.'

'Jocelyn?'

'The sadistic bitch. She told me to take care of you, make sure you faced the cameras. If I don't give them what they want, she will hurt me.' Indemira struggled to raise the sleeve of her dress. There were several bruises amongst the needle marks.

'You're an addict?'

She shook her head. 'Never. They give all the new girls a relaxant shot every night. It's supposed to make us more amenable and vital to the clients. Many of the older women have moved on to the harder stuff. My family would never forgive me.'

Charlie's expression softened. What had he been thinking? She was only a child, young enough to be his granddaughter. 'Where did you learn to speak such good English?'

'I come from a farming community in the north of Azerbaijan, near the Caucasian mountains. My father was a Dutch agronomist, but spoke English most of the time. I became the English teacher in the local school.'

'How on earth did you end up here?'

She moved off the toilet seat to sit down on the floor next to him. Her eyes roved around his face, as if searching for confirmation. 'Are you for real or is this some sort of trick to catch me out?'

Charlie reached for her hand and clasped it between his. 'Let me put it simply. This is what I think is happening. A friend of Darren Bateman doesn't like me and believes if he can arrange some compromising photos of me having sex with a prostitute, he can convince me to do what he wants or else he will show the photos to my wife. To make me more amenable, they put something in my drink, only I didn't drink it all, just a mouthful. But I'm feeling lightheaded and tired. I bet you've been told to make sure the camera gets a good look at my face while we're in the act.' He stopped. 'Believe me or not, it's the truth. Now, your turn.'

She nodded slowly, as if weighing up what to say. 'Gangs of people traffickers operate in the small towns around the area from where my family lives. Some people come to them willingly, refugees from the war-torn Middle East or Afghanistan. We are a Muslim country with many borders. These people believe they are going to relatives in the West but end up here or working as slaves in factories, so I am told.'

'You came as a refugee?'

She shook her head. 'Sometimes they just take people to satisfy an order. On the night I was captured, these men, mainly Georgians and Armenians, took young women from six villages in the valley. There were around twenty of us, some as young as fourteen, bundled into a lorry to take us across Europe.'

'How do they get away with it?'

'They bribe the local police to ignore them and warn the families that if they approach the authorities, their loved-ones will all be killed. We were told the same thing would happen if we tried to escape. To keep us quiet, we are given eighty pounds per week to send to our relatives and ordered to write and tell them everything is wonderful here in England.'

There was a knock on the room door and a hoarse male voice asking if everything was all right. She was on her feet in an instant, heading for the bedroom. 'Just looking for towels,' she shouted. 'Everything is fine.'

'Get on with it,' came the response.

She ran back into the bathroom. 'That was Eric, one of our minders. If I don't do what they say, he will hurt me.'

Charlie nodded. 'I'll lay there, and you pretend. Sit on top and tell me when to groan with satisfaction. No funny business. You understand?' He switched off the shower and checked the recorder on his mobile. It was still working, although the battery wouldn't last long.

She stopped him before they walked from the bathroom. 'Will you help me get out of this place? If you do, I'll tell your wife what a gentleman you were.'

He laughed. 'I'll see what I can do.'

'Jesus!' Darren said. 'What did you do, use him for batting practice? The state of him.' He looked closely through the window of the storeroom at the figure still bound to the upturned chair, the upper half of his body flat against the concrete floor. 'You're sure he's still alive?'

'Of course,' Morgan said. 'I gave him a couple of extra taps for fucking me about the other night when I was trying to screw the cow he lives with.' He held out the baseball bat. 'Anyway, you said you needed some of his blood on the end of this one and I was careful to keep the plastic cover over the other man's fingerprints on the handle before I smacked him with it.'

'Did he say who gave him the financial information that's got this old copper's knickers in a twist?'

Morgan laughed. 'He said he's telling me jack shit and why didn't I cut him loose, take the mask off, stand up and fight him like a man? I gave him another tap, and he fell over. He's still unconscious.'

'Did he recognise you?'

'I don't think so. I disguised my voice.'

Darren checked the message on his mobile. 'I've got no more time to waste on this guy. I'm doing Len a favour and now we've got some pics of Greaves getting his end away, the problem's solved. Get Eric to help you stick the Aussie in the boot of Greaves's car. Hide the bat under a blanket.'

Dominic crouched down in the driver's seat of the van so as not to be seen by the two men carrying the body around the perimeter of the car park. As they neared the Volvo, he sank even lower, his eyeline just above the dashboard. He had parked fifty metres away, head on, intending to wait for Lance and Charlie to emerge from the club, take some photos on his mobile, and let his mother and sister draw their own conclusions. What was happening now was definitely not in the script. God knows what these two thugs would do if they caught him watching. As if reading his thoughts, one of the two men glanced over in his direction. He took a step toward the van just as the other man called to him and waved a car key in the air. As the boot lid sprung open, the man retraced his steps and joined his colleague to lift the body unceremoniously into the void. There was a brief conversation concluding with the smaller of the two men angrily slamming the lid shut before walking to the driver's door, where he leaned inside and placed the key in the ignition. Dominic slowly raised his body to a sitting position as he watched them make their way back around the perimeter to the main building. He checked around as he eased the van door open. Nobody. The creak of the hinge seemed even louder than ever.

For a split second, he thought he heard a rustling of grass, as if someone was moving through the undergrowth that bordered the field beyond. He strained his eyes and ears, but there was no movement. He must have imagined it.

Alone in the darkness, the only sounds were of his shoes on the gravel and the chill, easterly wind whipping through the treeline and blowing strands of lank brown hair onto his forehead and eyes. In the space of fifty metres, he must have pushed the hair back into place six times.

The key fob in the ignition had a boot release button. The hunched body partially obscured the internal light, but in the dull glow, he could make out the wild eyes staring at him from the bloody mess that was Lance's face. He had taken a severe beating: a broken nose and two serious gashes, one near his temple, the other a deeper cut across his cheek. Both wounds were still bleeding, rivulets of red draining across his face onto his shoulder.

Recognition was mixed with both relief and pain. 'It's you. Thank God.' The words were barely intelligible. Two of his teeth were cracked, his tongue bruised. Dominic thought he sounded like one of those people with a speech impediment. 'I think my leg's broken. Get me out of here!' There was utter desperation in his voice.

Dominic stood back. He had not expected to feel the way he did – couldn't help himself. He was alarmed at his own reaction at seeing the one person for whom he had sacrificed everything curled up in agony. For an instant, the world stopped turning; he found it impossible to breathe; the pity he had expected to feel was not present or had evaporated into the ether. Instead, a tsunami of rage welled inside him, a torrent of anger at the ease of the betrayal, the casual way his hopes and dreams had been swept aside. He was nothing more to this beaten individual than the flotsam lying on the sand after the tide had retreated.

'For all that's holy, Dom, are you just going to stand there like a damn statue? I'm in pain. Do something!'

So, he did.

Morgan Priest opened the door to the overspill car park. A wedge of light illuminated a ten-metre pathway in front of him into the darkness. Beyond that, he needed the torch app on his mobile to find a way around the perimeter back to the Volvo. He had taken the car keys from the pocket of the Aussie's bomber jacket which had been left hanging in the staff rest room. The ever-unhelpful Eric had refused point blank to collect it and stick it in the boot. 'I'm not fetching and carrying for the filth,' he had said. 'Do your own dirty work and don't forget to bring back the bat. The boss says it's safer kept somewhere it can come to light as and when the law starts nosing around.'

'Bonehead,' Morgan said out loud, as he stumbled over a mound of grass on the verge.

He stopped. There was the sound of feet moving rapidly on gravel, too far away for the person to be caught by the torchlight. His first thought was that the Aussie had somehow come round and was making a dash for it. He discounted the idea on two counts. One, the boot was locked and two, the first blow he had administered with the bat had almost certainly broken a bone in the man's leg. The Aussie wasn't walking anywhere.

The noise had stopped. Had they witnessed what had happened? One thing at a time. He fumbled with the boot release and was about to toss in the jacket. The man's face seemed bloodier than it had done earlier, the baseball bat coated in red further down the shaft. He pulled at the man's arm. No pulse. He turned the body onto its back, wedged his hands together and began chest compressions.

He stopped at the sound of a car door slamming shut and an engine coming to life. The driver over-revved, causing the gravel to spin out from under the tyres as the vehicle raced away. Momentarily, the headlights were illuminated to identify the exit and then, extinguished, the driver relying on his sidelights to reach the main road.

Morgan rolled down his shirt sleeves. There was no point. His shirtfront was spattered in blood. The man was dead. Questions reverberated in his head. Was he responsible? What had the driver of the vehicle witnessed? Had he seen the body? Had he done something to it? Why did the head wounds look so much worse than he recalled? In a daze, Morgan retrieved the bat and stumbled back to the entrance. Eric was waiting outside. He listened, cursed long and hard, and secured the bat in a storage cupboard as Morgan watched on, head bowed, eyes glazed and hands shaking.

'Let's check the CCTV.' Eric grabbed the policeman's arm, leading him to the first-floor control room. It took less than ten minutes to verify the van's arrival shortly after eleven and although the camera had failed to identify the registration, the sign written name on the side was clearly visible.

Darren had entered the control room to be brought up to date with the chain of events. 'Was it you who killed him?' He turned to the disgruntled figure of Morgan. 'Or did the mystery man in the van finish him off?'

'I just meant to send him a warning not to go poking around in other people's business,' he said, disconsolately. 'I never meant for him to die.'

'Very admirable. I'm sure if he's looking down on you, he'll appreciate the sentiment. Now, pull yourself together.' He asked after the whereabouts of the baseball bat. 'Critical, that is now,' he continued. 'The police will eventually end up here and we need to make sure they find the murder weapon with Greaves's fingerprints all over it. Put a couple of stills from his bedroom adventure on the corpse. We can make it look like blackmail gone wrong.' His finger tapped the screen of the monitor, highlighting the side of the van. 'See the name?' He tapped the screen again. 'Call for Byte Man at Soft Touch IT Solutions.' He gave a knowing nod. 'Find out who the driver is and we've not only got our witness but, almost certainly, the guy who's been hacking into the offshore banking records of our friendly, retired Chief Inspector.'

The dawn light was filtering through the blinds in the executive office suite as Darren raised the glass to his lips. In the chair opposite, Eric sat legs apart, a bottle of beer couched between his hands.

'You know what?' Darren said. 'I get the sense our Mr Morgan might have difficulty in dealing with his conscience.'

'So do I.' Eric took a swig from the bottle.

'Dependent upon how things progress, if we don't get Greaves in the frame for murder, it might be desirable, even necessary to arrange a "can't live with myself anymore" suicide: typed note on the screen of his laptop, admission of guilt, overdose or slit wrists in the bath. Get somebody on the outside to give you a price. He'll need to react smartish when we give him the word. Understood?'

Eric nodded. 'Just say the word. I can't stand the man.'

FORTY-THREE

CHARLIE

Charlie awoke with a start, his heart beating fast, his eyes slowly focussing on the rain and wind beating on the bedroom window. Whatever the dream causing him to wake with palpitations, he could not remember. The sensation was one of melancholy, yet somehow tinged with excitement and anticipation.

There was nobody next to him in the bed; there was nobody in the room. With the effect of the drug in his system, he must have fallen asleep as soon as his head touched the pillow. Whatever the girl – what was her name? Indemira, that was it – whatever Indemira had needed to fake, she had done it over his unconscious body. Come to think of it, the tip of his nose was sore. She must have pinched it to stop his snoring. He managed a laugh out loud. A robust snort would hardly have been an appropriate response at the height of her performance.

His mobile was on the side table, switched off, out of battery, he discovered. There was a trickle charger in the Volvo. He needed to get out of here.

As he went to get up, his fist unclenched to reveal a slip of paper. There was a name, Emir Salmanov, and an address in Cardiff. Underneath, she had written "Please help me. I did as you asked. Indemira X"

The memories of their conversation in the bathroom came flooding back. There was no time to waste. Find Lance, return the Volvo to Cary, pick up his car, and drive to Wales.

There was nobody in reception and no way of knowing where the Australian had got to. He doubted there would be anybody but cleaners or croupiers in the club, and he really didn't fancy the idea of coming face-to-face with Bateman or his henchmen again.

Fortunately, the keys to the Volvo were in the ignition. Lance could find his own way back. Charlie had given his word to a frightened girl held against her will. Keeping it would ruffle more than a few feathers, including that scheming sonofabitch, Len Sheppard.

He was crossing central London before there was enough juice in the battery to activate his mobile. Both Lance's and Dominic's numbers went straight to message service. Sylvia had left three messages. She had been trying to contact Lance since early morning. Where were they both? By the tone of the last message, she was both hurt and angry. He sighed. Norma hadn't tried to contact him. If he was to have any chance with her, he would need to come clean about everything that had gone on. He put the thought out of his mind and tapped the voice recorder app. By the time he had parked outside Dominic's house, he had played back not only his conversation with Indemira, but a statement she had added whilst he was asleep. It was substantially a repeat of everything she had told him and would be turned over to the police as soon as he had contacted this Mr Salmanov in Cardiff.

Back at the house, Dominic had crashed out on the sofa in his underpants. The intermittent beep in the kitchen came from the washing machine, confirming the wash cycle was complete. There was no point in disturbing his son.

Charlie took a quick shower, changed, and closed the front door as quietly as possible. The smell inside the Mercedes reminded him of home. The tears seemed to come out of nowhere.

'Are you all right?' Cary sensed something was wrong as soon as she answered the phone and he tried to speak.

'Sorry,' he said. 'Bit of a cold, you know. Your car's fine. Nothing serious. Gave it a long run last night and this morning. I've left it parked outside your and Dominic's house.' He caught his breath. 'The keys are on the hall table.' There was another pause. 'Speak to him for me, will you? He's in a bad way. Made a lot of wrong choices he's now regretting. Be kind. It's what Norma would ask of you.'

'I know just how he feels,' Cary replied. She ended the call before he could ask her to explain.

FORTY-FOUR

LEN, TERRY, RANDY AND THE KUMARS

Flashing his warrant card in the face of a tired security guard at the entrance to the industrial estate coupled with talk of a drugs raid prompted a response none of the three could have hoped for.

Len nodded sagely as the man explained where he kept the master key to the units for safekeeping in case of an emergency. For a small financial inducement, the security staff would facilitate inward deliveries whenever the tenant could not be present. The Indian gentleman at number seventeen often used this service. He was not a generous tipper. The man produced a key and asked which drugs they were looking for and where had they come from. Terry's abrupt answer made Cocaine and Kolkata sound like a musical duo.

There were a dozen wooden crates scattered around the floor, some opened, others still nailed shut. Stencilled black lettering in both English and Hindu script described the contents as variously: Diwali Lamps, Brass Puja Sets, Incense sticks, Wedding Shera and Garlands.

'Over here,' Randy called out.

An overturned chair, severed plastic ties, and a baseball cap littered the rough cement floor.

'That's Nobby's,' Terry said. 'He was wearing it the last time we met.'

'They've taken him somewhere else. Call the woman and ask where it could be.' Len fingered the cap, rotating it in his hands. 'We need to find him and soon.'

'The agreement was I wouldn't contact her until we were ready to leave,' Terry said.

'We haven't got time to hang around,' Len snapped. 'You got him into this mess. You get him out of it.'

Terry moved out of earshot to make the call. 'She's dead nervous,' he reported a few minutes later. 'Asked if we were ready to go tomorrow. I said maybe the day after. I was gearing up for Wednesday.'

'Fuck your arrangements.' It was the first time Randy had spoken. 'What did she say about Nobby?'

'She doesn't know. The only thing she said was that last night, the women in the house were told to wait together in the lounge. There was activity in the hall. Afterwards, she heard her mother-in-law raise her voice to her husband. She said something about the cellar.'

Len was already on his way out of the warehouse. 'Let's go. What's the address?'

'Hang on,' Randy said. 'If they don't let us in, what are our grounds for forcing an entry without a warrant?'

'Show your ID and say we have reason to believe a serious crime has been committed and we have grounds to suspect there is evidence on the premises.' As he sat in the passenger seat, he turned to face Randy. 'You know the drill.'

'I could get kicked off the force for this. By rights, I should call it in and let uniformed or CID deal with it.'

'In the meantime, your friend and colleague could be in mortal danger. Call it in after we've got inside.'

The old woman who stood four-square in the doorway was plainly determined not to let them gain access. She represented an imposing barrier. Legs planted apart, she was dressed in a traditional sapphire blue *salwar kameez* trouser suit and tunic with her stern face framed in a matching *dupatta* scarf wrapped around her head and neck. The two younger women standing just behind her in more conventional dress were plainly apprehensive.

'My husband is not here. You may not enter,' was the reply as Randy proffered his police identification and politely asked to inspect the premises.

Len pushed Randy to one side as he faced the woman. 'Stand aside or I will arrest you for obstructing a police investigation. If you three do not allow us access, you will be charged, forcibly removed and taken to a cell in Wembley Police Station for interrogation.'

Terry could sense the old lady's resistance was crumbling as she reacted to the sobs of the two younger women behind her. They were backing off, pleading with her in mumbled sentences. He had to admire the old girl's persistence as she made one more attempt to hold her ground.

'My husband is General Badri Kumar, a diplomat and an associate of your Police Commissioner. He would not permit me to grant you entry.'

'We shall be more than happy to talk with the General when he comes to visit you in your cell.' Len turned to face Randy. 'Call uniform to come and take them away. Read them their rights.' He turned away, winked, and smiled in response to the look of dread on Randy's ashen face.

The two younger women had already retreated along the hallway and out of sight. The General's wife looked over her shoulder, bowed her head as she clasped her hands together and shuffled to one side, allowing the three men to push past.

All three knew exactly where they wanted to search, but Terry had insisted they scan every room in the house first before centring their attention on the cellar. No suspicion could be directed at Mahi as their informer. Len had reluctantly agreed.

Len felt the gentle tap on his shoulder. The old woman had regained some of her composure. 'Who told you to come to this house?' she asked bluntly.

'Nobody,' he replied. 'We were dealing with a complaint of a disturbance in a warehouse. Certain evidence was present which prompted us to discover the address of the tenant, Mr Vijay Kumar. I assume he's not here?'

She looked away and shook her head.

The three men had now congregated in front of a cellar door with a Yale lock. 'Key, please,' Len said.

The old woman shrugged and held up her hands. 'It is with my husband.'

Terry's foot was already raised. The door gave in with the sound of shattered timber accompanied by the scream of a man and the clatter of a body tumbling downstairs. Terry peered into the darkness, his hand feeling for a light switch. A neon glow illuminated a narrow staircase at the bottom. A man was stumbling to his feet.

'You said there were no men in the house.' Len looked past Terry at the figure in T-shirt and tracksuit bottoms, nursing a bleeding arm, and then back to the old woman. Her face was expressionless.

Randy stayed guarding the landing to ensure nobody tried to leave or enter the house. Len and Terry made their way gingerly downstairs, the injured man backing off as they neared the bottom. 'What do you want with us?' His voice was full of fear as his gaze fixed on Terry. 'I recognise you,' he said. 'You stopped me in the park. What's this all about?'

Terry pushed the man firmly in the chest, causing him to lose balance and fall awkwardly onto the floor. He yelped as he instinctively put down his injured arm to break the fall.

Len looked questioningly at Terry. 'He was following Mahi,' Terry explained. 'He's her brother-in-law, Vijay. I sent him packing.'

The man looked up in amazement. 'How do you know my name and Mahi?'

'My colleague is working with Mahi on a podcast. He told me.' Terry sniffed. 'That's why we're here. His name is Robin Clark, former policeman and our colleague. We need to trace him. You know where he is, I believe. So, talk.' Ignoring the protests, he pulled the man by the shirt collar to his feet.

The cellar entrance opened out into a large area, representing a footprint of the house. Len was already taking stock of the scene before him.

To one side was a table structure close to twenty square metres upon which was mounted a model railway setting, including a panoramic mountain with ravines, precipices, viaducts and tunnels leading into a series of lakes dotted with boats and water skiers. The railway line turned through a complex of sidings into a detailed village arrangement, complete with residents, vehicles and chalet-style houses.

'Jesus,' Len said, taking in the scene. 'Who put all this together? It must have taken years.'

'It did.' The female voice caused Len to turn to face one of the younger women. 'I am Danika.' She bowed her head to avoid his gaze. 'My brother, Neeraj, has had a problem with anger management since he was a boy. Our father discovered a few hours spent concentrating on the detail of his hobby had a calming influence. As Neeraj grew older, so the hobby grew with him.' She looked at the wounded figure of Vijay, wheezing, his body propped up against the wall. 'The women of the house: me, my mother and sisters, we are not allowed down here.' She pointed at the railway setting. 'I haven't seen this for years.'

'Why are you banned?'

She shrugged. 'Men like secrets. Don't ask me. Ask him.' The glance toward her brother showed no sympathy as she backtracked toward the staircase.

Len looked at the wine racks on the far wall, the bank of three chest freezers against the gable end, the table and four chairs alongside. 'It all looks fairly innocuous to me.' He pointed for Terry to lead his charge to sit on a chair. 'Vijay, isn't it? Why all the secrecy, Vijay?'

The man was regaining his composure. He raised his head to look at Len from the side of his eye. 'My father is an important man in the Embassy.' His tone hardened. 'As you will discover when he learns you forced your way into the house.'

'Untrue,' Len was quick to reply. 'Once your mother had listened to our argument, she stood aside and allowed us in. No force was applied. Just persuasion. You were saying?'

'My father advises on the border defences of the Punjab, east to Pakistan and west, to Nepal and China-controlled Tibet. It is highly confidential . . .' He broke off. Terry had lifted the lid of the first freezer and was shuffling through the contents.

'I'm listening,' Len said.

'He is obsessed with the idea everywhere is bugged, including the house.' His eyes followed Terry as he moved to the second freezer. 'He comes down here to deal with sensitive matters and, sometimes with Neeraj and I, to discuss family or community issues.'

Terry held up a muslin sack with three legs of lamb in it. 'Why all the meat?' he asked. 'Expecting a shortage?'

'Our requirements are prepared once per month by a *jhatka* butcher. It's similar to *halal* in that it's how the animal is slaughtered.' His voice took on an edge. 'Please don't keep opening and closing freezers.'

Len walked toward the third freezer as Terry lifted the lid. As with the other two, it was full, this one topped with bags of frozen vegetables. Len fished underneath and produced an identical muslin sack of legs of lamb. 'I would have thought you'd have kept similar meats together, wouldn't you, Terry?'

With the muslin sack in hand, he went over to the second freezer and removed the contents. 'Had to make room for something bulkier, did you?'

His eyes met Terry's in a moment of joint recognition. At the bottom of the freezer, wrapped in a white sheet, was a body. Len unwrapped the frozen form. 'You evil bastards,' he said. 'You killed him.' He turned toward Vijay; his fist clenched.

'It's not what you think.' The old lady was standing at the bottom of the steps, shielded by her daughters with Randy behind her. 'He was an honoured guest. He had a heart attack and died. My husband felt it best to store his body whilst he contacted next-of-kin and assisted with funeral arrangements.'

Terry hustled over to her, his face a mask of anger as he bent within inches of her. 'You lie easily. It must come naturally.' He rushed back to the freezer and lifted a rigid, bare arm upwards. 'Honoured guest! Is this the way you treat an honoured guest?' He indicated the mark around the wrist. 'Bind him with plastic restraints and keep him prisoner in a warehouse whilst you question him?'

'He *did* die of a heart attack,' Vijay said. 'We never meant to harm him.'

'When my husband learnt of his unfortunate experience at the hands of my sons, he ordered they bring Mr Clark here to receive a full apology and to be our guest at dinner once he had rested and cleaned himself.' Danika reached for her mother's elbow as the old lady faltered, then steeled herself once more. 'During the meal, he felt unwell, and we called our doctor to treat him. After strenuous attempts to revive him, he was pronounced dead. My husband felt it incumbent on us to seek his next of kin and assist in the funeral arrangements. The doctor has issued a death certificate.'

Terry continued to lean toward her. 'Well, how very convenient,' he said between gritted teeth. 'I suppose while he was held captive by your son here and his brother – where is Neeraj, by the way?'

'He is with my father,' Danika said. 'Speaking to the community leaders about this tragedy.'

Len blocked the way as Terry turned back to face Vijay. 'This is no time to let our emotions dictate our actions,' Len said. 'We can't bring him back. Let's deal with the issue.'

But Terry was in no mood to hold back. He pushed past and grabbed the limp arm dangling at Vijay's side. The man yelped. 'Why did you take him in the first place?' He squeezed the arm again. 'I expect he pleaded for his medication, and you ignored him? Tell me I'm wrong.'

Vijay's face was a mask of pain, sweat clouding his eyes. 'Neeraj was convinced the podcast was nonsense, that Clark was after his wife, and she was preparing to run away with him. My brother has a violent temper. He refused to accept his denials and held off providing his medicines to extract a confession.'

'Which never came,' Terry added.

Vijay nodded. 'Listen, I told Neeraj he was going too far. I called our father. Please, I need to go to a hospital.'

Terry was about to react when Len told him to stand aside. 'Randy, call the local force and wait for them.' Len walked to the rear of the cellar and gestured for Randy to join him. 'The way we agreed. Remember? You and some friends were looking for your colleague and ended up here after visiting the warehouse. When you discovered what had happened, you called it in.'

Randy nodded. 'Okay, but I've just received a message. I need to get back to the office to return a call to an inspector from the Spanish national police in Benalmadena. It'll be to do with the enquiry I put out about the death of Stanley Forbes.'

'Good man. Keep me posted.'

The printouts Len held in his hand were copies of two of the half dozen images Darren had loaded onto the cloud. There was no mistaking Charlie's enraptured features as he lay in bed, nor the purpose or profession of the young lady who sat astride him. They would be more than enough to ensure his adversary behaved himself from now on.

'Charlie done anything about that heap of scrap metal?' he asked Caroline.

'He phoned me to say there was no serious problem. In his words, the car is running sweet as a nut. I'll pick it up after work. I'm dropping the girls off with Gerry and Gloria for the weekend, so you won't have them getting under your feet.'

'Is that wise? Gerry's not a very desirable influence on young, impressionable minds. Anyway, I thought you were moving in with Alex this weekend?'

'Change of plans. The girls love the chance to see their uncle and it's wonderful therapy for him. It gives me the opportunity to talk everything over with Alex before I take the plunge. There are a few issues.'

'Sounds ominous.'

'I'm collecting the girls for Sunday lunch with their father. Apparently, the estate agents won't start marketing the property until both joint owners have signed their representation agreements. I'll send him your love.'

'Where do you get your sarcasm from? Can't be me, surely.' The phone vibrated in his ear. 'Got to go. Another call coming.'

Randy came straight to the point. General Kumar and Neeraj had returned to the family home as he had been waiting for the uniformed officers to arrive. They had obliged him to leave. The General had said he was invoking diplomatic privileges on behalf of his entire family and ordered him out. The stand-off continued, first with the officers in the squad car and then with the CID detective, who appealed unsuccessfully to gain entry.

After hanging around for two hours, Randy had been summoned to the Assistant Commissioner's office at Scotland Yard, questioned and made to sign a formal statement. He had stuck to the story agreed with Len, which appeared to have been accepted at face value.

'You weren't questioned?' Len asked.

'Not really. Apparently, my account supports what the General is claiming.'

'How come?'

'Kumar told his assistant commissioner golfing buddy that his sons found Nobby wandering around dazed, hands bound on the industrial estate, took him to their warehouse, sat him down, cut his restraints and took the confused man back to the house. Kumar claimed Nobby told him he had been mugged and bundled out of a car. As a fellow Indian with mutual family roots in the Punjab, the General took a special interest in their guest, allowing him to rest and organising with a doctor friend a visit later that evening with the medication Nobby required.'

'Crafty old man. It all sounds feasible, if only it were true. What about Vijay's confession to Terry?'

'The Assistant Commissioner forcibly suggested I omit any reference from my report. He said he did not want to confuse the issue with hearsay resulting from the use of force. It's political and embarrassing. I suspect the powers that be wanting to sweep it under the carpet. I doubt they will ask you or Terry for statements. Your presence will be conveniently ignored. There was an implied threat. You and Terry could be charged with impersonating acting police officers.'

Len did not react. 'Go on,' he said. 'What else did the General say?'

'Probably the truth. Nobby collapsed over dinner. The doctor arrived, tried to resuscitate him and failed.'

'So why not advise the authorities and let them deal with the death?'

Randy gave a cynical laugh. 'You'll like this. The General assumed patriarchal responsibility, insisting that Nobby be treated in traditional Punjabi fashion with a local undertaker summonsed tomorrow to collect and take responsibility for the body and eventual cremation.'

'There will have to be an autopsy.'

'All sorted. A police contractor will do it quietly at the undertaker's premises it, causing no offence to community sensibilities.'

'He certainly knows how to pull strings.'

'And how. He's also tracked down Nobby's second cousin in Chandigarh and paid for her to fly over as a family representative at the funeral. Mark my words, the Kumar clan will come out of this smelling of roses.'

'You'd better tell Terry to get his skates on. His woman's likely to be under house arrest once Nobby's funeral is over.'

'I have. It's all set for tomorrow. He'll collect her after work.'

Len nursed the cut-glass tumbler in both hands and sighed long and hard. He often found it comforting to sit alone in silence as dusk turned to night, but the events of the day had left him desperately sad, deeply frustrated and full of resentment. Old man Bateman's paranoia to attain social recognition: his hold over Len and the others, his unnecessary demands – they had rekindled emotions best left dormant and had brought about the death of a dearly loved colleague. There could be no more dancing to the old man's tune. One way or another, it had to end.

If Nobby's death had one positive outcome, it was to put his feud with Charlie Greaves into perspective. Enough damage had been done. His financial arrangements had been called into question and a potential problem resolved with the help of Caroline's new partner. Subject closed.

From his side, the threat of disclosing images of the man having sex with a prostitute should be sufficient leverage to curtail Greaves's links with Caroline and the twins. Len would try to avoid using what were only accusations of VAT fraud unless imperative, and there was no way he was going to bring into play Randy's latest piece of intelligence.

As he had listened to his colleague recount the details of a conversation with his Spanish police contact, Len had experienced a familiar hollow sensation in the pit of his stomach. One thing he had learned from the experience of being part of the team investigating a terrorist bombing in the financial centre of London was that if he wanted to avoid ending up kneeling on the floor to receive a bullet in the back of the head, it was sensible to keep a low profile where the IRA was involved.

And this was surely one of those occasions.

FORTY-FIVE

CARY, GERRY AND THE TWINS

'I can't find my Wellington boots with the daisies on,' Creedence complained. 'Gran is always tidying up. She says we're getting into bad habits.'

'Don't sound so accusatory. Gran likes to keep her house nice and clean.' Cary recognised the blank look of incomprehension on her daughter's face. 'We left your boots and raincoats in the car before it went away to be repaired.' She ruffled the girl's blonde curls. 'So, no need to blame your Gran. Are you ready? Where's Syracuse?'

'*You* told us to get in the car. She's waiting. She said she wants a piece of Auntie Gloria's chocolate cake.'

'Well, we'd better get a move on.' Cary opened the back door of the Volvo. 'Put your backpacks on the floor and into your car seat. Wave goodbye to Gran.'

Gerry and Gloria stood arm-in-arm as they watched the rear wheels of the Volvo churn up mud and come to a stop on the dryer grass stand where other cars were parked.

The twins fidgeted with excitement as they tried to release their safety belts and wave at the same time. Cary clicked the boot release button and removed the key from the ignition as Gerry opened the rear door to let out the twins.

'Uncle Gerry,' Creedence crooned. 'Auntie Gloria,' came the retort from Syracuse as she leapt from the car and buried her head in Gloria's bosom.

'She's shy around almost everybody,' Cary said. 'When your names are mentioned, she's like a flower in full bloom. No inhibitions.'

Gloria gave the girl a squeeze and kissed her head. 'She knows when it's time for a world of make-believe, of witches and giants, of fierce dragons and friendly lions. This one has a vivid imagination, don't you, my little darling?'

Syracuse looked up into the smiling face and nodded, her eyes full of adoration.

'Let's get out of this weather and have some pop and chocolate cake,' Gerry said, marching toward the chalet. 'It's too miserable to stand outside. Put your knapsacks over there, girls,' he said. 'Go into the kitchen with Gloria and get some goodies.'

He pulled Cary toward him out of earshot of the twins. 'As delighted as we are to have the girls stay with us, I understood you were moving in with your new man this weekend.'

Cary sat on the sofa. 'Bit of a hitch, I'm afraid.' She smiled as Gerry raised his bushy eyebrows. 'I've learned a few things about his past life which he should have mentioned and has kept to himself. He's still married, admittedly to a woman who is mentally and physically incapable. He also has an adult son from a previous relationship. The man was quite scathing about his father's attitude to women. I need to clear the air before we move on. And—'

'Most people,' Gerry interrupted, 'Especially successful businessmen, don't get to fifty-plus without a few skeletons in the cupboard. Maybe he feels vulnerable about telling you and is waiting for the right time.'

She nodded unconvincingly. 'I was about to say, to cap it all, he was released from custody this morning on police bail pending an investigation into the death of one of his clients.' She hesitated. 'I should add not just any client. The victim was my father-in-law's ex-partner, and I arranged the introduction.'

'He's not a suspect, I presume?'

'I don't know, but with everything that's going on.' She let the sentence trail off.

'You're getting cold feet?'

She nodded. 'Suddenly, life with Dom doesn't seem so bad anymore.'

'I thought you said his sexual preference had changed?'

'From what I understand, it appears to have been more an aberration than a serious transition into homosexuality. Life may have become boring for both of us, but, at least, I wasn't faced with the complications I now have to deal with.' She gave a forced laugh. 'I suppose it could have been even more confusing if he was involved with another woman. Anyway, I'm seeing him tomorrow to sign some paperwork. We'll have a heart-to-heart.'

Creedence marched toward them, a glass of a fizzy red soft drink in one hand and a hand full of melted chocolate cake. 'Give it here,' Cary said, 'and go wash your hands and face. You've got most of it around your mouth.'

Gerry put his arms around Cary and squeezed, his gaze following the twin as she skipped to the bathroom. 'You'll work it out, I'm sure. Applying common sense to emotions can be very confusing, but I have every confidence in you.'

They were still in an embrace as Creedence returned. 'Didn't you bring any wellingtons for them?' Gerry asked. 'It's muddy out there.'

'Silly of me,' Cary said, pulling away. 'I meant to get them out of the boot. Creedence, be an angel. Go to the car and get your and your sister's boots and raincoats, will you? I just want to finish chatting with Uncle Gerry.'

Creedence turned on her heels and made for the door.

'She's quite the little madam, isn't she?' Gerry said.

'She bosses everybody about, including her grandfather.'

'How does Len take that?'

'Stoically, but sometimes he can't disguise the spontaneous chief inspector reflex.'

Gerry laughed. He looked over Cary's shoulder. 'Back so soon, Creedence. Couldn't you find them? What in God's name?'

Cary wheeled around. Little fingers were covered in blood. 'What did you do, darling? Have you hurt yourself?'

Creedence shook her head as if absentmindedly. 'My daisies are all red. I tried to get them out from under the man.'

'What man?'

'The man who is asleep in the boot. He must have banged his head. His nose is bleeding. I'm sorry.' She started to sob.

FORTY-SIX

CHARLIE AND EMIR SALMANOV

It was nearly forty years since Charlie had crossed the Severn Bridge into South Wales. Now there were two bridges to choose from and no toll to pay. That was what he called progress.

As he looked down at the swirling waters of the River Severn, he recalled with a smile his one and only visit to the Principality; to a car auction in Newport where he had come away with the star prize of the day, a 1300cc Ford Capri and, as it transpired, a financial black hole. At the time, he was new to the used car game, a small pitch in Bermondsey, buying and selling locally, making a score here and there, sometimes as much as fifty pounds. Finding a somewhat rare Capri with a larger engine was a commission from a buyer who would pay a price that would give Charlie the chance to make a handsome profit.

Bidding had been intense, but Charlie's winning bid would, by his calculations, turn a profit of two hundred pounds after expenses. It was when he came to settle his account that elation turned to misery. Charlie had never bothered to register for the VAT he would have to pay, nor had he counted with the buyer's commission payable to the auctioneer. His profit had evaporated, leaving barely enough to pay his fuel bill for the journey home.

He gave a chuckle. It had been his first costly encounter with the VAT legislation, but he had got his own back in the end.

The sterile voice linked to the GPS told Charlie he had reached his destination. It was as much as Indemira had told him, a hairdresser near Adamsdown. He looked around. If the rest of Cardiff was like this, street-upon-street of two-up, two-down terraced houses, he was glad he didn't live here.

Now where? He would ask a local. Directions, nervously given in an accent he had difficulty in understanding, led him to a small parade of local, double-fronted shops and a hairdresser with a professionally painted sign above the door saying, *Caspian Curls – Hair Artistry*.

As he pushed open the door, a dozen female faces turned to stare at the intruder. The stylist manning the chair nearest the counter eyed him suspiciously. She was old, with long, peroxide-blonde hair and heavily made-up with foundation in a failed attempt to disguise blunt, unattractive features. Her high-heeled shoes scraped on the floor as she walked toward him, scissors in hand.

'Yes?' she said in a husky voice. 'What can we do for you, sailor?'

Her client, with hair bound into rows of small rollers, giggled. She said something in a strange language, causing a general outburst of laughter amongst staff and clients.

Charlie felt the heat in his cheeks. 'I'm looking for Mr Salmanov,' he said. 'I was given this address.'

'Who by?'

'It's a private matter I'd rather discuss with him.'

There was an ominous silence throughout the salon. 'There is no Mr Salmanov here. Do you know this man?'

Charlie had regained his composure. 'No,' he said. 'Not that it's any of your business. Can you point me in the right direction, please? He'll want to hear what I have to say.'

The stylist slowly looked him up and down. 'The door to the side of the salon leads upstairs. Go there and ask.' She turned back to her client.

Charlie made his way out. The solid wooden door she had described was firmly locked. A muted tap seemed wholly inadequate; a fist banging, unnecessarily aggressive. He did not have to choose. The hunched, wiry-looking man who opened the door eyed him carefully. 'Back to me, hands in the air, legs apart.'

He rattled out the instructions in heavily accented English with a strange Welsh twang that sounded totally out of place. His hands moved proficiently over Charlie's body.

Charlie climbed the narrow staircase, emerging into a room where four men were sitting, three watching a foreign-language movie on an enormous wall-mounted television, the fourth, studying a small monitor with a real-time image of the hairdressing salon below.

A push in the back sent Charlie toward another doorway and into a large, dimly lit office with curtains drawn. The room was sparsely furnished with a partner's desk set in front of a leather sofa. 'Wait,' the man said as he retreated out of the door, locking it from the outside. The cushion on the sofa had depressed under Charlie's weight and he had sunk so close to floor level that rising to stand would either involve somebody's help or having to twist onto his knees to gain traction.

Five minutes had passed, and his eyes had acclimatised to the shadowy surroundings. Beyond the desk, the far wall was clad in mahogany-style panelling, more in keeping with a stately home than these bland surroundings. The only other piece of furniture in the room was a large, stand-alone globe of the world, which he imagined would open to reveal a small drinks cabinet.

As he thought about helping himself to a drink, a section of the panelling creaked open to reveal a doorway. A breathless figure emerged, holding a blonde wig in its hand. 'Glad to get this off today. It's itching like. . .' The search for a simile proved fruitless.

Charlie recognised the stylist from the salon but now clearly identified from a partially cleansed face and short brown hair as a man in a blouse and slacks. He marched over to the desk, tossed the wig into a drawer, and scratched at his head as he sat. 'You're looking for Salmanov. You've found him. What's your business?'

Charlie stared up at the man towering above him. This frightening apparition of a burly man with haunting eyes in female clothing did not need the advantage of height.

'I'm here because of Indemira Taskin,' Charlie stuttered and swallowed hard.

Salmanov produced a towel and wiped his face. 'Who's she?' he asked.

'Your niece or a friend of your niece. I'm not sure. We didn't have the opportunity to get into discussing family trees.'

'Tell me about this Indemira Taskin and what you know about her.'

Charlie gave a blow-by-blow account of the background to his visit to the club, the circumstances surrounding the meeting with Indemira, and the story of how she came to end up as a virtual prisoner and sex slave.

'You took advantage of this young woman?' Salmanov had now transferred the remaining skin-coloured foundation from his face onto the towel.

Charlie was indignant. 'No, I did not. I fell asleep and I assume she must have pretended to be having sex with me to provide the photos intended to be used against me. She needed a performance to avoid getting a beating for non-compliance. I have a recording on my mobile of our entire conversation. Remember, I came here of my own free will to help the girl.'

Salmanov nodded as he stood up. 'You could do with a drink, I expect. You've had a long drive.' He poured them both a whiskey and sat down on the sofa next to Charlie. 'Tell me all about this club and who and how many are involved.'

By the time Charlie had related everything he had seen at Dreamlands, they were on their third whiskey and the atmosphere was relaxed.

'The girl who escaped is called Tulay and is the niece of one of my men,' Salmanov explained. 'She managed to contact us, and we picked her up. She is young, still at school, and was able to give us little information about the container or where it was heading. All she remembers is a thick-set man with a scar on his forehead. Somebody called to him from outside the container. She thinks the name was Bernie.'

'Another girl was shot, apparently?'

'I believe so. We don't know her name, but it was this Bernie who had the gun. My men are working on it.'

'Your men? I don't understand.' Charlie refused another top-up. 'I've got to drive home. I'll be paralytic at this rate.'

'Have you heard of Nagorno-Karabakh?'

Charlie shook his head. 'Sounds like a nasty disease.'

The other man reacted to the comment with a quizzical look. 'I know you English like a joke, but maybe there is some truth in your remark. Nagorno-Karabakh is a disputed region of my country which Armenia claims and has waged a bloody war with us over centuries. The hostilities continue to this day, provoked, many would say, by destabilising Russian interference.' He clambered to his feet and returned to his seat behind the desk. Sweat and the remaining foundation around his neck had stained the frilly blouse.

'In 2016, a band of Armenians invaded my village, and amongst their atrocities, raped my wife and left her for dead. Fortunately . . . maybe,' he reflected, 'my wife survived.' He stopped to compose his thoughts. 'I commanded a guerrilla troop of thirty men. We made a revenge attack through the Lachin Corridor into Armenia. The village we came upon was protected by six Armenian soldiers. They were well positioned in sniper locations and claimed eighteen of my men. We were – how can I say – over exuberant in victory. We cut off their heads and put them on poles at the entrance to the village.

'The charge levied against us was one of war crimes. Before the authorities could round us up, ten of my men and I escaped. One was arrested and executed before he could be put on trial and his country humiliated. Through dissidents in Turkey, we arranged new passports and identities and travelled independently to the UK. Here we are today, only I am not Emir Salmanov anymore. My name is Ali Binici, a Turkish/Italian concoction. You can see the suspicion you created by asking to speak to me.'

'That was the name Indemira gave me.'

'Of course. She would not know any different. She is a friend of the family, a teacher in the local school.'

'How did these girls come to be taken?'

'Armenian criminal gangs. They operate to order. You want somebody killed and have money. You want sex slaves or fruit pickers. Pay and it's yours.'

'So, how do you propose helping to free Indemira?'

An hour had passed before a plan was finalised and Charlie had downed a succession of black coffees to combat the relaxing effect of the alcohol. 'I don't wish to pry,' he said, 'But why do you dress up as a woman? I'm intrigued.'

Salmanov stood up to escort his guest out of the building. 'My wife never recovered from her experience. She died a year after we settled in Cardiff. There's a small but tightly knitted Azerbaijani community here. Ever since I was little, I had the urge to dress up as a girl. One day, one of my men caught me trying on one of my late wife's dresses and a wig I had bought on the internet. He asked me what I was up to, and I said the first thing that came into my head. You must remember, by this time I had taken a hairdressing course and set up the salon as a cover for certain other activities. So, I asked him that what authority would ever suspect a silly old transvestite dressing up to style ladies' hair as a wanted terrorist, which is how we are described.

'The idea caught on and now the salon attracts clients from all over the neighbourhood to come and witness the freak show.' He laughed. 'I'll tell you this. These high heels are bloody murder on the feet.'

FORTY-SEVEN

CARY, GERRY AND A VISITOR

'You're sure we're doing the right thing?' Cary's hands were trembling as she turned the steering wheel. 'I can't help thinking we should have called the police.'

Gerry loosened his seat belt and put a hand on her shoulder. He squeezed. 'I told you, inviting the police onto our trailer site to report a murder means curtains for the entire community. The press would hound us. Local action groups would be activated with unfounded accusations of criminal acts. Irrespective of the truth, we would be stigmatised and forced to leave the site. There are nearly fifty livelihoods at stake.'

'But it's a corpse. A person I met and talked to the night before last has been brutally murdered. He was Sylvia's boyfriend. We can't keep it a secret.' Her voice had risen an octave. 'Do you think her dad did it?'

Gerry shrugged. 'I've only met the guy twice, but I can't see it, can you? You don't top someone, put the body in the boot and wait for someone else to discover it. It makes no sense. I suspect he didn't even know it was there.'

'What if he comes out when we park in his driveway to investigate the problem?'

'Tell him or anybody else who comes to the door there is a knocking noise. You're in a dreadful hurry to get to a meeting and you have a lift.' He checked the wing mirror to ensure the car of a friend from the trailer park was close behind. 'If nobody is in, leave a note and we'll beat it.'

'I don't like it. The police are bound to question me. What do I say?'

'Tell the truth. The last time you opened the boot was before it went away to be repaired. There was nothing suspicious.'

She stopped the Volvo a hundred metres before the turn into the Greaves' driveway. 'I've had a terrible thought,' she said. 'Creedence's DNA will be in the boot, possibly on the corpse. We can't expect her to lie. She'll say what she saw.'

Gerry was lost for an answer. 'We'll think about that. Let's make sure we keep the girls out of this if we can.' It was the only thing he could think of to say.

Cary knocked gingerly on the door. Her heart leaped. There was no reply. She had just posted the keys through the letterbox and turned back to the waiting car as an upstairs window opened.

'Cary. What a pleasant surprise. Wait, I'll come down.' Norma pushed a hand through dishevelled hair and pulled the dressing gown tight around her neck.

Cary turned back and waved. 'Please, don't bother, Norma. I'm in a dreadful hurry. Can we talk later?'

'Is there a problem?'

'There's another problem with the Volvo. I thought Charlie could check it out.'

'I'm so sorry, Charlie's not here. Do you want to borrow my car? I'm not using it today.'

Cary cleared her throat. 'It's all right. I don't need it anymore.' She pointed along the driveway to where Gerry and his friend were waiting. 'My uncle has sorted out a replacement. I'm very grateful to you.'

'Are you sure you can't stop? I can make a cup of tea for you all.'

'Honestly,' Cary said. 'I need to see Alex this morning and I can't be late.'

'Of course, I forgot. You're moving in today.'

'No, it's on hold. We have a few things to sort out first. I really must be off.'

'Sounds intriguing,' Norma said. 'I won't hold you up. Call me later. Promise?'

'I promise. Just to let you know, I'm taking the twins over to see their father tomorrow. There's some paperwork to deal with regarding the sale of the house.'

As the diesel engine fired into life, Cary exhaled loudly and sank down in the back seat of the friend's Volkswagen. She crossed her arms. 'Thank God. I thought she was going to quiz me. I must see Alex. He'll know what to do. My life needs to be sorted out. It's become so complicated.'

Norma frowned as she closed the bedroom window. Cary was certainly not her laughing, confident daughter-in-law this morning. She seemed apprehensive, almost scared, as she talked. Perhaps she was having second thoughts about the relationship with her new man. If so, all might not be lost between her and Dominic. She needed to check out what her son was up to and make sure he was ready to play the caring husband and father when he next got together with his wife.

'Charlie, is that you? Are you driving?'

'I thought you'd never ring. I'm on the M4 on my way back to town. Can we talk?'

'No.' Her voice was chill. 'I didn't call about us. I want nothing to do with you. Adulterous husbands are not on my 'to do' list right now. I'm just calling to let you know Cary's got another problem with that wretched Volvo you got from Ludo. I'll leave the keys on the front tyre. Don't try to come in. The doors bolted.'

'For God's sake, Norma. We have to talk sometime.'

'Maybe we do, but not yet. I'm hurting and angry. Right now, you're the last person I want in front of me.'

Cary was feeling distinctly better disposed and more confident than she had since the discovery of the body the previous evening. A nourishing but slimming breakfast of various grains and a vegetable smoothie coupled with a rousing dose of common-sense talk from Gloria had improved her spirits no end. An added bonus was Creedence's approach to the new day. There was no mention of the sleeping man in the boot. She seemed far more concerned with probing Gerry to lay out the programme of activities and had put on her wellington boots without commenting on the blood which had yesterday stained the daisy relief and had since been cleaned off.

The Volkswagen was a lot easier to drive than the Volvo and as Cary turned off the M20 onto the winding B-road which would take her to Alex's estate, she was convinced the doubts about his past would be readily explained and put behind them. She must be positive because the future was looking better.

She was listening to the radio when the ring tone on her phone cut in. As she looked at the caller's name, her stomach fluttered.

'Cary, is that you?'

She was having palpitations. 'Hi, Sylvia, how you doing?'

'I'm out of my mind with worry. Lance went out with dad two nights ago from Dom's to a meeting with Len and no one's seen him since. Neither Dad nor Len knows anything, and Dom thinks he's just ditched me and scarpered. I'm just checking on the off chance he might have been in contact with you. I know he was using the Volvo you were driving.'

Cary gulped. 'I can't help you, Sylvia, I'm afraid. The last time we spoke was when he came around to pick the car up earlier in the week. The way he talked; he seems really keen on you.' She coughed.

'Are you all right? You sound stressed.'

'I'm driving in heavy traffic. If I hear anything, I'll be in touch.'

'Sorry to be a pest. I'm feeling deserted this weekend. Holly was supposed to be staying, the idea being for us to meet up with you.'

'I totally forgot. In all these new family arrangements, it slipped my mind.'

Sylvia's voice adopted a hurt and affronted tone. 'Well, don't worry about offending her. I had her dinner on the go when she phoned to say there had to be a change of plans. No explanation. Before I could say anything, she had rung off. Since when, she has gone off the grid. God knows where she is.'

Cary was grateful for the change of emphasis. 'I wouldn't be too worried. Remember, her mum has just died and there's her brother, Roddie, to think about now he's on his own. He's not a stable character.'

'Maybe you're right, Cary. I'm just uptight about everything. I'll speak soon.'

Cary heard the call disengage. She let out a sigh of relief.

Unusually, the remote-controlled, gated entrance to the drive was about to close as she drove up. The sensors reacted to the presence of her car and the gate started to re-open. Either somebody had just entered or just left. There was no sign of activity along the driveway or on the country road adjoining the property. The only vehicle in sight was a silver-coloured compact car parked half on the road, half on the verge, two hundred metres away.

She stopped alongside the Lexus and the Range Rover. Good. Alex was indoors, just as he had promised. Normally, either Saban or Abdyl would be outside, valeting one of the cars. Of course, Saban was still in custody. Could he really have been involved in Logan's death? It didn't seem possible. What motive could he have? Alex would explain.

Choosing the kitchen entrance rather than the front door, Cary made her way noiselessly across the granite stone floor along a corridor toward the annex added to the main building as office accommodation. The only sound was that of her heels on the woodblock flooring. Suddenly came the sound of a telephone ringing, followed by Alex's recorded voice telling the caller to leave a message.

She pushed at his office door. It only partially opened before something heavy on the floor blocked its passage. Tentatively, she squeezed sideways through the gap. Abdyl's unseeing eyes stared up at her. Blood was seeping from the hole in his forehead. Cary gasped and held on to the door for support. She felt as if she would faint. Her legs were weak, her body shaking.

Alex was in the chair behind his desk. His chin rested on his chest. Somehow, she drove herself forward to stagger into the room, her gaze taking in the scene. One side of his head no longer existed, a pulp of bone and muscle where his eye should have been. In his lap, a hand gripped a pistol with a silencer.

Cary closed her eyes, bent her head toward the floor and vomited. She retched until there was nothing left to discharge. Slowly, she wiped a hand across her mouth. Her throat was burning. She must have water.

There was a rustling noise behind her. She wheeled around and gasped in amazement. Alex's mother was standing on a chair propped against the wall.

They both spoke at the same time.

'Did you kill them?' Cary blurted.

'It wasn't you then?' Rose said.

Both said 'No' simultaneously.

'Didn't think so,' Rose said. 'You didn't seem like the vengeful type. Don't touch anything.'

'What's happened? Who did this? Why are you up there? Have you called the police?' Cary's eyes stayed fixed on Rose. There was no way she was turning around to look at the scene of carnage.

309

'What's happened is that both Alex and his manservant are dead from bullet wounds. Who did it is a moot point. It's been made to look like suicide. There's a typed message on his laptop saying he and the Albanians were responsible for Logan's death – whoever he is – and he can't go on any longer living a lie. It's all fabricated, if you ask me. Alex was far too selfish to kill himself, and why use a silenced gun? I doubt he was worried about offending my sensibilities with the noise. Let's get out of here and call the police. I've seen everything I need to. I'll make a cup of tea while we're waiting.'

Cary grasped a mug of tea between her hands. It stopped them from shaking. She responded weakly to Rose's reassuring smile. 'I don't get it,' Cary said, regaining some of her composure. 'Why aren't you in bits about the death of your son? You seem totally unmoved.'

'I've lived with the probability he would meet a sticky end for ages – kind of got used to the idea and come to accept it. Behind the veneer of respectability, the truth is he was a loan shark and loan sharks make lots of enemies. Why do you think he had the Albanians around? Professional colleagues or minders and enforcers? I know which I'd pick. Everything I dreaded came true this morning and when it did, I found I'd done all the weeping years ago. I had no more tears left. Maybe tomorrow or the next day, it will hit me.'

'You don't think it was suicide? Tell me what happened exactly.'

Rose sipped at her tea. 'He invited me down to stay overnight, ostensibly to be formally introduced to you, his real motive to coach me in the art of sterile conversation so that I said nothing about his past which could cause embarrassment. I was also expected to back up whatever he told you to circumvent what you already knew or suspected.'

'It was Rupert who was quite scathing about Alex's past relationships with women.'

'He's a good boy. Probably felt you were vulnerable and didn't want you to get hurt.' She looked out of the window. 'They will be here soon. Anyway, I was in my bedroom when I heard three popping noises sounding like a car backfiring, or so I thought. Thought no more of it and came down twenty minutes later to find the scene you witnessed.' She gave a weak smile. 'I've always been a fan of crime novels, so after pulling myself together, I read the message on his laptop. It didn't convince me. The man on the floor had been killed with a single shot to the head, as had Alex. That left one popping noise or silenced shot missing. I was standing on the chair looking for a bullet hole which I had just found when you came in. For a moment, I thought you were the guilty party, but when you started to throw up, I realised you had just walked in on the carnage.'

'And the third shot?'

'It confirmed my suspicions of a murderer trying to make it look like suicide. He must have placed the gun into Alex's hand after he had killed him and fired the shot into the wall, leaving evidence of gunshot residue on Alex's hands. Whoever it was had some prior in mock suicides.'

There was the sound of vehicles breaking hard on the driveway.

'Who do you think did this?' Cary asked.

'Look through his filing cabinet and take your pick.' There was a loud knock on the door. She stood up. 'Ready for some questioning by dumb and dumber?'

FORTY-EIGHT

LEN AND MURIEL

Len had to hand it to old man Kumar. He was a crafty and clever operator. The word from Randy was that the Assistant Commissioner at the Met had a draft press release ready for release as soon as the post mortem confirmed the cause of Nobby's death. It summarised the General's version of events and commended him for his community-spirited response in dealing with the funeral arrangements and, at his own expense, ensuring a family member from India could be present to attend. The padding was all to do with racial harmony and bringing the culprits to justice. Len might be a cynic, but he suspected it would be a press release worthy of a round of drinks the next time the two met up for a round of golf.

Now, the difficult bit.

'Muriel, we need to talk.'

There was silence. 'What about?' she said, eventually.

'For God's sake, we can't have a conversation through the bedroom door. Come downstairs. I've got some bad news.'

'Don't order me to do things. Ask politely.'

He clenched his fists in frustration. 'Okay. I apologise. Please come downstairs.'

The lock turned, and the door opened.

'You're dressed up to the nines, made up and all. Are you going out?' His jaw dropped. 'Are you meeting someone?'

She walked past him and started down the stairs. 'Yes, I'm going out and, yes, I'm meeting someone. Now, what is it you want to say?'

Len followed behind her. 'Would you mind telling me who you're seeing?' he called after her retreating figure.

She sat on a stool at the breakfast bar. 'Yes, I would. Be quick. I have an Uber booked.'

'What is wrong with you these days?' He took the stool opposite. 'What have I done to cause this hostility?'

'You're mistaking indifference for hostility. Now, please tell me what you have to say.'

Len repeated the sanitised version of the events surrounding Nobby's death.

'I'm saddened to hear that.' Her voice softened. 'On the few occasions I met him socially, he seemed like a friendly and gentle man. He was your colleague and I sympathise with your pain. I expect you are going to the funeral.'

She went to get up, but he held up his hand. 'Please wait. I won't keep you long.'

Muriel checked her watch. 'I have an appointment. Five minutes and I must go.'

'Please tell me why your attitude towards me has changed. I can't carry on like this.'

'Neither can I,' she replied. 'That's why I'm seeing a divorce lawyer this morning.'

'It's Saturday. Solicitors don't work on weekends.'

'There you go, challenging me. Instead of "Please don't do that, I love you and need you", you're effectively calling me a liar. Don't you see what you've become?' She hesitated. 'Maybe, always have been.'

'I was just pointing out. . .' He stopped in mid-sentence.

'She's a friend of Caroline's. They met at her wedding through Norma's daughter. Her name is Holly. She is up in London this weekend from the West Country. Her mother died recently. We're meeting in Kingston for lunch. I want to know where I stand financially if we go our own ways.' She raised her eyebrows. 'Happy with the answer? What did you think? That I was having a clandestine affair?'

'Don't be like that. We get on so well. Why not talk to somebody to see if you can get through this . . . difficulty?'

She thumped her fist on the counter. 'So now what? I need a psychiatrist, do I? It's me who's the problem. Let me tell you something, Leonard Sheppard. Beyond the first few years of our marriage when I was a career woman, and you were an up-and-coming DI in the force and when our relationship was very much of a couple in love, along came a surprise package named Caroline and everything changed.

'From the moment I gave up my position as a PA to the marketing director to stay at home and care for our child, the scales came down over my eyes and I entered a vacuum created and nurtured by you. I'll grant you it was insidious, a slow but steady progression of you exercising control and dominating the relationship.'

Muriel checked her watch again. 'Let the cab wait,' Len said. 'Say your piece. It will clear the air.'

'You really don't have a clue what I'm talking about, do you?' There was a hard edge to her voice. 'I accept part of the blame. I allowed myself to come under your spell. At first, it was easy. I was tired. Caroline was a difficult baby and I have never liked arguments. The trouble was total control also involved decision making without ever consulting me, telling yourself the breadwinner had the right to control our destiny by leaving me in the dark and treating my point of view as irrelevant.'

Len shook his head. 'I don't accept that. I've always kept you in the picture.'

'When it suited you and, without exception, after the event. Look at this house. You put down a deposit before you had even told me you were thinking of moving. And why? That's another thing. You're a frustrated snob who wants to mix it with the wealthy social movers and shakers. You really thought a house on a gated estate in Weybridge would be a passport to realise your entry into the world of candlelit dinner parties and chit-chat about corporate takeovers and the stock market. You stretched us financially and look where it got you. We live at the paupers' end of paradise row and the only people you know are your next-door neighbours, a chartered accountant and his wife, the most boring people who ever drew breath, and a casual nod to the undertaker across the road whose house alarm was going off and you went to check if anything was wrong.'

She looked at her reflection in the glass door of the built-in oven. Her cheeks were flushed, and her mascara had smudged. 'The worst thing about your social pretensions is the harm it has done to our daughter and her relationship. You kid yourself the feud with Charlie Greaves is about protecting the well-being of the twins.'

'It is just that.'

'Bullshit. You're so concerned about your grandchildren, you haven't even seen or asked after them over the last two days other than to tell them not to do or touch this and that. No wonder they were elated when they knew they were spending the weekend with Gerry.'

'Something I'm not in favour of. He's another bad influence.' He looked pointedly at her. 'And not only on the kids.'

'I don't know how he made it to the man he is with you as his brother. No, your problem with Greaves is the belief that he and his family are not worthy of mixing with yours. Over the years, you've been like a dripping tap in Caroline's ear, trying to control her and frustrate and destroy the relationship with Dominic. You've virtually forced her into the arms of a man who can certainly match your social ambitions but is almost old enough to be her father. You should let people flourish and display their personalities, not shut out the daylight and try to smother them. I expect you do the same thing to those you worked with.'

As if on cue, the mobile vibrated in his pocket. He checked the caller's identity. Paul Bateman. 'Sorry, I have to take this. Be back in a minute.' He moved from the kitchen into the conservatory.

The call lasted barely a minute, but when he returned, she was nowhere to be seen. He was about to call out when he heard a car pulling away from the house.

FORTY-NINE

NORMA AND SEAMUS

The sun glinted on the gloss paintwork of the car as it pulled up in the road alongside the house. Norma smiled. There had been a time when she knew almost every popular make and model on the road and the trade price for each spanning the last five years. Her knowledge had developed over their married life together, not because she had any deep-seated interest in cars, but as a counter to Charlie's early cavalier approach to used car buying. Sometimes his enthusiasm to do a deal needed tempering, and she had applied an excellent memory to provide concise background support. The bug had stuck. Even now, she would pick up a car magazine and flick through the pages. Couldn't help herself. Old habits die hard, and they had made a good team. Once upon a time.

The driver had made no attempt to exit the vehicle, but she had a fair idea who was about to pay her a visit. 'Let's put it this way,' she said to herself. 'The car is the three-door model in quartz grey with that distinctive new shoulder line running along the side. That makes it this year's model. Odds are it's a rental picked up at the airport. That narrows it down to just one person. Is he stealing himself to get out of the car and face me?'

The butterflies in her stomach fluttered as he finally walked toward the house. She opened the front door before he was halfway along the path. 'I've been expecting you,' she said.

He looked over at the parked Volvo. 'New car?' he said.

'Long story. You're looking old and you've put on weight.'

'I could say the same about you.'

'Flatterer. You don't always have to tell the lady the truth, you know. Speak to Charlie. He'll tell you all about lying.'

He looked askance at her. 'Have I called at a bad time?'

'Atrocious. As before, your timing is impeccable. Come in, Seamus.'

She stepped aside as he entered and accepted the brief kiss on her cheek. He smelt just like he used to. Intoxicating. She ushered him into the lounge. 'Are you having the funeral here or taking Ludo's body back to Ireland?'

Seamus pushed his fingers through a mop of silver-grey hair and gave her what she had once called his leprechaun smile. 'Back to Cork. We'll scatter his ashes alongside mum's grave. They're releasing the body tomorrow. I plan to leave around the middle of next week as soon as I've completed the arrangements.'

Norma poured two large servings of Jamiesons into cut glass tumblers. 'I won't insult you by asking if you would prefer tea or coffee. *Sláinte is táinte,* if I remember correctly,' she said. She sat on the sofa and held up her glass.

He returned the gesture. 'Health and wealth to you, as well.' He took a sip. 'I am driving, you know. We must obey the law.'

She took a large swig. 'I expect it will be out of your system by the time you leave.'

Seamus raised his eyebrows in mock surprise. 'I take it Charlie's not around?'

'You know my husband had nothing to do with your brother's death? He was fucking his mistress at the time and using a fictitious dinner date with Ludo as his cover. I've sent him packing until the urge to kill him passes. He's already committed me to one life sentence. I don't want another.'

He nodded. 'This is unreal,' he said. 'It's like déjà vu.'

'Same woman as well.'

'The affair's been going on for twelve years?'

'No. Their paths crossed again over the historic VAT problem, and he couldn't resist getting into her knickers for old time's sake.'

Seamus tut-tutted in mock disgust. He had a kind face, she thought, soft features and sensuous eyes with those heavy, devil-like turned-up eyebrows. You would never guess from his face he had been an IRA terrorist responsible for God knows how many knee-cappings and ritual executions in the bad old days holistically referred to as 'The Troubles'.

'Makes me mad thinking about it,' she added. 'Let's change the subject. Are the police any closer to catching the killer?'

'They're heading in the right direction. There's still one loose end to tie-up.'

'Somebody's in for a lengthy prison sentence, don't you think?' she probed.

His expression was serious. 'It won't come to that.'

She nodded. 'Summary justice?'

'Best you don't insist on an answer. I'd hate to lie to you.' He hesitated. 'You know somebody in the police has been asking questions about that incident twelve years ago?'

'Stanley Forbes?'

He nodded. 'It's not official, apparently. An individual initiative from a DI Randall Compton on whose behalf I don't know. My source in Spain says this Compton is with the City of London force, Economic Division.'

'So was Len Sheppard, Dominic's father-in-law, and soon not to be.'

'A divorce?'

Norma nodded. 'Charlie's convinced Len is trying to dig up dirt on him to warn us off from having anything to do with our granddaughters once the divorce comes through.'

'Sounds petty and spiteful.' Seamus held his glass out for the offered refill. 'I don't normally drink during the day.' He watched as she topped up her own glass.

Norma laughed. 'I thought that line was what the girl was supposed to say.' She could have sworn she saw his eyes twinkle. 'It's a smokescreen, really,' she went on. 'Len's a closet snob, an Alpha male who considers Charlie to be a big-mouthed lout whom he doesn't want to have anything to do with.'

'Ungracious.'

'Charlie is a big-mouthed lout, but he can be a loveable, self-opinionated big mouth on occasions. Though I'm not awarding him that accolade at present.' She twisted on the sofa, lifting her legs to rest on the cushions. 'Will you answer a question?'

He watched the manoeuvre. 'Maybe,' he said. 'Depends on the question.'

'Why were you and Ludo so eager to see Forbes eliminated from the scene?'

319

He moved from the armchair to perch at the end of the sofa. His hands grasped her bare foot. He kneaded his thumbs into the hard skin on the base of her foot. 'If I tell you, I might be forced to . . .'

'To what? To kill me?'

'No. To make love to you.'

She sighed at the pleasure of his firm touch. 'I'm sure that can be arranged. So, tell me.'

He massaged the other foot. 'You remember you told Ludo how concerned Charlie was about Forbes spilling the beans to the VAT people about his scam? You asked Ludo if he could do anything about it?'

The ecstasy of the moment was stilled by the question. She nodded.

'It put Ludo in a difficult position. You raise your eyebrows, but it's true. My brother was a lovely man, a mechanic who never had a cent to his name. He came to see us asking for money to invest in a half share of Charlie's used car business. We wanted something in return. Ludo had the perfect cover for shipping clandestine material all over Europe. He was buying and selling cars. All he had to do was extend their operations across the Channel and convince Charlie there was a market in left-hand drive cars in the UK.'

'And is there?'

'God knows. I expect so. We created one.'

'How come?'

'We packed a few models in Spain with some gear we required transporting to the UK and sent some people to buy the cars from Charlie, all at a handsome profit. Charlie told Ludo he was a genius and from that moment on we had a reliable fetcher and carrier of equipment we wanted moved around Europe.'

'And what? Forbes found out?'

'No. Forbes developed a conscience about Charlie's scam and wanted to tell all to the VAT man.'

'VAT woman,' Norma corrected stiffly.

Seamus laughed and moved his hands toward her calf and knee. 'Don't get annoyed. After all, you're not pure white yourself.'

She put her head back and closed her eyes. 'A couple of black dots, that's all,' she moaned. 'Go on.'

'We knew if the authorities poked their noses into Charlie's company, our clandestine activities through Ludo would likely come to light. So, we staged a fatal accident. Our friends in ETA in Spain were only too willing to help in exchange for some of our American hardware and they produced a willing candidate.'

'The young man who drove the car?'

His hands moved under the hem of her dress and pushed her thighs apart. 'The poor soul hanged himself in prison, so I'm told. The question then became could we trust you to keep quiet once you had put two and two together.'

She raised her head. 'You bastard. You bedded me just to guarantee I wouldn't talk?'

His fingers picked at the elastic on her briefs. 'On the contrary, I made love to the sexiest woman I had ever met.' He moved closer to her. 'And the sexiest I am ever likely to meet.'

'You're just saying that. You wanted to guarantee Charlie never found out about Forbes.'

'Did he?'

'Absolutely not. Charlie would never have sanctioned killing Forbes in a million years. He would rather have gone to jail. To this day he believes it was a tragic, but fortuitous accident.'

He moved his fingers inside her briefs. 'Enough talking, don't you think?'

'Yes.' She could barely get the word out.

He had his elbow propped on the pillow, hand under his chin, staring at her as she slept. He felt the warmth of her body against his. He eased away and out of the bed. The mobile had dropped from her jumper pocket onto the floor alongside the dressing table as he had pulled at her clothes to undress her. He picked it up and took it to the kitchen. Five minutes later, he had cloned her contacts onto a new burner phone retrieved from the rental car.

Norma was still sleeping when he returned to the bedroom. His fingers stroked her cheek. Her eyelids fluttered, her gaze questioning her surroundings, the realisation as she turned toward him. 'You are the most wonderful, caring lover,' she said. 'How can somebody so sensitive and tender be so cold and callous?'

'Live in compartments,' he said. 'Never let one life bleed into another or you'll drive yourself crazy.'

'I don't want to think about your other life. Let me just savour the past hours.'

'As much as I'd like to, I'm afraid I can't. There is a problem you need to resolve. You may need my help to do so.'

'You're talking in riddles.'

'You were quick to tell me Charlie had nothing to do with my brother's death. When I arrived a couple of days ago, he was my prime suspect. I realised he wasn't living here after I'd spent eighteen hours watching the house. He turned up in the afternoon while you were out, stayed for ten minutes and reappeared with a suitcase. I followed him to what I now know is your son's house.'

'That's creepy. Charlie would never do anything to hurt Ludo. He'd just helped him out of a scrape by buying that Volvo out there for cash.'

'I had to make sure. Forgive me. Anyway, I followed Charlie to a gambling club in Essex. Another guy was with him, the driver. They parked the Volvo in an overspill area; I chose the main car park alongside the motel. Charlie and this younger man went into the club, and I never saw your husband again.'

'Why was Charlie there? It sounds like he was with Lance?' She reached for a dressing gown. 'What on earth was he up to? He only gambles on horses. Casinos aren't his style. Come downstairs. I'll make some coffee.'

'I'll cut to the chase.' Seamus nursed the cup between his hands. 'By the time I walked from the motel to where Charlie had parked, I noticed your son's work van had also turned up. Your son was sitting in it, presumably waiting for Charlie to reappear.'

'Dominic was there too? I have no idea what this is about.'

Seamus left the kitchen and returned a minute later, holding three postcard-sized photographs. 'I have a fancy American camcorder with high-resolution night vision kindly supplied by sympathisers in Boston. I took these stills from the video stream.' He offered them to her. 'The only illumination was the moonlight, but you can make out the stature of the men and a partial of their features. Do you recognise any of them?'

She studied the photos intently. The first print showed a grainy image of two men carrying a body to the car. The next, a man leaning into the boot, and a third of another man standing next to the Volvo with a bomber jacket over his arm.

After a full minute, she looked up warily at him. 'This one,' she held up the second, 'looks very much like Dominic. The others, I don't know who they are. Please tell me what's going on.'

'In the early hours and with your son still parked up, two men appear from the club carrying a body. Initially, it was impossible to tell who the victim was, but there was enough moonlight to run a video as they loaded the victim into the boot of the Volvo. They went back inside the club. Dominic had been watching this unfold, walked over to the Volvo, and thrashed around inside the boot. I assumed he was trying to resuscitate the victim. He stopped when he heard the club door open, ran to the van and drove off. One of the men who had carried the body reappeared with the distinctive bomber jacket Charlie's driver had been wearing and tossed it into the boot. He waited a minute, then I heard him say. "Jesus, the fucker's dead."'

Norma had her hands clasped in front of her. 'Oh, my God! It sounds like it was Lance, Sylvia's boyfriend. What happened next?'

'I don't know. Five minutes later, I got a message from our contact at the Met and left. The police had a lead on the man who attacked Ludo; Forbes' brother, Roddie, as it turns out. He's gone to ground, but I'll find him.'

'He killed Ludo?'

'No. Left him for dead, but Ludo was alive. A debt collector acting on the instructions of some loan shark turns up and finishes the job by putting a plastic bag over his head. The boss man claimed he knew nothing about it and his stooge had acted independently. Can't prove or disprove it right now as the employee is in custody, but I'll find out.'

'How do you know all this?'

'A confession, shall we say? I'm not going into details.'

She turned on him, her eyes blazing in anger. 'Don't treat me like some dizzy blonde. Why didn't you tell me all this when you first arrived?' Tears trickled down her cheeks.

323

'And spoil the opportunity to rekindle a relationship I've dreamed about for all these years?'

'You selfish man. You had no right to keep me in the dark. Are you saying Charlie and Dominic are involved in a murder?' She wiped the back of her hand across her cheek. 'And Lance is dead?'

He reached for her hand. She did not resist. 'I've no idea if Charlie is involved. Probably not, if what you say about his relationship with Sylvia's boyfriend is true. And Dominic appears to have been trying to help, it seems.'

'How can we establish if it was Lance?'

'I suggest we open the trunk. My guess is the body is still inside.'

She walked toward the back door, but hesitated. The tears were gone, and her eyes were wide open. 'You're right. One way or the other, Cary got back the Volvo and must have opened the boot. Not knowing what to do, she drove it back here and complained of a new mechanical problem. She was acting strangely and couldn't wait to leave.' She looked straight at Seamus. 'What do we do if Lance's body is in the boot, phone the police?'

He shook his head. 'That's why I said you will need my help to resolve it, but I can't be seen to be involved.' He tugged at her arm. 'Come on. Let's see what awaits us.'

FIFTY

LEN AND THE BATEMANS

Old man Bateman's words were ringing in Len's ears. 'Your little vendetta with this car dealer has created an unnecessary and distasteful problem which I shall have to clear up. It will cost you and your mates the ten grand I proposed. I expect to see you at the club tomorrow night. Be there.' He had rung off before Len could object.

He was none the wiser and now Muriel had stomped off in a strop to meet a lawyer. This entire business was getting out of hand. What was going on? He had spent all morning waiting for her to return. Her mobile went straight to messaging. Now, more than ever, he needed her support.

He made the call from a pay-as-you-go burner. It rang six times before a voice full of sleep answered. 'Jesus, Len! I told you to only use this number in an emergency. It's Sunday, for fuck's sake, and I'm trying to get some kip.'

'It's two o'clock in the afternoon, Darren, and this is an emergency. I've had a call from your dad. He talked about a problem and said he was coming to the club tomorrow to sort it out. What's he talking about?'

'Can't it wait until he's here? I had an hour's earful from him at six this morning. He's worried the Queen's going to plunge the sword into his chest rather than tap him on the shoulder.'

'Stop talking in riddles and tell me what's happened.'

There was a loud sigh of resignation. 'The night Greaves was here, he turned up with a young Aussie who had been involved in a set-to with a copper from your old force who just happened to be in the club. Apparently, there was an altercation that resulted in a fatality.'

'The Australian?'

'Correct. We have made it appear Greaves was implicated, if you get my drift?'

Len was conscious the conversation was about to become more specific, and caution told him not to pursue the matter further. 'I don't, but I'll pick up on it later when I meet up with your father.'

'You got the snaps I sent to you?'

325

'I did. They're fine.'

'I told you I'd help if you did the same.'

'We played our part and I expect you to honour your side of the agreement. Terry needs his share urgently. He'll be paying you a visit tomorrow to collect, so make sure you've got ten grand available in cash.' There was silence at the end of the line. 'Did you hear me, Darren? I'm not joking.'

'There's always cash on the premises.'

'That wasn't what I asked you.'

Darren's voice became more animated as he changed the subject. 'Do you want to hear something to make you laugh?'

'What?'

'Your man Greaves enjoyed himself so much, he's made a booking at the motel for tomorrow night. He's coming along with eight of his motor trader mates. He's even asked for the same girl to be available for him; randy old bastard.'

'That's all I need,' Len said. 'There's no way I want to meet up with him. Get your doorman to take me straight to the office, will you?'

Len ended the call and sank back into an armchair. He had never experienced such a sense of loneliness as he felt at that moment: Muriel was planning to leave him, Cary was with her new man, the twins staying with Gerry and Gloria, Nobby, dead, Terry, about to live abroad. Little by little, his world was falling apart. All those people who had meant something to him no longer needed him around.

There was still Randy. They might not be as close as he had been with Nobby and Terry, but they were still colleagues of long-standing and he needed to hear a friendly voice.

'You sound down, Len. Are you all right?'

'I'm fine. You eating? Have I interrupted something?'

'Just finishing a pizza for lunch. Thought about what I dug up on this Greaves character?'

'The IRA connection?'

'It ties in the hit and run in Spain all the way back to Greaves's partner. I just need to convert a little conjecture into fact.'

326

'Forget it. Take my advice. When you get involved with the Provisionals, nasty things can happen.'

'It's all history, Len. You remember it as it was. This is a straightforward conspiracy to commit murder. Greaves will go down for the rest of his life along with his partner.'

'Don't you follow the news? His partner's dead. Somebody topped him.'

'You suspect the IRA? If I'm right, they've killed one of their own.'

'I don't know who did it? You're best positioned to make some enquiries.'

'I'll check it out and come back to you.'

'And back off with your snooping. I've got enough on Greaves to keep him quiet without involving the Irish connection.'

Len heard the "okay", but he wasn't convinced.

FIFTY-ONE

THE TWINS, CARY, DOM AND NORMA

Was there such a thing as normality anymore? Cary doubted it. When bad things happened, her mind erected defences of which she was not even conscious. A haze of calm had developed in front of her eyes. She could see the policeman's lips moving, but the sound percolated through the mist in blurred, slow motion. You've asked that question before, she thought, and he acknowledged the fact, claiming there might be a detail in the recounting she had not remembered. What detail? She had stumbled into a room with two corpses hours after discovering another in the boot of a car; simple as that, although she hadn't mentioned Sylvia's lover to the police. Poor Sylvia. She never had much luck with men.

It was Cary's choice to return to Gerry's place and not the family home. She really couldn't stand the thought of facing the clinical policeman's reaction of her father or the sympathetic hangdog look of her mother as she suggested a cup of tea as a suitable remedy for the mental trauma. No. She would sit holding the girls and listen to another of Gloria's reality checks, drink alcohol and, eventually, pass out.

When she awoke, the birds were singing, the sky was cloudless, and she wasn't sure the way she felt was self-deception or the something Gerry might have been putting in the stream of drinks she had consumed the previous night. Whatever it was, her overriding sensation was one of relief. The decision had been taken away from her by a phony suicide, because that is surely what it was. Alex was too self-assured, too egotistical to take his own life. Somebody had murdered him; she was certain. There were doubtless plenty of candidates to keep the police busy.

Cary checked her body in the mirror; still firm and curvaceous enough to seduce a man, even one who believed his sexual preferences were changing. If the truth were told, she had treated Dom badly, criticising and belittling his manhood and breadwinner status as she mentally compared his failings to the qualities she had recognised – better to say, thought she had recognised – in her new lover. Making Dom feel inadequate as a man had provided her with the justification she had needed to get back at the men in her professional life who downgraded her simply because she was a woman. The bitter truth was the man for whom she was prepared to sacrifice her marriage had been a fraud and had deliberately put on an act to hide his true personality. Dom would never do that.

The twins were excited about the prospect of seeing their father. She was too. There would be enough time to call by her parents' house, change into something a little more provocative and put on some make-up. She needed a fighting chance to resurrect her marriage.

Dom was completing his mission to have the house spotless by the time Cary arrived with the twins, when a key turned in the front door and he looked up to see his sister standing in the hall.

'You look like shit,' he said.

Sylvia flung a canvas bag onto the armchair and sat draped alongside it. 'You were right about him,' she said. 'Looks like he ditched me and disappeared.'

Dom looked away, walked to the other side of the room, and puffed up some cushions on the sofa.

'Got nothing to say?' she insisted. 'You were the one who told me to call it off before I got hurt.'

'You'll find somebody else. Forget him.'

'Easier said than done. I honestly believed he was keen on me.'

He continued attending to the cushions. 'Last time I saw him, he was taking Dad to some girlie casino joint in Essex. Maybe the temptation was too great. He wasn't exactly the steadfast type.'

'Wasn't?' she queried.

'"Wasn't" in the sense that he's apparently gone from our lives. Good riddance, as far as I'm concerned.' He took a deep breath.

'Is Dad around?' Her eyes darted around the room.

'In our bedroom. He's still sleeping off a long drive from somewhere yesterday. He's being very secretive about his movements. God knows what's got into him.'

'I need to talk to him. Maybe he knows something about Lance.'

'He said he didn't want to be disturbed.'

'He won't mind if it's me.' She took to the stairs as the sound came of a car coming to a stop on the road outside. 'Who's that?' There was expectation in her voice.

Dom parted the curtains. 'It's Mum,' he said. 'What is this, a family get-together?'

Sylvia continued her climb. 'Oh God, Dom. Keep her amused. I'm not in the mood for twenty questions. Don't tell her I'm here.'

'A little tricky with your car parked in the drive, don't you think?' But she had gone. He heard the door to the bedroom open and close behind her.

'Hello, Mum.'

Norma ignored the greeting and pushed past him, grabbing his arm as she did so. 'Where's your sister?'

He looked bemused. 'Upstairs, waking up Dad.'

'Kitchen,' she ordered and pulled him along with her.

'What is this, Mum? Have you lost the plot?'

Norma perched on the edge of a stool, leaning across the breakfast bar to where he stood. 'Does she know?'

'Know what?'

'Don't play games, Dominic. I don't have the time or the patience to humour you. There's the dead body of Sylvia's boyfriend in the boot of the Volvo and I've seen a video of you exerting yourself over it in some deserted car park. Explain yourself.'

It was difficult to tell whether his expression was one of confusion, fear, or disbelief. 'A video?' he protested.

'That's right. Somebody was watching you and taking pictures. What was going on?'

'Who was taking pictures?'

'It doesn't matter. Somebody who has your best interests at heart. It's impossible to see exactly what you were doing, but it looks like an attempt to resuscitate a mortally wounded man. Why were you there in the first place?'

Dom slumped onto a stool, elbows on the breakfast bar, hands cupped under his chin. His voice was a whispered monotone. 'Dad had a call from Len, suggesting a meeting to clear the air at this casino place in Essex. He asked Lance to go with him, share the driving.' He wiped the saliva from the

331

corner of his mouth. 'It pissed me off. Why didn't he ask me? He had more faith in some transient opportunist than his own son. I decided to follow in the firm's van. They parked in an overspill car park. I waited for a couple of hours. Two guys appeared carrying a body. They dumped it in the boot of the Volvo. I waited until they had gone and went to see who it was.'

Norma studied him. 'They left the boot open?'

He shook his head. 'The keys were in the ignition. I used the boot release.'

'And?' She raised her eyebrows.

He blinked rapidly. 'Like you say. I saw him there, curled up and lifeless. I tried the CPR procedure I remembered from the training corps, but I heard the men coming back, so I ran back to the van and drove off.'

'Did they see you?'

'I don't think so. They obviously heard the van leaving.'

'Did you recognise them?'

'One was built like a bouncer. The other guy was just ordinary looking. I'd never seen either of them before.'

Norma leaned closer to him. 'At some point, the police are going to get involved and see the video. Take the initiative and approach them.' She recognised the petulant look on his face. 'At least get your story straight.'

'What story does he have to get straight?' Sylvia was standing at the doorway to the kitchen. 'You two look as though you've been plotting to blow up the Houses of Parliament.'

Norma slid off the stool and went to greet her daughter. 'Lovely to see you.' She gave Sylvia a hug. 'I was just saying Cary and the girls will be around at sometime today. If he's going to appeal to her good nature, he's going to have to get his story straight as to why his father is here and sleeping in their bedroom. I don't want my marital problems gossiped about by Len and his cronies.'

Sylvia gave a weak smile of acknowledgement. 'I haven't seen or heard from Lance. Dad says the last time he saw him was at a casino in Essex. They parted company and when dad went looking for him, he was nowhere to be found. He'd left dad the car and vanished into thin air.'

Dom looked over at Norma. 'I told her the man was . . . is a waste of space and she's better off without him.'

332

Norma looked from one to the other, resting a smile on Sylvia. 'Let's not prejudge anybody until we know what's happened, shall we? I really must be going. I only popped in to see what time the girls were arriving.'

Sylvia blocked her path. 'Dad heard you were here. He wants to know if you'll talk to him face to face.'

'Tell him not now, darling. I'll deal with your father when I'm sure I won't lose my temper with him. Right now, I'm likely to say something I'll regret.' She turned as she reached the front door. 'Call me, Dominic, when the family has left. I want to know how you all got on and what are your plans. Understand?'

'Yes.'

'Promise you will call?'

'Promise.'

She turned to Sylvia. 'You're my witness. I'll speak to you as well, later, or perhaps tomorrow.'

'I'm thinking about taking the day off tomorrow and finding this casino place in Essex to see if anybody knows what happened to Lance. Somebody must have seen him.'

'Call me,' Norma said. 'If you decide to go, I'd like to come along for the ride; keep you company and have some genuine mother/daughter heart to hearts. It's been a long time.'

Sylvia's brow ceased. 'Seriously?'

'Deadly serious,' Norma replied.

The twins could not control the excitement at returning to their bedroom and rediscovering the cache of toys they had rejected taking with them a few days earlier. The emotion of the moment was too much for Syracuse who, according to Creedence's attempt to imitate her mother's tone when annoyed, ". . . had damn well wet herself and would need to change her pants!" It was the first time their parents had laughed together in months, which somehow seemed to embarrass them both.

As they looked at each other, Dom spoke first. 'Sorry to laugh,' he said. 'I didn't mean to trivialise the pain you must still be feeling. Stumbling into such a scene . . . I can't imagine.'

Cary shook her head. 'Hardly your fault for the words that come tumbling out of our daughter's mouth. She's a little madam sometimes.' The humour of the moment left her face. 'The snapshot of the room when I realised what had taken place is something I am going to have to learn to deal with by counselling and the support of those around me. I know that much. What concerns me more is my reaction as the afternoon unfolded.'

'How do you mean?'

She hesitated; her attention drawn to the sound of the twins playing upstairs. Her voice hardened. 'I've not said this to anybody, but the emotions I expected to feel: distraught at the loss of a man I loved, emptiness, sadness, the anger of feeling robbed of my future happiness. I experienced none of these. Instead, and it's a callous thing to say, I felt a sense of relief. Shameful, isn't it?'

'I don't know.'

'I've tried to analyse it. I don't like myself very much.'

'That's ridiculous.' He stopped as he registered her expression.

'Let me finish. Please. I didn't mean to come over so abruptly.' She squeezed his hand. 'After years of attempting to emasculate you and, dare I say it, succeeding, I saw in Alex an equal on all levels, physical and mental, and a means of shedding the mantle of living a boring, conventional, suburban, family life. For a while, I craved the unconventionality of an older man full of energy and surprises. I told myself it was a lifestyle destined to stimulate the girls.'

His shoulders slumped. She knew it was a tough listen, but it had to be said. 'The novelty wore off. The weird, resigned indifference displayed by his mother at the sight of her dead son; the hostility of his own son to the treatment of women by his father; the existence of a wife he let me believe was dead; all this took solid ground from underneath my feet. The revelation that this loving, happy-go-lucky man could be a murdering loan shark, as I heard someone call him, made me realise what I should have seen with my own eyes if I had taken off the rose-tinted glasses.'

'Where does that leave me and the girls?'

'Are you still looking for a gay relationship?'

'Heavens, no. These last six months feel like an aberration. Faced with what I saw as your intention to finish our relationship, I had felt inept and insecure in the idea of appealing to another woman. I was well and truly seduced by an indiscriminate sexual predator and found it a complete cop-out to become totally involved. It was the last thing I really wanted. That was for us to stay together and work at restoring what we once had.'

'You were talking about Lance? Do you know where he is?' She looked down at the floor.

He sucked in air noisily. 'No. Sylvia hasn't seen or heard from him. More than likely run off with a richer prospect.'

There was a moment's hesitation. 'We both made mistakes,' she breathed. 'But no long-term relationship is founded solely on shifting sand. There were many positives I was simply willing to overlook to justify my actions. Over the years, I've listened to Dad too much and related to the idea I was superior with a bigger income, adopting the mantle of a breadwinner and treating you as somehow unworthy of our partnership. It was totally out of order, and I apologise. I need to know if you'll take us back and we can set our sights on restoring our relationship to something like it was when the twins were young.' She sighed. 'There, I've said it. What do you say?'

He walked toward her; arms outstretched. 'It's exactly what I wanted to hear. Of course. I can't believe my luck.' He hugged her. 'The girls will be thrilled.'

'I need to collect their things from Dad's.'

He broke away. 'I'll come with you. Why don't we stop for a pizza on the way back?'

'Great idea,' she said. 'It'll be my treat, okay?'

FIFTY-TWO

RANDALL COMPTON

Sunday evening for a man who was a creature of habit meant a stroll to The Farmer's Inn, a couple of pints and an hour listening to the Irish Folk Music trio who played at the pub two nights a week. He really enjoyed the organised and predictable nature of the occasion, much as in the same way as he lived his organised and predictable life. From bitter experience, he had come to realise how an intimate relationship could challenge and demolish these two bastions of his credo and just how far he was at odds with the nickname by which everybody called him. In real life, randy, he had never been. Deranged might be more apt.

Tonight, he might move into uncharted territory, stay beyond his allotted hour – he was finishing his second pint – and chance a third. It was all in a good cause. He was waiting to meet a man whom he knew by name only. Earlier that afternoon, as he sat in front of the TV watching a soccer match, his mobile had registered a call from an unknown number.

Part curious and part annoyed at the intrusion, he had asked gruffly who was calling and sat up at the answer.

'How did you get my number, Mr Greaves?' he asked.

'My son's in computer systems, ain't he? Get the drift?'

'What can I do for you, Mr Greaves?'

'A little bird told me you're asking questions about the accident in Spain involving Stanley Forbes. I thought you might like to get the true story from the man who knows the facts. Interested?'

Randall had set up the meeting at The Farmer's Inn for nine o'clock. It was now past ten. His various attempts to call the mobile number went to unavailable, and he had lost patience. Why set up a meeting and then not turn up? Greaves was obviously a worried man, and he would shortly have a reason to be really concerned. He downed the remnants of his third pint and said his goodbyes.

As far as the suburb of Kidbrooke in South London was concerned, having a pub with a name suggesting an agricultural connection was probably

337

a hundred years out of date. The place was a concrete jungle, high-rise blocks and countless rows of identical terraced and semi-detached houses. The only greenery he could recall was the children's recreational area and the school playing fields.

Randall retraced his steps. The quickest way back home was along the lane with the one car garages on either side. Parking was a real problem in the area and garages changed hands for ridiculous sums, often equivalent to the value of a three-bedroom house in some parts of the country.

He heard the car engine behind him and stepped to one side, turning as he did so. A headlight on full beam was the last thing he saw as the car ploughed into him and sent him headlong into the air.

Seamus watched the body land in front of the Volvo. He sniffed. The car had the distinctive smell of the Big Mac and fries he had consumed as he waited for Randall to leave the pub. He could do with a drink, but he'd give the Farmer's Inn a miss.

Probably, the man was already dead, but just to be sure, he gunned the engine, engaged low gear and picked up the revs as the car struggled to rise over the body. The corpse in the boot thumped up and down as the car finally reared over the human speed bump and glided forward toward the main road.

He was more than satisfied with his day's work. His task to protect the network of IRA activists and sympathisers in England had been secured by the elimination of a nosey copper and, by good fortune, an opportunity to implicate Norma's husband in the hit-and-run.

Opening the boot and setting eyes on the bloodied corpse had visibly shocked Norma. The stoicism she had displayed until the moment those staring, dead eyes seemed to follow her startled retreat two steps back from the car was instantly replaced by a look of horror. Although she appeared to listen as he outlined his plan, Seamus doubted she had taken in one word of what he said.

Initially, he had intended to leave his rental car at the hotel where he was staying and come back for the Volvo later that day, drive it to Essex and leave it in the car park at the club. Norma would follow in her car, stopping in the lane beyond the club out of CCTV range and wait for him to reappear and return him to his hotel. On the following day, an anonymous call would be made to the police, coupled by the post on a bogus Instagram account of the clip of the two men carrying the body to the Volvo. Having seen how fragile Norma had now become, he would prefer to leave her out of the arrangement and plot a different course of action. As fate would have it, luck was on his side.

It must have taken a full hour for Norma to regain her composure with the help of two large gin and tonics. There was no way she could stay around the house with that ghastly corpse yards away from her. She would call an Uber and visit her son to see what he had to say for himself. There was also Sylvia to think about.

Seamus tailed her hire car to the small, detached house in the leafy, suburban cul-de-sac. The driveway was occupied by an older model Volvo and a sign-written van. A Mercedes saloon was parked half on the verge, half on the road, alongside a red compact.

Twenty minutes had passed when Norma and a younger woman reappeared. They hugged as a taxi pulled up to collect Norma, leaving the other woman – would this be daughter, Sylvia? – to drive off in the compact.

Instinct told Seamus to hang around. The seeds of a new plan were formulating in his mind. Manoeuvring Charlie into taking the initiative for him meant reducing the options on one level and increasing them on another.

Strolling casually past the Mercedes, he bent, jabbing the stiletto blade of his pocketknife firmly into the wall of the rear tyre. As he withdrew it, there was the satisfying hiss of air as the tyre deflated. For good measure, he repeated the process with the front tyre, causing the car to sit at a sharper angle with the chassis almost touching the asphalt. The vehicle would need to be lifted before any jack could be inserted to assist a wheel change and tyre emergency foam was unlikely to be of any practical use with the weight of the car settled on the rims of both wheels.

The plan was simple: to wait until Charlie discovered the problem and abandoned the car, leave a suitable time interval before using the cloned contact detail from Norma's phone to call her son's mobile and pretend to be the garage where Cary had supposedly left the Volvo for repair. Seamus would ask the son for a delivery address, anticipating that Charlie would be only too grateful for a substitute vehicle.

As it transpired, the plan worked in a modified form. Once Charlie discovered the punctures, he re-emerged from the house with a small suitcase and was driven away by his son in the van and unceremoniously dropped off at a budget hotel some two miles away. The phone call to Dominic went to plan. Seamus parked up the Volvo at Charlie's hotel and left the keys with the receptionist.

The one thing left for him to do, hopefully before he returned to Ireland with his brother's body, involved tailing Charlie Greaves. He would resume surveillance at the hotel the following morning. Seamus gambled that Greaves's life was under threat from Ludo's attacker, Roddie Forbes, who had, so far, eluded the police search. If this fugitive was as mentally unstable as his contact had suggested, chances are he would want to continue to avenge his brother's death by going after Greaves.

If he did, Seamus would be waiting for him.

FIFTY-THREE

SHOWDOWN

With a whispered goodbye, Terry briefly acknowledged Len's nod of the head and left the Hindu temple just as the priest began the cremation ritual. The three Kumar males, seated in the front row with Nobby's confused-looking cousin wedged between the old man and Vijay, looked anxiously at each other as they watched Terry's departure. He tried to dismiss the feeling they were aware of his secret and would leap out of their seats to follow and curtail him.

As he reached his car, he turned to look, fully expecting them to be close behind. Nobody was tailing him. He chided himself for the uncharacteristic attack of paranoia.

Mahi was sitting at a table in the café, her fingers drumming on the melamine surface. She exhaled visibly as she saw him, her smile weak and fearful. Terry beamed. 'You came,' he said.

'Did you doubt me?' She pulled his arm toward her and kissed the back of his hand. 'I've been so afraid they would find out. Now, you're here.'

He shook his head. 'I left them lording it at Nobby's funeral. Even in death, he's helping us out.' He checked around her chair. 'No luggage, as requested?'

'There is no reason to keep anything to remind me of all those wasted years.'

He pointed at her handbag, which she handed to him. 'No mobile phone?' he questioned.

'Nobby said to take out the sim card and flush it away. The handset was to be broken into pieces and discarded. I did as he asked.'

Terry rummaged in the inside pocket of his raincoat, pulling out an envelope and a new, inexpensive mobile. 'There's one number on it. Mine. Use it only in an emergency.' He reached into another pocket, producing an identical mobile. 'I'll do the same.'

There was a look of panic on her face. 'What do you mean? We're not staying together?'

'Keep calm. I'll explain. When the General realises you're missing, I'm assuming he's got plenty of contacts in the right places to trace you. I booked us on an Aer Lingus flight to Dublin in the morning. I've no doubt he'll be waiting at Heathrow for us.'

Her brow creased. He stopped her from asking the obvious question. 'You don't spend a lifetime in the police force without coming across some very accomplished criminals.' He shook the envelope, allowing two blue, biometric passports to rest on the table. 'These cost me a pretty penny, but they will get us out of the country. As of now, you are Patricia Grant and I'm your husband, Jules. We are booked on the midnight ferry from Harwich to the Hook of Holland. Tomorrow, we take the KLM flight from Amsterdam to Bangkok, where we'll organise visas to travel on to Australia and the start of a new life.'

'Where did the money come from for all this?' She flicked through the pages of her passport. 'Nobby took this picture of me,' she said. 'He said it would look good alongside his bogus article.' She laughed. 'I should have realised.'

'That's why we must split up for a few hours.' He handed her two ferry tickets. 'Hang onto these. I'm going to put you on a train to Harwich whilst I go to an address in Essex to collect a large sum of money I'm owed. I'll meet up with you at the ferry terminal sometime around eleven.'

She was back to looking worried. 'Do you have to? Can't we stay together?'

'Believe me, it will be quicker and easier for me to handle it on my own. It's best if you don't know who my contacts are. They are not nice people.'

'Don't tell me after all this, you are going to put yourself in danger. It's not worth it. I told you, I *do* have some money.'

'I'm not in any danger. My ex-boss is handling the transaction. It will all be over in minutes.'

She hesitated, obviously unsure of whether she should test the relationship by pressing her argument. 'Can't you borrow it from your ex-boss and let him collect what you're owed?'

He smiled. 'I understand your concern for me, but it'll be fine. He's under internal scrutiny by the force. He can't risk being traced handling large sums of cash. Besides, nobody is after me. I'll be in and out in no time. We'll crack open a bottle of champagne on the boat.'

The car pulled into the station forecourt at Stratford. Terry leaned across her to open the passenger door. To her surprise, he kissed her full on the lips. 'I'll be as quick as I can,' he said.

She pulled back; her eyes were full as she turned her head to avoid him seeing. 'Be careful,' she whispered as the car door closed behind her. 'I just want to know peace for once in my life.'

Joel Barnett had seen nothing like it in his six months working on the reception desk at the Dreamlands Motel. As the group of new arrivals received their room keys with a smile and made their way to the block accommodation on the upper floor level, he pined for a suggestive wink or some sign that one or other of these Adonis-like men would welcome his attention. Apart from the old guy who was checking them in and one or two of the others whom Joel dismissed as middle-aged, the other half-dozen could be no older than mid-thirties and extremely fit. He could easily have fallen for any of them.

'Why all the luggage?' he asked the old guy. 'You're only staying one night.'

The man looked as if he was about to tell him to mind his own business, but a smile cracked his lips. 'We're here to warm up for a stag weekend in Amsterdam,' he explained with a knowing look. 'They'll need a frequent change of underwear, I expect.'

Joel warmed to the Cockney accent, sensing he could be less than discreet. 'You're not going to tell me they're all straight? I'd be gutted.'

'Afraid so,' Charlie replied. 'You're out of luck with this lot.'

Joel feigned disappointment. 'Surely not. It defies the law of averages or some such theory.' He checked the computer screen. 'If your group is typical of the guys running the motor trade, I'm going to be looking for a new job selling cars.'

Charlie took the stylus from the counter and signed the screen of the tablet, acknowledging his credit card could be debited for the extras charged by the group. He picked up his overnight bag. 'I'll tell them you're available,' he said, looking over his shoulder. 'But I'll think you'll find they'll be otherwise occupied.' He turned back as if remembering something. 'I was here last week. Don't think it was you on duty. Could you contact Indemira and, if she's free, ask her to come to room two-eleven?'

Joel smiled and nodded. 'Dirty old man,' he said under his breath.

The young man intercepted Len as he made his way from the temple back to his car. 'It's Len Sheppard, isn't it?'

'Who wants to know?' He had found the entire funeral service an over-the-top extravaganza he knew Nobby would have detested. Watching the Kumars stand in line at the exit to the temple to receive both commiserations and plaudits from the assembled congregation he found nauseating. His silent vow to Nobby to make things right seemed hollow when he considered the options open to him.

'I'm DS Priest from City CID. Your wife said I'd find you here.'

Len went immediately on the defensive. 'I've answered all Brannigan's questions. What does the IOPC want now?'

'I don't know what you're talking about. I'm here to speak to you about DI Randall Compton.'

Len's brow creased. 'What about him?'

'You haven't heard? DI Compton was the victim of a hit-and-run incident last night.'

'God! No, I had no idea. Is he all right?'

'I'm afraid he died at the scene. The Super wants to speak with you.'

Len leaned heavily on the car, head bowed, his hands covering his eyes. 'Was it an accident?'

Priest avoided eye contact. 'It's being treated as suspicious pending post-mortem results. First reading is somebody struck your former colleague from the front and then ran over the body. The car involved did not stop, but as the area in south London where it occurred is awash with CCTV cameras, identifying the vehicle should be possible.'

Len shook his head. What he suspected, he could not dare to voice. 'It was near to his home?'

'I've no more information. You'll have to ask the Super. He knows you two were close. I expect he wants to ask if you can shed any light on who might have wanted to kill him if it turns out to be a murder enquiry. We'll take my car. Somebody will drop you back for yours.'

Seamus checked his watch. It had been ninety minutes since he had tailed Charlie in the Volvo to the motel adjoining the casino. In half-an-hours' time, through a series of proxy servers, a video entitled 'Dumping a Body in the Boot of a Volvo' would air on YouTube and several other social media sites. At some stage during the night, the police were bound to ask for the video to be taken down but, by then, who knows how many hits it would have had. He was confident by midnight there would be flashing blue lights surrounding the premises.

His left leg had cramped. Standing behind the trimmed hedgerow leading to the first tee, he had an uninterrupted view of the main casino and motel entrances and the rear emergency/private doorway at the rear of the premises leading to the overspill carpark. The trouble was, he wasn't thirty anymore and a stake-out meant a progression of aches and pains in various body parts. He rubbed his calf muscle and grimaced at the pain, more so when he cast his mind back to the thought of a welcoming double bed and Norma at his side.

Charlie had sat in the parked Volvo until the arrival at the motel of a hired coach from which emerged a burly, middle-aged man in a black leather jacket. He greeted Charlie with an expansive hug and gestured for the passengers inside the vehicle to disembark. Make no mistake, Seamus thought as he watched the line of men leave the bus and retrieve their baggage: this is no boys' night out. These guys carry themselves like hardened combat troops, fit and resilient, attentive to the detail around them as they assess their surroundings. And, as for their baggage; too large for standard holiday requirements; too small for a golfer's needs. If he had to guess, experience told him that amongst the change of clothing, there would be plenty of armaments and, by the weight on their shoulders, some potent semi-automatic weapons in the mix. He was definitely hanging round to watch events pan out tonight.

Charlie had left the Volvo in the main car park, presumably still blissfully unaware of the body in the boot. That was all about to change. In five minutes, the video would go live. He made the phone call to the Assistant Commissioner's mobile number his contact had provided. He put on his best neutral English accent, leaving the policeman in no doubt what his next move should be.

Seamus turned his attention to the overspill car park. Two cars had pulled up and parked within a minute of each other. Both drivers were alone and of late-middle-age. They shook hands warmly before the taller and slenderer of the two put his arm around the stockier man's shoulder and encouraged him toward the casino entrance.

Their passage was interrupted by the arrival of a third vehicle. Nerve endings in Seamus's body tingled. No mistaking the stature and gait of this man: he was one of the two who had carried the body to the Volvo.

Seamus checked his watch again and smiled. 'Now here's the *craic*,' he said to himself. 'Charlie, my friend, you are about to experience your five minutes of fame.'

Len waited as Terry hurried across the carpark toward him and offered his hand. 'I don't think I've ever felt so nervous, even when we were dealing with a gang of armed villains.'

Len put an arm around his friend's shoulder. He had decided not to say anything about Randy's death. Terry was stressed enough and the news, coming so soon after Nobby's funeral, would most likely stop him in his tracks. 'Eloping is a big step,' Len said with a broad smile. 'Especially for someone who's led a conventional and solitary life in recent years. Come on. Let's go and get your cash sorted out, and you two lovebirds can be on your way. Hope you've chosen somewhere hot and steamy to hide away until the smoke clears.' They walked toward the doorway and the solitary security guard on duty.

'Do you think the old man will pay up without a fuss?' Terry said.

'I don't see how he can refuse, do you? You've effectively got the ear of the only person who can prey on his paranoia about the ownership of the impounded vehicle.'

They both turned as another vehicle entered the car park and braked heavily, sending a volley of gravel into the air. Len stopped in his tracks as he recognised the driver. 'Go on and wait for me at the door, Terry. I need to speak with this guy.'

He walked toward the driver. 'What the fuck! Are you following me?'

346

Priest pressed the door lock on his key fob. 'Mr Bateman asked me to come. He wants me to meet his father.' He hesitated. 'As if it's got anything to do with you.'

'How are you tied in with the Batemans?'

'I did a small favour for Darren, and he gave me free access to the club.' He moved to pass Len, who took a step sideways to block his path. 'Nothing on your scale.' Priest reacted to the move with a smirk. 'The word in the nick was how the old man had you and your cronies in his pocket. So, it should hardly surprise me you're here tonight. By the way, your mate's death is being treated as murder. The NCA is on the case. You're a person of interest, so you can expect a knock on the door.'

'Any developments?'

'The word is they've identified the vehicle involved. I know no more.'

'Listen.' Len poked him hard in the chest. 'Not a word here tonight about Randall's death. All right? You'll spook everybody and tonight's just a friendly get together, so keep schtum. You understand?'

Priest raised his eyebrows. 'I had no intention of mentioning it. Anyway, it'll be all over the morning papers in a few hours. They'll have the perp in custody by the morning.'

Len stepped aside. If his suspicions were correct, he doubted Priest's optimism was well founded.

Charlie had nothing but admiration for the way the operation was being handled. Before taking a seat at the bar of Lovers' Nook, the dimly lit seating area leading to the access door into the motel, he had passed through the bars, casino, and restaurant. One or two of Salmanov's men had taken up strategic positions in each location, waiting for the order to proceed. The two security guards responsible for monitoring the girls, along with the three casino reception staff, had already been immobilised and were sitting bound and gagged on the floor of one of the motel rooms. Both front and emergency doors of the club had been locked.

Indemira had followed Charlie's instructions and, on Salmanov's command, herded some twenty of the girls into two of the reserved bedrooms. Three other girls, more inured into a way of life and substance dependency they could not resist, had failed to follow Indemira's urgings and remained socialising with the members. Salmanov was not leaving anyone behind. At some point, they would join the group by force, if it were necessary.

There was only one thing not going to plan. Neither Darren Bateman nor his principal henchmen were on the casino floor. Indemira had told Charlie she had glimpsed a man identified as Darren's father and they were at a meeting in the control room, a secure area with reinforced doors and shutters where the treasury operations were carried out and money and valuables were locked away in a strongroom. Through an internal door was the surveillance room with a direct view over the casino floor through one-way glass and a series of screens relaying live video from CCTV cameras throughout the club.

Charlie shrugged. Salmanov might want a face-to-face confrontation with the Batemans, but he was content to let the police deal with the aftermath once the confusion was in full momentum. In fifteen minutes, the police and fire brigade would be summoned to a disturbance, the fire alarms triggered to provoke a stampede toward the exits as lighted cloths soaked in kerosene filled the corridors with thick, evil-smelling smoke. In the confusion, the girls would be led from the motel to the coach, accompanied by the Karabakh. The plan was for them to travel to a refuge in South Wales where the girls would remain under the care and control of the Azerbaijan immigrant community until arrangements were made to repatriate them. Indemira would stay in London with Salmanov, who had instructed a specialist lawyer to arrange a meeting with a senior officer at Scotland Yard's SCD9 branch for the following day. Indemira's statement was guaranteed to see the Batemans in custody and fill in the blanks surrounding the bloodstains found in the refrigerated lorry in which she had been a prisoner.

Charlie called the barman over and ordered another drink.

'A quiet night, tonight,' the young man said as he nestled the tumbler on the coaster.

Charlie smiled. 'You never know,' he said. 'Things could liven up.'

'Get Darren up here,' Bateman barked at Eric. He held the door open to let Len and Terry through, his arm blocking the entrance once they had passed. 'You would be?' He looked at the younger man over the top of his glasses.

'I'm Morgan Priest,' he said. 'Darren asked me to come.'

348

'You wait out there until my son arrives. I need a private word with these gents.' He shut the door before Priest could acknowledge the order.

'This is a fucking mess.' He indicated the two men should sit. 'Your bloody vendetta, Len, has given me nothing but problems.' He sucked in air between gritted teeth. 'I ask you to do a simple job—'

'Which we did,' Len interrupted.

'And you press me for a favour because you want to fuck off your daughter's father-in-law.'

Terry had remained standing. 'I don't know about all this, but I did what you asked of me. Your minor difficulty is resolved and I'm here to collect the cash you agreed to pay.'

Bateman's mouth opened in feigned surprise as he turned to address Terry. 'You expect me to give you money? Because of your mate, Len here, a man was murdered on these premises and his body unceremoniously dumped in the boot of a car. You should pay me for handling this mess.'

'I haven't got a clue what you're talking about,' Len said. He looked anxiously at Terry, his teeth gritted, hands constantly flexing into fists. 'Let's just relax, understand what's going on, and we can sort it out.'

'Nothing to sort out,' Bateman said dismissively. 'The fact is this Greaves character you've got a grievance with turned up here with an Australian he's been using to dig up dirt on your past which, coincidentally and unacceptably, implies digging up dirt on me.

'According to Darren, this Aussie gets into a set-to over some bird he fancies with the copper you just came in with and it comes to blows with a baseball bat. The copper is a little too enthusiastic and ends up topping the Aussie. They've tried to make it look like Greaves was the culprit by dumping the body in the boot of his car and ensuring his fingerprints are on the murder weapon, but I'm guessing the police will see right through it and come knocking at our door for an explanation.' He wrinkled his nose as he sniffed, an expression of contempt on his face as he held Len's gaze. 'Now you see what harm your petty little vendetta has caused, and you come here expecting me to tell you everything's rosy and shower you with pound notes? Don't make me laugh.'

349

Len sank down in a chair. 'Jesus, I never meant for any of this to happen.' He shook his head. 'I just wanted to exert some pressure on the guy. Nobby, Randy and now, this.'

Bateman took a step back as Terry moved toward him, their faces barely inches apart. He poked the older man hard in the chest. 'I don't know or care about any of this. You asked me to help you out for ten grand. I performed. Now, it's your turn to pay up. I'm not interested in excuses.'

Bateman retreated another step, the desk barring any further movement. 'Do you know who you're talking to?' He watched the raised fist. 'Len,' he said, forcefully. 'Get your man under control.'

'Leave it, Terry.' Len was on his feet. 'You get on your way. I'll see what I can sort out when this mess is over. You've got somewhere to be.'

Terry turned; his fist still raised. 'I'm counting on this money. My place is all tied up with mortgages and legals. God knows when I'll get any dough out of it.' His expression changed from despair to anger. 'You said you'd see me right, Len. We've had each other's backs for over twenty years. I was relying on you.'

'Circumstances have changed. We need to hold fire until this problem has been resolved. Let me get it under control. I'm sure Mr Bateman will be reasonable.'

'Damn you!' Terry's fist thumped on the desk. 'You said I'd get my money, Len. Don't you understand? I will not start off a new life with a fucking begging bowl.'

Len looked for some gesture from Bateman. All he got was a stony, disinterested stare. 'Let me handle it, will you?'

Terry broke away and walked to the door. 'So, you're on his side, are you, Len? Showing your true colours at last? You two had better remember I know enough to send you both away for the rest of your natural. Just bear that in mind.' He kicked the leg of a chair, sending it flying across the room. 'I did what you asked of me and I expect you both to keep to your side of the bargain.' He hesitated and shook his head. 'If not, all bets are off. I'll see myself out.' The metal reinforced door rang like a bell as he slammed it behind him.

Bateman sat back in his chair. He raised his eyebrows and stared at Len.

350

'Leave him be,' Len replied to the questioning look. 'He'll calm down and I'll fix it. You'll need to pay him something.'

'I don't like threats, Len, and I'm not paying a penny.' He looked down at the screen as the banging on the security door started. 'What's the problem, Darren?'

'Let me in,' came the anxious voice through the intercom.

Darren, followed by Eric, hustled into the room. ''Chelle's been on the phone.' He pushed Eric toward the laptop on the cashier's table.

'Chelle?'

'Michelle. My wife, your daughter-in-law, for God's sake.' The panic in his voice was apparent. 'She says there's a video doing the rounds on YouTube showing two guys carrying a body across our car park and dumping it in the boot of a car. It's already had six thousand hits. You got it, Eric?'

Eric sat back as they crowded round the laptop.

Darren combed his fingers through gel-fixed hair and looked nervously at the reaction on his father's face. 'It's night vision and grainy, but you can tell from his stature and the way he's walking.'

'Tell what?' Bateman asked quietly.

'That it's the copper, the one who's waiting outside. The other guy's our man from security.'

A screen refresh showed a new total of fifteen thousand hits. 'You made contingency plans?' Bateman continued. 'I hope so.'

Darren nodded. 'I have somebody on standby.'

Bateman whispered something into his son's ear. Darren nodded and motioned for Eric to join him as he went to leave the room.

'What the hell is going on?' Len asked. 'Is this what you were talking about? He pointed at the image on the screen as, suddenly, it vanished and the message "video removed" took its place.

Without warning, the screens relaying live images from the security cameras around the club went blank; lights and power circuits ceased to function, and the fire alarm sounded.

'What the . . .' Bateman said as the emergency generator kicked into action with a thud and the lights flickered on. Whatever had been used to cover the security cameras was removed from one of the lenses, revealing a pall of smoke and people running across the casino floor toward the exits. The microphone picked up the feint sound of emergency sirens.

A Dali mask filled one screen. The demonic smile did not match the gruff, accented man's voice. 'I trust you can hear me, Mr Paul Bateman and his son.' Smoke swirled around the mask, causing the man to rattle a cough. 'As you can hear, time does not allow me to find you in your bolthole, but I promise you we will meet, to your intense disadvantage. Keep looking over your shoulders. I will seek you out when you least expect it so that you may pay for your barbaric crimes. Believe me, you can hide, but I will find you. I make this commitment to the girls and women whose lives you have destroyed.'

The face was gone, replaced by a blank screen.

For the last twenty minutes, it had been eerily quiet in both parking locations outside the venue. The last activity had been a dark coloured Lexus which had been parked alongside the car belonging to one of the three men who had entered the club minutes before. A man of Asian appearance had exited from the passenger seat, bent down out of sight alongside the neighbouring car and returned to the Lexus with something in his hand.

Seamus felt a sense of unease. He had checked his smartphone.

The video was online as arranged. Something needed to happen.

The door to the overspill carpark crashed open and the stout man he had watched enter the club stormed out, knocking the security guard to one side as he did so. Seamus clearly heard the exchange of profanities.

The man walked over to his car and was about to open the door when the passenger in the Lexus exited and rushed toward him, shouting in English for him to stop with an accent which Seamus interpreted as coming from India or Pakistan. The intended target ignored the demand and continued to fumble with his key fob.

From the driver's side of the Lexus, a second man stumbled to his feet and careered the twenty metres toward his target, shouted something unintelligible and launched himself into a rugby tackle around the victim's waist. It was the wrong move. With both hands free, the stout man delivered an uppercut under the chin with such force, his attacker released his grip and howled in pain, grasping his chin with both hands as he writhed on the ground.

Seamus smiled at the amateurish behaviour. He watched as the victim turned to defend himself against the second man. He was too late. The taser poked into his stomach sent him arcing backwards to slam into the frame of his car door. He slid to the floor in a sitting position, his chin bumping into his chest.

There was shouting: one voice filled with panic seeming to bark orders, the other in pain and cursing. Helped to his feet, the first man kicked the unconscious victim between the legs and made his way slowly back to the Lexus. The second man dragged his victim toward the car. With what seemed to Seamus as an adrenalin, supercharged effort, the second man slowly hoisted his victim into the boot. Tyres spun in the gravel as the car sped up toward the exit. There was nearly a head-on collision as it swerved to avoid the car entering the venue.

Seamus turned his attention to the new arrival. The compact moved slowly into a parking spot close to the entrance to the casino. Two women emerged from the car.

Seamus cleared his throat, preparing to shout. He could feel sweat trickling down his neck. What on earth was Norma doing here alongside the woman he now knew to be her daughter, Sylvia? Norma was motioning frantically. Momentarily, thoughts of intimate moments distracted him. He forced himself to concentrate on the present, but events overtook both his desperate need to call out and Norma's attempt to enter the casino.

Each of the doors at the front of the venue and the side entrance in the overspill car park crashed open and people emerged, at first in ones and twos then, in increasing numbers until a crowd of confused and distressed individuals had congregated in front of the building. People turned toward the sound of multiple sirens, many coughing, some bent doubled gasping for breath, mobile phone screens lighting up in the dusky gloom. A wispy trail of smoke followed the last of the people to exit.

Seamus followed the progress of Norma and Sylvia as the stream of people shunted them toward the front entrance and the main car park. He turned his attention to the motel. Charlie had just emerged and stationed himself to block the automatic glass entrance door from closing. Behind Seamus, a convoy of three police cars and two fire engines with blue lights flashing and sirens blaring pulled into the overspill car park. A group of firemen rushed toward the casino entrance whilst six uniformed policemen attempted to move the crowd away and form a cordon as far back as space would allow.

Seamus realised his vantage point was about to be invaded. Time to find Norma amongst the crowd.

Charlie had one last task to perform. He motioned the coach driver to swing the vehicle into the reception bay at the front of the motel. With the hydraulic hiss as the door opened, Charlie waved forward a waiting line of girls and women dressed in a mix of cocktail dresses and flimsy lingerie. They boarded the coach. Finally, the group of Karabakh men moved forward, six of whom were forcibly manoeuvring three semi-conscious women between them.

Salmanov stood with Indemira at the deserted reception desk. His thumbs up said everybody was accounted for. Charlie motioned to the driver, and the coach pulled away.

'That was a close call,' Charlie said to himself as he watched a group of uniformed and plainclothes police feed into the area. They seemed to be looking for a particular vehicle. Time to leave. He waved a goodbye to Salmanov and Indemira and made his way to the Volvo. A sensation of satisfaction and well-being overcame him as he walked. He would find Norma, explain everything, and return to the comfort of his own home and her good graces. He was confident she would forgive him.

As he pressed the open-door symbol on his key fob, a hand grasped his arm and held it tight.

'We'll do that if you don't mind.' The man pointed a warrant card at Charlie's face without releasing his grip. A uniformed officer leaned into the car and popped the boot release. He led Charlie round to the rear of the car.

'Open it, please,' the detective said.

As he lifted the lid, Charlie recoiled at the smell. 'Jesus Christ,' he said. 'How in God's name . . .' He pulled back the jacket to reveal the gaunt, white features of the corpse. 'What the fuck!' he exclaimed.

A woman burst through the crowd, wriggling past the outstretched arm of the uniformed policeman. She peered into the boot and screamed.

'Lance!' she cried, rounding on her father. 'How could you do this to me?'

FIFTY-FOUR

WHO NEEDS MEN? – 18 MONTHS LATER

Two of the young men in hard hats working on the replacement water main looked at each other and raised their eyebrows as the woman hesitated outside the entrance to the restaurant.

She had become a stranger to dining out. In fact, the last time she could recall doing so was that disastrous dinner engagement when Norma's husband had lobbed a baked apple at Len. That would be over eighteen months ago, and such a lot had happened in the meantime. In fact, Muriel could say the events had been life changing.

The folds in her loose-fitting kaftan style dress swirled around her ankles as she turned and gave a cheeky wave to the two men before moving toward the wooden and glass-panelled revolving door at forty-five Jermyn Street, Fortnum and Mason's elegant brasserie in London's St James.

Her eyes roamed around the interior, taking in the retro style décor with the flock wallpaper, rust-coloured, curved and padded bench seating, the woodblock flooring and highly polished wooden tables. Yet, there was a contemporary feel to this 1950s setting as the servers glided between tables with their trays of artistically prepared dishes.

She spotted Norma at a more private circular seating arrangement alongside the bar and returned the wave of recognition as she handed her wrap to the cloakroom assistant.

'You look fantastic, Muriel,' Norma said, nursing a tumbler of what looked like a Bloody Mary. 'I swear I would have walked past you in the street. Sit down and tell me everything. Do you fancy one of these? It's potent. You're not driving, are you?'

'I'll have a gin tonic, please.' The server smiled and retreated. 'I came down by train,' she added. 'I couldn't resist your invitation.'

'So lovely to see you after such a long time,' Norma said. 'I barely spoke to you at the church, and it was family only at the crematorium, as you know. In the circumstances, I didn't fancy hosting a wake and having to deal with awkward questions.'

'It must have been a very testing time for you.' Muriel acknowledged the server as he set her drink on a coaster. She took a large swig. 'I needed that.' A menu was placed in front of her. She ignored it. 'Without wishing to sound inquisitive or intrusive, what do you mean by "awkward questions?"'

Norma twiddled a cocktail stick pinned to a half-moon lemon slice between her fingers. 'The circumstances around Charlie's death were hushed up by us at the time – embarrassment, mainly – but like most secrets, eventually they see the light of day. In a way it's comic.'

'Intriguing.'

'You will recall when Lance's corpse was discovered in the boot of the car Charlie was driving, he was arrested. When the police discovered it was also the vehicle involved in a hit and run killing . . .'

'That was Len's mate, Randall, something or the other,' Muriel interrupted.

'That's right. Well, the police thought they had a double killer on their hands. Charlie spent seventy-two hours under interrogation before they concluded they had the wrong man. By this time, they had not only discovered the other body but the young Azerbaijani woman who had been forced into prostitution gave a statement describing how Charlie had been pivotal in her release and that of the other women held against their will.'

'You must have been proud of him?'

Norma treated the remark as an observation rather than a question, in her view, a non sequitur. 'Have you looked at the menu? I'm going for a starter of the Portland Crab Salad followed by the Dover Sole. Remember, it's my invitation. Lunch is on me.'

Muriel shook her head. 'I won't hear of it. It's a fifty/fifty deal or I'm sticking to bread and water. But do finish your story; I'm fascinated.'

Norma relaxed back in the chair, massaging the padded arms of the carver with her hands as she thought about her choice of words. 'Charlie had the most objectionable ego. His five minutes of fame turned into a week-long procession of newspaper and magazine interviews, television appearances and sycophantic followers, mostly female, and did he milk it for all it was worth. He completely forgot he had a wife and family and as his public appeal intensified, so he became even more obnoxious than normal.'

'You really had a down on him?'

'He was unbearable. I cringed as I listened to or read the ever-exaggerating storyline. Of course, the world moved on, but Charlie remained in a time warp of high-living, boozing until all hours, and taking God knows what else.'

'He didn't ask you to take him back?'

'Good Lord, no! He knew I would bring him back down to earth with a bump and that was the last thing he wanted. Whereas . . .' She gave a wry smile at the memory. 'He had in that slut of a mistress a willing partner who enjoyed her cameo performance in the limelight. In the end, she got what she deserved. One night whilst he was fucking, his heart gave out, and he laid like a beached whale on top of her. Dead as a dodo and weighing a ton, she could not move from under him.' Norma stopped and drained the Bloody Mary, licking the tomato juice remnants from around her lips. 'Let's order some wine, shall we?'

'How long did she stay like that?'

'Hours, I expect, whilst she enjoyed the rigor mortis, I shouldn't wonder. In the end, she managed to reach her mobile and, as she apparently had no friends to call upon, resorted to the fire brigade. I expect it will be a folk legend in the fire station and retold for years to come.'

'How awful for you.' The statement did not match the amused expression on her face.

'Every cloud, as they say. Thankfully, Charlie had a healthy insurance policy. Why do you think I suggested we eat here? Anyway, back to the menu. What are you going to have?'

In between mouthfuls of crab salad and caramelised onion risotto, washed down with a white Musar, the attention turned to Muriel and her life since Len had been imprisoned.

With the elder Bateman turning Queen's evidence, the corrupt activities of Len and his colleagues were brought sharply into focus. The judge was scathing in his remarks, condemning Len for his role in facilitating human trafficking as "one of the most despicable acts perpetrated by a serving senior police officer he had ever come across". It was no surprise when the judge imposed the maximum sentence of ten years, but there was an intake of breath in the Court when he stipulated a mandatory minimum of eight years, nine months along with a fine of a quarter of a million pounds.

Muriel filed for a divorce within weeks of her husband's committal on the grounds of unreasonable behaviour and the application was speedily granted.

'Did you ever visit him in prison?' Norma asked.

Muriel shook her head. 'Beyond a solitary visit by Caroline early on and contact from his appeal lawyer, he has had no visitors as far as I know.'

'Not even his colleagues?'

Again, she shook her head. 'Of the three men mentioned in the indictment, Nobby and Randy were dead, and the third cohort, Terry, has disappeared from the face of the earth. The last sighting of him was an altercation with two men in the car park at the club, but there was so much confusion. Of course, you know that. You were there when everybody piled out.'

Norma sighed. 'Regrettably. Sylvia was at her father's shoulder the moment Lance's body was discovered. By accusing him so vehemently, she rather attributed the guilt before the police had really taken stock of the situation.'

'Understandable,' Muriel said as she fished in her handbag and drew out an envelope. 'I'd welcome your opinion on what you think I should do with the content of this letter sent to Len, which he has had forwarded to me.'

Norma hesitated while the server cleared the starter plates. 'Tell me more.'

'It's from a woman whom I assume from her name to be Indian. Mahi Kumar. She writes about how she intended to escape from an oppressive relationship by running away with Terry, who had been a former boyfriend. It happened on the same night it all kicked off. She waited for him at Harwich, but he never showed up. Assuming it was the repetition of cold feet – apparently, a similar thing had happened in their previous relationship – she got on the ferry alone, put Terry out of her mind and started a new life. She's in Turin now and in a relationship with a violinist in the local orchestra.'

'Good for her. Wasting time waiting around for men to decide is utterly pointless.'

'I'm afraid the rest of the letter is more sinister and although it's circumstantial, I don't know whether I should pass it on to the police.'

Norma filled their wineglasses. 'Now you have really got my attention.'

'Apparently, Mahi was in touch with her parents in New Delhi to let them know she was alive and well. They came back to her with the surprising news that the Ministry of External Affairs had urgently summoned her father-in-law, a former General and important politician, together with his son, back to India. From a position of influence as an attaché on military issues at the Embassy in London, the General found himself in the city of Patna, capital of one of India's poorest regions, Bihar, responsible for coordinating the recruitment of reservists for the army. Such a demotion is normally linked to a recall through diplomatic channels when an individual is suspected of having committed a crime and needs to be removed and professionally shamed before a scandal breaks.'

'She suspects this General and his son were responsible for Terry's disappearance?'

'Mahi got a friend at the government department where she worked to investigate for her. He came across the CCTV images of the set-to between Terry and two men. Although they were both younger than the General, on video enlargement, they were certainly of Indian appearance. Coupled with that, the car they were driving had a 175D number which she learned was a diplomatic plate assigned to the Indian embassy.'

'Are you going to give the letter to the police?'

'I don't know. Right now, I'm leaning toward getting Mahi's okay before I do so. The one thing holding me back is the likelihood that the police already know more than we do and forced the hand of the Indian authorities to repatriate the General and his family. What do you think?'

Norma nodded, leaving Muriel in doubt whether she was agreeing with her or acknowledging the plate of rib-eye beef with Bearnaise sauce which had just been placed in front of her. She let the subject drop as her dish of spinach and tofu dumplings with a side order of cumin roasted carrots made its appearance.

'We'll not put on weight with these portions,' Muriel said. She drained her glass. 'Shall we move onto a red? I'm really enjoying filling in the blanks.'

Norma agreed. 'Tell me, do you plan on visiting Len to discuss what to do about the letter?'

'Lord, no, too far to travel, even if I had the inclination to do so, which I don't.' Muriel said, replacing her knife and fork on the tablecloth and holding Norma's inquisitive gaze. 'Len started off as a Category B offender in Thameside, but his lawyer kicked up a fuss following a fatal stabbing at the prison. He was concerned Len would be next in line.'

'Why was he at risk?'

'Accepting the fact that bent cops, especially CID officers, are always in danger from the mafia network of criminals they nicked, it turned out that there was a tenuous link between the victim and Len. He was an Albanian who worked for Alex Quentin, the man Caroline was involved with and who helped Len cover up his dodgy dealings.

'Coupled with a mild heart attack, for which he needed a pacemaker, the stabbing incident was enough to get Len reclassified as a category D, low-risk offender and transferred to an open prison on the Isle of Wight.'

Despite her curiosity, Norma left her next question on hold and suggested they pick up the conversation once their main courses were done. 'It looks too good to leave sitting on the plate,' she said.

As they finished studying the dessert menu and Norma settled on rhubarb crumble and Muriel, a knickerbocker glory, the conversation drifted back to the passage of events over the preceding months.

Muriel explained that in framing his appeal to the Home Office for a reclassification of prisoner category status, Len's lawyer had also laboured the point of how his client's cooperation and testimony had led to the conviction of Bateman senior on several charges relating to people-trafficking and a custodial sentence of thirteen years. Whilst the old man might pose no threat, the authorities were reminded that upon receiving a life sentence for murder, Bateman's son, Darren, had threatened in open court to see Len's throat cut from ear to ear.

'What with Charlie's passing and trying to tidy up his affairs, I'm afraid I didn't follow the trial. I needed a break, so I travelled.' Norma poked at the corner of her mouth with a napkin. 'When you talk about this Darren committing murder, you're referring to Lance, the Australian?'

'Lord, no. It was the policeman who killed Lance; the one who committed suicide.' Muriel hesitated. 'Although the coroner adjourned the inquest into his death pending the ongoing police investigation. Sounds like that business is far from cut and dried. No, I'm referring to the evidence of that brave young woman who was trafficked for sex. It was her compelling testimony that did for that nasty piece of work, Darren Bateman. One of the girls in the lorry tried to escape and was shot. Although he didn't pull the trigger, he was complicit and had provided the firearm.'

Norma nodded reflectively. 'You know, the young woman you're talking about phoned me when she heard Charlie had died. She wanted to impress on me just how Charlie had acted the absolute gentleman; nothing had gone on between them and her and the other girls' salvation really was down to him. Without Charlie, she'd still be a virtual prisoner.' She sighed. 'Sylvia accused me of being the complete bitch for not taking him back, quit her job, moved away, to where I don't know, and hasn't spoken to me since, other than to hold me responsible for his death.'

'How does that make you feel?'

'What do you think? A totally inadequate wife and mother, but I can't turn the clock back. I have to make the most of my life whilst I'm still able.'

Muriel reached across the table to pat her hand. 'If it's any consolation, I know Caroline is totally disillusioned with us, more so with Len, but I know I figure in her list of "How could yous?".'

'She'll come around.'

'I don't think so. She was always more into you than me. To tell the truth, she's been quite vindictive.'

'I'm sorry to hear that.'

'I'm not in Weybridge anymore. I was forced to sell the house.'

'It crossed my mind when you talked about travelling down to London and a long way to the Isle of Wight. Where are you living now?'

'Near Morecambe.'

'That's Blackpool way, isn't it? A bit of a drastic change?'

Muriel studied the collection of metal bracelets around her lower arm as she played with them. 'I'll come back to that. When Len tried to cover up the source of the protection money he had received from Bateman, he arranged a phony loan agreement with Caroline's boyfriend to evidence that we had borrowed the funds to complete the house purchase. Of course, no money had ever changed hands. With Quentin dead, his executor, who happens to be his son, Rupert, claimed repayment of the loan as a matter of course.'

'You had to pay back money you had never borrowed?'

'That's the long and the short. With penalty interest, we are talking about three hundred thousand pounds.'

'A perfect storm. You couldn't convince the son?'

'I couldn't. Caroline could have done and almost certainly did. She kept Rupert as a client. In fact, they seem quite close. She told me Rupert knew and acknowledged the deception. He was willing to forgo the debt, but Caroline insisted he press for repayment. We deserved to be punished, she told me, for the evil deeds Len had committed and I had done nothing to stop. She accused me of spending a lifetime with my head buried in the sand. I should have stood up for myself.' Muriel smiled to herself. 'The fact is, she's right.'

'Don't be so hard on yourself. It sounds callous and not like Cary.'

'She's changed. They've both changed, her and Dom. They don't seem like the same people. Don't you agree?'

Norma looked around. 'We're almost the last diners here. They'll be wanting to close.' She waited as a fastidious waitress cleared their dessert plates. 'Shall we order coffee, cognac and ask for the bill?' She acknowledged Muriel's agreement. 'What you were saying about the kids, I can't say I see them as often as I'd wish and when I do, they're certainly less communicative than they used to be. Of course, that business with the Forbes man spying on the house and stalking the twins, accosting them with questions – it was very unsettling for them.'

'The police arrested him in the end?'

'Only after he had broken into the house and threatened them all if they didn't reveal Charlie's whereabouts. Having already assaulted Ludo, this man, Roddie, was convinced Charlie had ordered his brother's death and wanted to avenge him.'

'What happened to him?'

'Last I heard, they had him locked away in a secure facility undergoing psychological evaluation,' Norma said. 'He must be due for sentencing. His sister Holly was lucky. Harbouring an offender can get you locked up. She got away with a fine and a caution from the magistrate for hiding him in a friend's vacant apartment.'

Checking her watch, Muriel apologised. She would have to leave in ten minutes if she was to make her train back to Morecambe.

'What on earth possessed you to move up north?'

Muriel laughed. 'You make it sound like the Outer Hebrides. They're quite civilised, you know, in that part of the world; no more spears and woad-painted faces.'

'I didn't mean that,' Norma countered. 'But we were both so much suburban Londoners, you with your status pad in Weybridge.'

'I know. And a lot of good it did us, right? Husbands dead or as good as, dysfunctional families, lies and deception – it was Len's half-brother, Gerry, I can thank for making me come to my senses and see exactly what sort of person I had become. Decades of having my self-respect eroded until I was about as dependent as one of Pavlov's dogs; make a noise and I'd come running. Gerry and his friends re-instilled my self-confidence, showed me how to attribute value to my beliefs, feel exhilaration and show compassion – emotions I had forgotten how to display.'

'You make it sound attractive,' Norma conceded.

'More than enough to opt to join their commune.'

'But Cary told me they had a site in the Hounslow area.'

Muriel smiled with a shake of the head. 'That was ages ago. A private contractor involved with the Heathrow Airport extension came along and offered millions for the site. Gerry et al gratefully accepted, and we moved on.'

'Why Morecambe?'

'We managed to find a site next to an area previously designated for fracking before the moratorium was imposed by the government. Our land just happens to be blocking access as and when approval is granted. The local community sees us as activists and applauds our stand.'

There was a wry smile on Norma's face. 'This commune you have joined. Are the motivations social or financial?'

'We don't see the two as mutually exclusive. Gloria says if you can galvanise public opinion and make money at the same time, what's to complain about?'

'I'm fascinated. What do you do with the money?'

'It's organised by Harry, one of the commune elders who was a lawyer and used to be a margin trader, whatever that is. He established an offshore trust in which everyone in the commune has a stake. Newcomers can invest in quotas based on the current value of the trust. I put in all the proceeds from my half share of the house and my quotas will grow with every deal the commune does. In the meantime, every commune member gets a weekly allowance to pay their expenses. Gerry says he started with next to nothing and now has savings in the trust of over one million.' Muriel concluded with a self-satisfied smirk. 'If the fracking licence ends up being granted, our fight is both lost and won. We'll be forced to negotiate a sale. I could double my investment.'

Norma shook her head. 'You could be described as a bunch of opportunists, exploiting socially sensitive issues.'

'That would be unkind and unjust. I prefer Harry's description of a group of similarly minded, concerned individuals having a social conscience with an embracing financial bandwidth.' They both laughed. 'Sounds pretentious, doesn't it?'

'I notice the "we" in your comments,' Norma said. 'You sound committed to this new life.'

'It's nice to be appreciated and have your opinions listened to and considered.' Muriel lowered her voice and leaned forward. 'Just between us, I've started a relationship with somebody.'

'Good for you.'

'He's a younger man, a medium, who believes he met me before in an earlier life when I was a seamstress in a Bavarian tailor's shop, and he was a huntsman who adored me.' She winked. 'It makes for good bedtime theatre.'

They hugged outside the restaurant. Muriel checked her watch again before speaking. 'I didn't ask you how Dominic was getting on in his new job; high powered, I heard.'

Norma nodded. 'I think he feels the pressure, but he's coping well, he says. It's a lot more money working for big pharma, as he calls it. He really feels like the breadwinner now.'

'Cyber security, isn't it?'

'Yes. A sea change from what he was doing.'

Muriel hesitated, plainly searching for the right words. 'Keep your eye on him. Remind him that work isn't everything.'

Norma's brow creased. 'Why do you say that?'

'A great deal was made at Len's trial of the admissibility of testimony derived illegally from hacking the offshore lawyer's files to establish how Len had secreted the bribes he took from the Batemans. The defence accused Dominic of acting on behalf of your late husband. His name was banded about the media and must have come to the attention of several influential prospective employers concerned with protecting their computer systems.'

'Is there something wrong with that? I don't understand.'

'Dominic, quite rightly, never admitted responsibility for the hacking. He wasn't on trial. He never had to lie or admit the truth. Overnight he achieved a precious notoriety.'

'What are you saying?'

Muriel took a deep breath and exhaled sharply. 'Dominic never hacked into Len's offshore holdings. I should be surprised if he even knows how. I was the person who told the authorities all about Len's clandestine bank account.'

'You?'

'I sent Police Standards copies of bank statements and correspondence Len thought he had hidden away from me. They must have been prepared to accept the anonymous source as the hacker once Len's legal team had put Dominic in the frame.'

'But, why? You must have realised what the consequences would be?'

Muriel hailed a taxi. 'Two reasons. Over the years, Len treated me not as a wife and lover, but as an appendage to his needs and ambitions who needed no insight into his control over our lives. He looked on me as cook, cleaner and baby bottle washer, did as he wanted and considered that giving me a fancy house to live in was reward enough. I would have lived in a hovel had he treated me as a loving partner with a mind of her own.'

'Even so, you had Len's fate in your hands and chose to expose him?'

'Absolutely. I knew everything that was going on. I overheard conversations, examined his secret papers – including the ones where he had forged my signature – and did nothing to counter his despicable behaviour. He needed to pay for all those poor people he stood by and watched being trafficked over the years. I'm not sorry for what I did.' She opened the taxi door. 'Can I drop you off somewhere? I'm heading for Euston.'

'No thanks,' Norma replied. 'Now Charlie's life insurance has paid out, I'm thinking of upping sticks and moving to Ireland. It's a lovely part of the world and I've found the people so welcoming.'

She waved a goodbye as the taxi pulled away.

Geoff Cook

Geoff grew up in South London, the latch-key child of a widowed mother who struggled in post-war Britain to turn a place to live into a loving home. And she succeeded. Love you, Rita. RIP.

Geoff has had a varied commercial and financial career, living and working in countries with a Latin flavour (South America, Southern Europe) as well as London and the Welsh Valleys in the UK. His experiences extend from professional accounting, investment banking and pop music management to running a ceramic tile factory and retail outlets, managing a leisure complex, operating a restaurant ship, and owning and cheffing in restaurants on the Portuguese Algarve.

As a child, he opened a street lending library and developed an interest in literature and writing, turning his hand to numerous articles and projects over the years. In 2010, he published his first full-length novel as an e-book and has written several plays and novels of which *Irreconcilable Differences* is his latest offering.

Novels: Pieces for the Wicked – 2010 (e-book)

The Sator Square – 2017

'You should read it and follow the loops and tangles' – Booklore

Deaf Wish – 2019

'Twists and turns make this an interesting whodunnit' – Goodreads

The Last Rights – 2020

'If you like a good story & believable plot, then I would thoroughly recommend this book.' - Amazon

Irreconcilable Differences - 2022

Plays: The Painful Truth – 2015

The Last Chapter – 2016

Current projects include *Octogen*, a futuristic novel about life in 2060 without oil and the internet, and *Deguello*, a thriller set in Korea with a man who keeps on discovering surprising facts about his recently deceased wife.

For more information, visit www.geoff-cook.com

THE LAST RIGHTS

**Read an extract from Geoff's
last novel – the story of a
Holocaust survivor with a deadly secret**

* * *

**What people are saying about
The Last Rights**

'. . . engrossed by this compelling book.'

'. . . still reading at 3am. Absolutely brilliant.'

'. . . of considerable historical significance.'

The Last Rights is available in paperback,
on Kindle or as an audio book, narrated by Amanda
Parrott on Audible

SEVENTEEN

THE ALGARVE, PORTUGAL

Wednesday, 29 March 1989

An early dinner, he suggests. Easter has passed and he feels like a little celebration. After all, we have a great deal to be grateful for, and splashing out a little of our now meagre resources on a special bottle is fully justified.

Do we have a great deal to be grateful for? Do we have anything to be grateful for? Tonight, he intends to kill me and commit suicide. The bottle of bubbly, nothing more than the means to administer the sleeping draught or whatever he has put in my glass to make sure I pass out before the dreaded moment. It's not death I fear, but I don't want to be unconscious throughout whatever method he chooses to finish me. Fortunately, we have a strange ritual whereby Raus eats when we do, and his bowl alongside the table is handily placed for me to tip in my glass of bubbly whilst Kirchner is absent from the table. On his return, I ask for a top-up, confident that as he's drinking from the same bottle, whatever drug he used was already in my glass and is now in the dog.

The die is cast. He cannot bring himself to look up from the table. Head bowed, he pretends to concentrate on dissecting the salad. I know him too well. If he allows himself to meet my gaze, he believes I will see right into his soul and lay it bare. No comment is needed, no question implied. He cannot allow this to happen, even if it means imposing his will over me until the end.

He has not sought my agreement to mark this day as our last on earth together as ... what? A man and a woman, conqueror and vanquished, master and mistress, allies in survival, an unholy partnership ... how does he see it? He often refers to me in front of others as his wife, but such a relationship implies a freedom of choice I have never had and a range of emotions rarely felt and never expressed. Do I really mean something to him? It certainly sounded that way on the phone call with Richter, or were his protestations the simple manifestation of guilt? I cannot allow myself to dwell on this tender notion without exposing a weakness in myself. Tears now would serve no purpose, nor asking questions that might weaken his resolve.

The caterpillar spares us such a confrontation. Almost indistinguishable from the lettuce leaf from under which it appears, the tiny creature contracts and extends its body as it moves across his plate; the colouring, the detail, the sheer perfection of its form. Strangely, it gives me a sense of well-being about what is to come. Whatever science may dictate, however logical the explanation, how can we doubt the presence of a dimension beyond our comprehension capable of structuring such a perfect equilibrium between the creatures, plants and environment in which we all co-exist? Perhaps, at the moment of death we will discover the answer. Perhaps, in a blinding flash of realisation it will all be so apparent, a simplicity so obvious, yet beyond the understanding of mere mortals.

What slides across his plate and occupies his attention is a symbol of the intricate and delicate balance of co-existence which he and millions like him had tried to change and failed.

It is too late now. The experiment ended in disaster, years of anguish and wasted lives he would excuse as in the pursuit of a noble cause. He raises his fork and takes the last mouthful of salad. Is this to be his final act of defiance, a pointless demonstration as the end approaches to show that the destiny of this helpless insect is at the whim of the man who once held in his hands the fate of tens of thousands?

With no cover left under which to hide, the caterpillar appears confused, changing direction, but finding nothing before him but a flat expanse of white porcelain.

He smiles to himself. Flicking over the caterpillar, he slices it into two, spikes both pieces onto his fork and puts them into his mouth. The cutlery is placed neatly together in the centre of the empty plate.

For the first time, he looks up and sees I am smiling too. 'Did you enjoy that?' I ask.

It is nearly eight. As I suspected, the dog is fast asleep, snoring and breaking wind in random order. I am playing my part, apparent doziness transcending into crafted unconsciousness. How am I to die? He gathers me up from the couch with more difficulty than I imagine, even considering his poor state of health and my portly figure. Exhaling loudly, he lays me on the rug, carefully arranging me and placing my right hand in a closed fist against my stomach. So, it is to be a knife. I hear the sound of metal on glass as he places the weapon on the side table which he then pulls towards him.

'Shit,' he says. He raises himself from his knees, steadies himself and walks into the hall to retrieve the phone. From somewhere he has produced an extension lead and is bringing the handset over to the side table. He checks for a dialling tone and grunts his satisfaction.

Raus is stirring with a sort of whining noise and jerky paw movements. I can see him from the floor, my head turned away from Kirchner. The dog is in my direct line of sight. From the reflection on the copper coal scuttle, I can watch Kirchner without him realising my eyes are partially open. He takes the long, thin-bladed knife from the table and studies it. The handle is rubbed clean with a handkerchief which he then ties around the blade, just above the hilt. He kneels over me, prising my fist apart just enough to force the handle between my fingers to rest in my palm. The handkerchief he has used to complete this manoeuvre is unwound from around the blade. My eyes close as he wheels my head around to face him and the last thing I see is the small blue cross inked onto the vest he is now wearing. From now on, I can rely only on my hearing.

He is much thinner and lighter than he used to be, but the weight as he goes to lie on top of me takes me by surprise and the breath out of my body. Involuntarily, I gasp.

'Through the sternum,' I hear him say to himself. 'Penetrate the right ventricle with a five millimetre wound and sever the right coronary vein. Five minutes to bleed out.'

He clasps his hand around my fist and forces himself down onto me. The blade shudders as it penetrates skin and bone. He cries out in pain. The blade slides further in until his chest is flat against mine. The sigh is like a child's and I start to feel the warm, sticky sensation seeping through the dress fabric onto my skin.

He rolls off me and reaches for the handset. I can see the handle of the knife protruding from his chest. He must have put the phone onto speed dial. 'Sergeant Pedro Rodrigues. It's urgent.' The Portuguese is rehearsed. Even after all these years, his grasp of the language is little more than basic.

'He's where? Tell him it's Senhor Kirchner, his neighbour. Tell him to come quickly. My wife is trying to kill me. She has a knife. Oh no! She is going to stab me! Please!' He presses the 'call end' button and collapses onto his back.

My reflex action is to reach for his hand and hold it tight. He is trying to speak. Blood seeps from between his lips. 'It's the only way,' he says, strands of red spittle between his lips as he forces out the words. 'If the police arrest you, Richter won't be able to get to you. It's the only thing I could think of to do.' He is fighting for breath. 'Whatever you think of me, I really do care about you. I always have. Without you, my life has never had any meaning.' He stops and starts to raise his arm. 'We have to make it look authentic, a fight.' He closes his hand into a fist and before I can react, it is swinging towards my head.

Printed in Great Britain
by Amazon

87106165R00220